Everything's Archie®

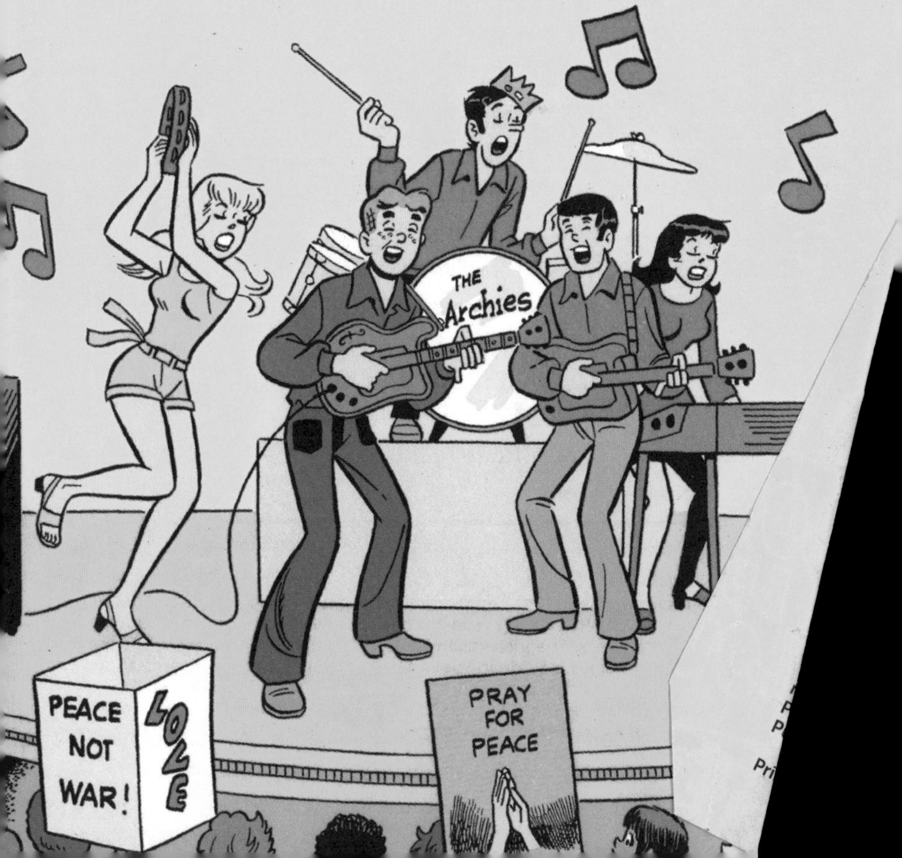
THE Archies
PEACE NOT WAR!
LOVE
PRAY FOR PEACE

Everything's Archie

Publisher / Co-CEO: Jon Goldwater

Co-President / Editor-In-Chief: Victor Gorelick

Co-President: Mike Pellerito

Co-President: Alex Segura

Chief Creative Officer: Roberto Aguirre-Sacasa

Chief Operating Officer: William Mooar

Chief Financial Officer: Robert Wintle

Director: Jonathan Betancourt

Art Director: Vincent Lovallo

Production Manager: Stephen Oswald

Lead Designer: Kari McLachlan

Associate Editor: Carlos Antunes

Editor / Proofreader: Jamie Lee Rotante

Co-CEO: Nancy Silberkleit

Printed in USA. First Printing. December, 2019. ISBN: 978-1-68255-807-2

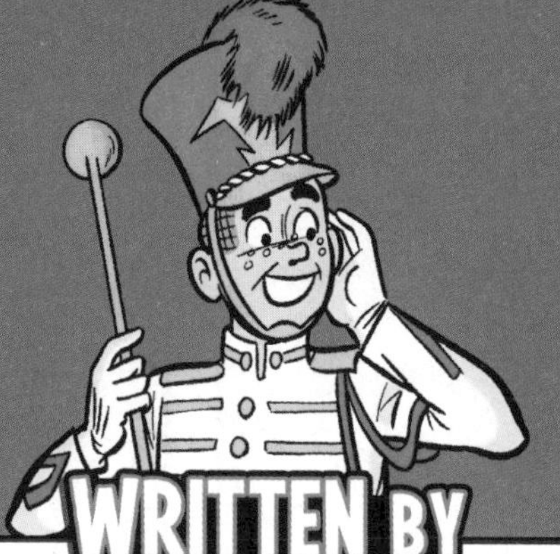

WRITTEN BY

Frank Doyle, Bob Bolling,
George Gladir, Al Hartley, Dick Malmgren,
Bob White & Gus LeMoine

ART BY

Dan DeCarlo, Harry Lucey, Samm Schwartz,
Bob Bolling, Stan Goldberg, Al Hartley, Bill Vigoda,
Bob White, Dick Malmgren, Gus LeMoine, Jon D'Agostino,
Rudy Lapick, Chic Stone, Mario Acquaviva, Bill Yoshida,
Sal Contrera & Barry Grossman

This book contains some material that was originally created in a less socially sensitive time in our society and reflects attitudes that may be interpreted as being unacceptable today. The stories are reprinted here without alteration for historical reference.

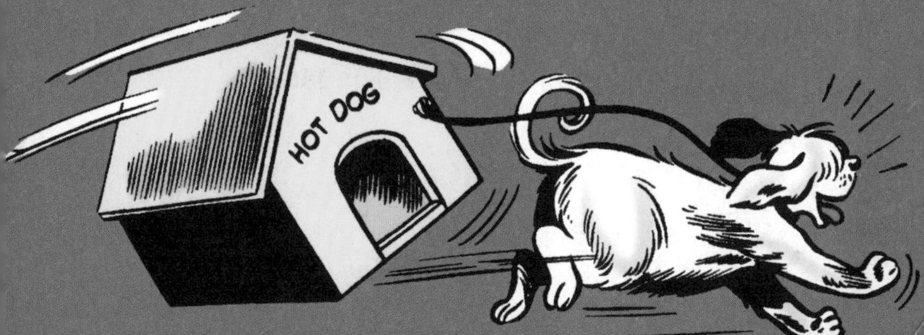
HOT DOG

Everything's Archie

TABLE OF CONTENTS

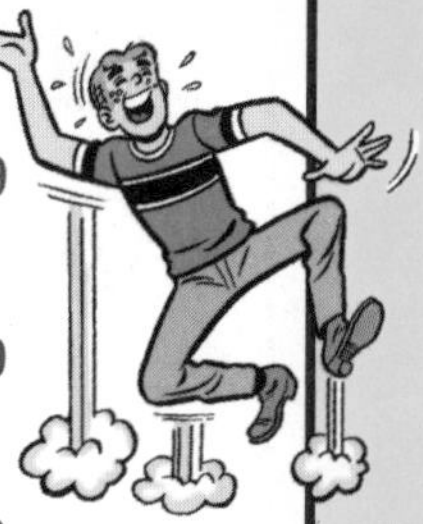

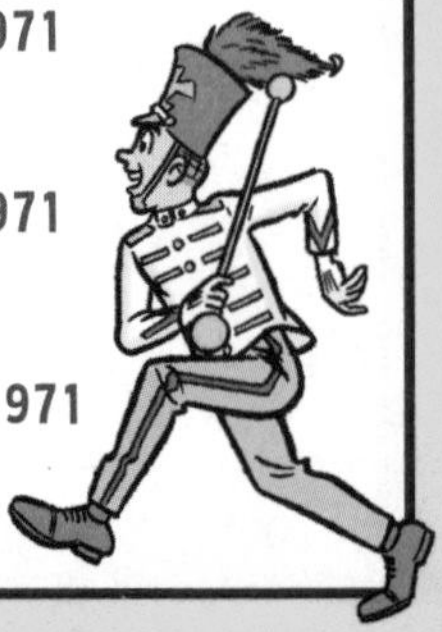

Everything's Archie®

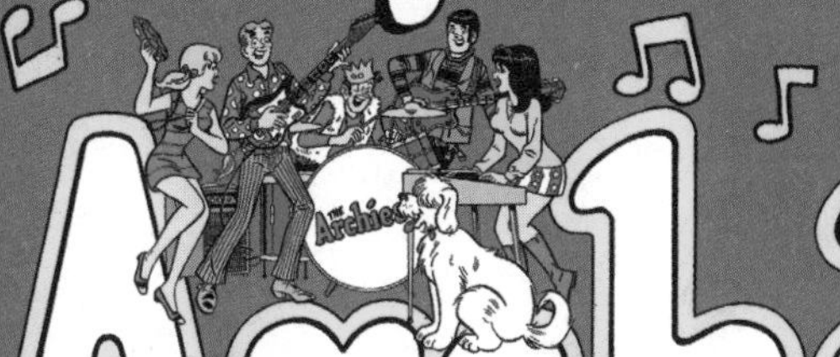

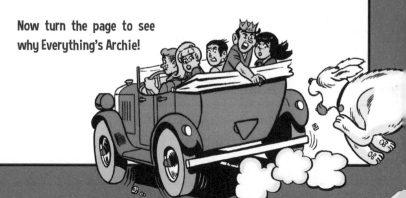

The *Everything's Archie* comic series was originally created to showcase Archie Andrews' band The Archies, following them from meetings with record labels to concerts and tours. Of course, a band composed of high school students means there still needs to be time for school and family-life, leading to plenty of stories featuring the extended Archie cast, including Moose, Mr. Weatherbee, Mr. Lodge, and Jughead's furry best friend, Hot Dog!

In this second volume of *Everything's Archie* you'll find stories about double dating drama, magical mischief, a rowdy pair of roller skates, a rogue marching band member, a problematical pole vault contestant, a riveting rehearsal and even a panic-stricken piranha—and that's just a sampling, there are way more outrageous and outlandish tales where that came from!

Now turn the page to see why Everything's Archie!

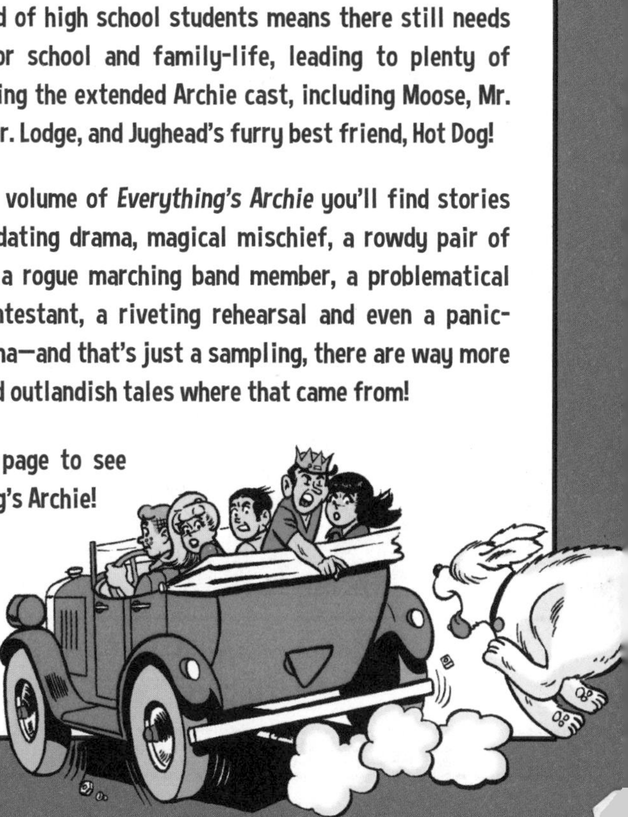

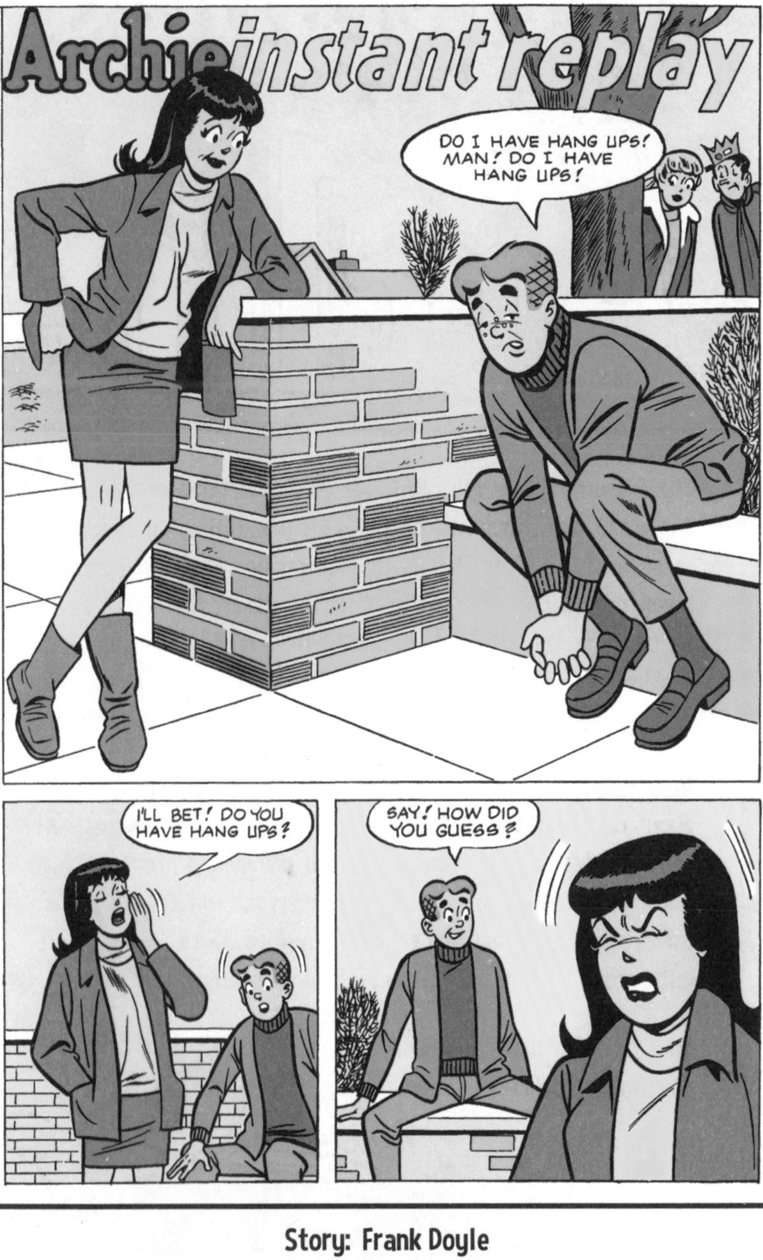
Archie instant replay
DO I HAVE HANG UPS! MAN! DO I HAVE HANG UPS!
I'LL BET! DO YOU HAVE HANG UPS?
SAY! HOW DID YOU GUESS?

Story: Frank Doyle
Art & Letters: Samm Schwartz

Originally printed in EVERYTHING'S ARCHIE #1, MAY 1969

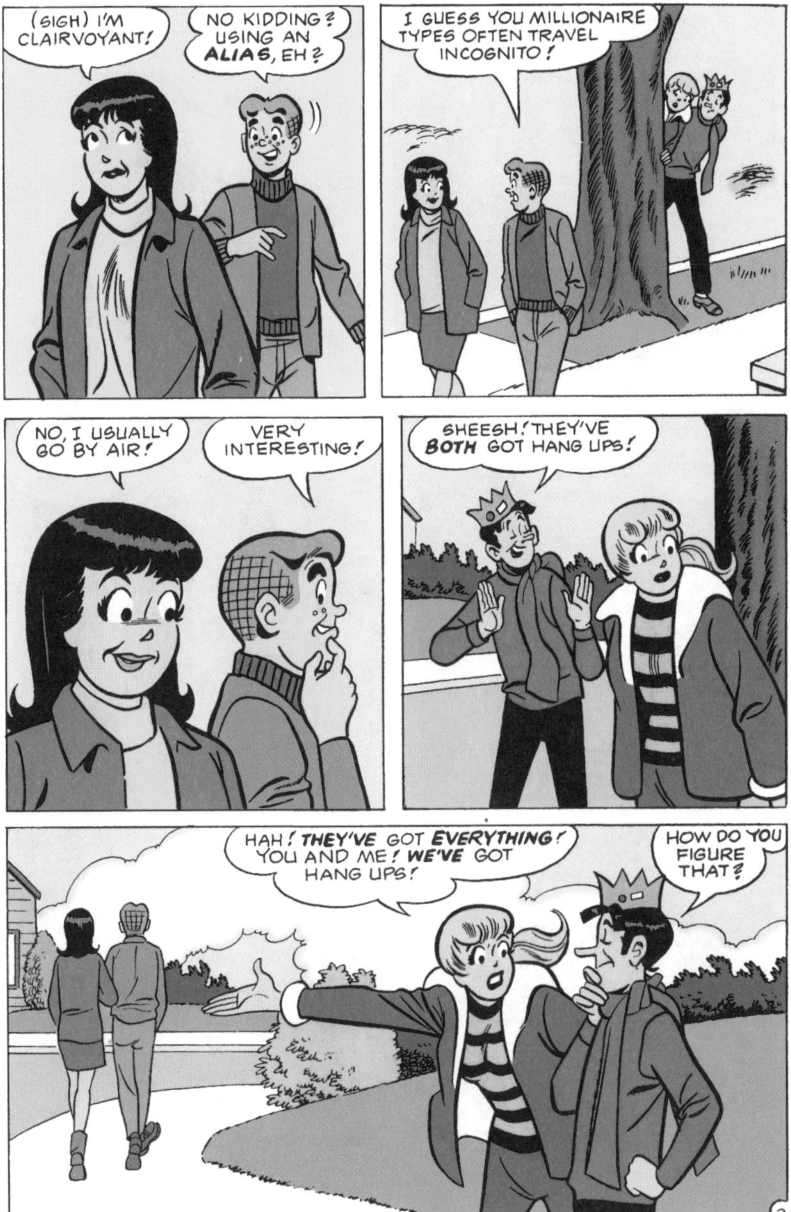
(SIGH) I'M CLAIRVOYANT!
NO KIDDING? USING AN ALIAS, EH?
I GUESS YOU MILLIONAIRE TYPES OFTEN TRAVEL INCOGNITO!
NO, I USUALLY GO BY AIR!
VERY INTERESTING!
SHEESH! THEY'VE BOTH GOT HANG UPS!
HAH! THEY'VE GOT EVERYTHING! YOU AND ME! WE'VE GOT HANG UPS!
HOW DO YOU FIGURE THAT?
2

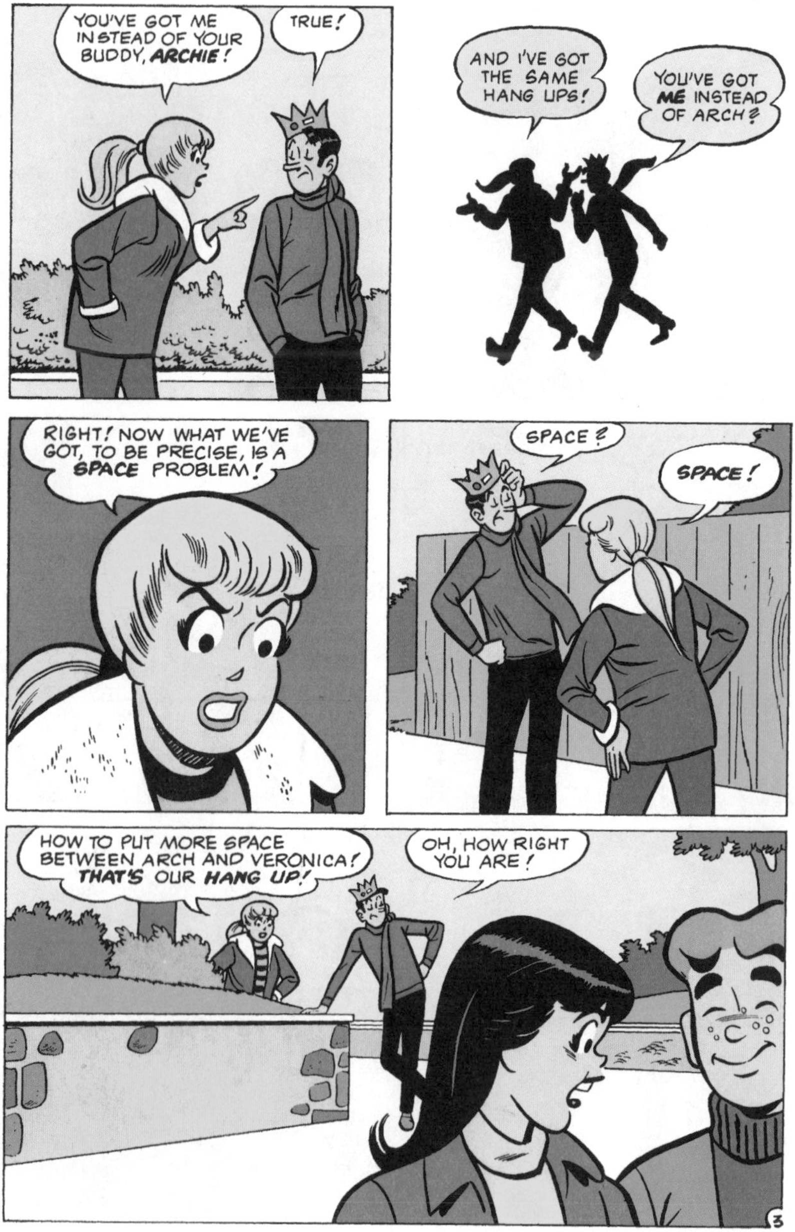
YOU'VE GOT ME INSTEAD OF YOUR BUDDY, ARCHIE!
TRUE!
AND I'VE GOT THE SAME HANG UPS!
YOU'VE GOT ME INSTEAD OF ARCH?
RIGHT! NOW WHAT WE'VE GOT, TO BE PRECISE, IS A SPACE PROBLEM!
SPACE?
SPACE!
HOW TO PUT MORE SPACE BETWEEN ARCH AND VERONICA! THAT'S OUR HANG UP!
OH, HOW RIGHT YOU ARE!
3

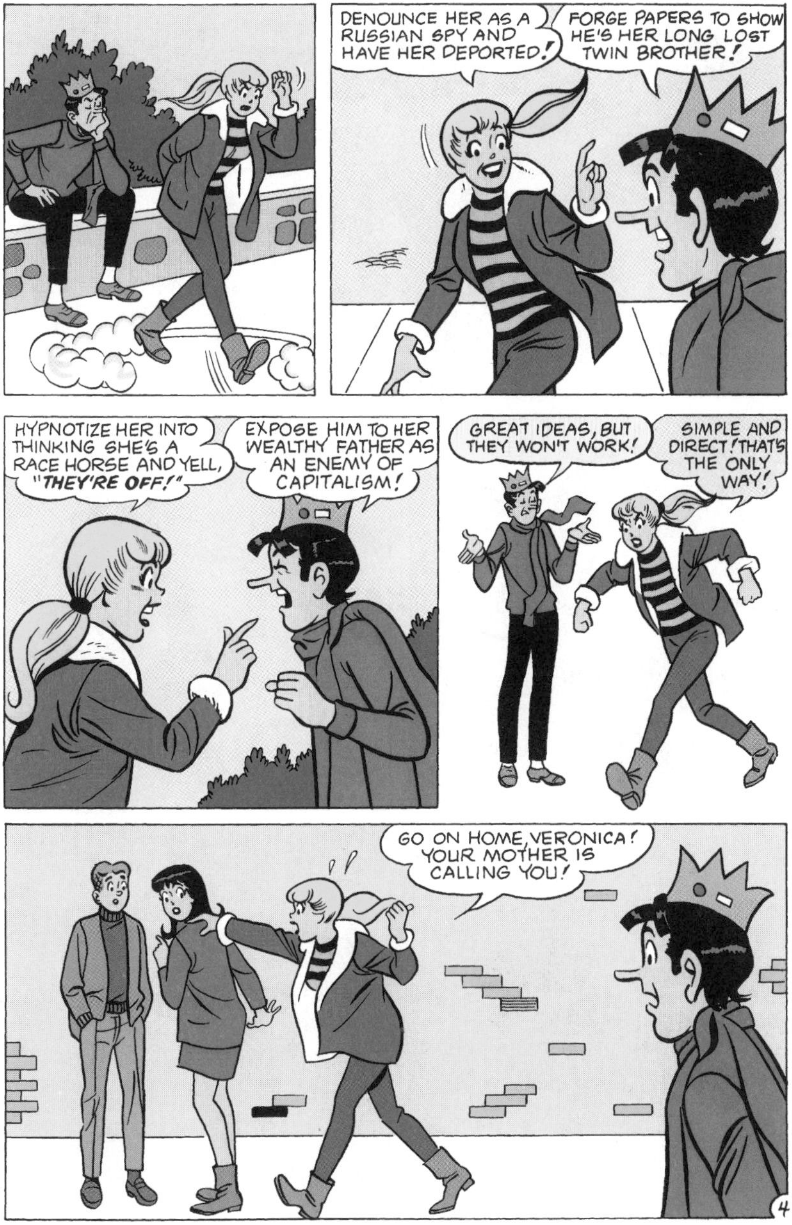
DENOUNCE HER AS A RUSSIAN SPY AND HAVE HER DEPORTED!
FORGE PAPERS TO SHOW HE'S HER LONG LOST TWIN BROTHER!
HYPNOTIZE HER INTO THINKING SHE'S A RACE HORSE AND YELL, "THEY'RE OFF!"
EXPOSE HIM TO HER WEALTHY FATHER AS AN ENEMY OF CAPITALISM!
GREAT IDEAS, BUT THEY WON'T WORK!
SIMPLE AND DIRECT! THAT'S THE ONLY WAY!
GO ON HOME, VERONICA! YOUR MOTHER IS CALLING YOU!
4

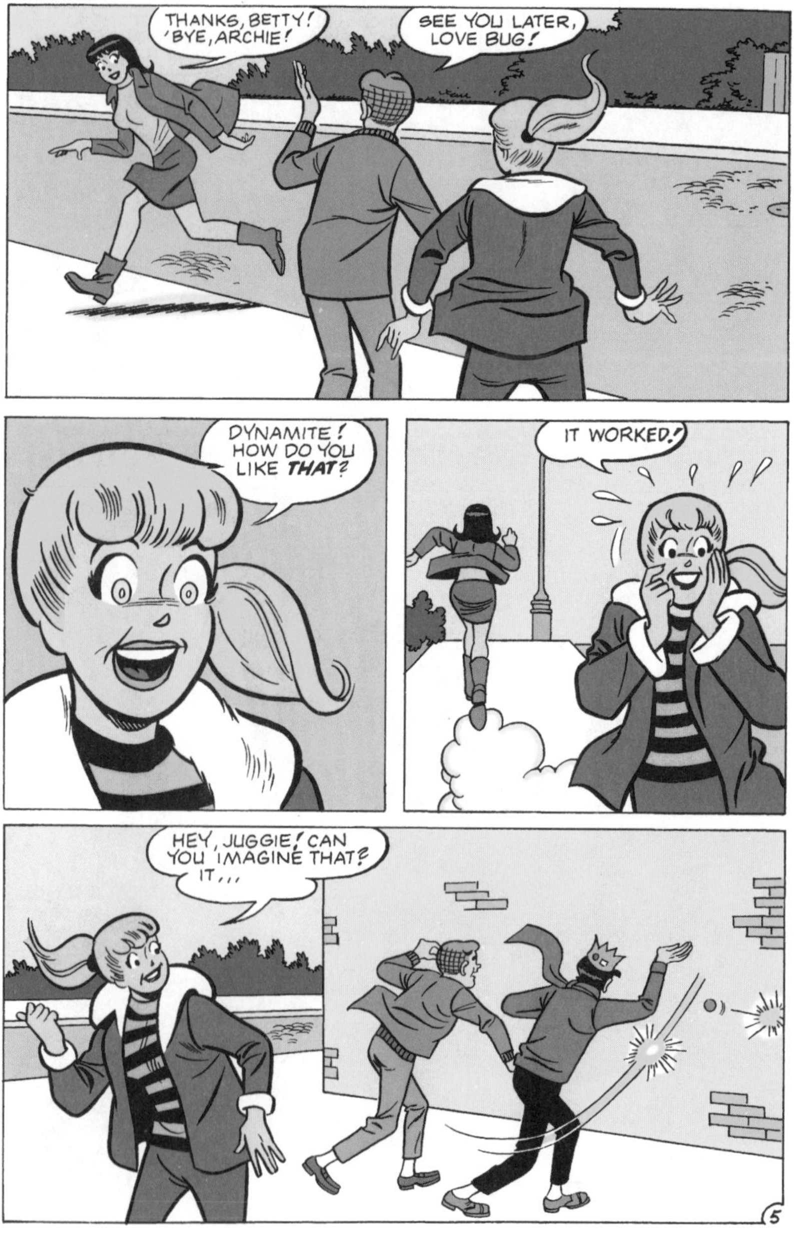
THANKS, BETTY! 'BYE, ARCHIE!
SEE YOU LATER, LOVE BUG!
DYNAMITE! HOW DO YOU LIKE *THAT*?
IT WORKED!
HEY, JUGGIE! CAN YOU IMAGINE THAT? IT...
5

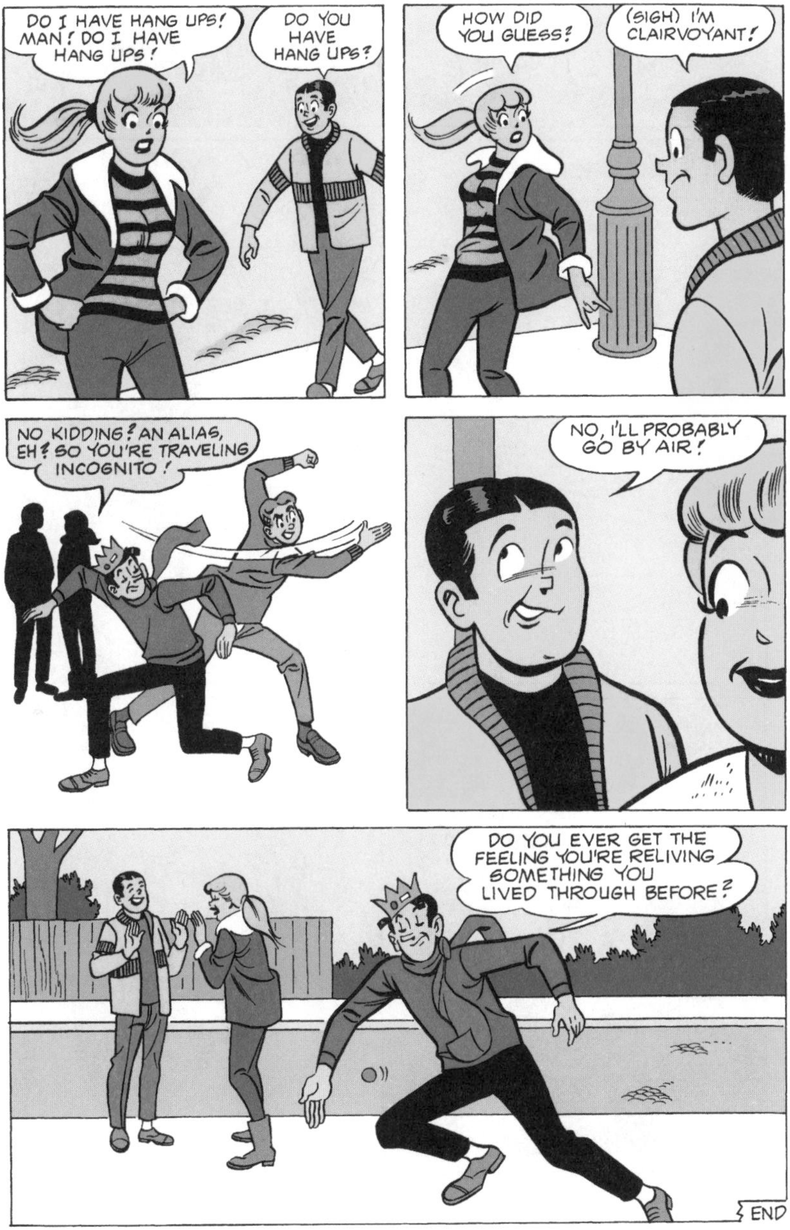
DO I HAVE HANG UPS! MAN! DO I HAVE HANG UPS!
DO YOU HAVE HANG UPS?
HOW DID YOU GUESS?
(SIGH) I'M CLAIRVOYANT!
NO KIDDING! AN ALIAS, EH? SO YOU'RE TRAVELING INCOGNITO!
NO, I'LL PROBABLY GO BY AIR!
DO YOU EVER GET THE FEELING YOU'RE RELIVING SOMETHING YOU LIVED THROUGH BEFORE?
END

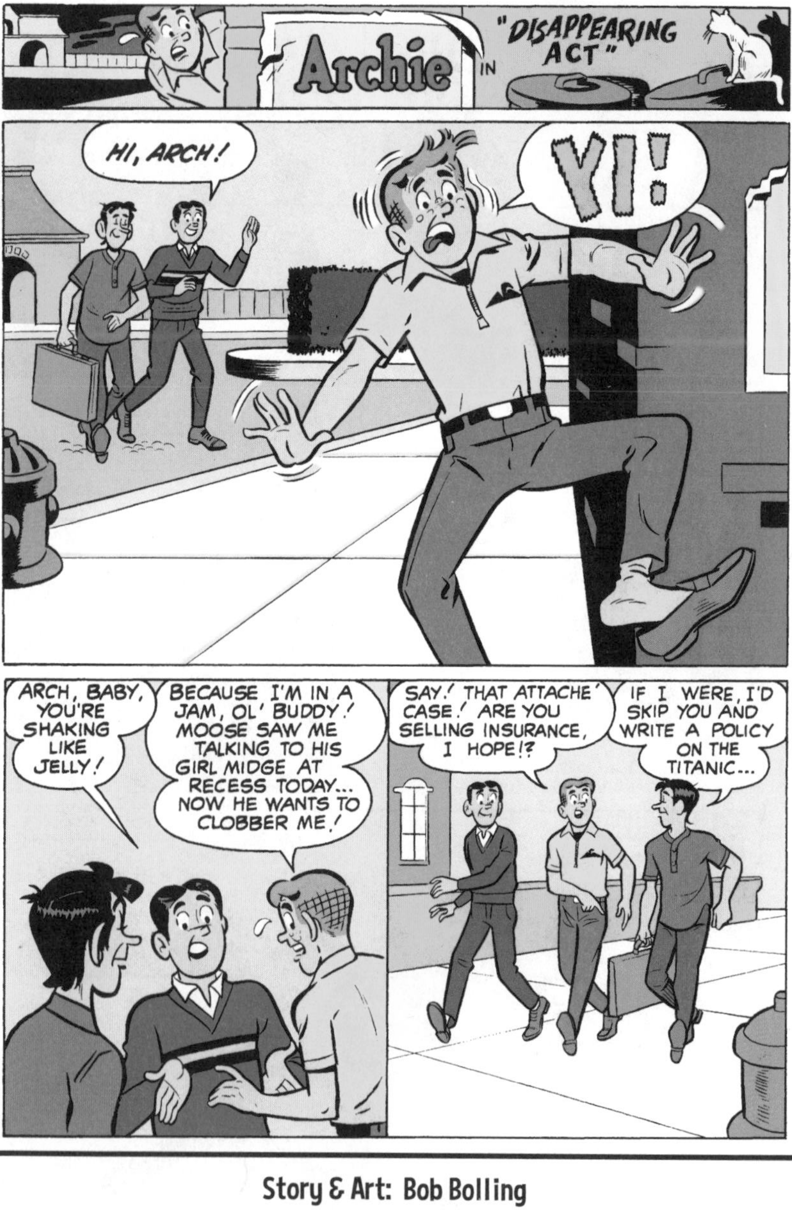
Archie IN "DISAPPEARING ACT"
HI, ARCH!
YI!
ARCH, BABY, YOU'RE SHAKING LIKE JELLY!
BECAUSE I'M IN A JAM, OL' BUDDY! MOOSE SAW ME TALKING TO HIS GIRL MIDGE AT RECESS TODAY... NOW HE WANTS TO CLOBBER ME!
SAY! THAT ATTACHE' CASE! ARE YOU SELLING INSURANCE, I HOPE!?
IF I WERE, I'D SKIP YOU AND WRITE A POLICY ON THE TITANIC...

Story & Art: Bob Bolling
Letters: Bill Yoshida

Originally printed in EVERYTHING'S ARCHIE #1, MAY 1969

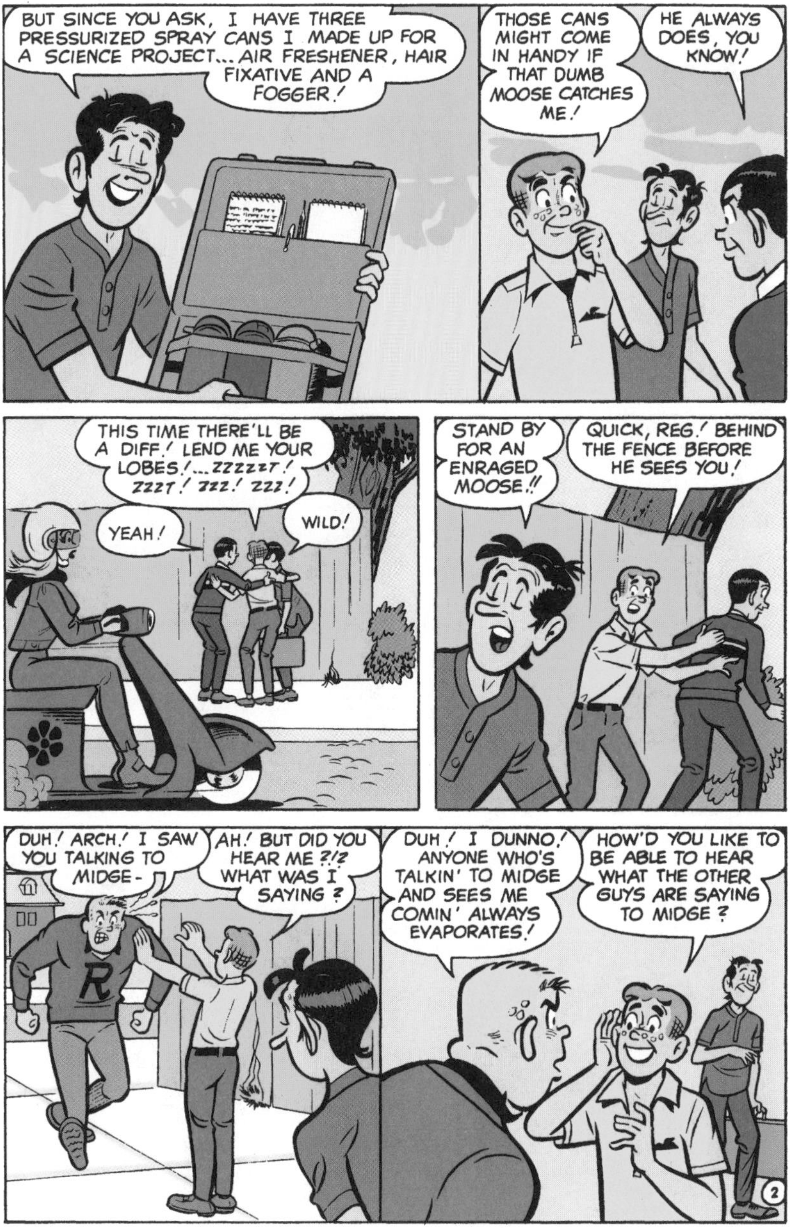
BUT SINCE YOU ASK, I HAVE THREE PRESSURIZED SPRAY CANS I MADE UP FOR A SCIENCE PROJECT... AIR FRESHENER, HAIR FIXATIVE AND A FOGGER!
THOSE CANS MIGHT COME IN HANDY IF THAT DUMB MOOSE CATCHES ME!
HE ALWAYS DOES, YOU KNOW!
THIS TIME THERE'LL BE A DIFF! LEND ME YOUR LOBES!...ZZZZZT! ZZZT! ZZZ! ZZZ!
YEAH!
WILD!
STAND BY FOR AN ENRAGED MOOSE!!
QUICK, REG! BEHIND THE FENCE BEFORE HE SEES YOU!
DUH! ARCH! I SAW YOU TALKING TO MIDGE-
AH! BUT DID YOU HEAR ME ?!? WHAT WAS I SAYING ?
DUH! I DUNNO! ANYONE WHO'S TALKIN' TO MIDGE AND SEES ME COMIN' ALWAYS EVAPORATES!
HOW'D YOU LIKE TO BE ABLE TO HEAR WHAT THE OTHER GUYS ARE SAYING TO MIDGE ?
2

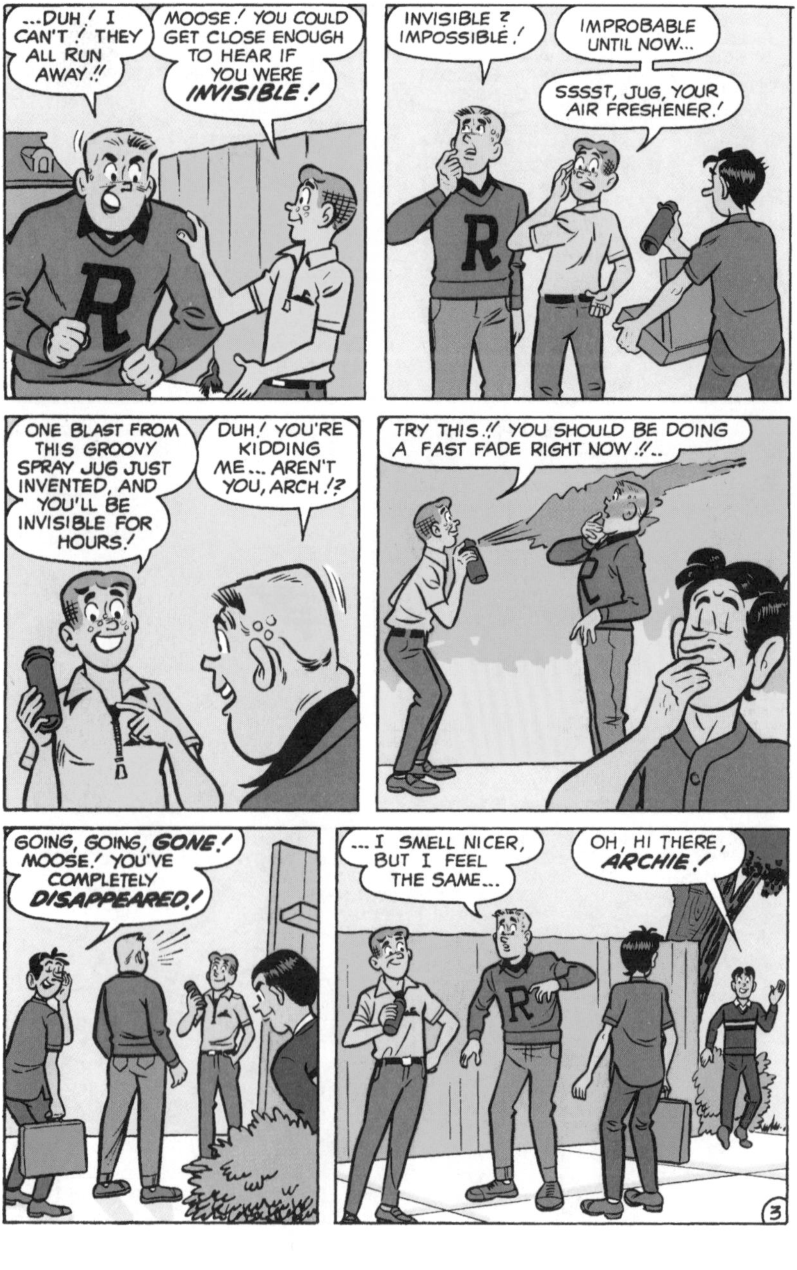
...DUH! I CAN'T! THEY ALL RUN AWAY!!
MOOSE! YOU COULD GET CLOSE ENOUGH TO HEAR IF YOU WERE INVISIBLE!
INVISIBLE? IMPOSSIBLE!
IMPROBABLE UNTIL NOW...
SSSST, JUG, YOUR AIR FRESHENER!
ONE BLAST FROM THIS GROOVY SPRAY JUG JUST INVENTED, AND YOU'LL BE INVISIBLE FOR HOURS!
DUH! YOU'RE KIDDING ME... AREN'T YOU, ARCH!?
TRY THIS!! YOU SHOULD BE DOING A FAST FADE RIGHT NOW!!..
GOING, GOING, GONE! MOOSE! YOU'VE COMPLETELY DISAPPEARED!
... I SMELL NICER, BUT I FEEL THE SAME...
OH, HI THERE, ARCHIE!
3

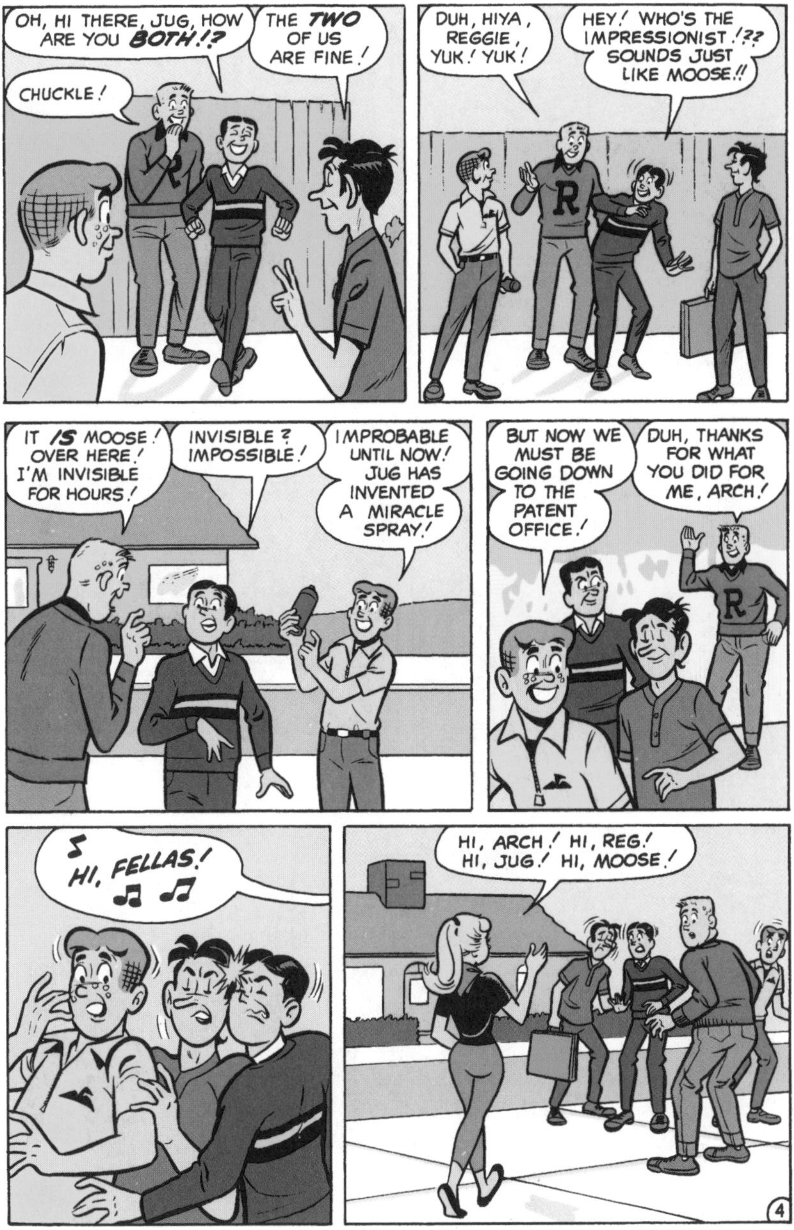
OH, HI THERE, JUG, HOW ARE YOU BOTH!?
CHUCKLE!
THE TWO OF US ARE FINE!
DUH, HIYA, REGGIE, YUK! YUK!
HEY! WHO'S THE IMPRESSIONIST!?? SOUNDS JUST LIKE MOOSE!!
IT IS MOOSE! OVER HERE! I'M INVISIBLE FOR HOURS!
INVISIBLE? IMPOSSIBLE!
IMPROBABLE UNTIL NOW! JUG HAS INVENTED A MIRACLE SPRAY!
BUT NOW WE MUST BE GOING DOWN TO THE PATENT OFFICE!
DUH, THANKS FOR WHAT YOU DID FOR ME, ARCH!
HI, FELLAS!
HI, ARCH! HI, REG! HI, JUG! HI, MOOSE!
4

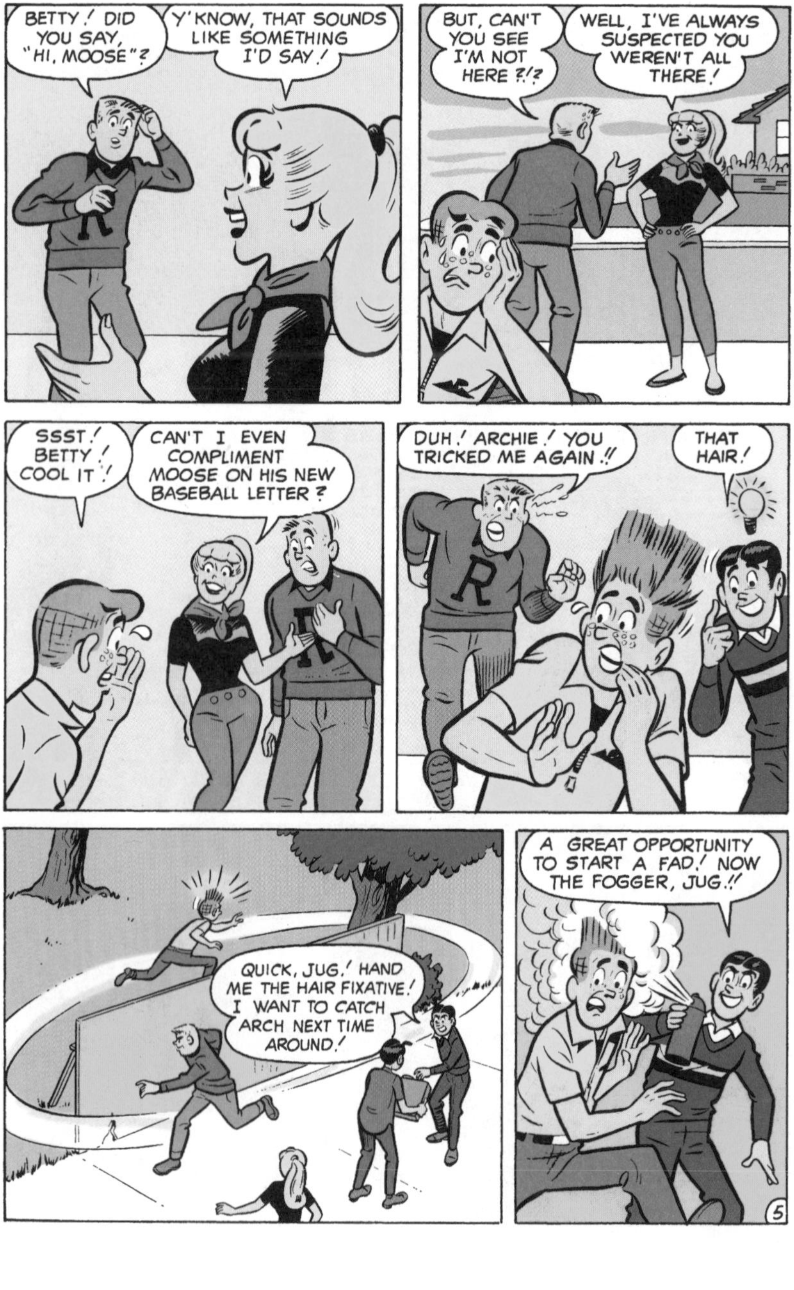
BETTY! DID YOU SAY, "HI, MOOSE"?
Y'KNOW, THAT SOUNDS LIKE SOMETHING I'D SAY!
BUT, CAN'T YOU SEE I'M NOT HERE ?!?
WELL, I'VE ALWAYS SUSPECTED YOU WEREN'T ALL THERE!
SSST! BETTY! COOL IT!
CAN'T I EVEN COMPLIMENT MOOSE ON HIS NEW BASEBALL LETTER?
DUH! ARCHIE! YOU TRICKED ME AGAIN!!
THAT HAIR!
QUICK, JUG! HAND ME THE HAIR FIXATIVE! I WANT TO CATCH ARCH NEXT TIME AROUND!
A GREAT OPPORTUNITY TO START A FAD! NOW THE FOGGER, JUG!!
5

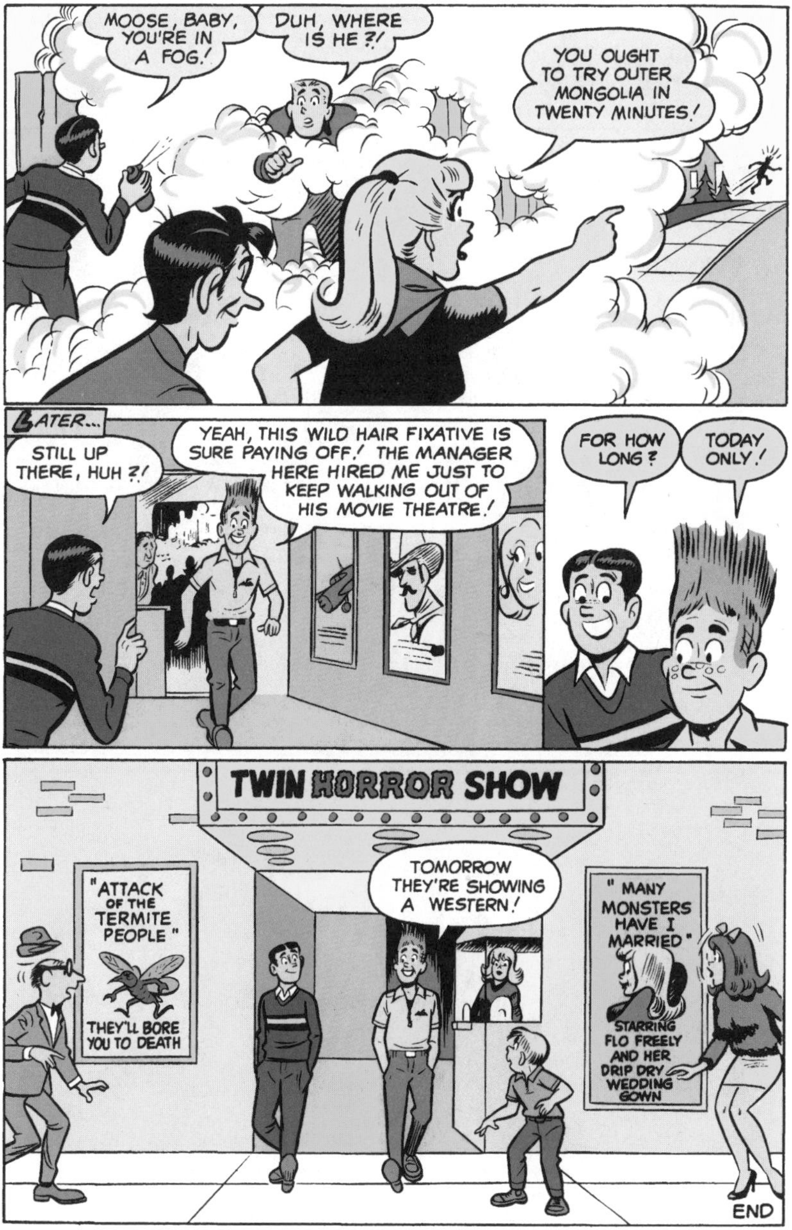
MOOSE, BABY, YOU'RE IN A FOG!
DUH, WHERE IS HE ?!
YOU OUGHT TO TRY OUTER MONGOLIA IN TWENTY MINUTES!
LATER...
STILL UP THERE, HUH ?!
YEAH, THIS WILD HAIR FIXATIVE IS SURE PAYING OFF! THE MANAGER HERE HIRED ME JUST TO KEEP WALKING OUT OF HIS MOVIE THEATRE!
FOR HOW LONG ?
TODAY ONLY!
TWIN HORROR SHOW
"ATTACK OF THE TERMITE PEOPLE"
THEY'LL BORE YOU TO DEATH
TOMORROW THEY'RE SHOWING A WESTERN!
" MANY MONSTERS HAVE I MARRIED"
STARRING FLO FREELY AND HER DRIP DRY WEDDING GOWN
END

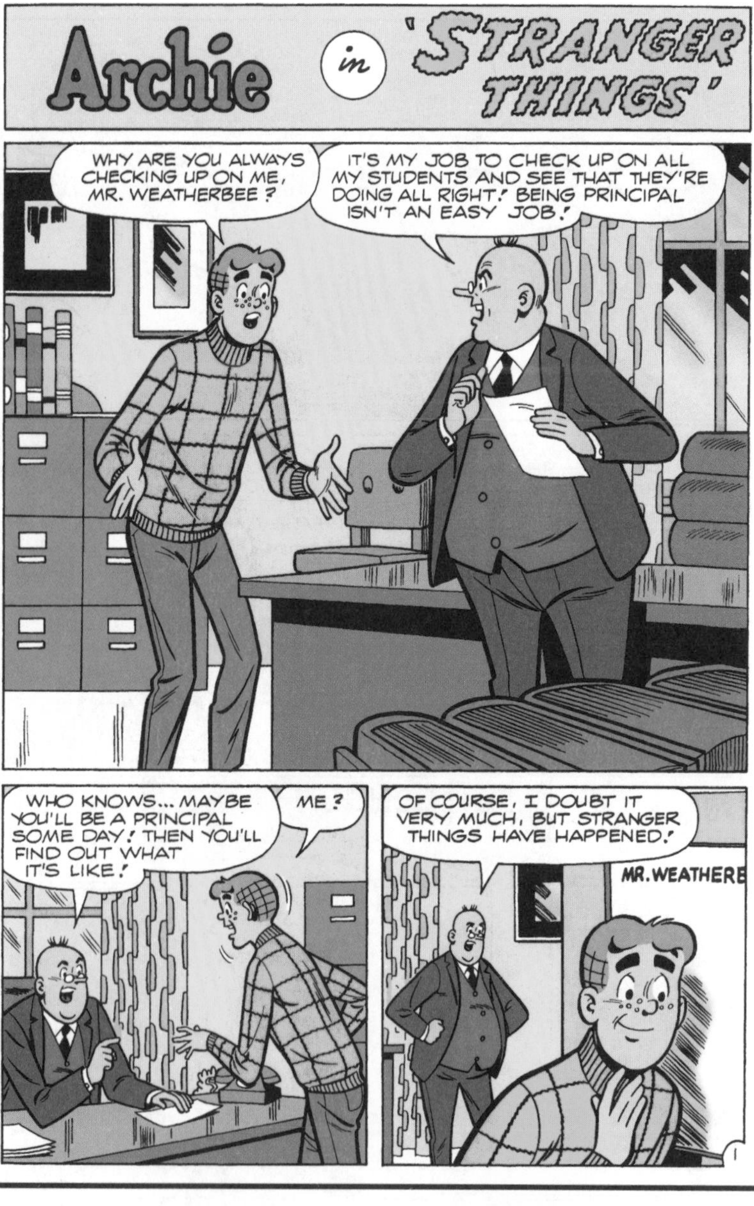
Archie in 'STRANGER THINGS'
WHY ARE YOU ALWAYS CHECKING UP ON ME, MR. WEATHERBEE ?
IT'S MY JOB TO CHECK UP ON ALL MY STUDENTS AND SEE THAT THEY'RE DOING ALL RIGHT! BEING PRINCIPAL ISN'T AN EASY JOB!
WHO KNOWS... MAYBE YOU'LL BE A PRINCIPAL SOME DAY! THEN YOU'LL FIND OUT WHAT IT'S LIKE!
ME ?
OF COURSE, I DOUBT IT VERY MUCH, BUT STRANGER THINGS HAVE HAPPENED!
MR. WEATHERE
1

Story: George Gladir Pencils: Stan Goldberg
Inks & Letters: Jon D'Agostino

Originally printed in EVERYTHING'S ARCHIE #1, MAY 1969

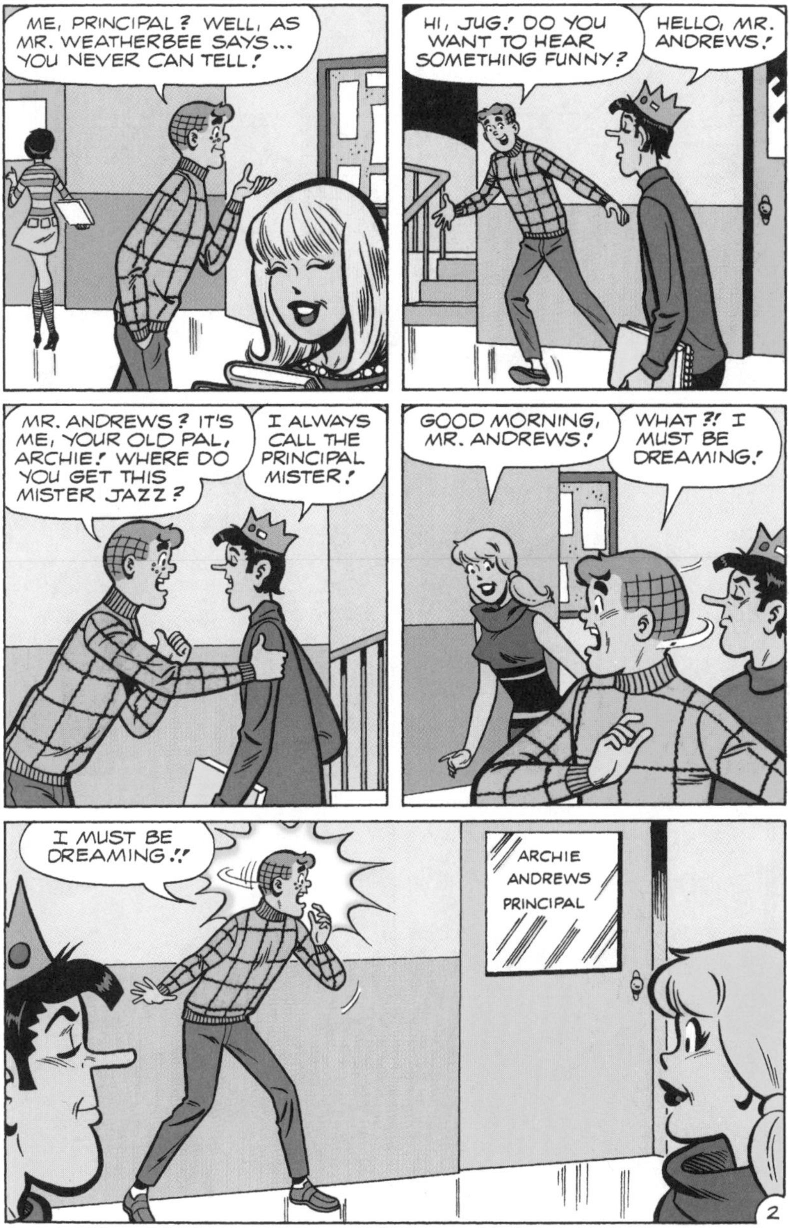
ME, PRINCIPAL? WELL, AS MR. WEATHERBEE SAYS... YOU NEVER CAN TELL!
HI, JUG! DO YOU WANT TO HEAR SOMETHING FUNNY?
HELLO, MR. ANDREWS!
MR. ANDREWS? IT'S ME, YOUR OLD PAL, ARCHIE! WHERE DO YOU GET THIS MISTER JAZZ?
I ALWAYS CALL THE PRINCIPAL MISTER!
GOOD MORNING, MR. ANDREWS!
WHAT?! I MUST BE DREAMING!
I MUST BE DREAMING!!
ARCHIE ANDREWS PRINCIPAL
2

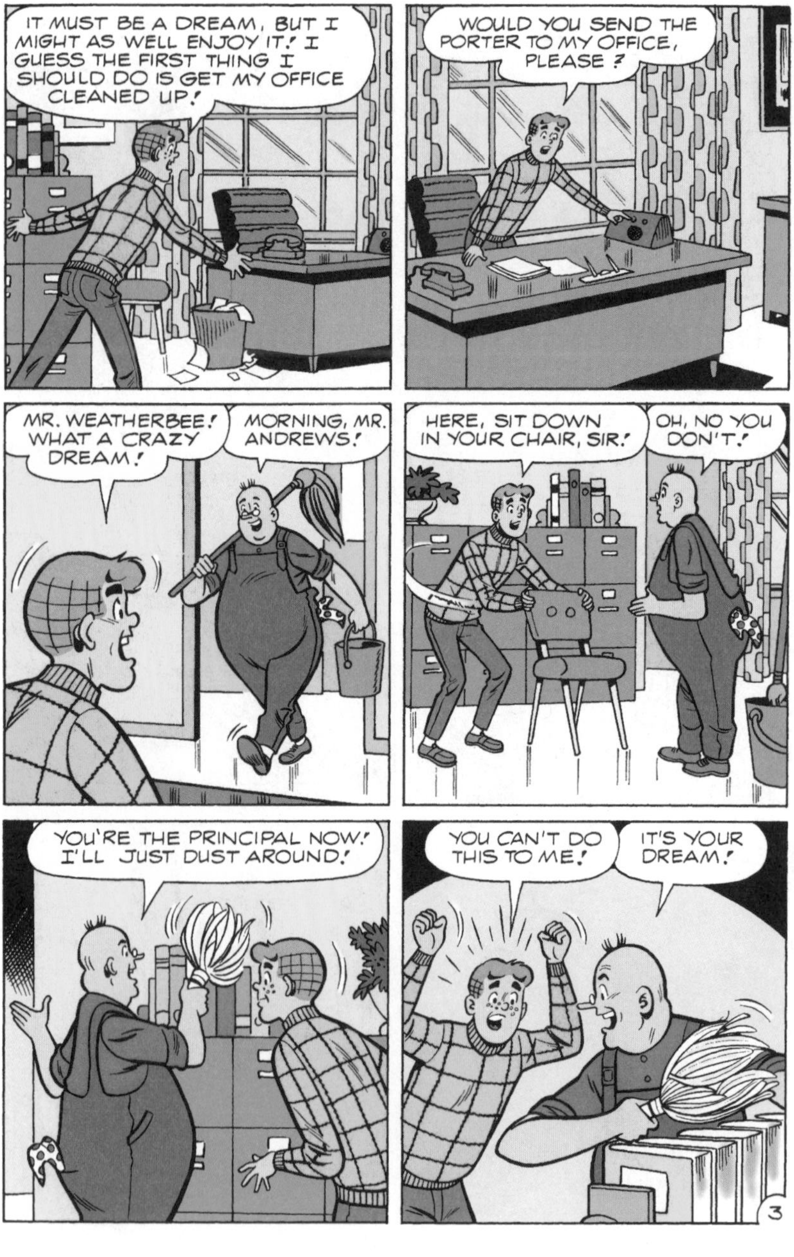
IT MUST BE A DREAM, BUT I MIGHT AS WELL ENJOY IT! I GUESS THE FIRST THING I SHOULD DO IS GET MY OFFICE CLEANED UP!
WOULD YOU SEND THE PORTER TO MY OFFICE, PLEASE?
MR. WEATHERBEE! WHAT A CRAZY DREAM!
MORNING, MR. ANDREWS!
HERE, SIT DOWN IN YOUR CHAIR, SIR!
OH, NO YOU DON'T!
YOU'RE THE PRINCIPAL NOW! I'LL JUST DUST AROUND!
YOU CAN'T DO THIS TO ME!
IT'S YOUR DREAM!
3

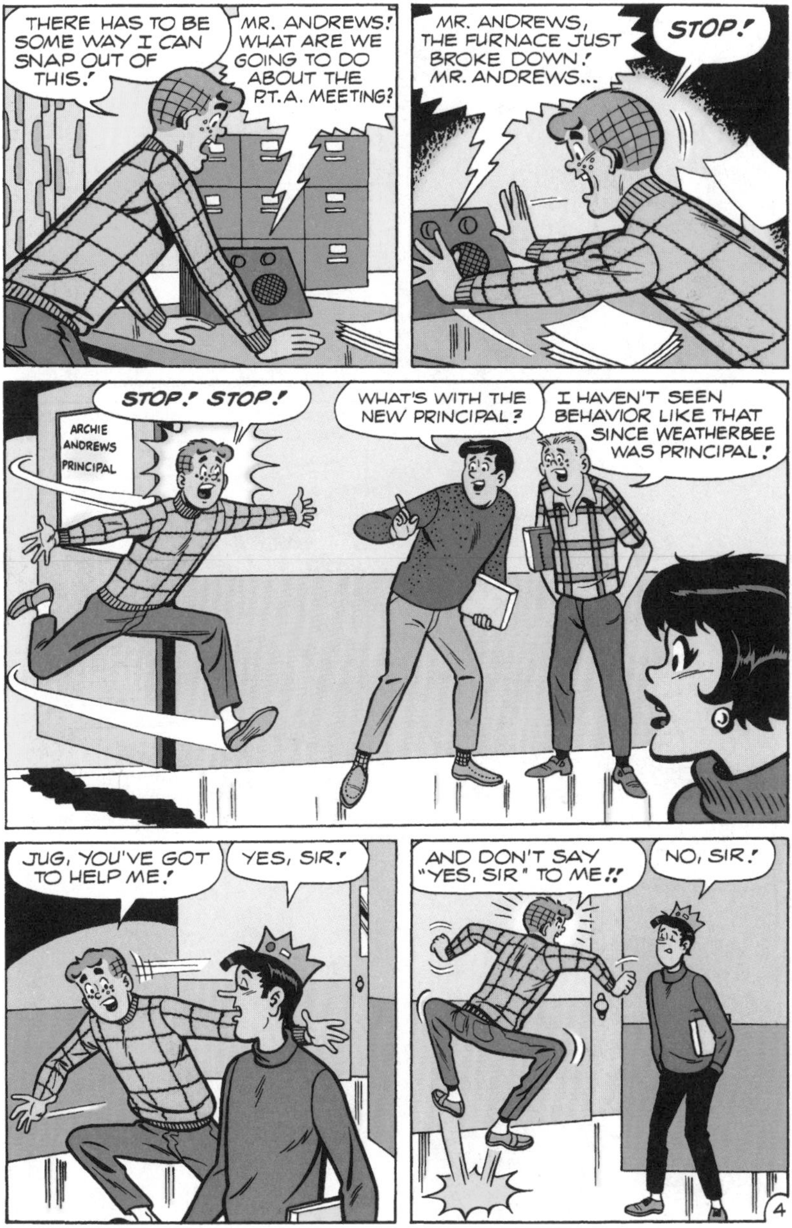
THERE HAS TO BE SOME WAY I CAN SNAP OUT OF THIS!
MR. ANDREWS! WHAT ARE WE GOING TO DO ABOUT THE P.T.A. MEETING?
MR. ANDREWS, THE FURNACE JUST BROKE DOWN! MR. ANDREWS...
STOP!
ARCHIE ANDREWS PRINCIPAL
STOP! STOP!
WHAT'S WITH THE NEW PRINCIPAL?
I HAVEN'T SEEN BEHAVIOR LIKE THAT SINCE WEATHERBEE WAS PRINCIPAL!
JUG, YOU'VE GOT TO HELP ME!
YES, SIR!
AND DON'T SAY "YES, SIR" TO ME!!
NO, SIR!
4

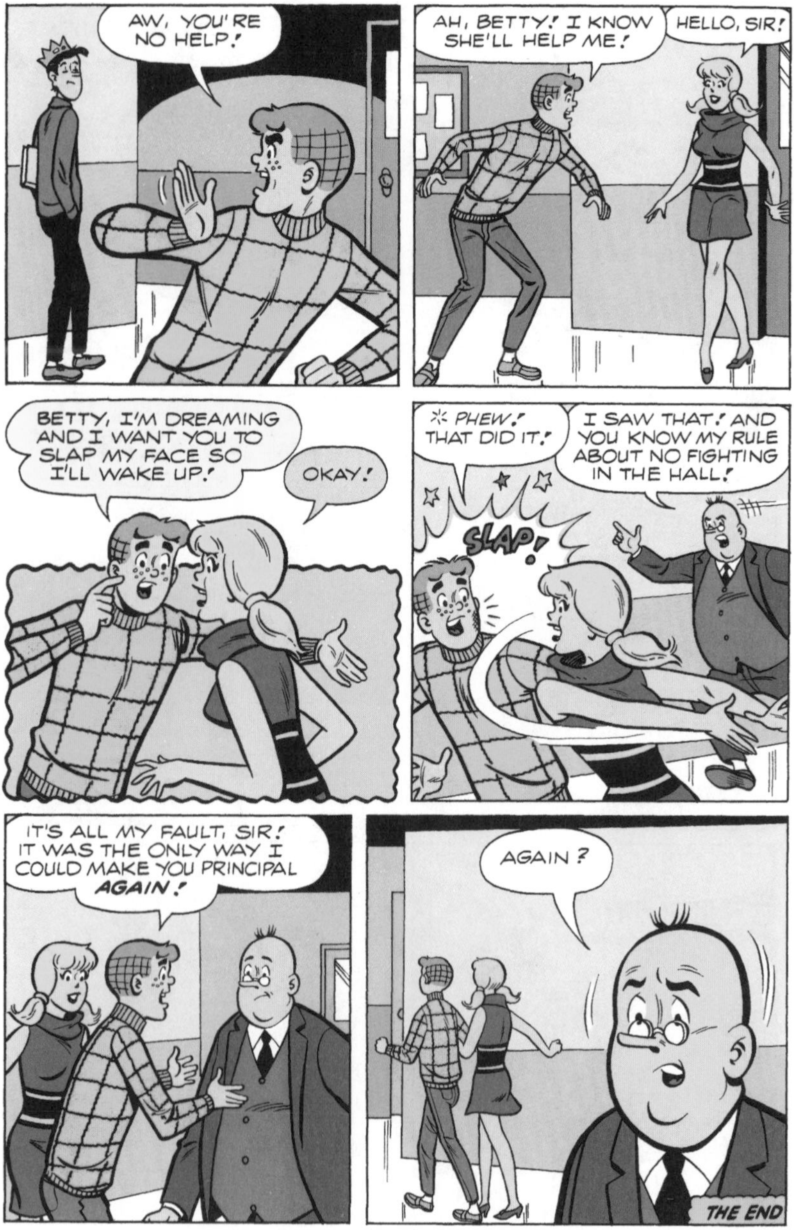
AW, YOU'RE NO HELP!
AH, BETTY! I KNOW SHE'LL HELP ME!
HELLO, SIR!
BETTY, I'M DREAMING AND I WANT YOU TO SLAP MY FACE SO I'LL WAKE UP!
OKAY!
SLAP!
PHEW! THAT DID IT!
I SAW THAT! AND YOU KNOW MY RULE ABOUT NO FIGHTING IN THE HALL!
IT'S ALL MY FAULT, SIR! IT WAS THE ONLY WAY I COULD MAKE YOU PRINCIPAL AGAIN!
AGAIN?
THE END

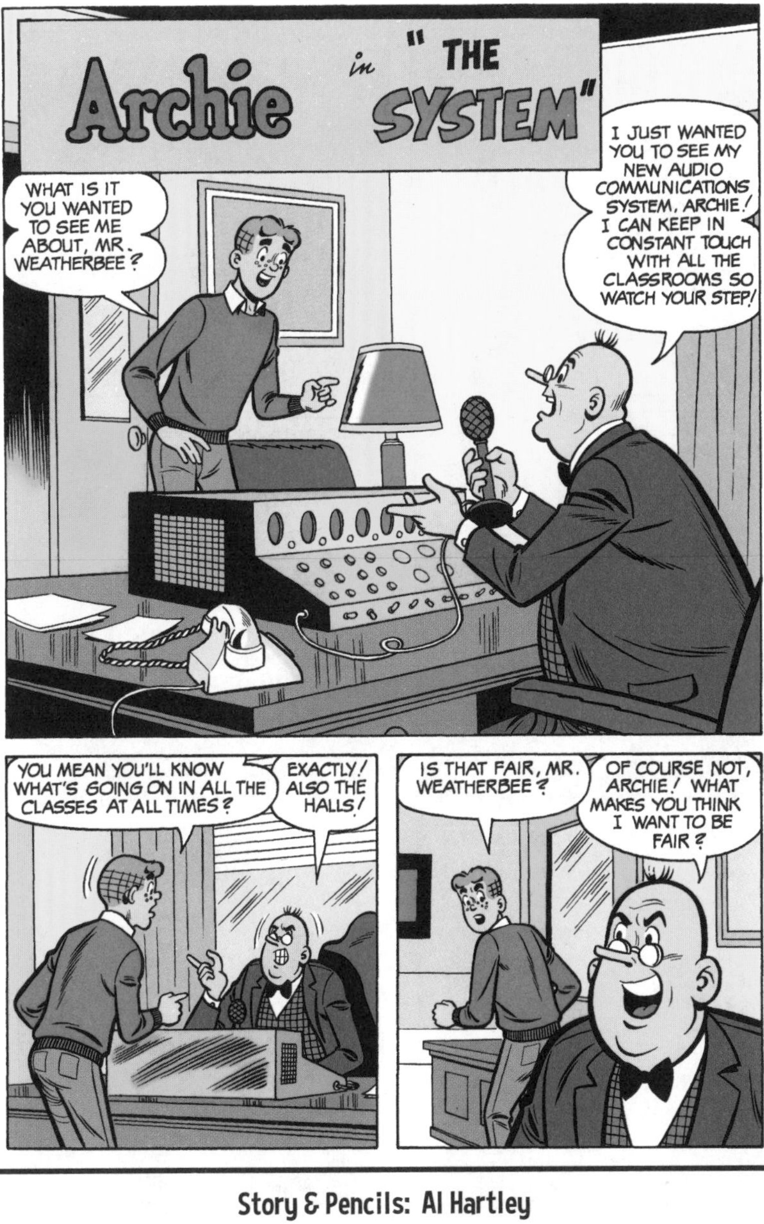
Archie in "THE SYSTEM"
WHAT IS IT YOU WANTED TO SEE ME ABOUT, MR. WEATHERBEE?
I JUST WANTED YOU TO SEE MY NEW AUDIO COMMUNICATIONS SYSTEM, ARCHIE! I CAN KEEP IN CONSTANT TOUCH WITH ALL THE CLASSROOMS SO WATCH YOUR STEP!
YOU MEAN YOU'LL KNOW WHAT'S GOING ON IN ALL THE CLASSES AT ALL TIMES?
EXACTLY! ALSO THE HALLS!
IS THAT FAIR, MR. WEATHERBEE?
OF COURSE NOT, ARCHIE! WHAT MAKES YOU THINK I WANT TO BE FAIR?

Story & Pencils: Al Hartley

Inks: Jon D'Agostino   Letters: Bill Yoshida

Originally printed in EVERYTHING'S ARCHIE #1, MAY 1969

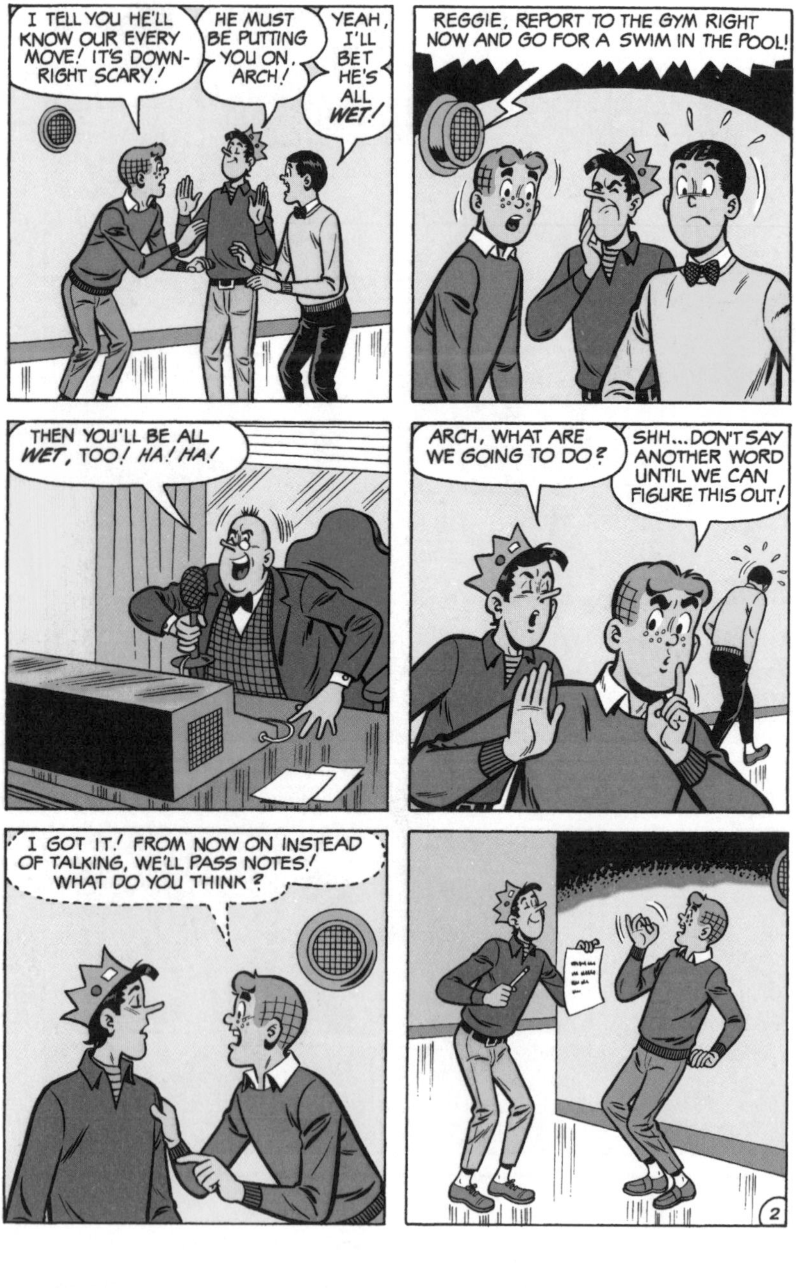
I TELL YOU HE'LL KNOW OUR EVERY MOVE! IT'S DOWN-RIGHT SCARY!
HE MUST BE PUTTING YOU ON, ARCH!
YEAH, I'LL BET HE'S ALL WET!
REGGIE, REPORT TO THE GYM RIGHT NOW AND GO FOR A SWIM IN THE POOL!
THEN YOU'LL BE ALL WET, TOO! HA! HA!
ARCH, WHAT ARE WE GOING TO DO?
SHH...DON'T SAY ANOTHER WORD UNTIL WE CAN FIGURE THIS OUT!
I GOT IT! FROM NOW ON INSTEAD OF TALKING, WE'LL PASS NOTES! WHAT DO YOU THINK?
2

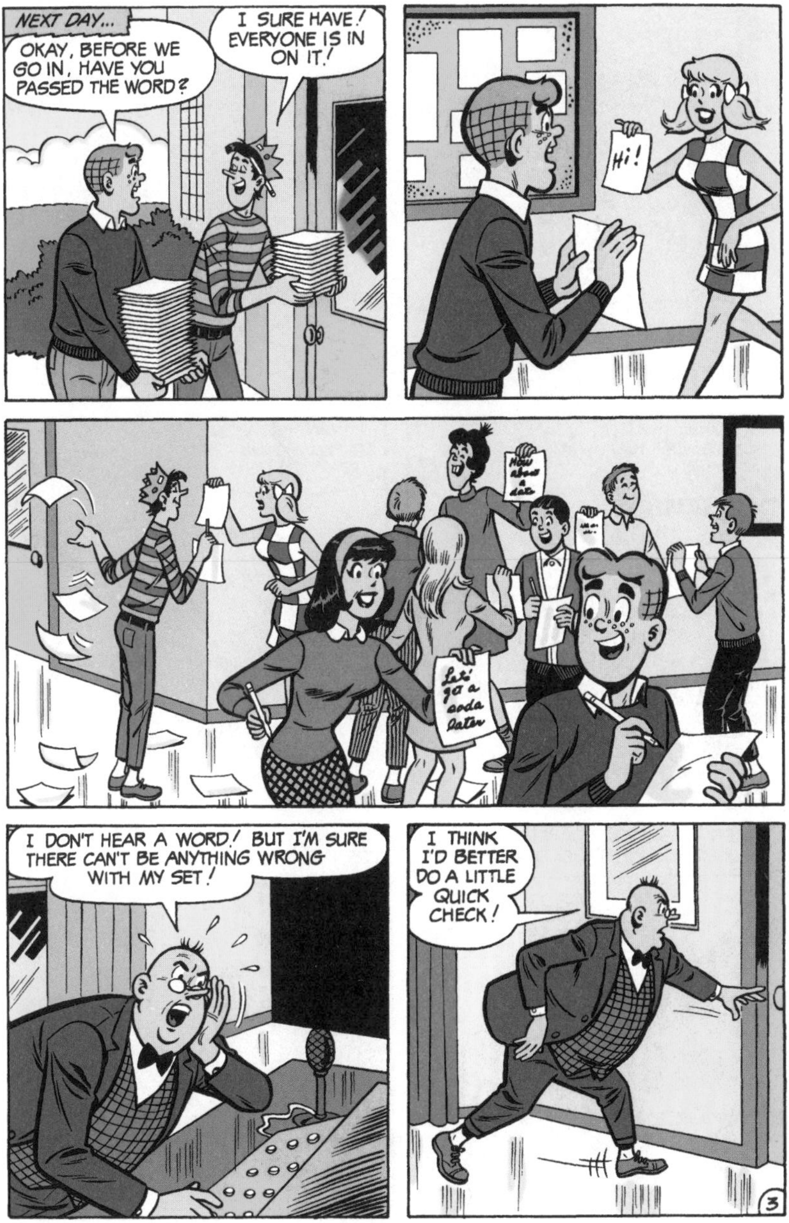
NEXT DAY...
OKAY, BEFORE WE GO IN, HAVE YOU PASSED THE WORD?
I SURE HAVE! EVERYONE IS IN ON IT!
Hi!
How about a date
Let's get a soda date
I DON'T HEAR A WORD! BUT I'M SURE THERE CAN'T BE ANYTHING WRONG WITH MY SET!
I THINK I'D BETTER DO A LITTLE QUICK CHECK!
3

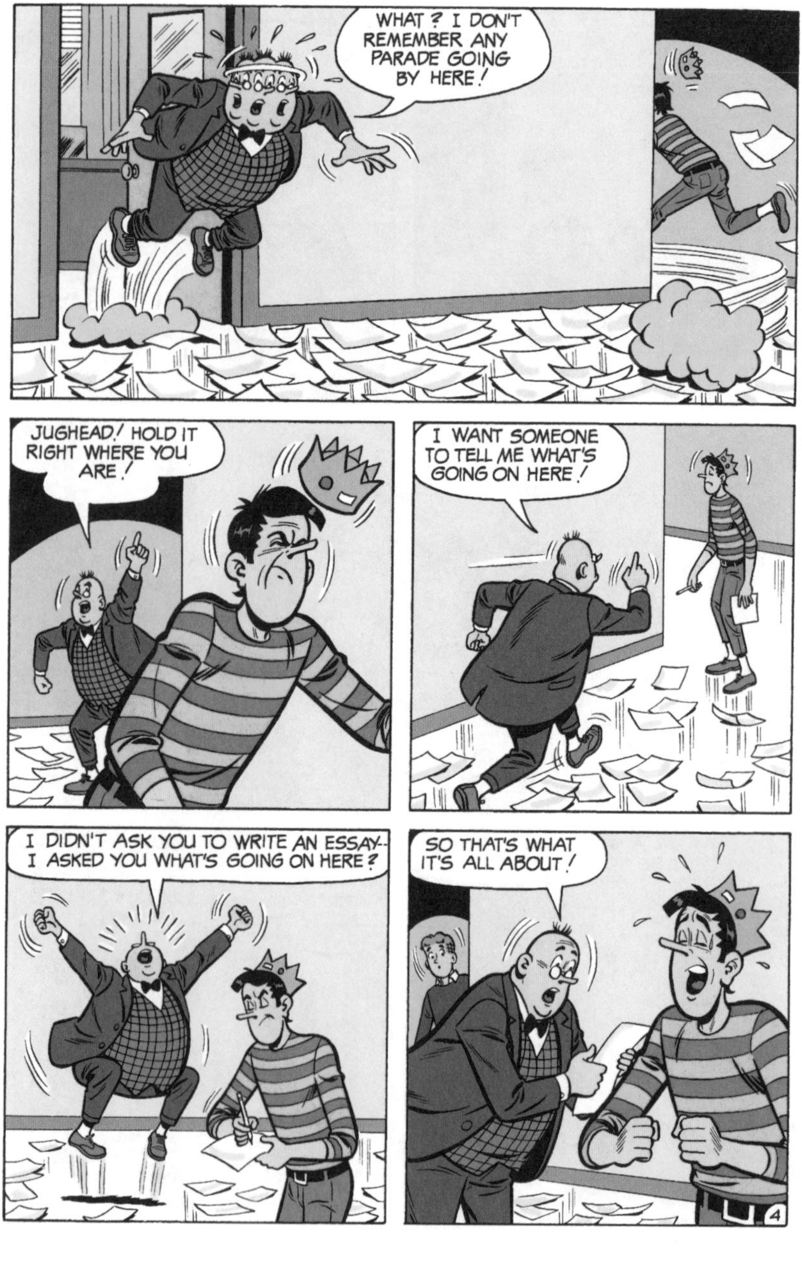
WHAT ? I DON'T REMEMBER ANY PARADE GOING BY HERE !
JUGHEAD! HOLD IT RIGHT WHERE YOU ARE !
I WANT SOMEONE TO TELL ME WHAT'S GOING ON HERE !
I DIDN'T ASK YOU TO WRITE AN ESSAY-- I ASKED YOU WHAT'S GOING ON HERE ?
SO THAT'S WHAT IT'S ALL ABOUT !
4

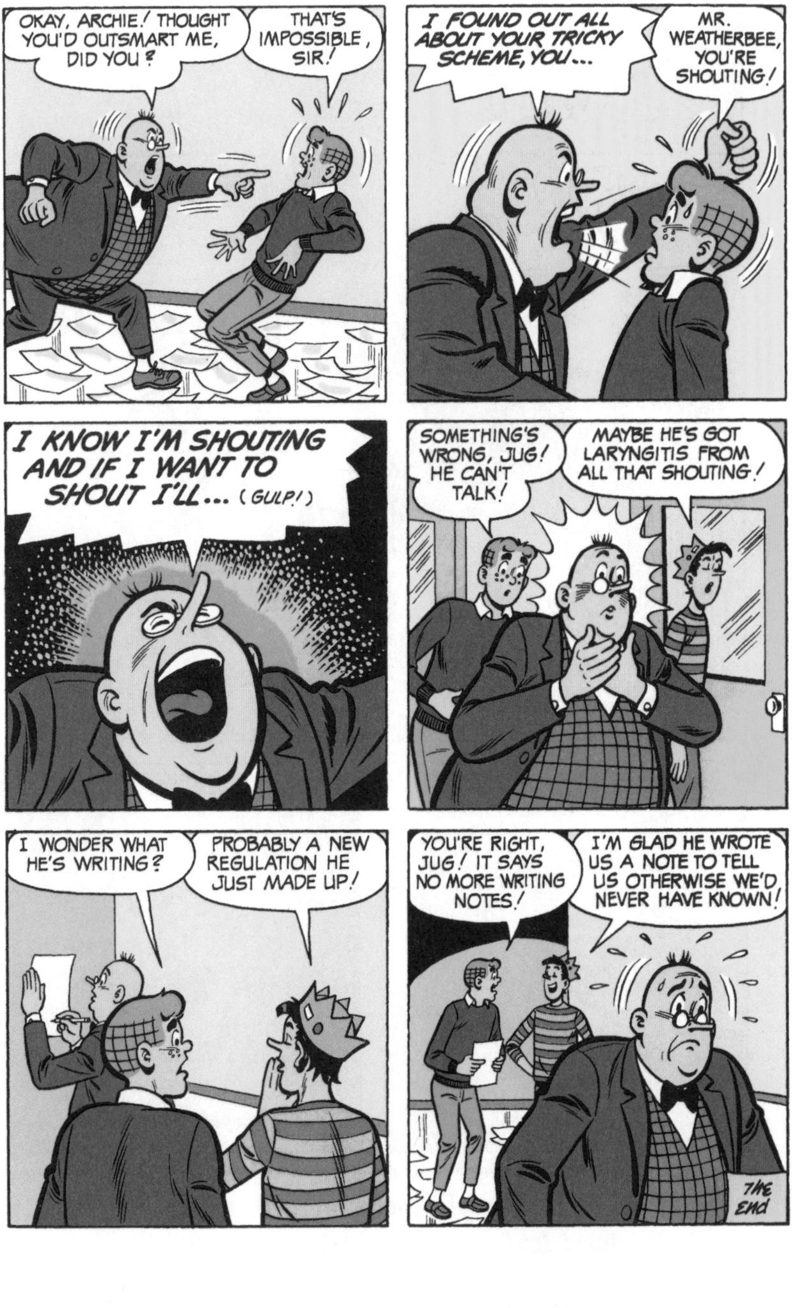
OKAY, ARCHIE! THOUGHT YOU'D OUTSMART ME, DID YOU?
THAT'S IMPOSSIBLE, SIR!
I FOUND OUT ALL ABOUT YOUR TRICKY SCHEME, YOU...
MR. WEATHERBEE, YOU'RE SHOUTING!
I KNOW I'M SHOUTING AND IF I WANT TO SHOUT I'LL... (GULP!)
SOMETHING'S WRONG, JUG! HE CAN'T TALK!
MAYBE HE'S GOT LARYNGITIS FROM ALL THAT SHOUTING!
I WONDER WHAT HE'S WRITING?
PROBABLY A NEW REGULATION HE JUST MADE UP!
YOU'RE RIGHT, JUG! IT SAYS NO MORE WRITING NOTES!
I'M GLAD HE WROTE US A NOTE TO TELL US OTHERWISE WE'D NEVER HAVE KNOWN!
THE End

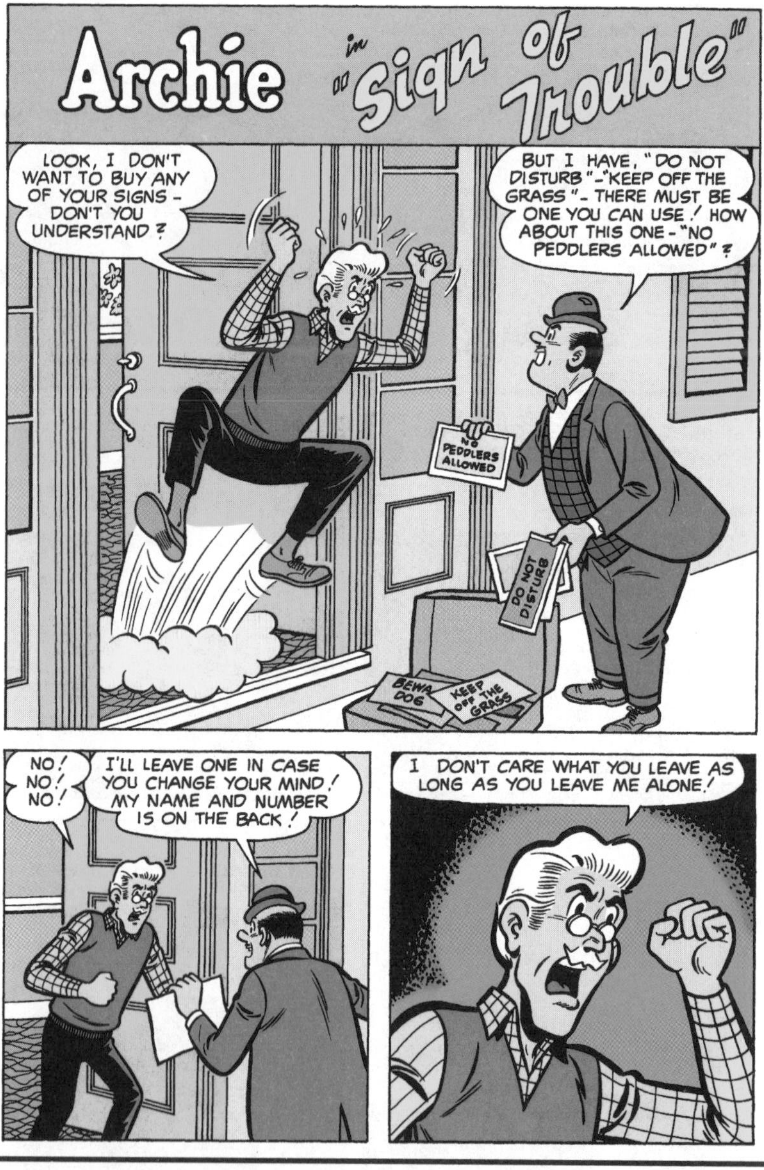
Archie in "Sign of Trouble"
LOOK, I DON'T WANT TO BUY ANY OF YOUR SIGNS - DON'T YOU UNDERSTAND ?
BUT I HAVE, "DO NOT DISTURB" - "KEEP OFF THE GRASS" - THERE MUST BE ONE YOU CAN USE! HOW ABOUT THIS ONE - "NO PEDDLERS ALLOWED" ?
NO PEDDLERS ALLOWED
DO NOT DISTURB
KEEP OFF THE GRASS
NO! NO! NO!
I'LL LEAVE ONE IN CASE YOU CHANGE YOUR MIND! MY NAME AND NUMBER IS ON THE BACK!
I DON'T CARE WHAT YOU LEAVE AS LONG AS YOU LEAVE ME ALONE!

Story & Pencils: Al Hartley
Inks: Jon D'Agostino Letters: Bill Yoshida

Originally printed in EVERYTHING'S ARCHIE #2, JULY 1969

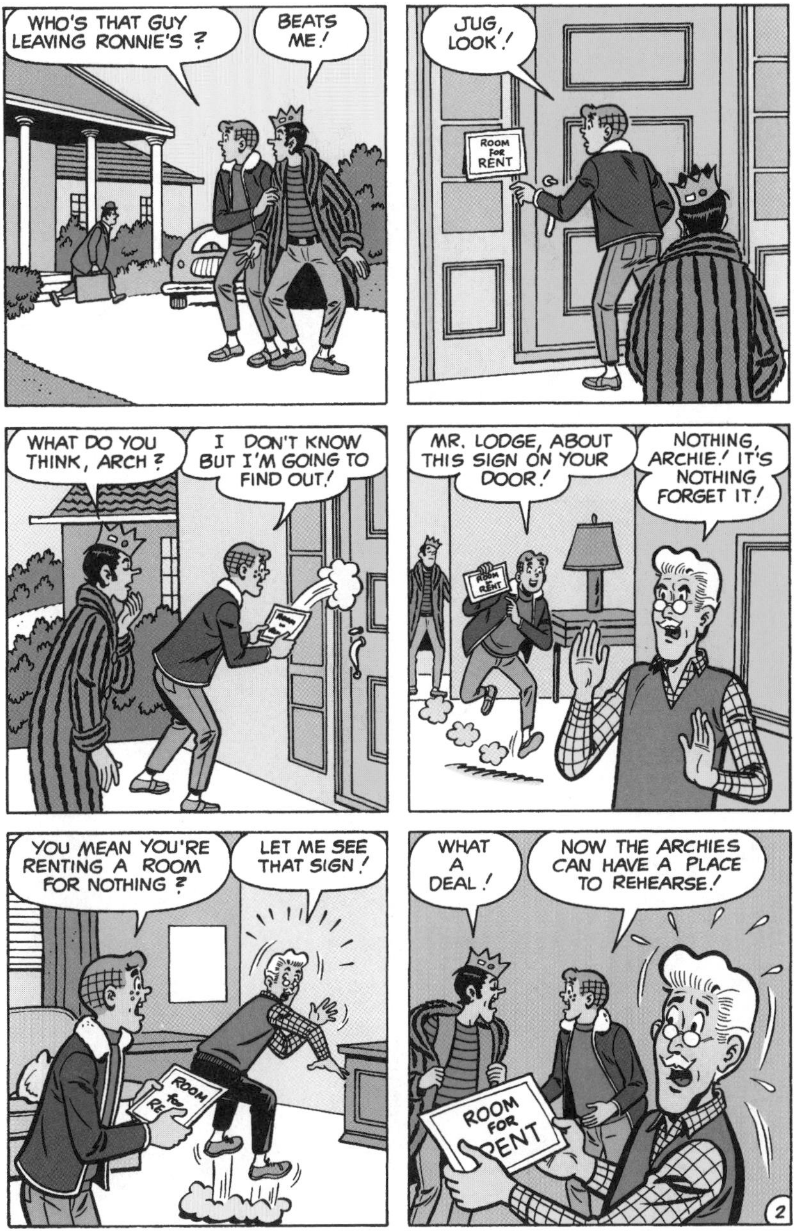
WHO'S THAT GUY LEAVING RONNIE'S ?
BEATS ME!
JUG, LOOK!
ROOM FOR RENT
WHAT DO YOU THINK, ARCH ?
I DON'T KNOW BUT I'M GOING TO FIND OUT!
MR. LODGE, ABOUT THIS SIGN ON YOUR DOOR!
NOTHING, ARCHIE! IT'S NOTHING FORGET IT!
YOU MEAN YOU'RE RENTING A ROOM FOR NOTHING ?
LET ME SEE THAT SIGN!
WHAT A DEAL!
NOW THE ARCHIES CAN HAVE A PLACE TO REHEARSE!
2

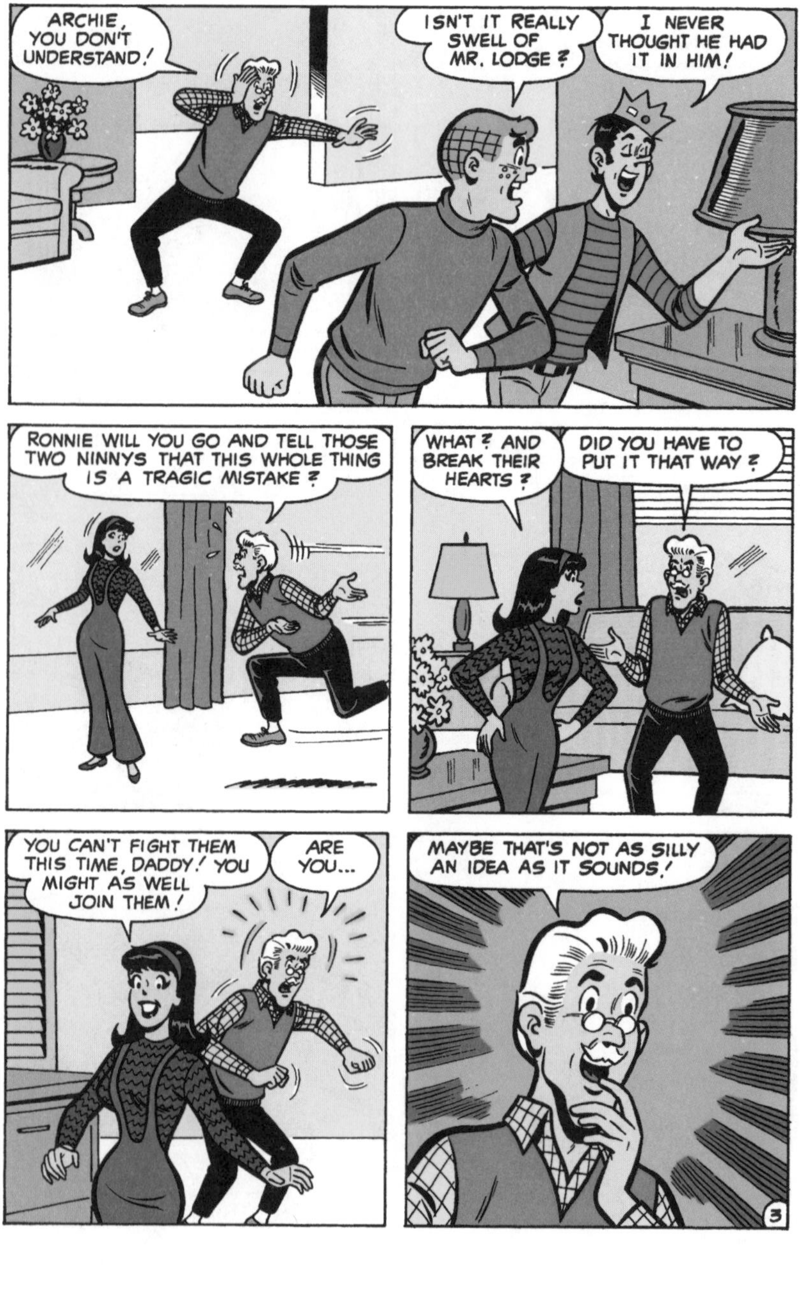
ARCHIE, YOU DON'T UNDERSTAND!
ISN'T IT REALLY SWELL OF MR. LODGE?
I NEVER THOUGHT HE HAD IT IN HIM!
RONNIE WILL YOU GO AND TELL THOSE TWO NINNYS THAT THIS WHOLE THING IS A TRAGIC MISTAKE?
WHAT? AND BREAK THEIR HEARTS?
DID YOU HAVE TO PUT IT THAT WAY?
YOU CAN'T FIGHT THEM THIS TIME, DADDY! YOU MIGHT AS WELL JOIN THEM!
ARE YOU...
MAYBE THAT'S NOT AS SILLY AN IDEA AS IT SOUNDS!
3

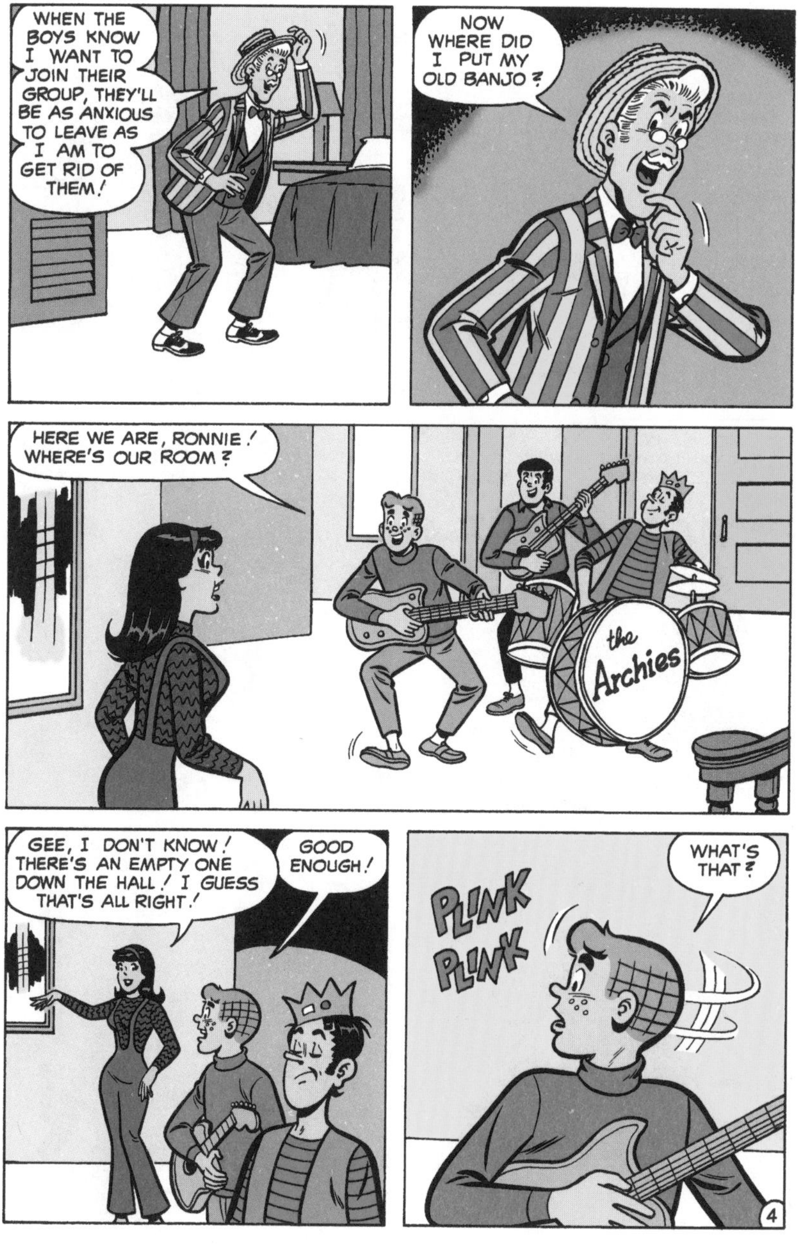
WHEN THE BOYS KNOW I WANT TO JOIN THEIR GROUP, THEY'LL BE AS ANXIOUS TO LEAVE AS I AM TO GET RID OF THEM!
NOW WHERE DID I PUT MY OLD BANJO?
HERE WE ARE, RONNIE! WHERE'S OUR ROOM?
the Archies
GEE, I DON'T KNOW! THERE'S AN EMPTY ONE DOWN THE HALL! I GUESS THAT'S ALL RIGHT!
GOOD ENOUGH!
PLINK PLINK
WHAT'S THAT?
4

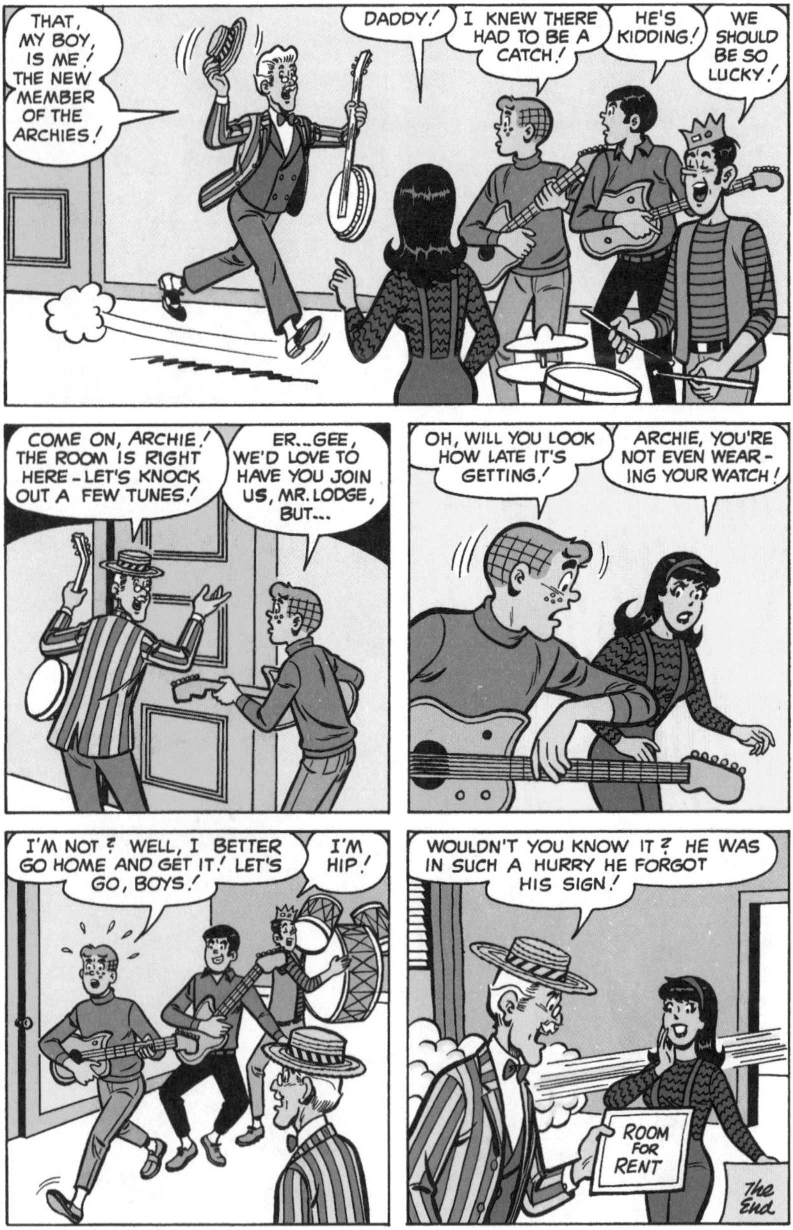
THAT, MY BOY, IS ME! THE NEW MEMBER OF THE ARCHIES!
DADDY!
I KNEW THERE HAD TO BE A CATCH!
HE'S KIDDING!
WE SHOULD BE SO LUCKY!
COME ON, ARCHIE! THE ROOM IS RIGHT HERE-LET'S KNOCK OUT A FEW TUNES!
ER...GEE, WE'D LOVE TO HAVE YOU JOIN US, MR. LODGE, BUT...
OH, WILL YOU LOOK HOW LATE IT'S GETTING!
ARCHIE, YOU'RE NOT EVEN WEAR-ING YOUR WATCH!
I'M NOT? WELL, I BETTER GO HOME AND GET IT! LET'S GO, BOYS!
I'M HIP!
WOULDN'T YOU KNOW IT? HE WAS IN SUCH A HURRY HE FORGOT HIS SIGN!
ROOM FOR RENT
The End

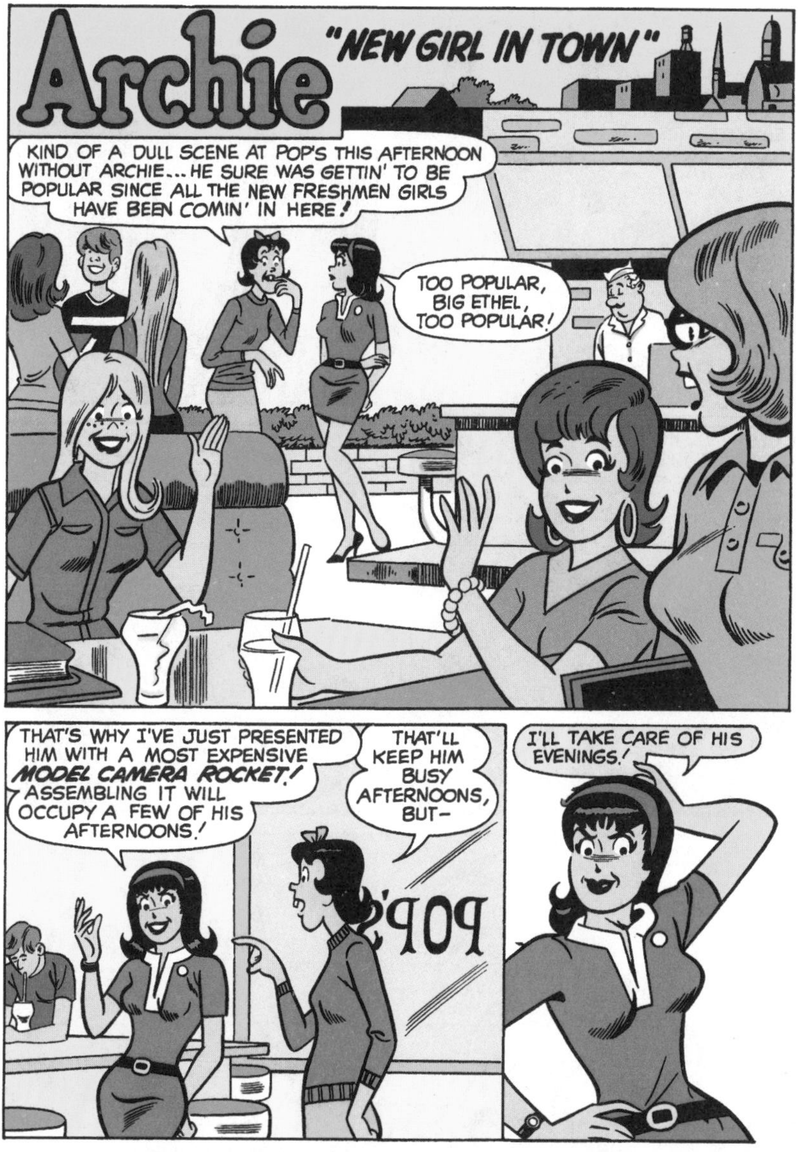
Archie
"NEW GIRL IN TOWN"
KIND OF A DULL SCENE AT POP'S THIS AFTERNOON WITHOUT ARCHIE... HE SURE WAS GETTIN' TO BE POPULAR SINCE ALL THE NEW FRESHMEN GIRLS HAVE BEEN COMIN' IN HERE!
TOO POPULAR, BIG ETHEL, TOO POPULAR!
THAT'S WHY I'VE JUST PRESENTED HIM WITH A MOST EXPENSIVE MODEL CAMERA ROCKET! ASSEMBLING IT WILL OCCUPY A FEW OF HIS AFTERNOONS!
THAT'LL KEEP HIM BUSY AFTERNOONS, BUT–
POP'S
I'LL TAKE CARE OF HIS EVENINGS!

Story & Pencils: Bob Bolling

Inks: Rudy Lapick Letters: Bill Yoshida

Originally printed in EVERYTHING'S ARCHIE #2, JULY 1969

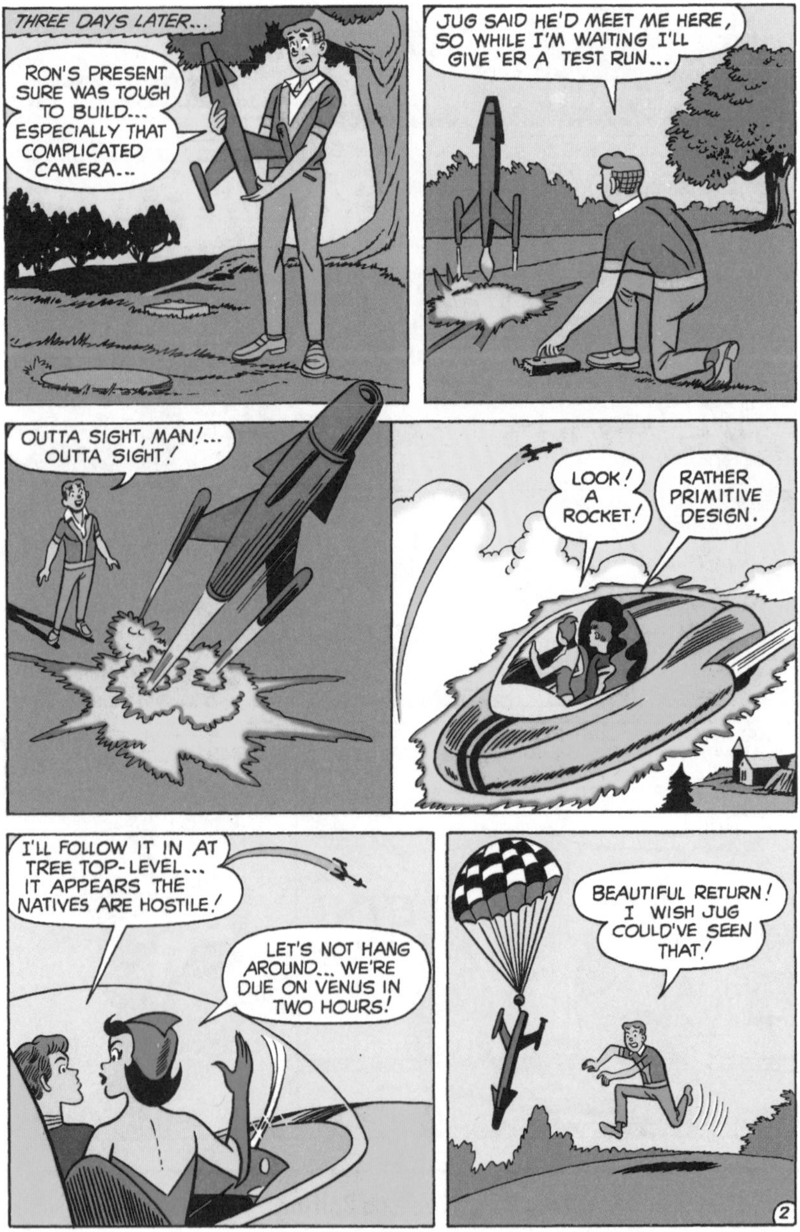
THREE DAYS LATER...
RON'S PRESENT SURE WAS TOUGH TO BUILD... ESPECIALLY THAT COMPLICATED CAMERA...
JUG SAID HE'D MEET ME HERE, SO WHILE I'M WAITING I'LL GIVE 'ER A TEST RUN...
OUTTA SIGHT, MAN!... OUTTA SIGHT!
LOOK! A ROCKET!
RATHER PRIMITIVE DESIGN.
I'LL FOLLOW IT IN AT TREE TOP-LEVEL... IT APPEARS THE NATIVES ARE HOSTILE!
LET'S NOT HANG AROUND... WE'RE DUE ON VENUS IN TWO HOURS!
BEAUTIFUL RETURN! I WISH JUG COULD'VE SEEN THAT!
2

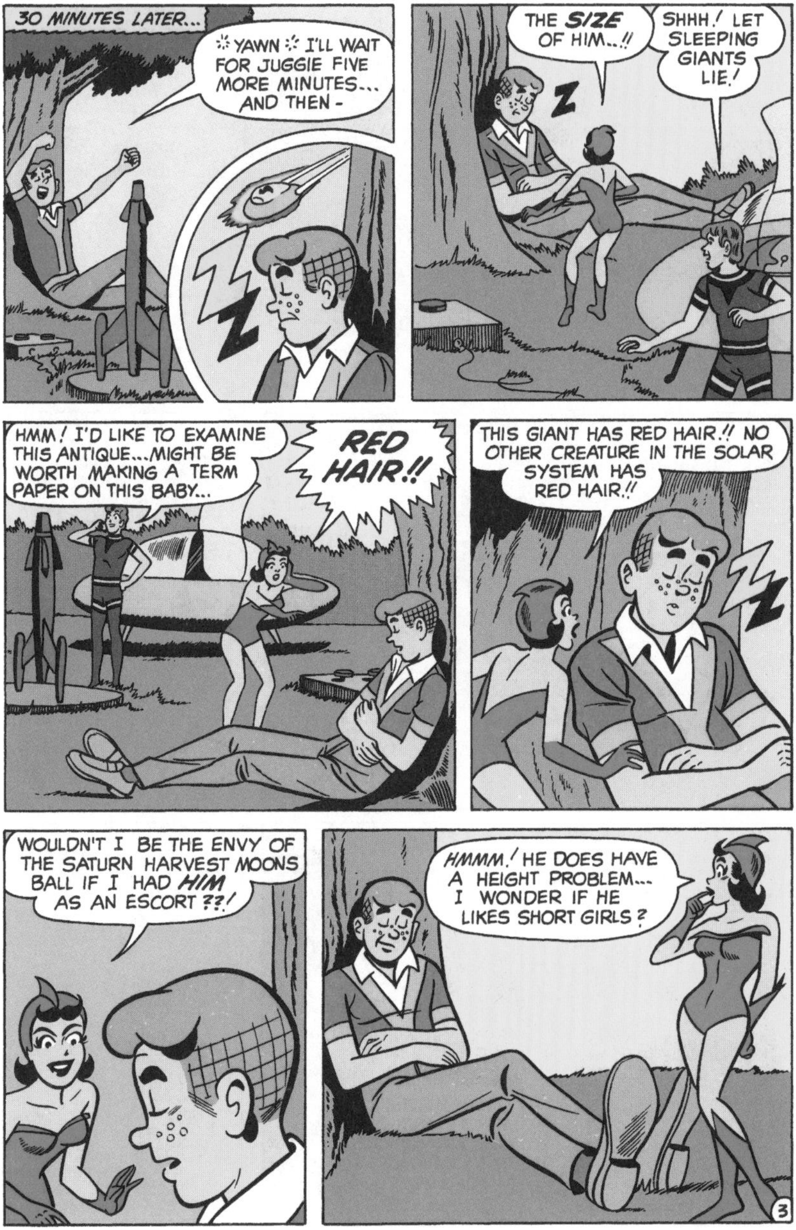
30 MINUTES LATER...
YAWN I'LL WAIT FOR JUGGIE FIVE MORE MINUTES... AND THEN -
THE SIZE OF HIM..!!
SHHH! LET SLEEPING GIANTS LIE!
Z
HMM! I'D LIKE TO EXAMINE THIS ANTIQUE...MIGHT BE WORTH MAKING A TERM PAPER ON THIS BABY...
RED HAIR!!
THIS GIANT HAS RED HAIR!! NO OTHER CREATURE IN THE SOLAR SYSTEM HAS RED HAIR!!
WOULDN'T I BE THE ENVY OF THE SATURN HARVEST MOONS BALL IF I HAD HIM AS AN ESCORT ??!
HMMM! HE DOES HAVE A HEIGHT PROBLEM... I WONDER IF HE LIKES SHORT GIRLS ?
3

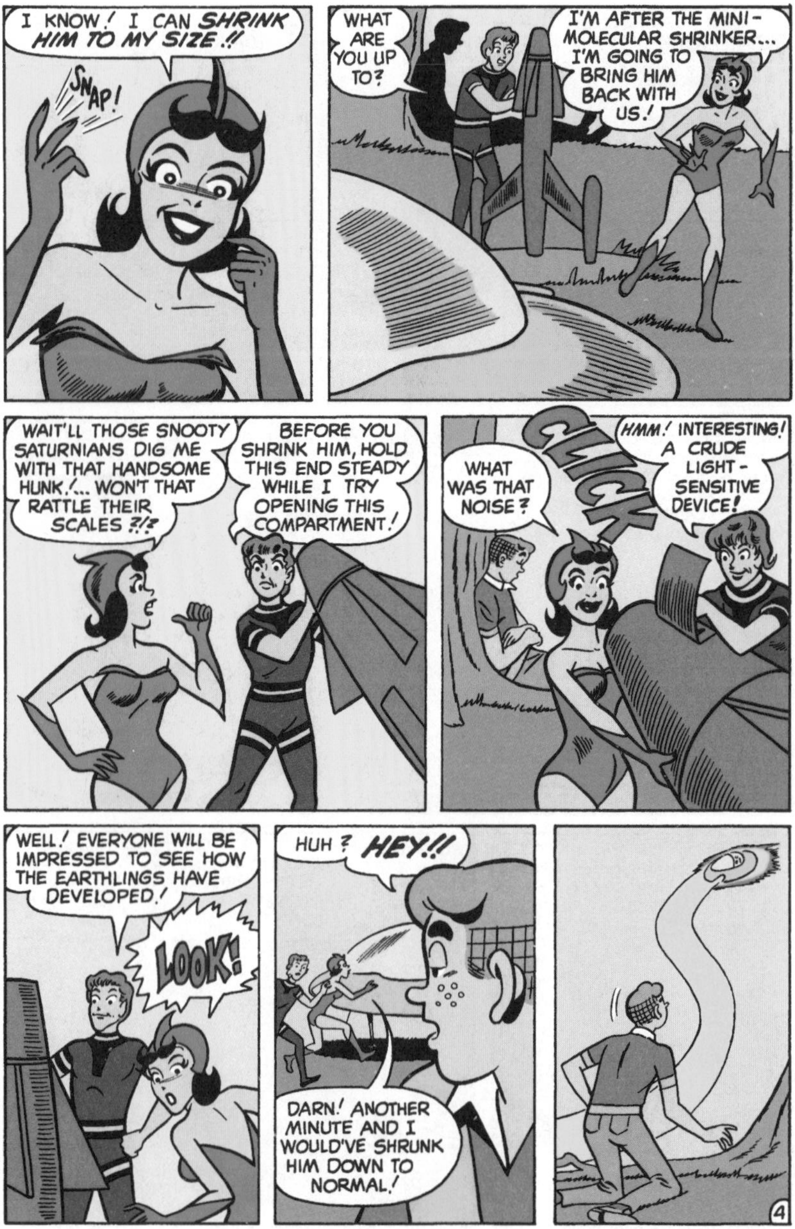
I KNOW! I CAN SHRINK HIM TO MY SIZE!!
SNAP!
WHAT ARE YOU UP TO?
I'M AFTER THE MINI-MOLECULAR SHRINKER... I'M GOING TO BRING HIM BACK WITH US!
WAIT'LL THOSE SNOOTY SATURNIANS DIG ME WITH THAT HANDSOME HUNK!... WON'T THAT RATTLE THEIR SCALES?!?
BEFORE YOU SHRINK HIM, HOLD THIS END STEADY WHILE I TRY OPENING THIS COMPARTMENT!
CLICK
WHAT WAS THAT NOISE?
HMM! INTERESTING! A CRUDE LIGHT-SENSITIVE DEVICE!
WELL! EVERYONE WILL BE IMPRESSED TO SEE HOW THE EARTHLINGS HAVE DEVELOPED!
LOOK!
HUH? HEY!!
DARN! ANOTHER MINUTE AND I WOULD'VE SHRUNK HIM DOWN TO NORMAL!
4

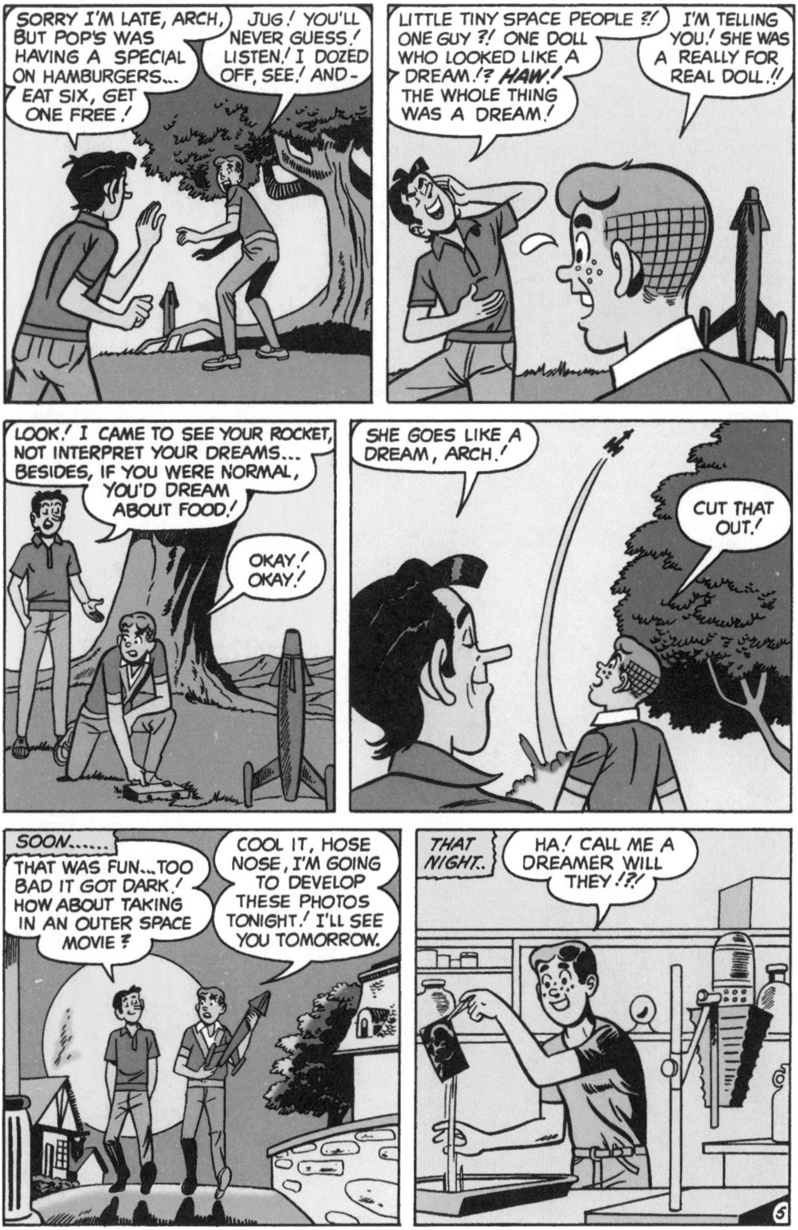
SORRY I'M LATE, ARCH, BUT POP'S WAS HAVING A SPECIAL ON HAMBURGERS... EAT SIX, GET ONE FREE!
JUG! YOU'LL NEVER GUESS! LISTEN! I DOZED OFF, SEE! AND-
LITTLE TINY SPACE PEOPLE ?! ONE GUY ?! ONE DOLL WHO LOOKED LIKE A DREAM !? HAW! THE WHOLE THING WAS A DREAM!
I'M TELLING YOU! SHE WAS A REALLY FOR REAL DOLL!!
LOOK! I CAME TO SEE YOUR ROCKET, NOT INTERPRET YOUR DREAMS... BESIDES, IF YOU WERE NORMAL, YOU'D DREAM ABOUT FOOD!
OKAY! OKAY!
SHE GOES LIKE A DREAM, ARCH!
CUT THAT OUT!
SOON......
THAT WAS FUN...TOO BAD IT GOT DARK! HOW ABOUT TAKING IN AN OUTER SPACE MOVIE?
COOL IT, HOSE NOSE, I'M GOING TO DEVELOP THESE PHOTOS TONIGHT! I'LL SEE YOU TOMORROW.
THAT NIGHT..
HA! CALL ME A DREAMER WILL THEY!?!
6

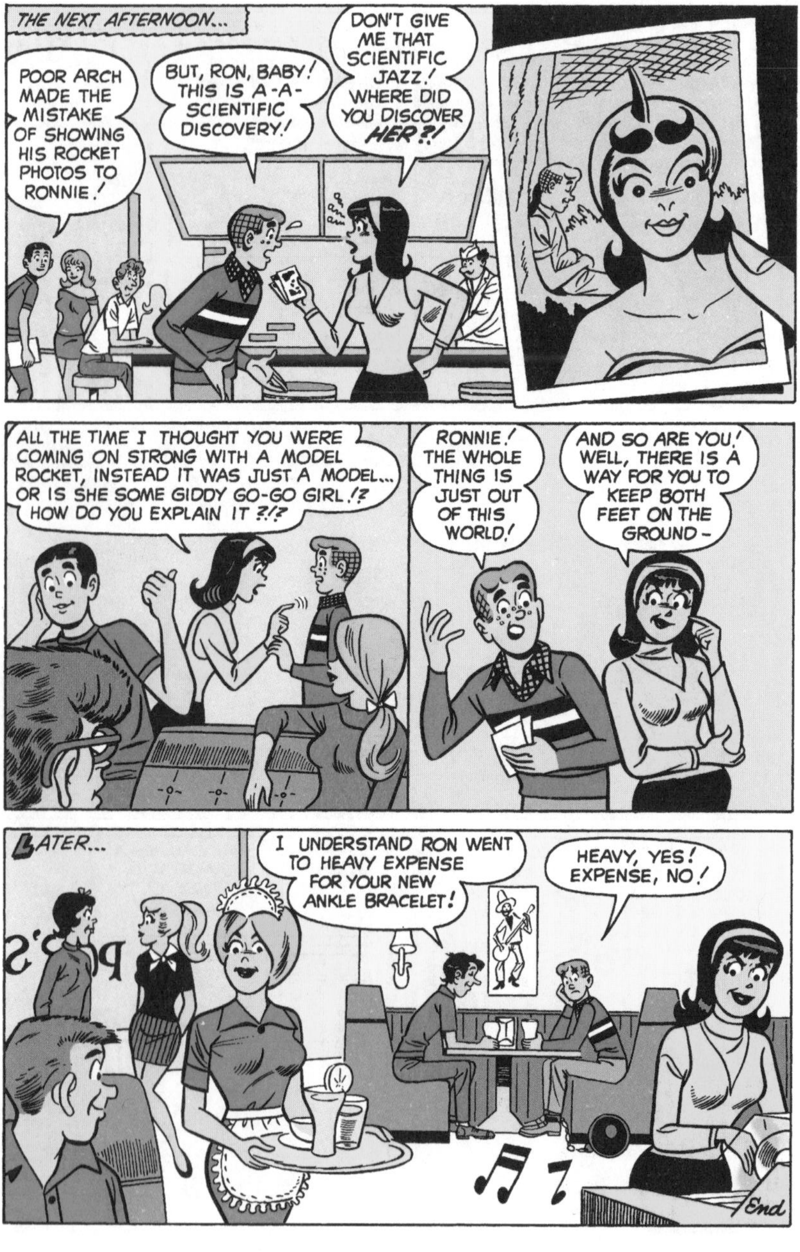
THE NEXT AFTERNOON...
POOR ARCH MADE THE MISTAKE OF SHOWING HIS ROCKET PHOTOS TO RONNIE!
BUT, RON, BABY! THIS IS A-A-SCIENTIFIC DISCOVERY!
DON'T GIVE ME THAT SCIENTIFIC JAZZ! WHERE DID YOU DISCOVER HER?!
ALL THE TIME I THOUGHT YOU WERE COMING ON STRONG WITH A MODEL ROCKET, INSTEAD IT WAS JUST A MODEL... OR IS SHE SOME GIDDY GO-GO GIRL!? HOW DO YOU EXPLAIN IT?!?
RONNIE! THE WHOLE THING IS JUST OUT OF THIS WORLD!
AND SO ARE YOU! WELL, THERE IS A WAY FOR YOU TO KEEP BOTH FEET ON THE GROUND -
LATER...
I UNDERSTAND RON WENT TO HEAVY EXPENSE FOR YOUR NEW ANKLE BRACELET!
HEAVY, YES! EXPENSE, NO!
End

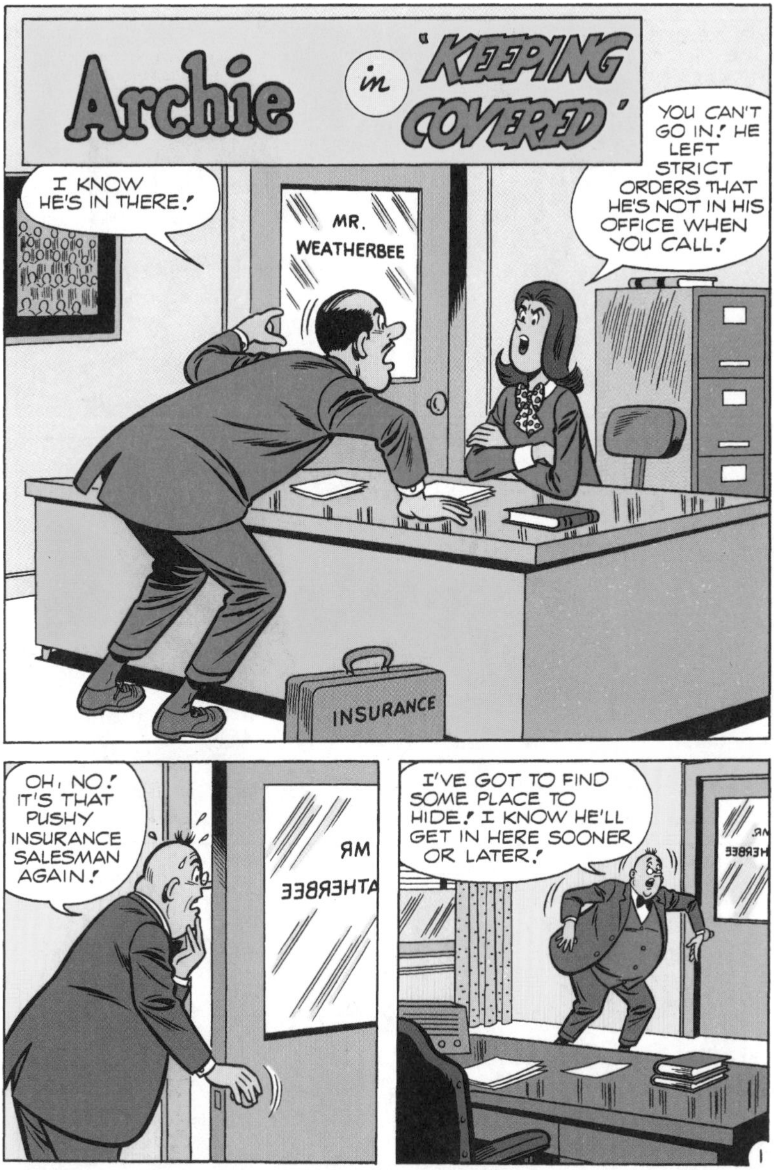
Archie
in
'KEEPING COVERED'
I KNOW HE'S IN THERE!
YOU CAN'T GO IN! HE LEFT STRICT ORDERS THAT HE'S NOT IN HIS OFFICE WHEN YOU CALL!
MR. WEATHERBEE
INSURANCE
OH, NO! IT'S THAT PUSHY INSURANCE SALESMAN AGAIN!
I'VE GOT TO FIND SOME PLACE TO HIDE! I KNOW HE'LL GET IN HERE SOONER OR LATER!

Story & Pencils: Al Hartley
Inks & Letters: Jon D'Agostino

Originally printed in EVERYTHING'S ARCHIE #2, JULY 1969

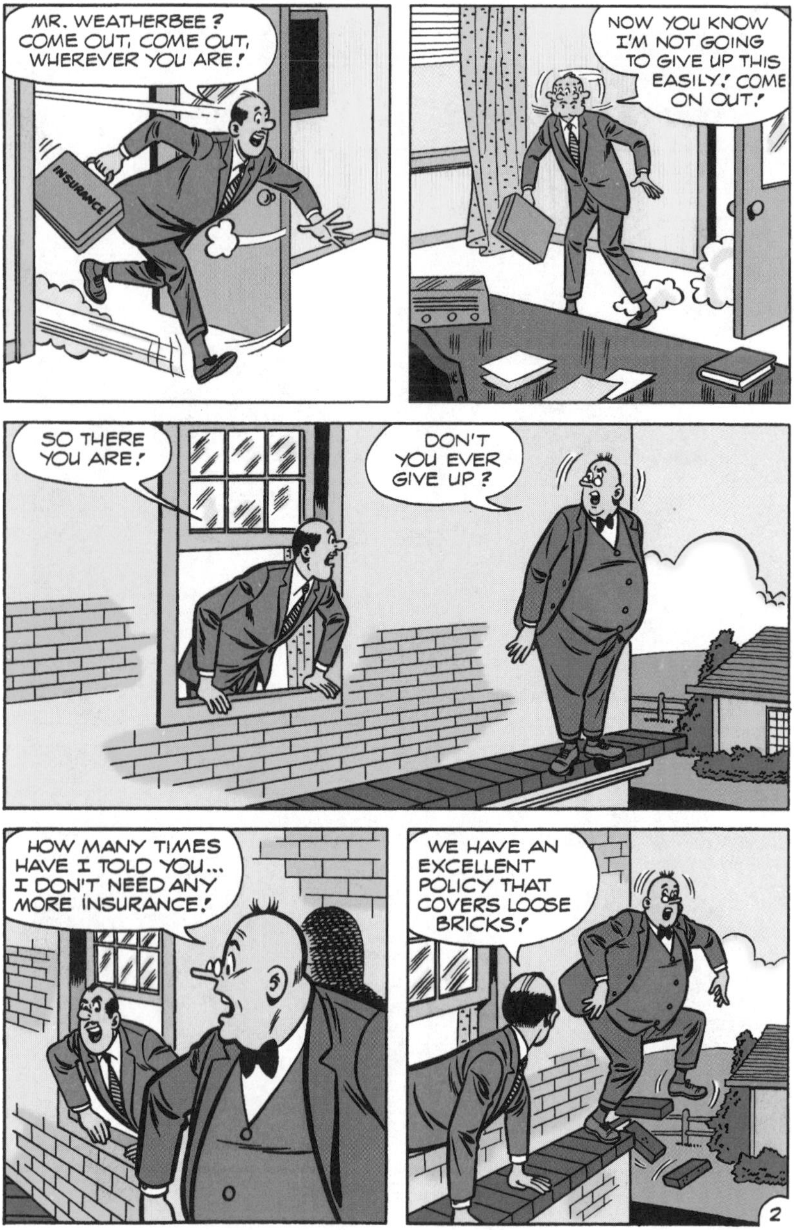
MR. WEATHERBEE? COME OUT, COME OUT, WHEREVER YOU ARE!
INSURANCE
NOW YOU KNOW I'M NOT GOING TO GIVE UP THIS EASILY! COME ON OUT!
SO THERE YOU ARE!
DON'T YOU EVER GIVE UP?
HOW MANY TIMES HAVE I TOLD YOU... I DON'T NEED ANY MORE INSURANCE!
WE HAVE AN EXCELLENT POLICY THAT COVERS LOOSE BRICKS!
2

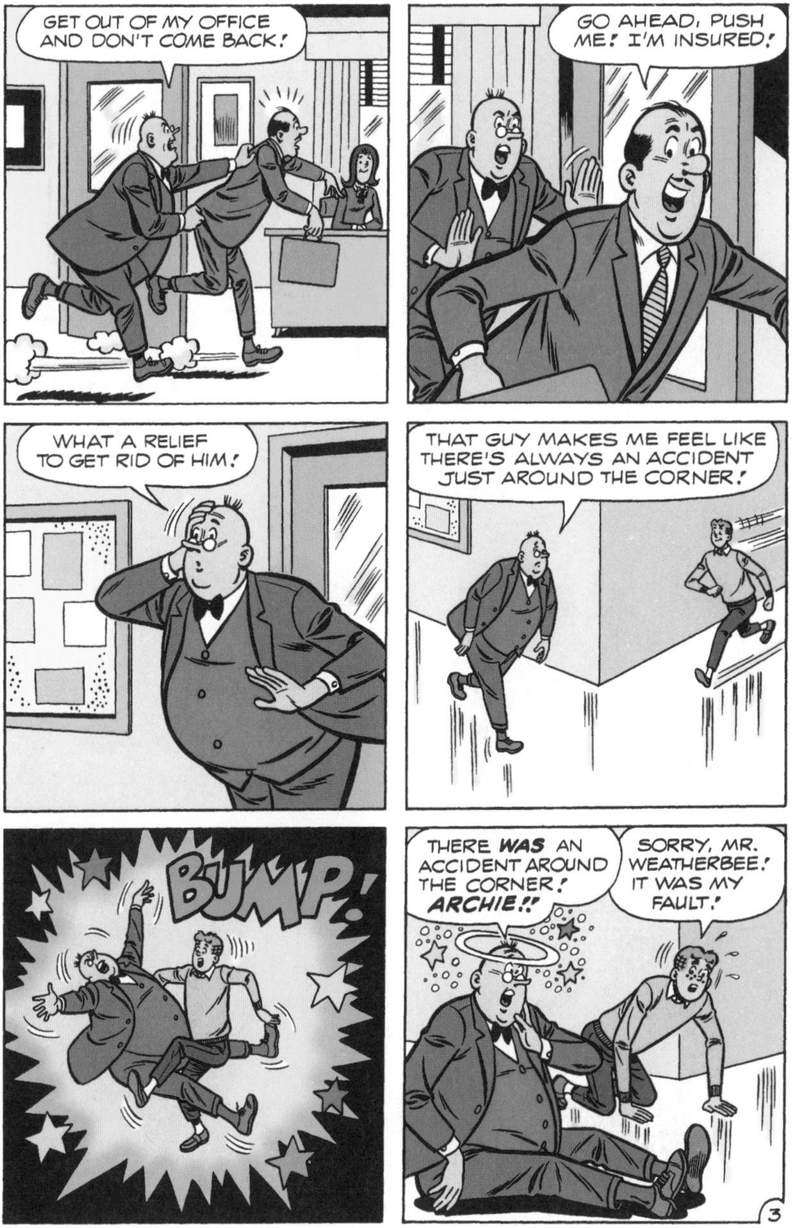
GET OUT OF MY OFFICE AND DON'T COME BACK!
GO AHEAD, PUSH ME! I'M INSURED!
WHAT A RELIEF TO GET RID OF HIM!
THAT GUY MAKES ME FEEL LIKE THERE'S ALWAYS AN ACCIDENT JUST AROUND THE CORNER!
BUMP!
THERE WAS AN ACCIDENT AROUND THE CORNER! ARCHIE!!
SORRY, MR. WEATHERBEE! IT WAS MY FAULT!
3

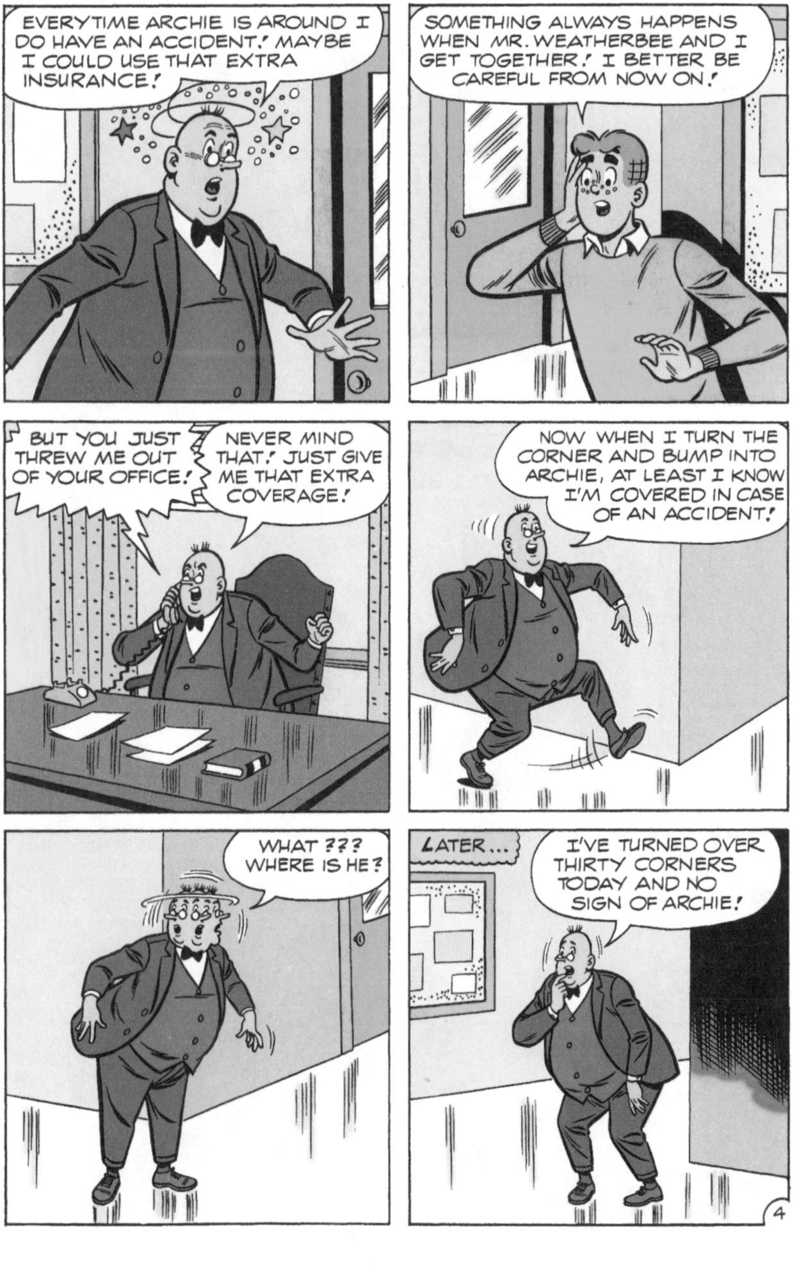
EVERYTIME ARCHIE IS AROUND I DO HAVE AN ACCIDENT! MAYBE I COULD USE THAT EXTRA INSURANCE!
SOMETHING ALWAYS HAPPENS WHEN MR. WEATHERBEE AND I GET TOGETHER! I BETTER BE CAREFUL FROM NOW ON!
BUT YOU JUST THREW ME OUT OF YOUR OFFICE!
NEVER MIND THAT! JUST GIVE ME THAT EXTRA COVERAGE!
NOW WHEN I TURN THE CORNER AND BUMP INTO ARCHIE, AT LEAST I KNOW I'M COVERED IN CASE OF AN ACCIDENT!
WHAT ??? WHERE IS HE?
LATER...
I'VE TURNED OVER THIRTY CORNERS TODAY AND NO SIGN OF ARCHIE!
4

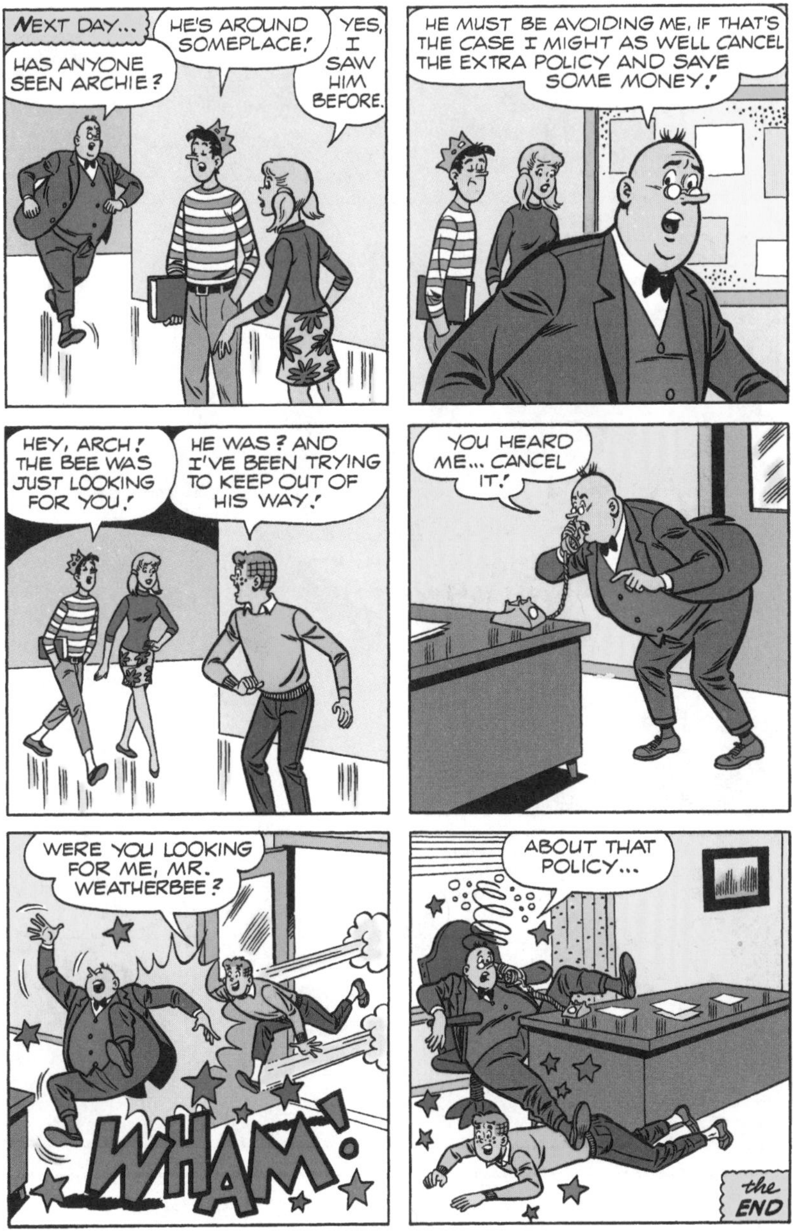
NEXT DAY...
HAS ANYONE SEEN ARCHIE?
HE'S AROUND SOMEPLACE!
YES, I SAW HIM BEFORE.
HE MUST BE AVOIDING ME. IF THAT'S THE CASE I MIGHT AS WELL CANCEL THE EXTRA POLICY AND SAVE SOME MONEY!
HEY, ARCH! THE BEE WAS JUST LOOKING FOR YOU!
HE WAS? AND I'VE BEEN TRYING TO KEEP OUT OF HIS WAY!
YOU HEARD ME... CANCEL IT!
WERE YOU LOOKING FOR ME, MR. WEATHERBEE?
WHAM!
ABOUT THAT POLICY...
the END

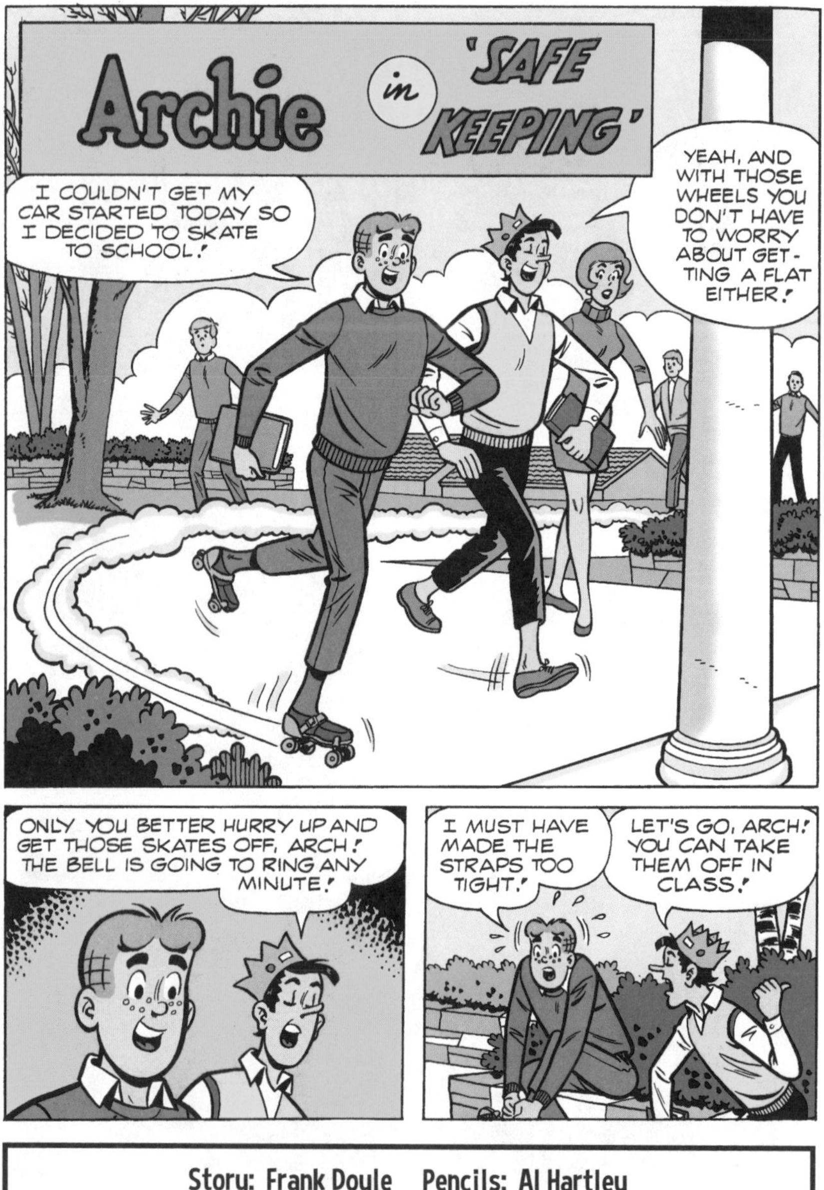
Archie in 'SAFE KEEPING'
I COULDN'T GET MY CAR STARTED TODAY SO I DECIDED TO SKATE TO SCHOOL!
YEAH, AND WITH THOSE WHEELS YOU DON'T HAVE TO WORRY ABOUT GET-TING A FLAT EITHER!
ONLY YOU BETTER HURRY UP AND GET THOSE SKATES OFF, ARCH! THE BELL IS GOING TO RING ANY MINUTE!
I MUST HAVE MADE THE STRAPS TOO TIGHT!
LET'S GO, ARCH! YOU CAN TAKE THEM OFF IN CLASS!

Story: Frank Doyle Pencils: Al Hartley
Inks: Jon D'Agostino Letters: Bill Yoshida

Originally printed in EVERYTHING'S ARCHIE #3, AUGUST 1969

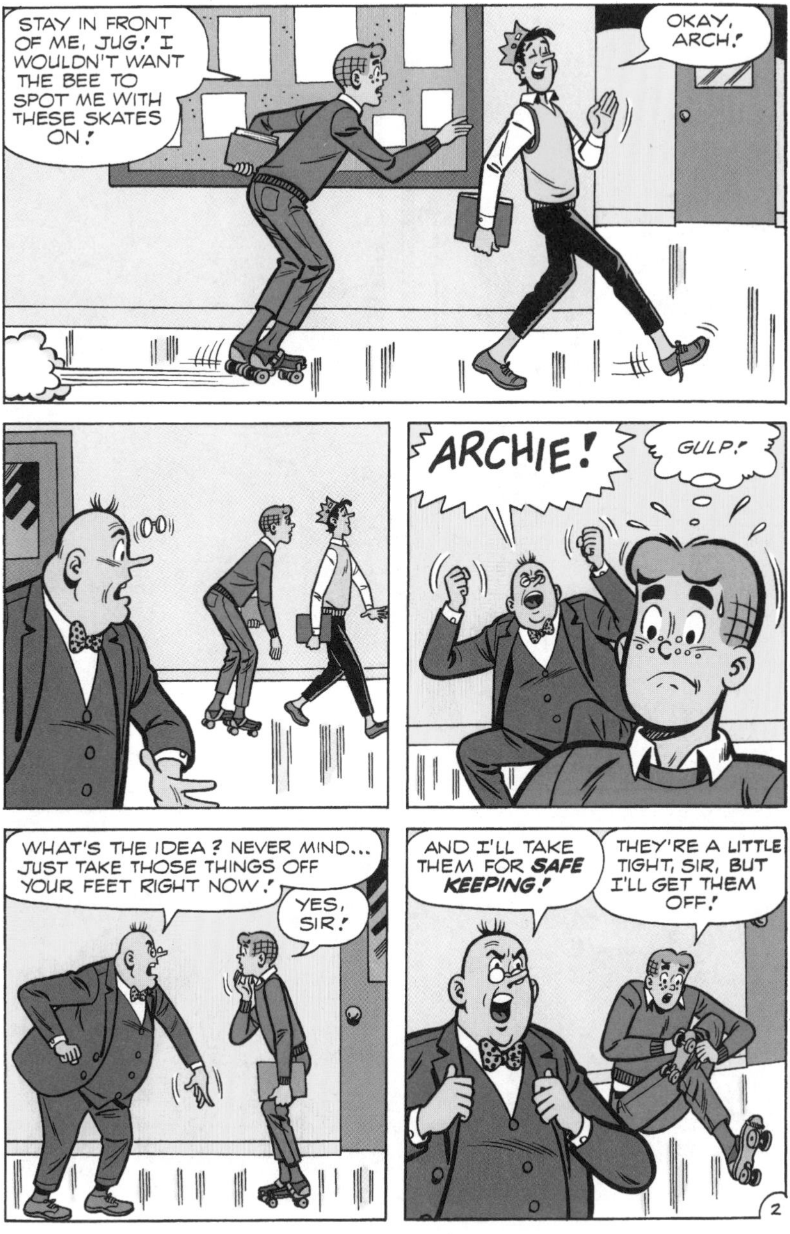
STAY IN FRONT OF ME, JUG! I WOULDN'T WANT THE BEE TO SPOT ME WITH THESE SKATES ON!
OKAY, ARCH!
ARCHIE!
GULP!
WHAT'S THE IDEA? NEVER MIND... JUST TAKE THOSE THINGS OFF YOUR FEET RIGHT NOW!
YES, SIR!
AND I'LL TAKE THEM FOR SAFE KEEPING!
THEY'RE A LITTLE TIGHT, SIR, BUT I'LL GET THEM OFF!
2

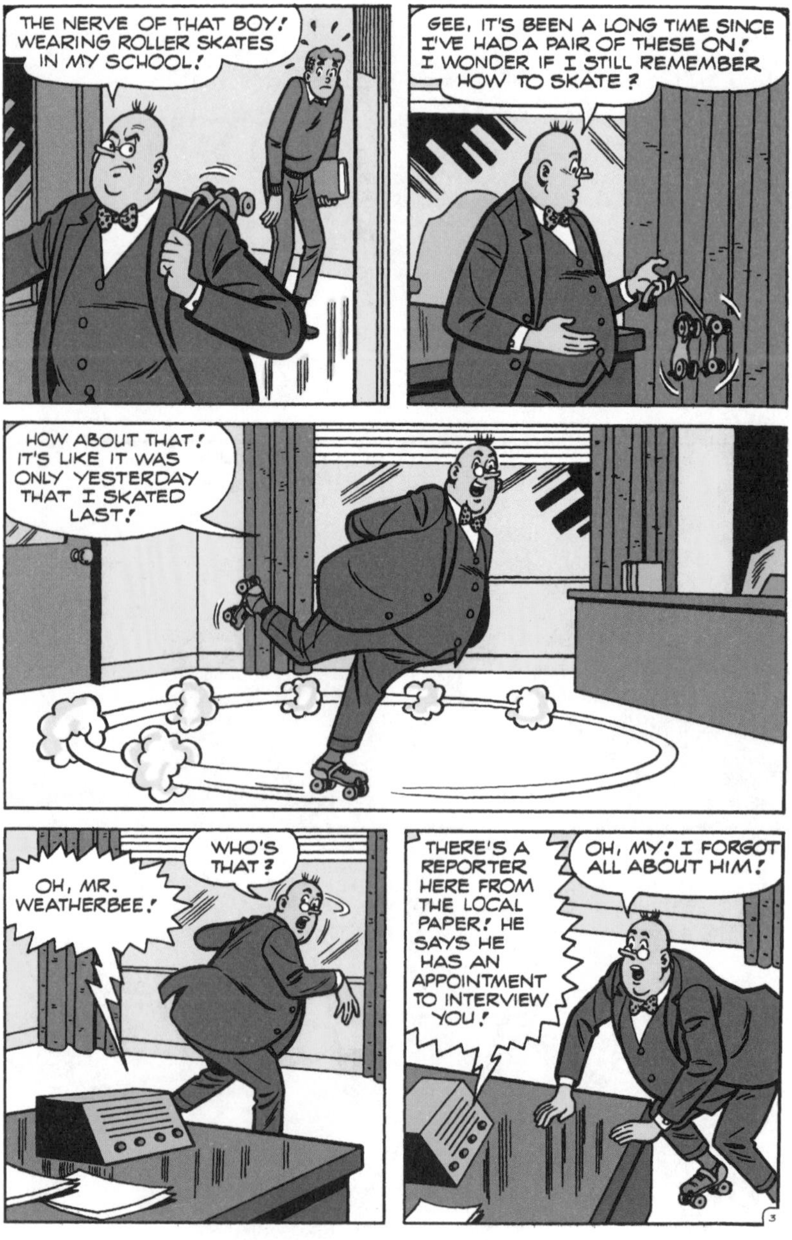
THE NERVE OF THAT BOY! WEARING ROLLER SKATES IN MY SCHOOL!
GEE, IT'S BEEN A LONG TIME SINCE I'VE HAD A PAIR OF THESE ON! I WONDER IF I STILL REMEMBER HOW TO SKATE?
HOW ABOUT THAT! IT'S LIKE IT WAS ONLY YESTERDAY THAT I SKATED LAST!
OH, MR. WEATHERBEE!
WHO'S THAT?
THERE'S A REPORTER HERE FROM THE LOCAL PAPER! HE SAYS HE HAS AN APPOINTMENT TO INTERVIEW YOU!
OH, MY! I FORGOT ALL ABOUT HIM!
3

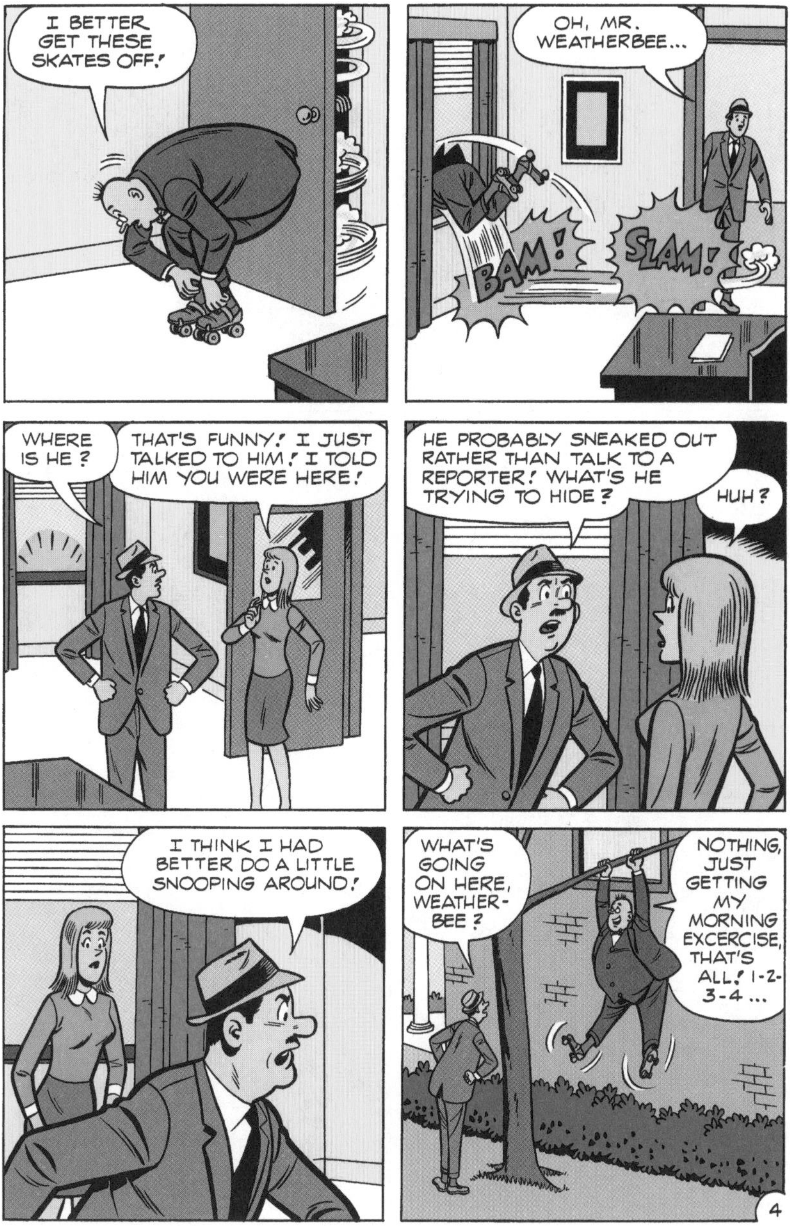
I BETTER GET THESE SKATES OFF!
OH, MR. WEATHERBEE...
BAM!
SLAM!
WHERE IS HE ?
THAT'S FUNNY! I JUST TALKED TO HIM! I TOLD HIM YOU WERE HERE!
HE PROBABLY SNEAKED OUT RATHER THAN TALK TO A REPORTER! WHAT'S HE TRYING TO HIDE ?
HUH ?
I THINK I HAD BETTER DO A LITTLE SNOOPING AROUND!
WHAT'S GOING ON HERE, WEATHER-BEE ?
NOTHING, JUST GETTING MY MORNING EXCERCISE, THAT'S ALL! 1-2-3-4 ...
4

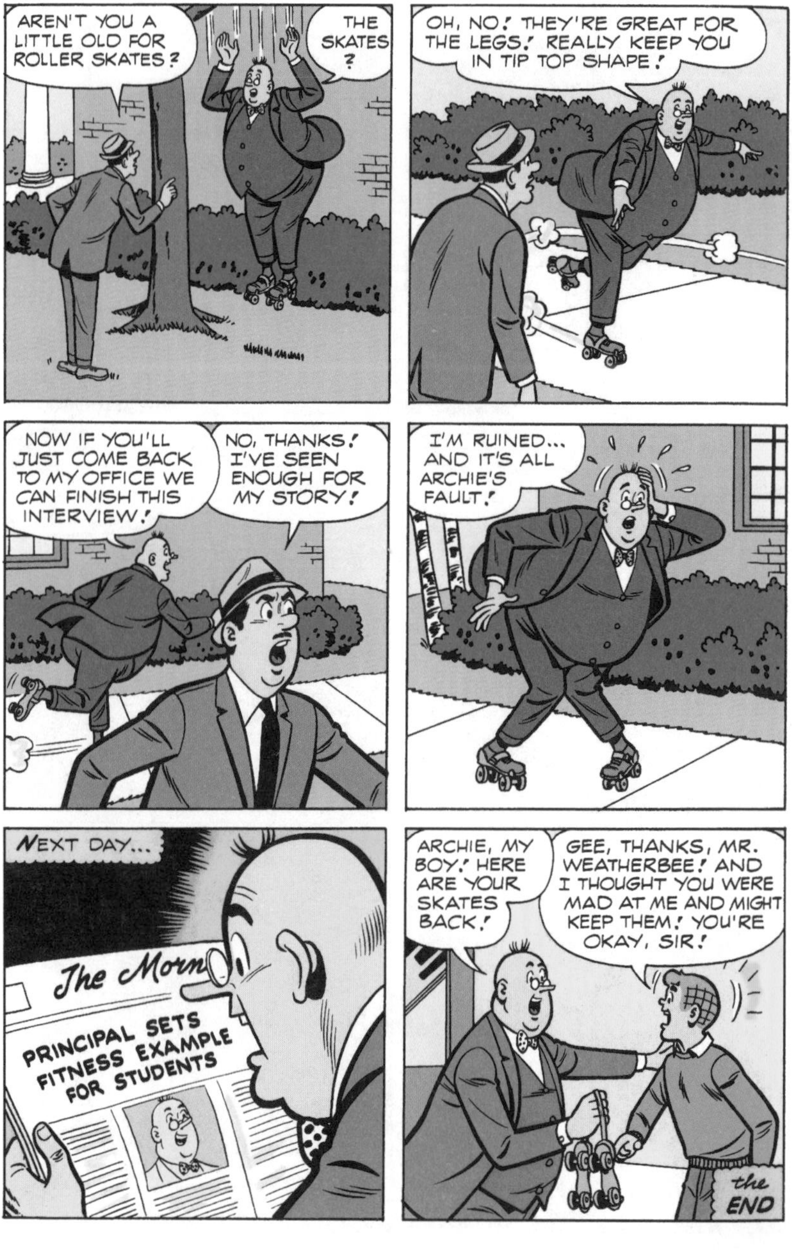
AREN'T YOU A LITTLE OLD FOR ROLLER SKATES?
THE SKATES?
OH, NO! THEY'RE GREAT FOR THE LEGS! REALLY KEEP YOU IN TIP TOP SHAPE!
NOW IF YOU'LL JUST COME BACK TO MY OFFICE WE CAN FINISH THIS INTERVIEW!
NO, THANKS! I'VE SEEN ENOUGH FOR MY STORY!
I'M RUINED... AND IT'S ALL ARCHIE'S FAULT!
NEXT DAY...
The Morn
PRINCIPAL SETS FITNESS EXAMPLE FOR STUDENTS
ARCHIE, MY BOY! HERE ARE YOUR SKATES BACK!
GEE, THANKS, MR. WEATHERBEE! AND I THOUGHT YOU WERE MAD AT ME AND MIGHT KEEP THEM! YOU'RE OKAY, SIR!
the END

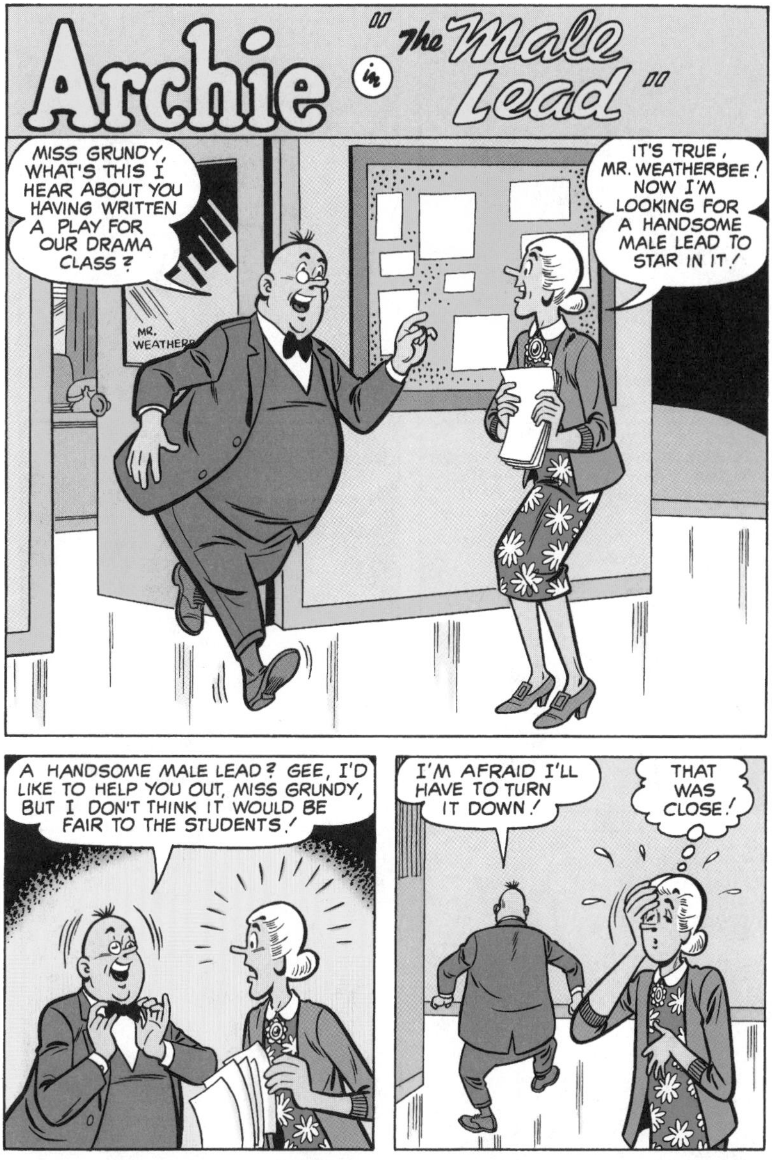
Archie in "The Male Lead"
MISS GRUNDY, WHAT'S THIS I HEAR ABOUT YOU HAVING WRITTEN A PLAY FOR OUR DRAMA CLASS?
IT'S TRUE, MR. WEATHERBEE! NOW I'M LOOKING FOR A HANDSOME MALE LEAD TO STAR IN IT!
A HANDSOME MALE LEAD? GEE, I'D LIKE TO HELP YOU OUT, MISS GRUNDY, BUT I DON'T THINK IT WOULD BE FAIR TO THE STUDENTS!
I'M AFRAID I'LL HAVE TO TURN IT DOWN!
THAT WAS CLOSE!

Story & Pencils: Al Hartley Inks: Jon D'Agostino
Letters: Bill Yoshida Colors: Barry Grossman

Originally printed in EVERYTHING'S ARCHIE #3, AUGUST 1969

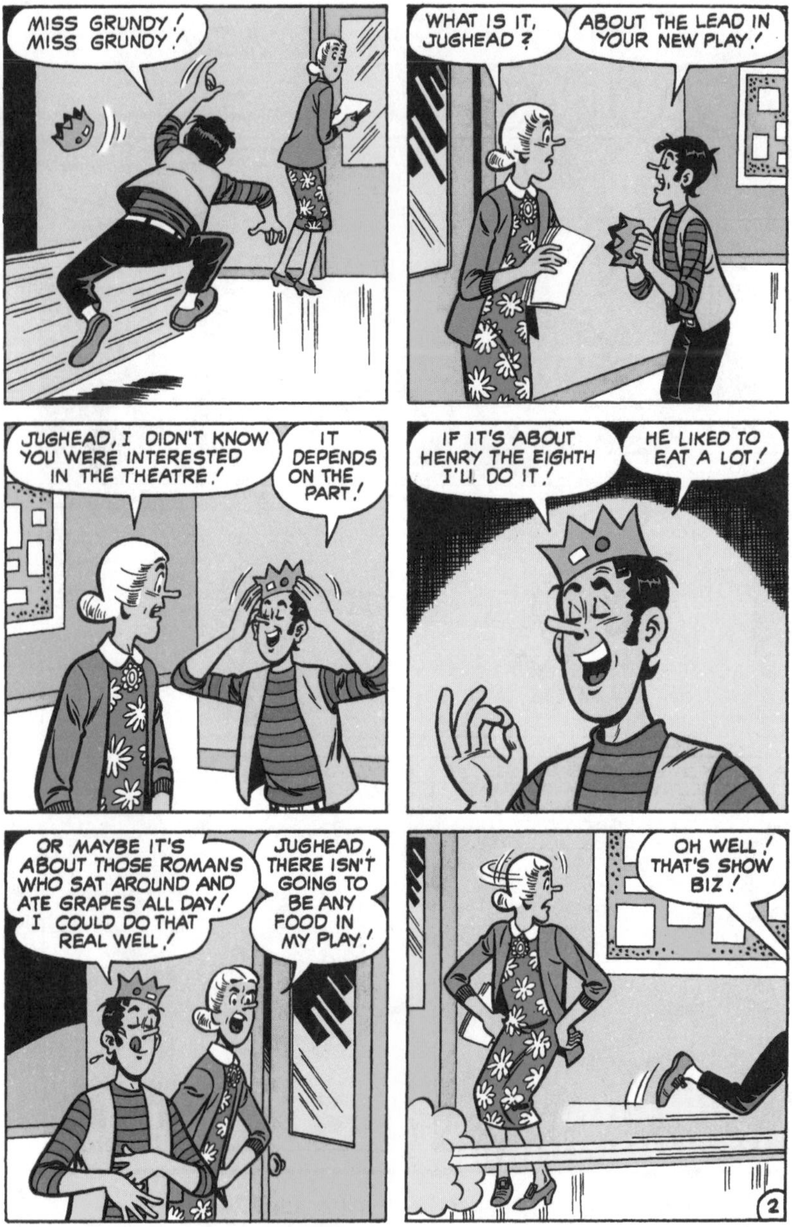
MISS GRUNDY! MISS GRUNDY!
WHAT IS IT, JUGHEAD?
ABOUT THE LEAD IN YOUR NEW PLAY!
JUGHEAD, I DIDN'T KNOW YOU WERE INTERESTED IN THE THEATRE!
IT DEPENDS ON THE PART!
IF IT'S ABOUT HENRY THE EIGHTH I'LL DO IT!
HE LIKED TO EAT A LOT!
OR MAYBE IT'S ABOUT THOSE ROMANS WHO SAT AROUND AND ATE GRAPES ALL DAY! I COULD DO THAT REAL WELL!
JUGHEAD, THERE ISN'T GOING TO BE ANY FOOD IN MY PLAY!
OH WELL! THAT'S SHOW BIZ!
2

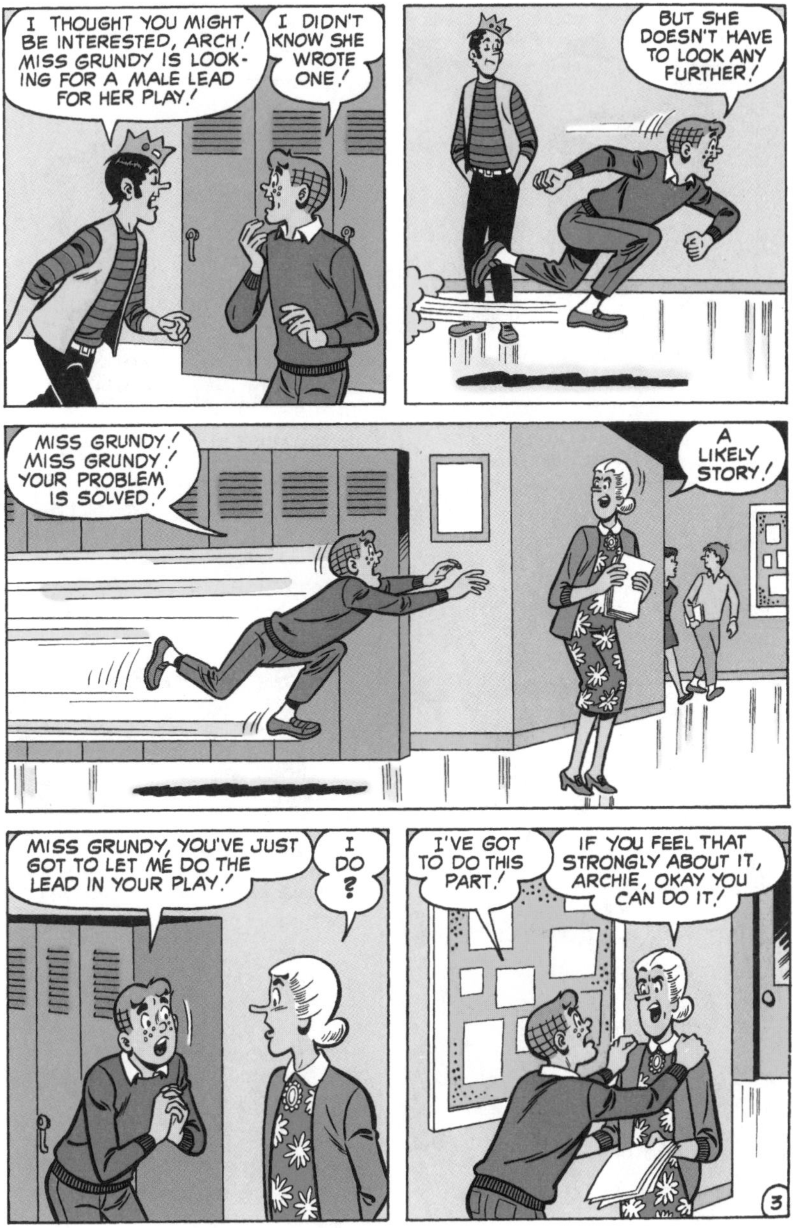
I THOUGHT YOU MIGHT BE INTERESTED, ARCH! MISS GRUNDY IS LOOKING FOR A MALE LEAD FOR HER PLAY!
I DIDN'T KNOW SHE WROTE ONE!
BUT SHE DOESN'T HAVE TO LOOK ANY FURTHER!
MISS GRUNDY! MISS GRUNDY! YOUR PROBLEM IS SOLVED!
A LIKELY STORY!
MISS GRUNDY, YOU'VE JUST GOT TO LET ME DO THE LEAD IN YOUR PLAY!
I DO?
I'VE GOT TO DO THIS PART!
IF YOU FEEL THAT STRONGLY ABOUT IT, ARCHIE, OKAY YOU CAN DO IT!
3

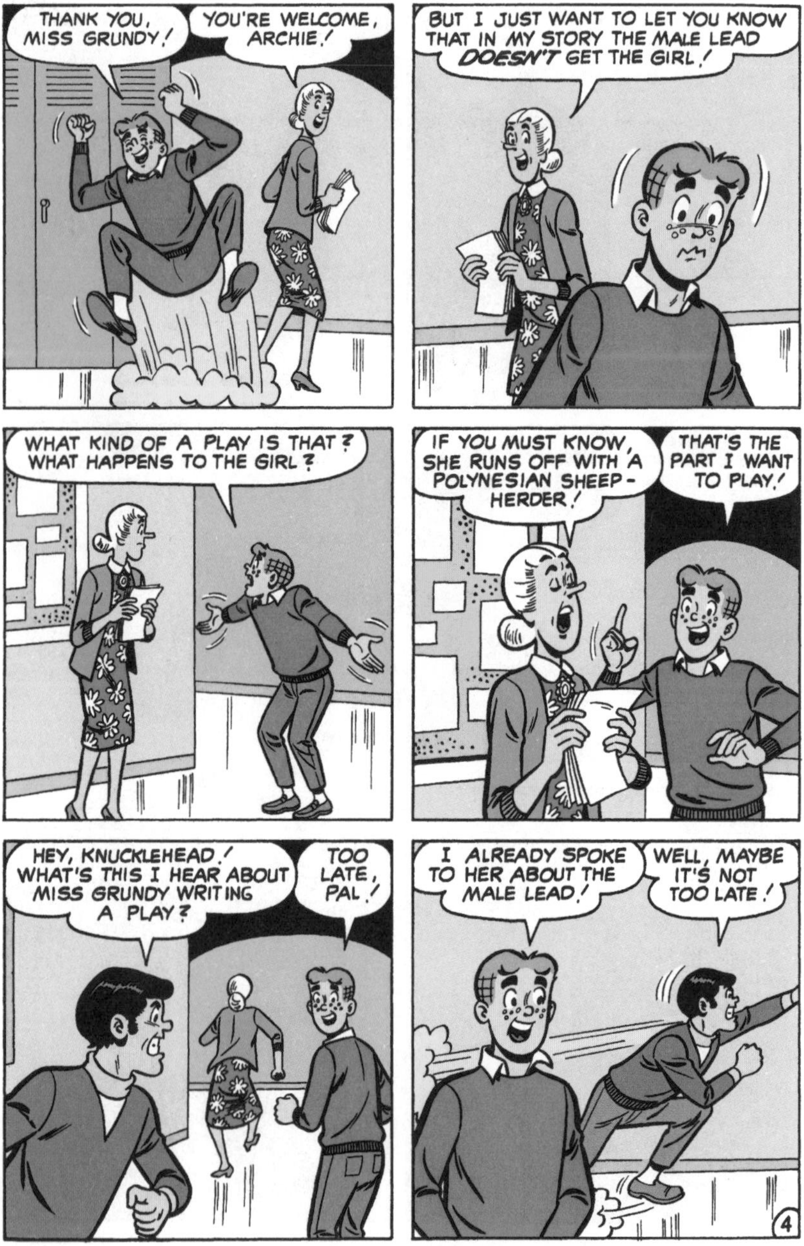
THANK YOU, MISS GRUNDY!
YOU'RE WELCOME, ARCHIE!
BUT I JUST WANT TO LET YOU KNOW THAT IN MY STORY THE MALE LEAD DOESN'T GET THE GIRL!
WHAT KIND OF A PLAY IS THAT? WHAT HAPPENS TO THE GIRL?
IF YOU MUST KNOW, SHE RUNS OFF WITH A POLYNESIAN SHEEP-HERDER!
THAT'S THE PART I WANT TO PLAY!
HEY, KNUCKLEHEAD! WHAT'S THIS I HEAR ABOUT MISS GRUNDY WRITING A PLAY?
TOO LATE, PAL!
I ALREADY SPOKE TO HER ABOUT THE MALE LEAD!
WELL, MAYBE IT'S NOT TOO LATE!
4

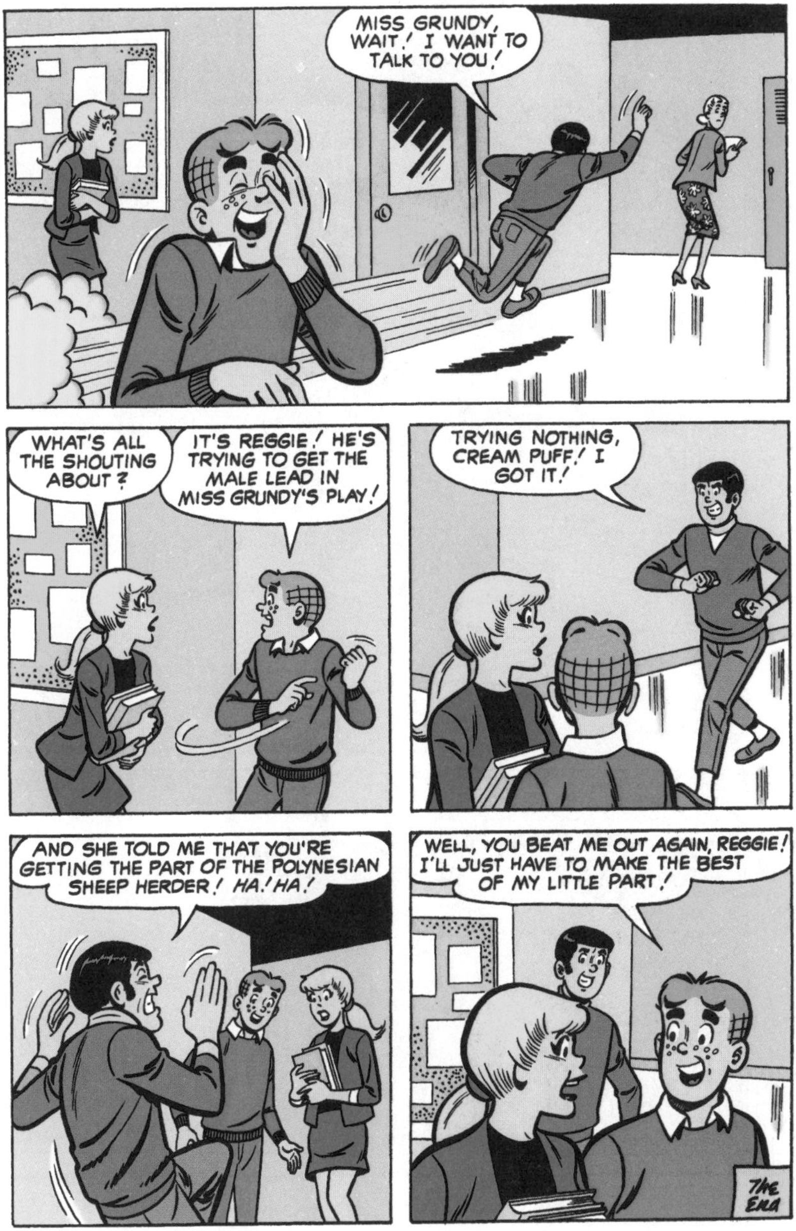
MISS GRUNDY, WAIT! I WANT TO TALK TO YOU!
WHAT'S ALL THE SHOUTING ABOUT?
IT'S REGGIE! HE'S TRYING TO GET THE MALE LEAD IN MISS GRUNDY'S PLAY!
TRYING NOTHING, CREAM PUFF! I GOT IT!
AND SHE TOLD ME THAT YOU'RE GETTING THE PART OF THE POLYNESIAN SHEEP HERDER! HA! HA!
WELL, YOU BEAT ME OUT AGAIN, REGGIE! I'LL JUST HAVE TO MAKE THE BEST OF MY LITTLE PART!
THE END

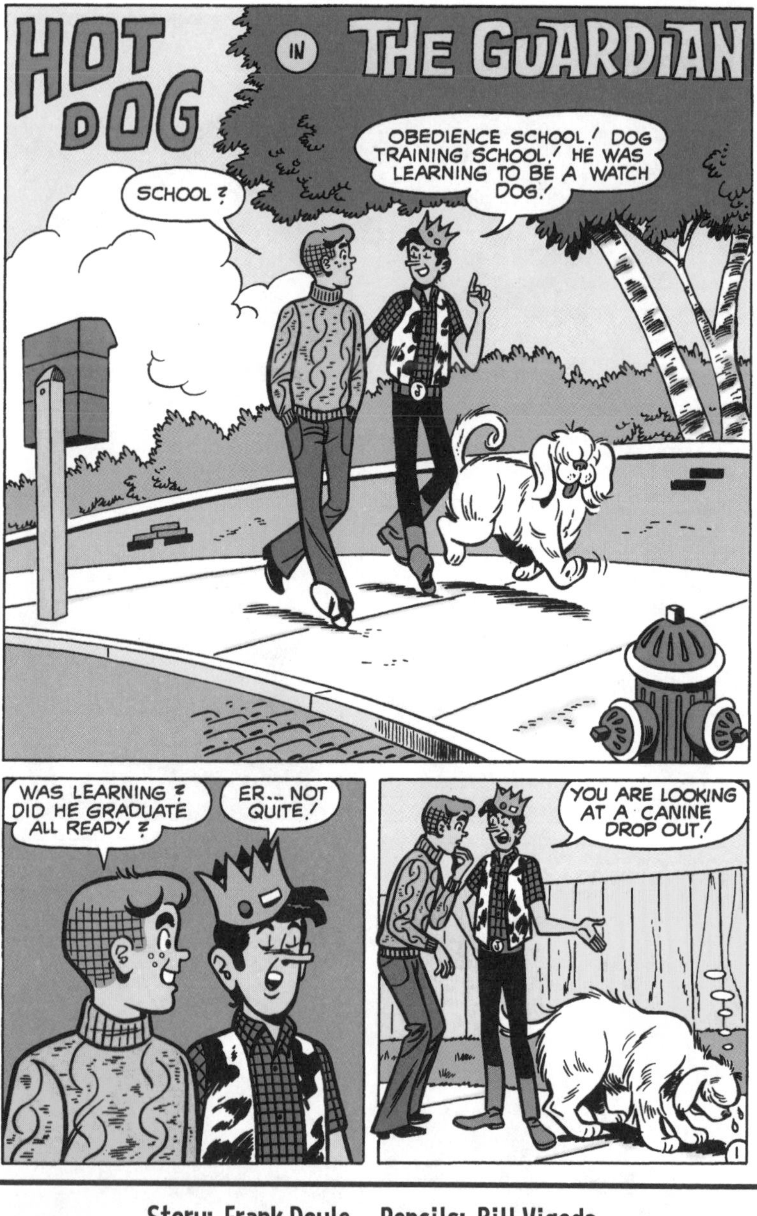
HOT DOG
IN
THE GUARDIAN
SCHOOL ?
OBEDIENCE SCHOOL! DOG TRAINING SCHOOL! HE WAS LEARNING TO BE A WATCH DOG!
WAS LEARNING ? DID HE GRADUATE ALL READY ?
ER... NOT QUITE!
YOU ARE LOOKING AT A CANINE DROP OUT!

Story: Frank Doyle   Pencils: Bill Vigoda
Inks: Rudy Lapick   Letters: Bill Yoshida   Colors: Barry Grossman

Originally printed in EVERYTHING'S ARCHIE #3, AUGUST 1969

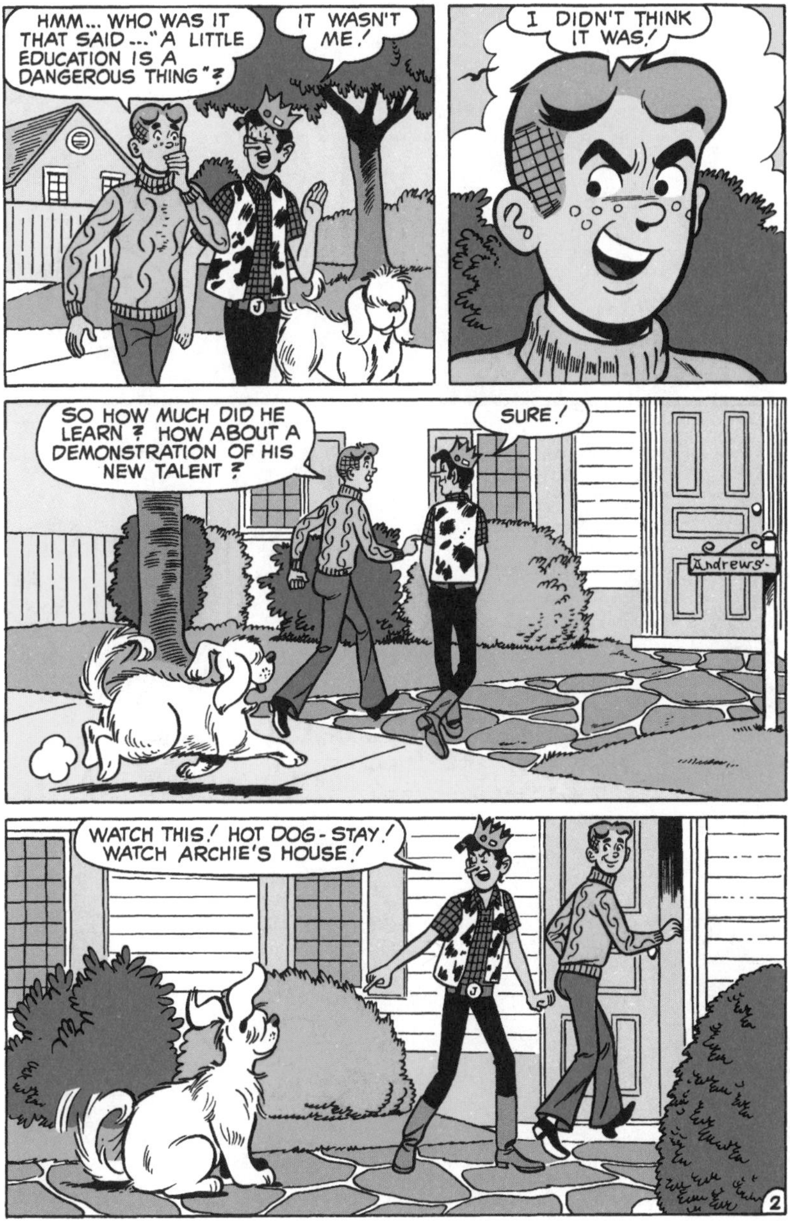
HMM... WHO WAS IT THAT SAID..."A LITTLE EDUCATION IS A DANGEROUS THING"?
IT WASN'T ME!
I DIDN'T THINK IT WAS!
SO HOW MUCH DID HE LEARN? HOW ABOUT A DEMONSTRATION OF HIS NEW TALENT?
SURE!
Andrews
WATCH THIS! HOT DOG-STAY! WATCH ARCHIE'S HOUSE!
2

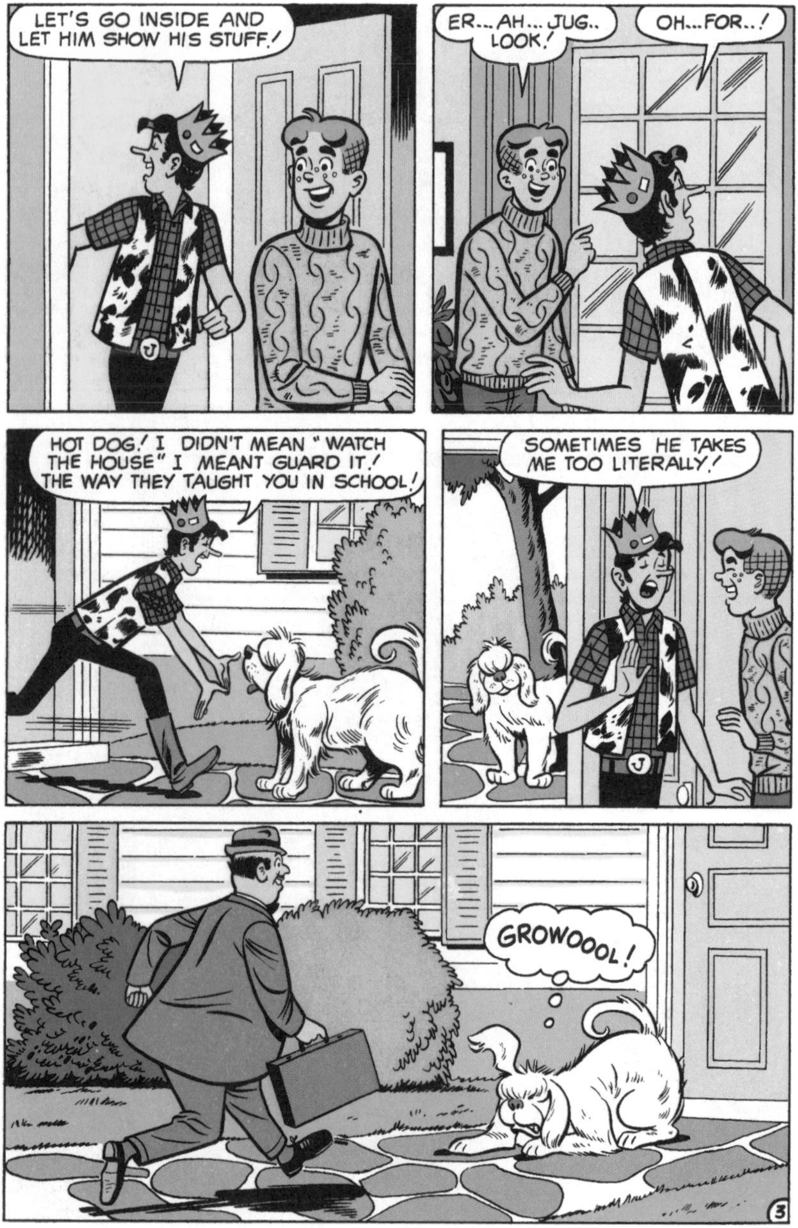
LET'S GO INSIDE AND LET HIM SHOW HIS STUFF!
ER... AH... JUG.. LOOK!
OH...FOR..!
HOT DOG! I DIDN'T MEAN "WATCH THE HOUSE" I MEANT GUARD IT! THE WAY THEY TAUGHT YOU IN SCHOOL!
SOMETIMES HE TAKES ME TOO LITERALLY!
GROWOOOL!
3

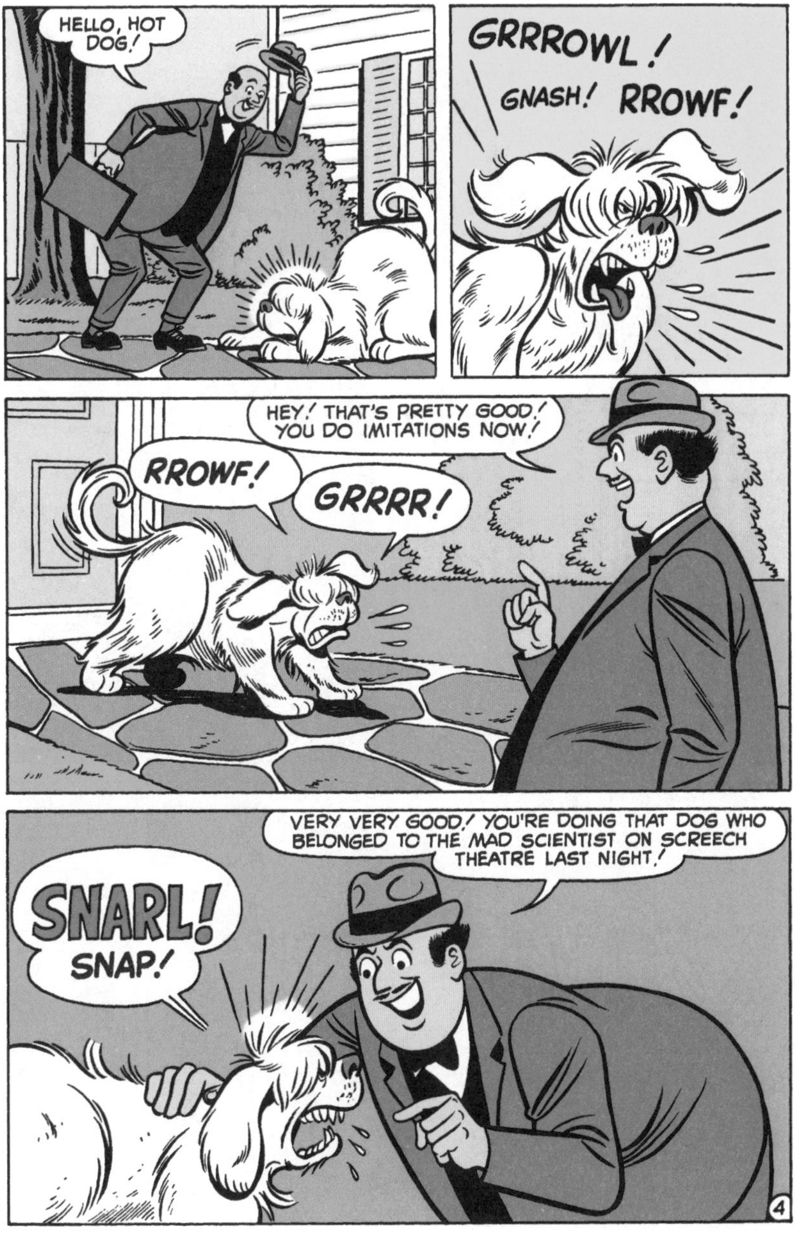
HELLO, HOT DOG!
GRRROWL!
GNASH! RROWF!
HEY! THAT'S PRETTY GOOD! YOU DO IMITATIONS NOW!
RROWF!
GRRRR!
VERY VERY GOOD! YOU'RE DOING THAT DOG WHO BELONGED TO THE MAD SCIENTIST ON SCREECH THEATRE LAST NIGHT!
SNARL! SNAP!
4

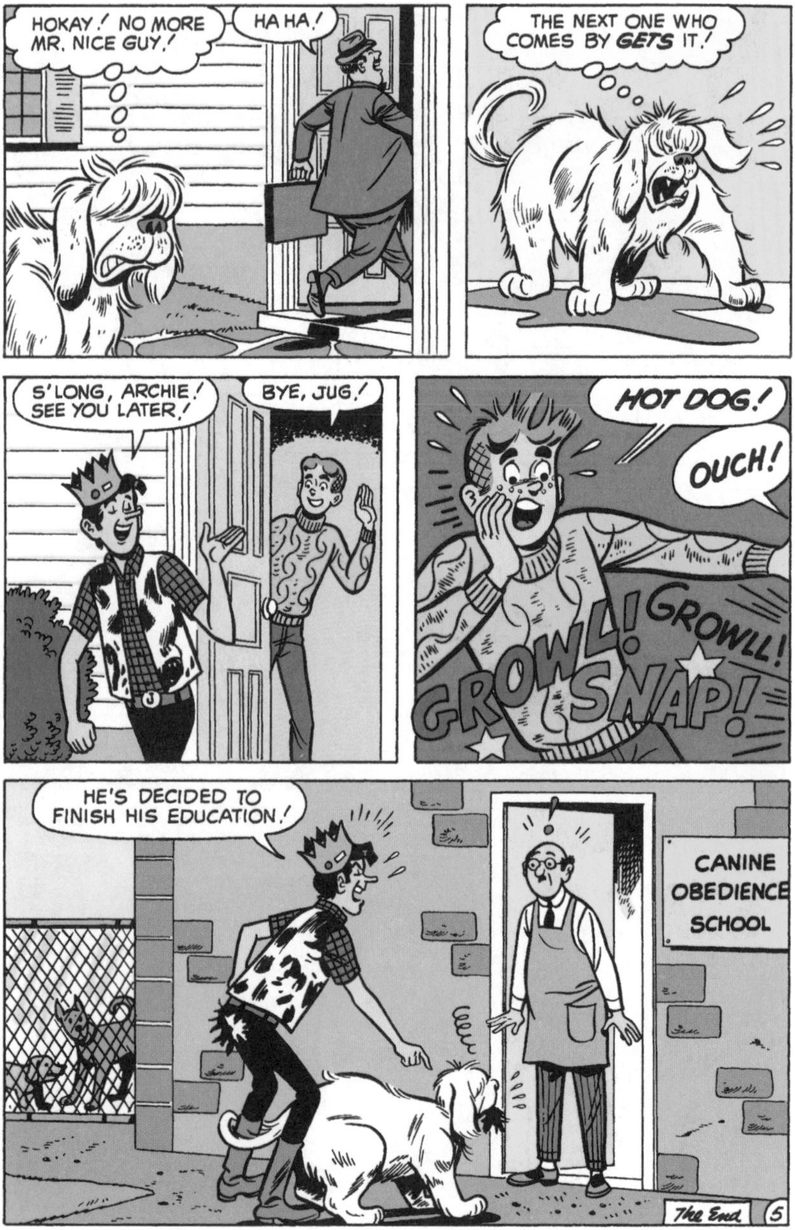
HOKAY! NO MORE MR. NICE GUY!
HA HA!
THE NEXT ONE WHO COMES BY GETS IT!
S'LONG, ARCHIE! SEE YOU LATER!
BYE, JUG!
HOT DOG!
OUCH!
GROWL! GROWLL!
SNAP!
HE'S DECIDED TO FINISH HIS EDUCATION!
CANINE OBEDIENCE SCHOOL
The End
5

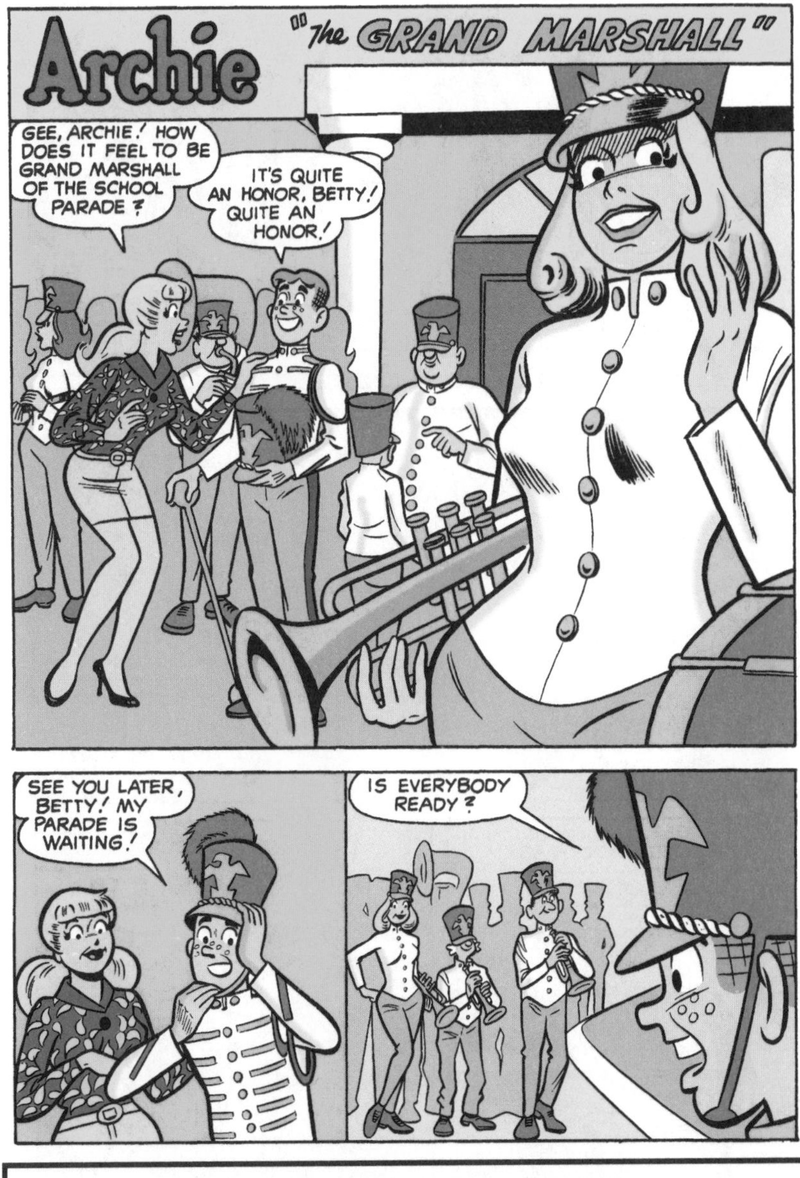
Archie
"The GRAND MARSHALL"
GEE, ARCHIE! HOW DOES IT FEEL TO BE GRAND MARSHALL OF THE SCHOOL PARADE?
IT'S QUITE AN HONOR, BETTY! QUITE AN HONOR!
SEE YOU LATER, BETTY! MY PARADE IS WAITING!
IS EVERYBODY READY?

Story: Dick Malmgren Pencils: Bob Bolling
Inks: Rudy Lapick Letters: Bill Yoshida Colors: Barry Grossman

Originally printed in EVERYTHING'S ARCHIE #3, AUGUST 1969

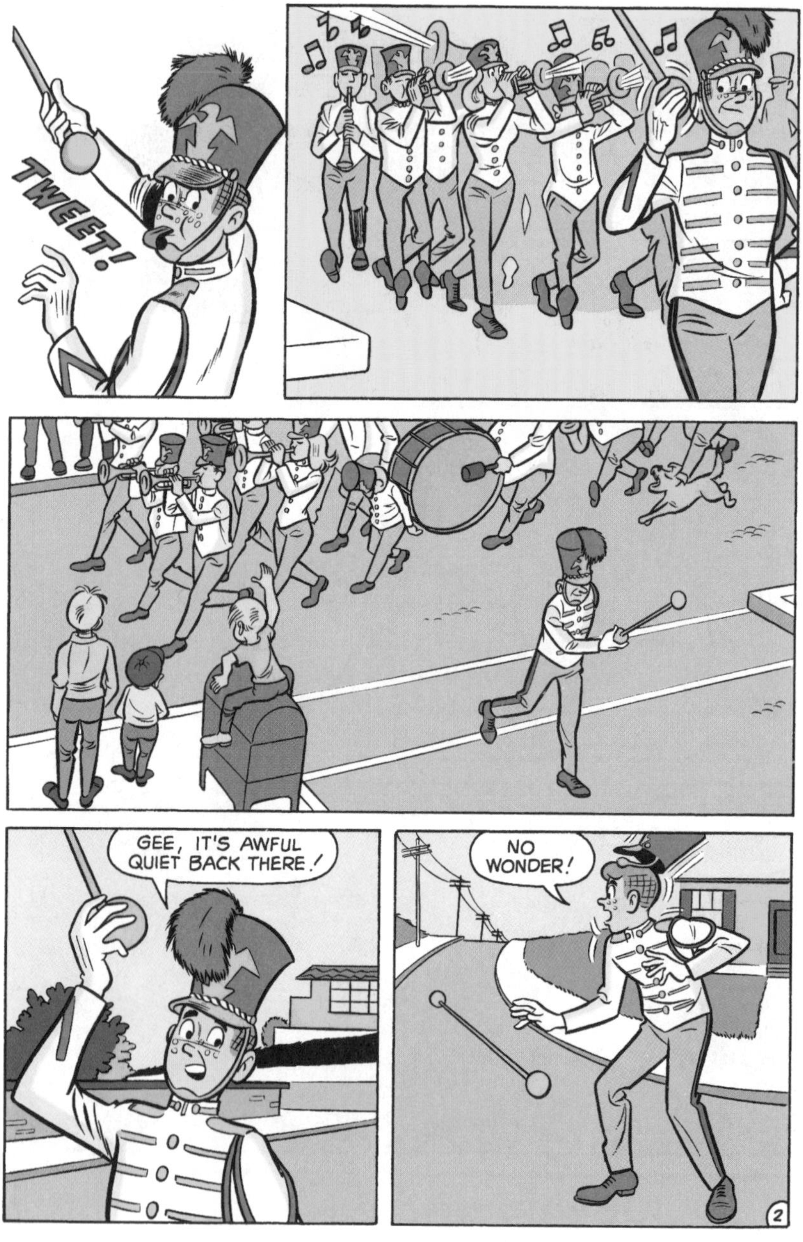
TWEET!
GEE, IT'S AWFUL QUIET BACK THERE!
NO WONDER!
2

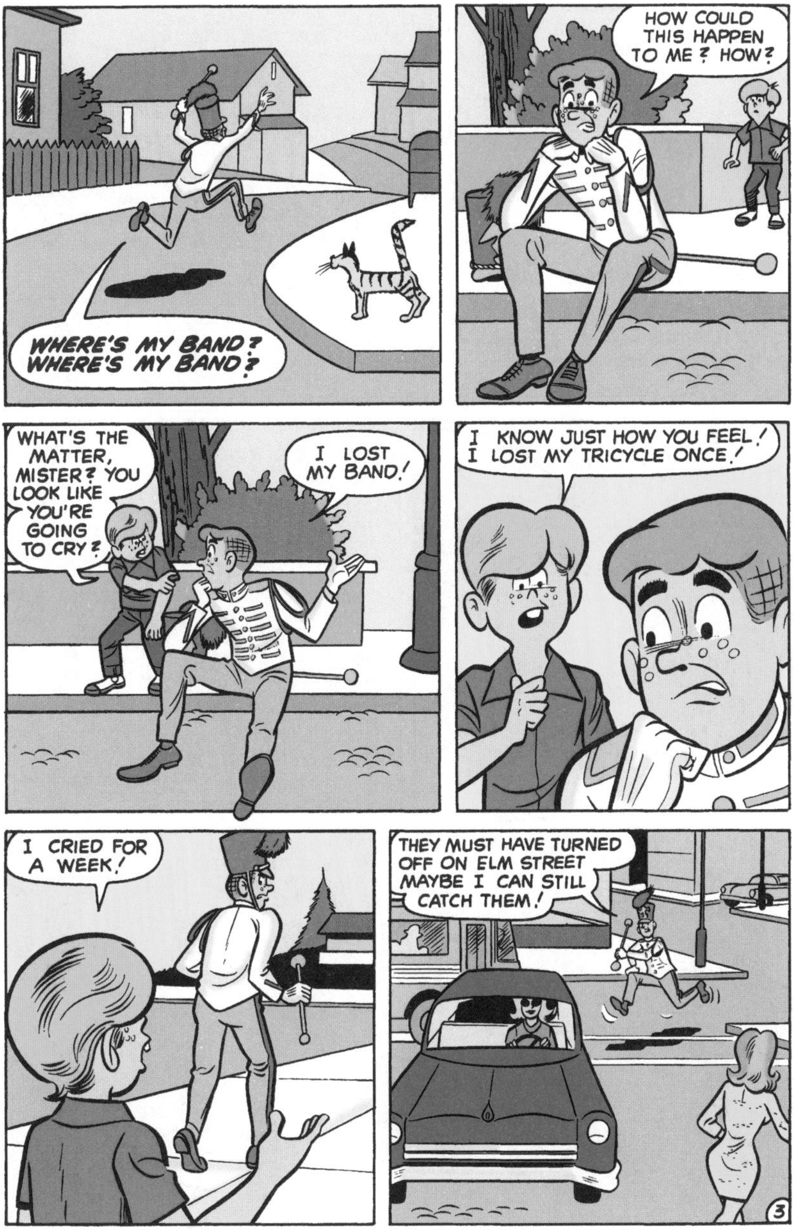
WHERE'S MY BAND? WHERE'S MY BAND?
HOW COULD THIS HAPPEN TO ME? HOW?
WHAT'S THE MATTER, MISTER? YOU LOOK LIKE YOU'RE GOING TO CRY?
I LOST MY BAND!
I KNOW JUST HOW YOU FEEL! I LOST MY TRICYCLE ONCE!
I CRIED FOR A WEEK!
THEY MUST HAVE TURNED OFF ON ELM STREET MAYBE I CAN STILL CATCH THEM!
3

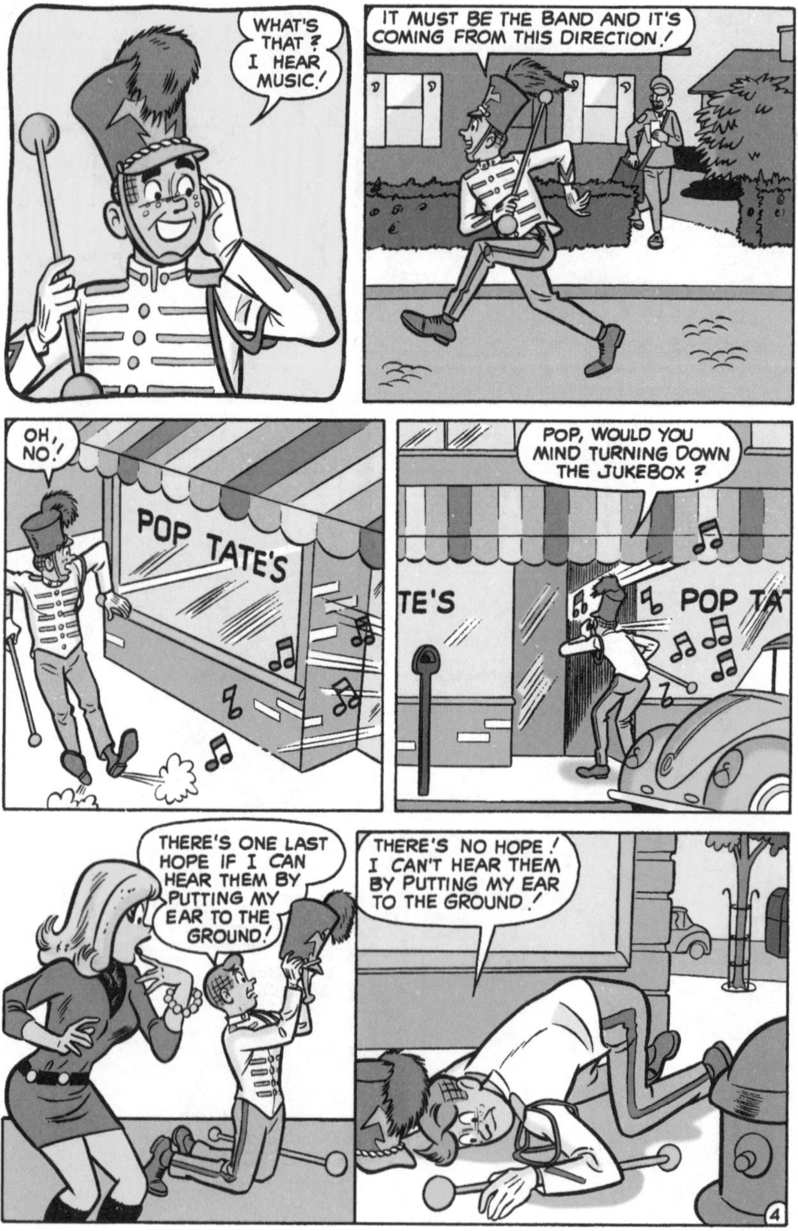
WHAT'S THAT? I HEAR MUSIC!
IT MUST BE THE BAND AND IT'S COMING FROM THIS DIRECTION!
OH, NO.!
POP TATE'S
POP, WOULD YOU MIND TURNING DOWN THE JUKEBOX?
TE'S
POP TA
THERE'S ONE LAST HOPE IF I CAN HEAR THEM BY PUTTING MY EAR TO THE GROUND!
THERE'S NO HOPE! I CAN'T HEAR THEM BY PUTTING MY EAR TO THE GROUND!
4

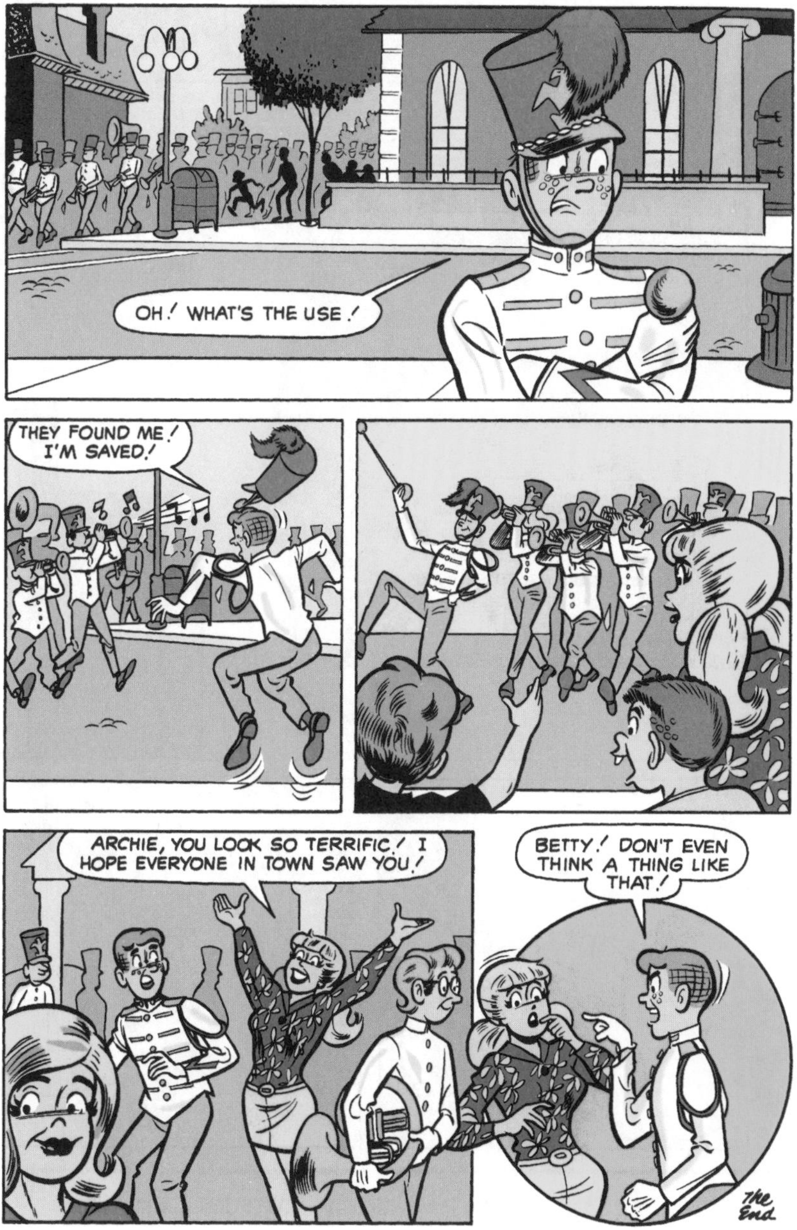
OH! WHAT'S THE USE!
THEY FOUND ME! I'M SAVED!
ARCHIE, YOU LOOK SO TERRIFIC! I HOPE EVERYONE IN TOWN SAW YOU!
BETTY! DON'T EVEN THINK A THING LIKE THAT!
The End

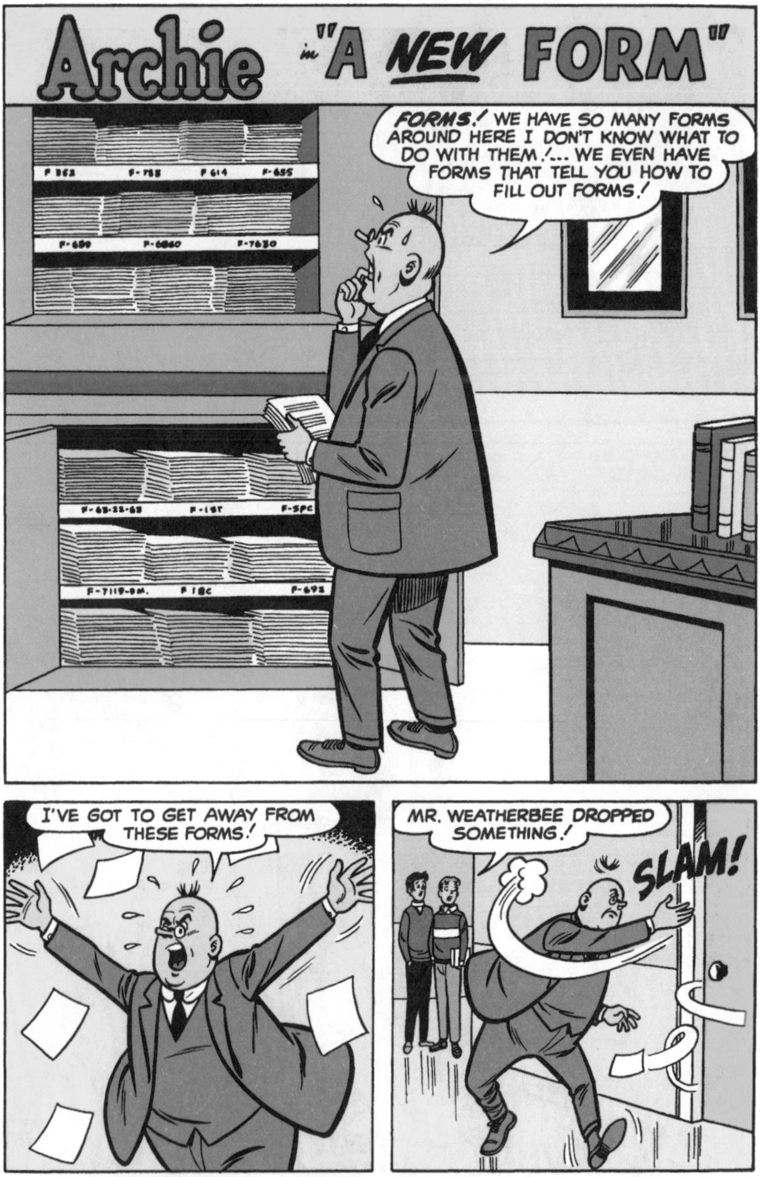
Archie in "A NEW FORM"
FORMS! WE HAVE SO MANY FORMS AROUND HERE I DON'T KNOW WHAT TO DO WITH THEM!... WE EVEN HAVE FORMS THAT TELL YOU HOW TO FILL OUT FORMS!
I'VE GOT TO GET AWAY FROM THESE FORMS!
MR. WEATHERBEE DROPPED SOMETHING!
SLAM!

Story & Pencils: Dick Malmgren Inks: Jon D'Agostino
Letters: Bill Yoshida Colors: Barry Grossman

Originally printed in EVERYTHING'S ARCHIE #3, AUGUST 1969

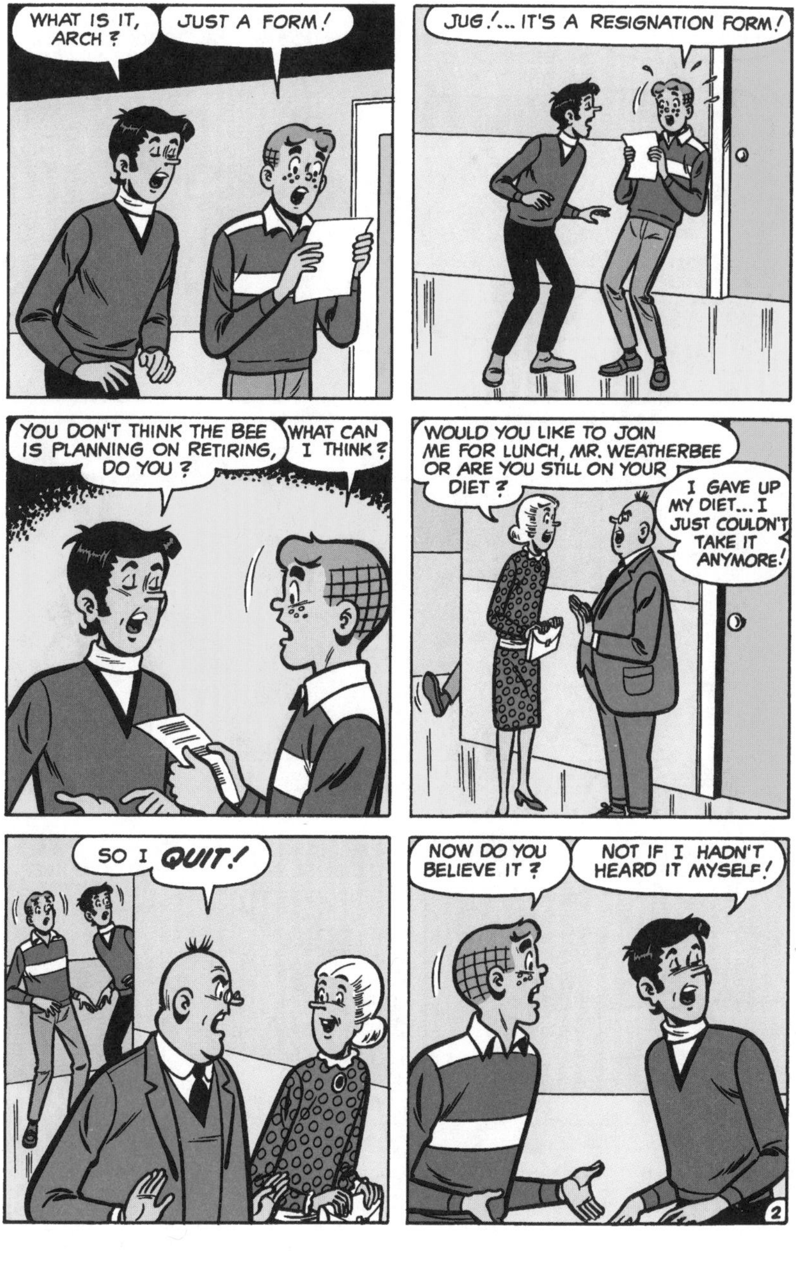
WHAT IS IT, ARCH ?
JUST A FORM!
JUG!... IT'S A RESIGNATION FORM!
YOU DON'T THINK THE BEE IS PLANNING ON RETIRING, DO YOU ?
WHAT CAN I THINK ?
WOULD YOU LIKE TO JOIN ME FOR LUNCH, MR. WEATHERBEE OR ARE YOU STILL ON YOUR DIET ?
I GAVE UP MY DIET... I JUST COULDN'T TAKE IT ANYMORE!
SO I QUIT!
NOW DO YOU BELIEVE IT ?
NOT IF I HADN'T HEARD IT MYSELF!
2

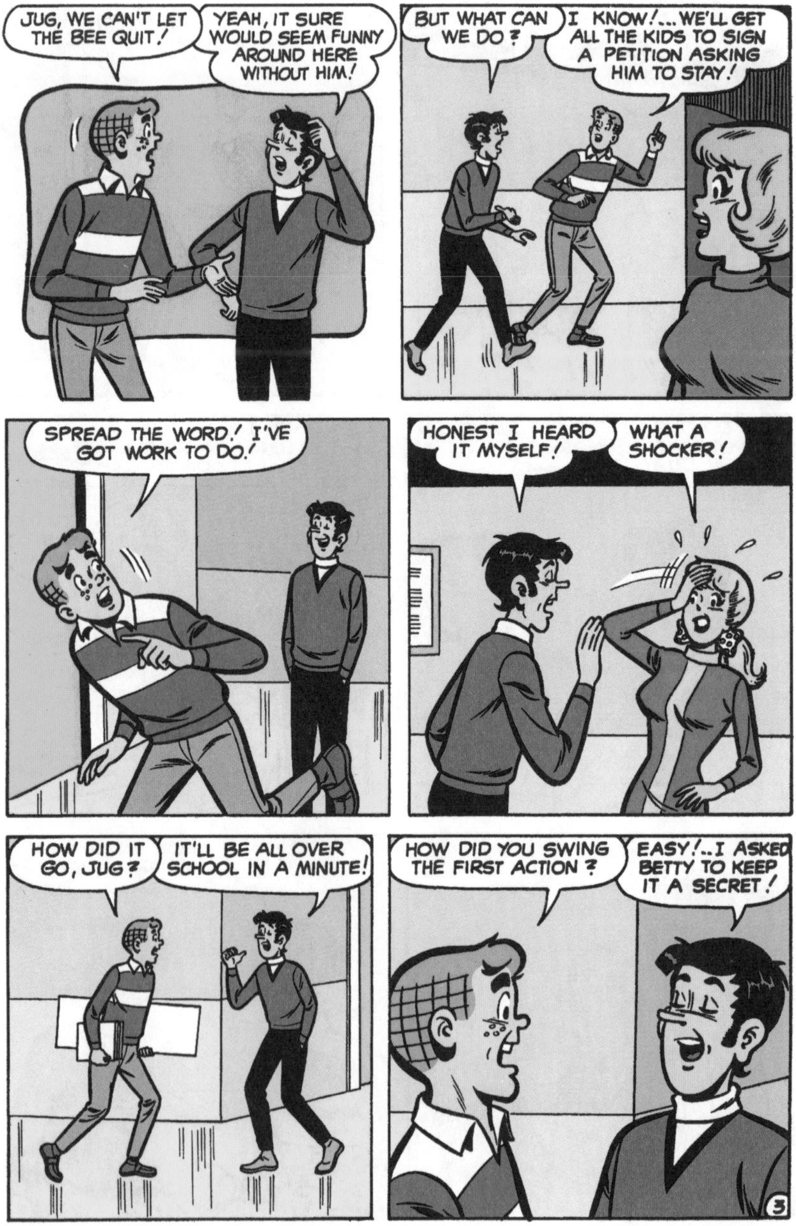
JUG, WE CAN'T LET THE BEE QUIT!
YEAH, IT SURE WOULD SEEM FUNNY AROUND HERE WITHOUT HIM!
BUT WHAT CAN WE DO?
I KNOW!...WE'LL GET ALL THE KIDS TO SIGN A PETITION ASKING HIM TO STAY!
SPREAD THE WORD! I'VE GOT WORK TO DO!
HONEST I HEARD IT MYSELF!
WHAT A SHOCKER!
HOW DID IT GO, JUG?
IT'LL BE ALL OVER SCHOOL IN A MINUTE!
HOW DID YOU SWING THE FIRST ACTION?
EASY!..I ASKED BETTY TO KEEP IT A SECRET!
3

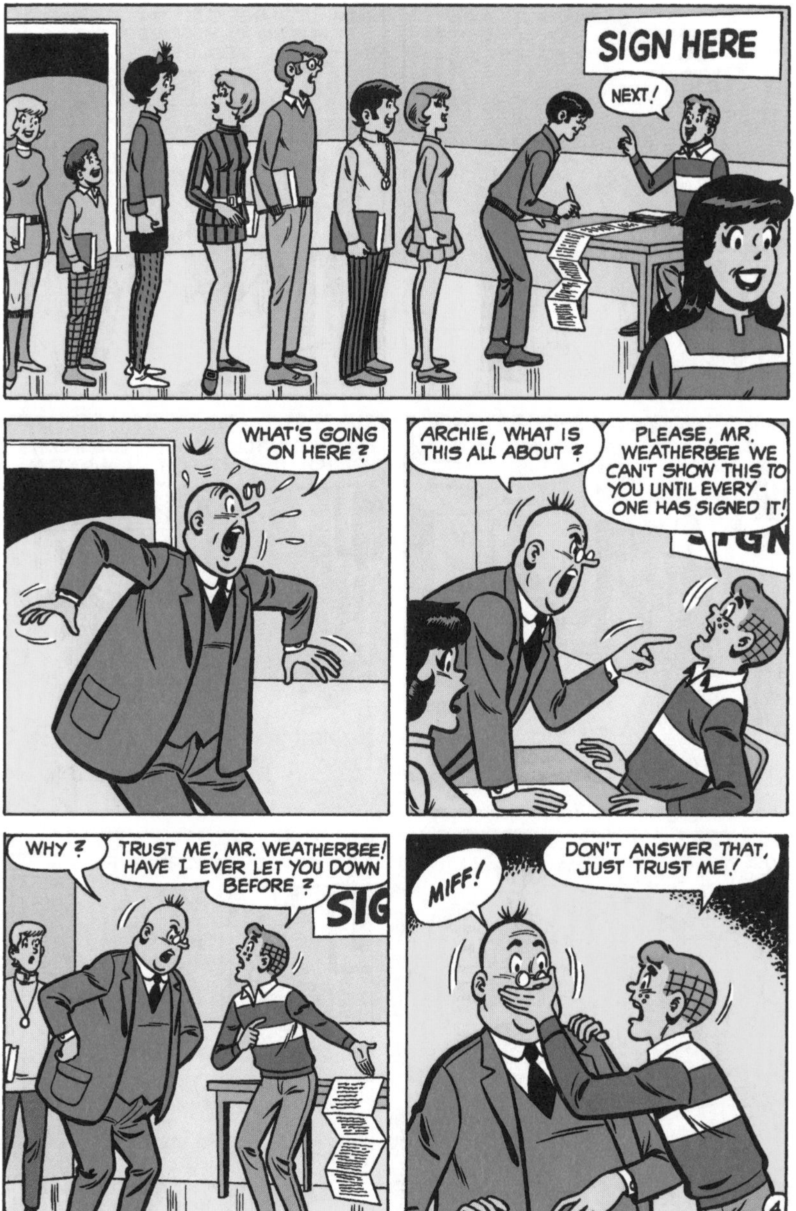
SIGN HERE
NEXT!
WHAT'S GOING ON HERE?
ARCHIE, WHAT IS THIS ALL ABOUT?
PLEASE, MR. WEATHERBEE WE CAN'T SHOW THIS TO YOU UNTIL EVERY-ONE HAS SIGNED IT!
WHY?
TRUST ME, MR. WEATHERBEE! HAVE I EVER LET YOU DOWN BEFORE?
MIFF!
DON'T ANSWER THAT, JUST TRUST ME!
4

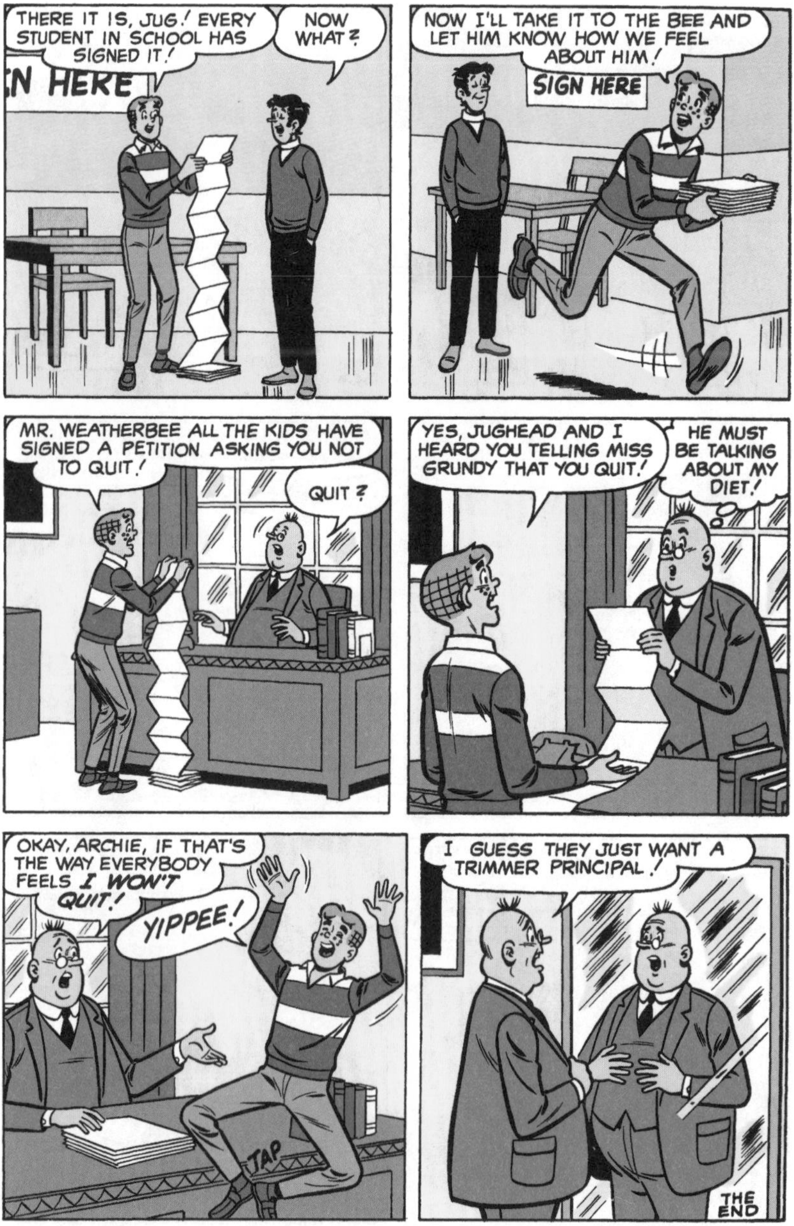
THERE IT IS, JUG! EVERY STUDENT IN SCHOOL HAS SIGNED IT!
NOW WHAT?
N HERE
NOW I'LL TAKE IT TO THE BEE AND LET HIM KNOW HOW WE FEEL ABOUT HIM!
SIGN HERE
MR. WEATHERBEE ALL THE KIDS HAVE SIGNED A PETITION ASKING YOU NOT TO QUIT!
QUIT?
YES, JUGHEAD AND I HEARD YOU TELLING MISS GRUNDY THAT YOU QUIT!
HE MUST BE TALKING ABOUT MY DIET!
OKAY, ARCHIE, IF THAT'S THE WAY EVERYBODY FEELS I WON'T QUIT!
YIPPEE!
TAP
I GUESS THEY JUST WANT A TRIMMER PRINCIPAL!
THE END

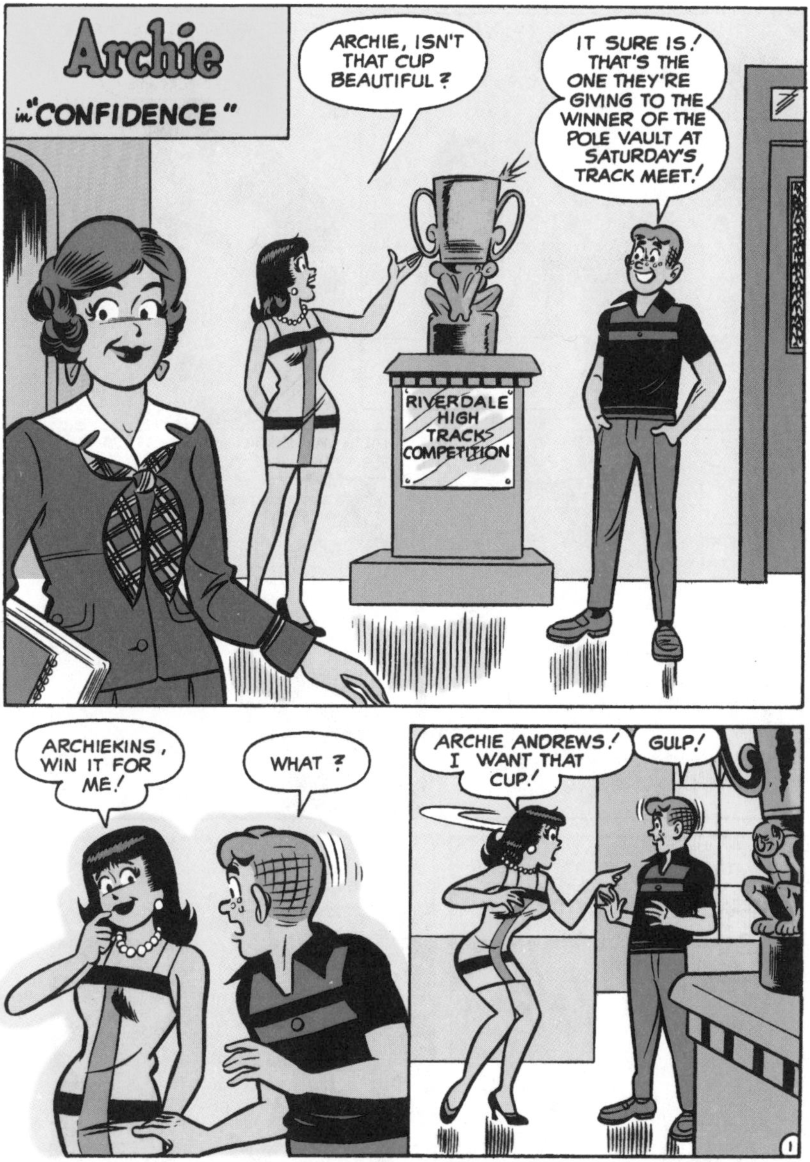

Archie
in "CONFIDENCE"
ARCHIE, ISN'T THAT CUP BEAUTIFUL?
IT SURE IS! THAT'S THE ONE THEY'RE GIVING TO THE WINNER OF THE POLE VAULT AT SATURDAY'S TRACK MEET!
RIVERDALE HIGH TRACKS COMPETITION
ARCHIEKINS, WIN IT FOR ME!
WHAT?
ARCHIE ANDREWS! I WANT THAT CUP!
GULP!
1

Story & Art: Bob Bolling

Letters: Bill Yoshida Colors: Barry Grossman

Originally printed in EVERYTHING'S ARCHIE #3, AUGUST 1969

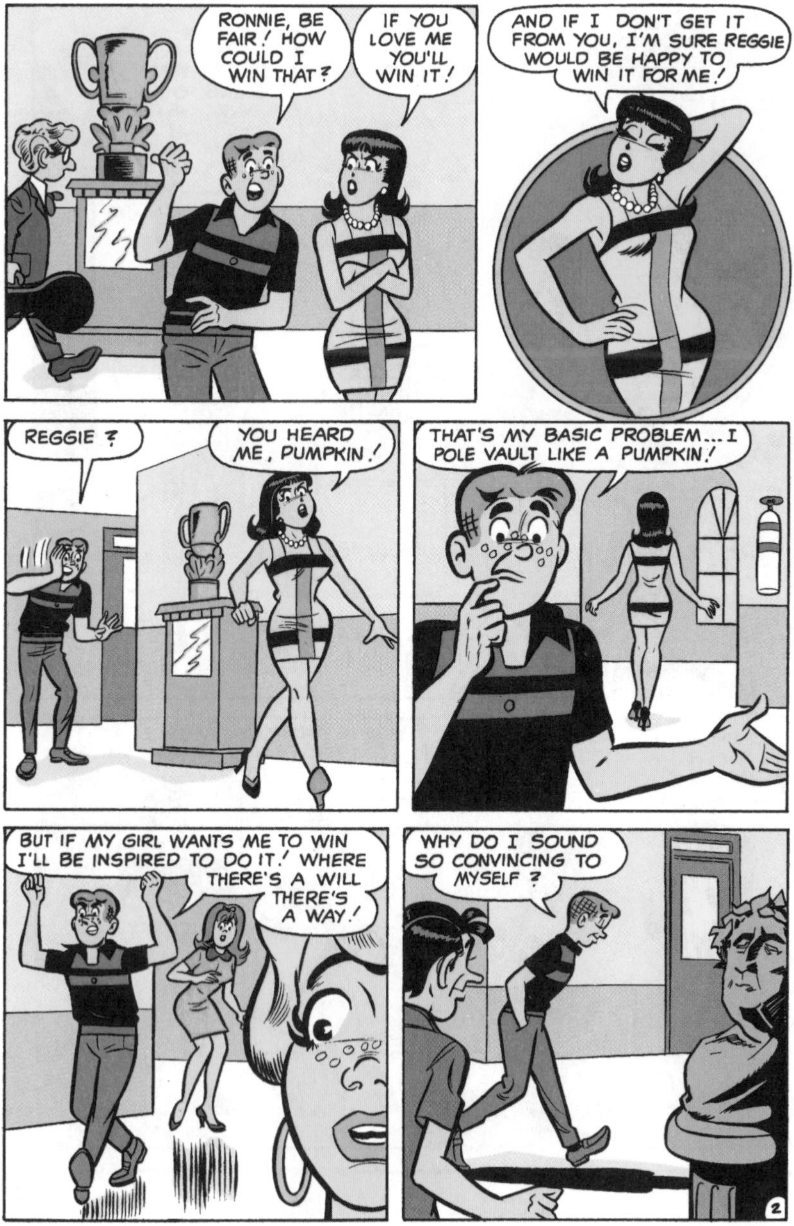
RONNIE, BE FAIR! HOW COULD I WIN THAT?
IF YOU LOVE ME YOU'LL WIN IT!
AND IF I DON'T GET IT FROM YOU, I'M SURE REGGIE WOULD BE HAPPY TO WIN IT FOR ME!
REGGIE?
YOU HEARD ME, PUMPKIN!
THAT'S MY BASIC PROBLEM... I POLE VAULT LIKE A PUMPKIN!
BUT IF MY GIRL WANTS ME TO WIN I'LL BE INSPIRED TO DO IT! WHERE THERE'S A WILL THERE'S A WAY!
WHY DO I SOUND SO CONVINCING TO MYSELF?
2

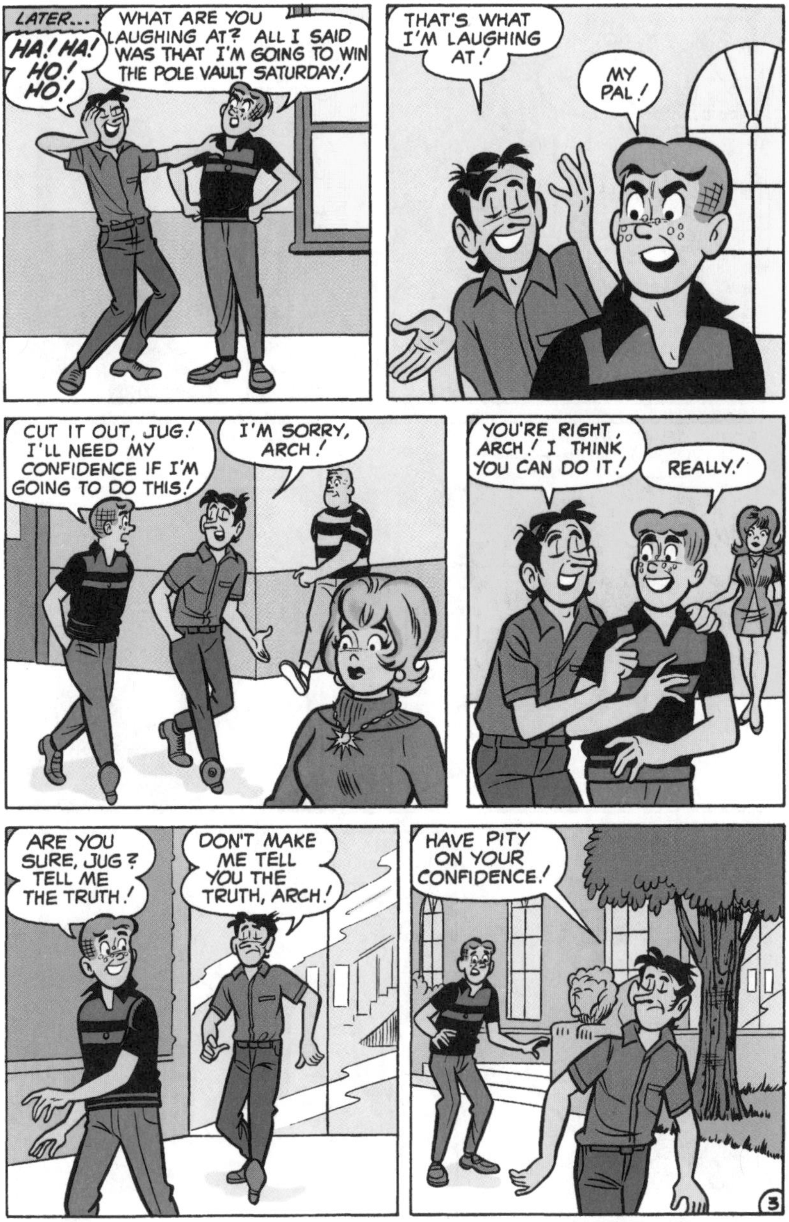
LATER...
HA! HA! HO! HO!
WHAT ARE YOU LAUGHING AT? ALL I SAID WAS THAT I'M GOING TO WIN THE POLE VAULT SATURDAY!
THAT'S WHAT I'M LAUGHING AT!
MY PAL!
CUT IT OUT, JUG! I'LL NEED MY CONFIDENCE IF I'M GOING TO DO THIS!
I'M SORRY, ARCH!
YOU'RE RIGHT, ARCH! I THINK YOU CAN DO IT!
REALLY!
ARE YOU SURE, JUG? TELL ME THE TRUTH!
DON'T MAKE ME TELL YOU THE TRUTH, ARCH!
HAVE PITY ON YOUR CONFIDENCE!
3

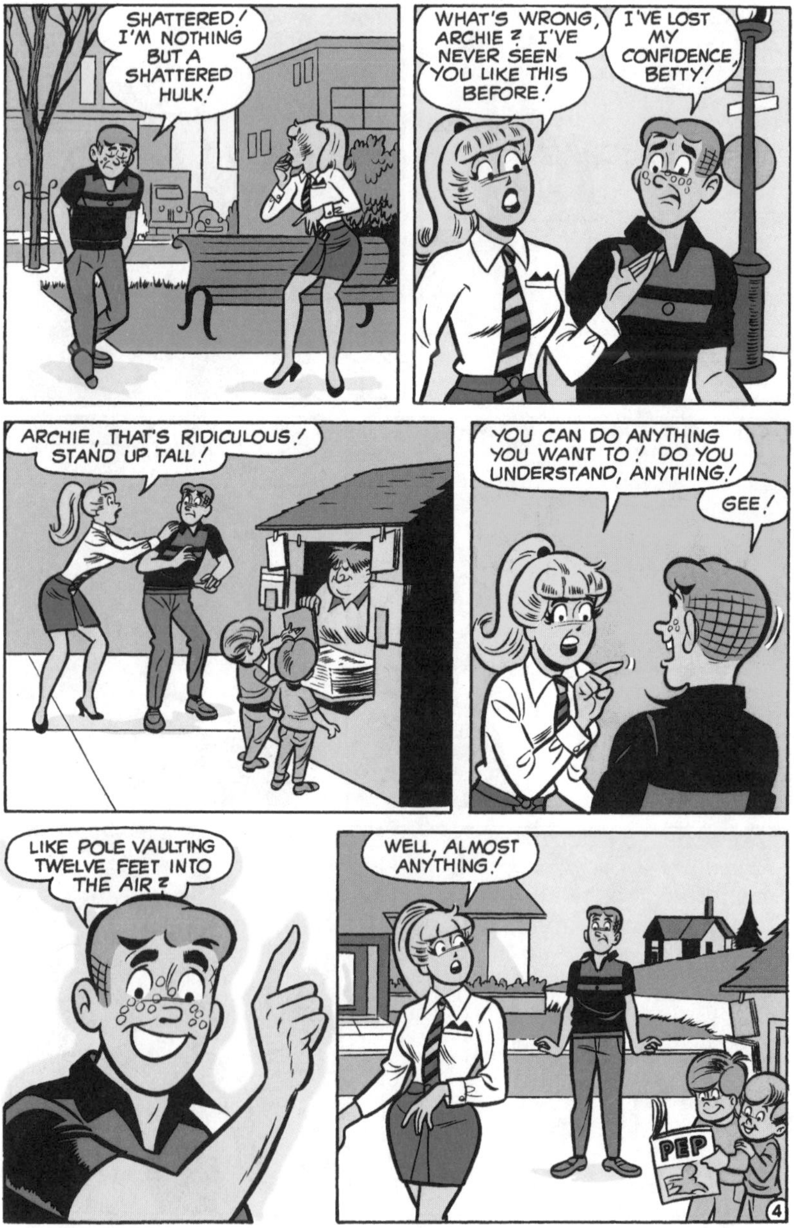
SHATTERED! I'M NOTHING BUT A SHATTERED HULK!
WHAT'S WRONG, ARCHIE? I'VE NEVER SEEN YOU LIKE THIS BEFORE!
I'VE LOST MY CONFIDENCE, BETTY!
ARCHIE, THAT'S RIDICULOUS! STAND UP TALL!
YOU CAN DO ANYTHING YOU WANT TO! DO YOU UNDERSTAND, ANYTHING!
GEE!
LIKE POLE VAULTING TWELVE FEET INTO THE AIR?
WELL, ALMOST ANYTHING!
PEP
4

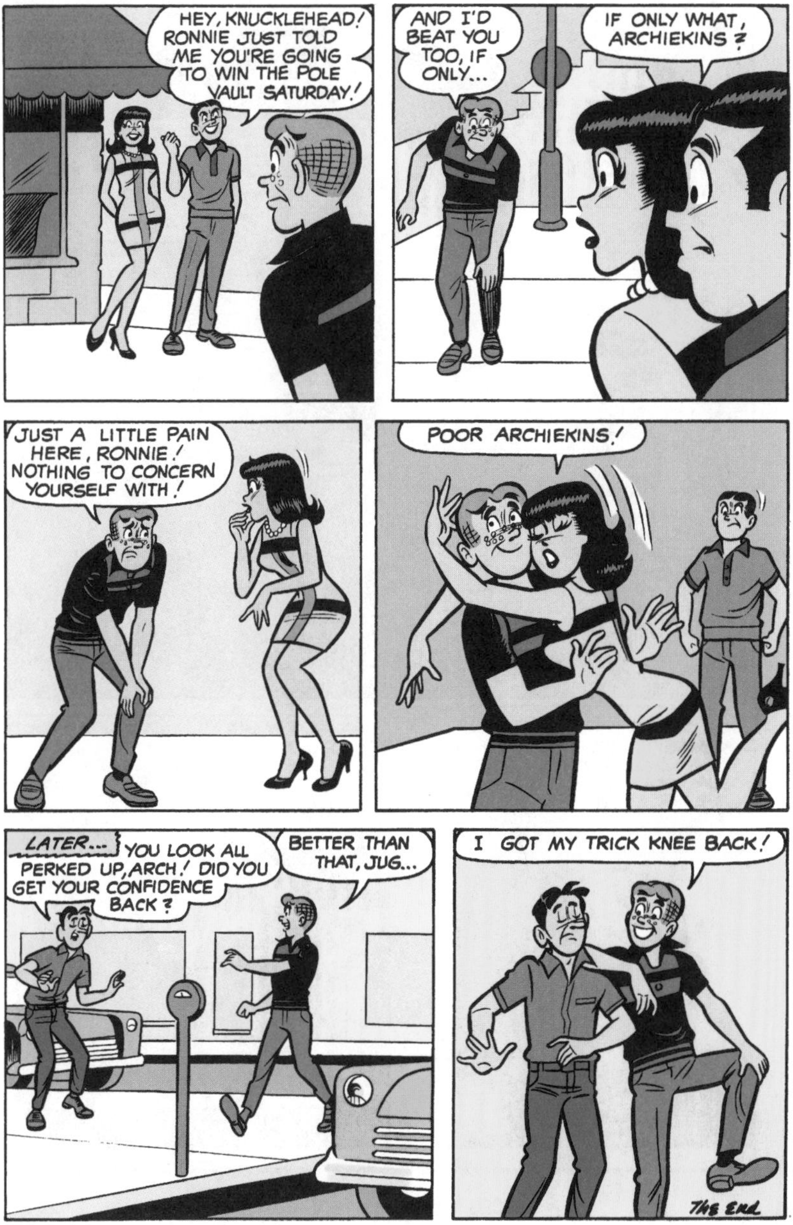
HEY, KNUCKLEHEAD! RONNIE JUST TOLD ME YOU'RE GOING TO WIN THE POLE VAULT SATURDAY!
AND I'D BEAT YOU TOO, IF ONLY...
IF ONLY WHAT, ARCHIEKINS?
JUST A LITTLE PAIN HERE, RONNIE! NOTHING TO CONCERN YOURSELF WITH!
POOR ARCHIEKINS!
LATER...
YOU LOOK ALL PERKED UP, ARCH! DID YOU GET YOUR CONFIDENCE BACK?
BETTER THAN THAT, JUG...
I GOT MY TRICK KNEE BACK!
The End

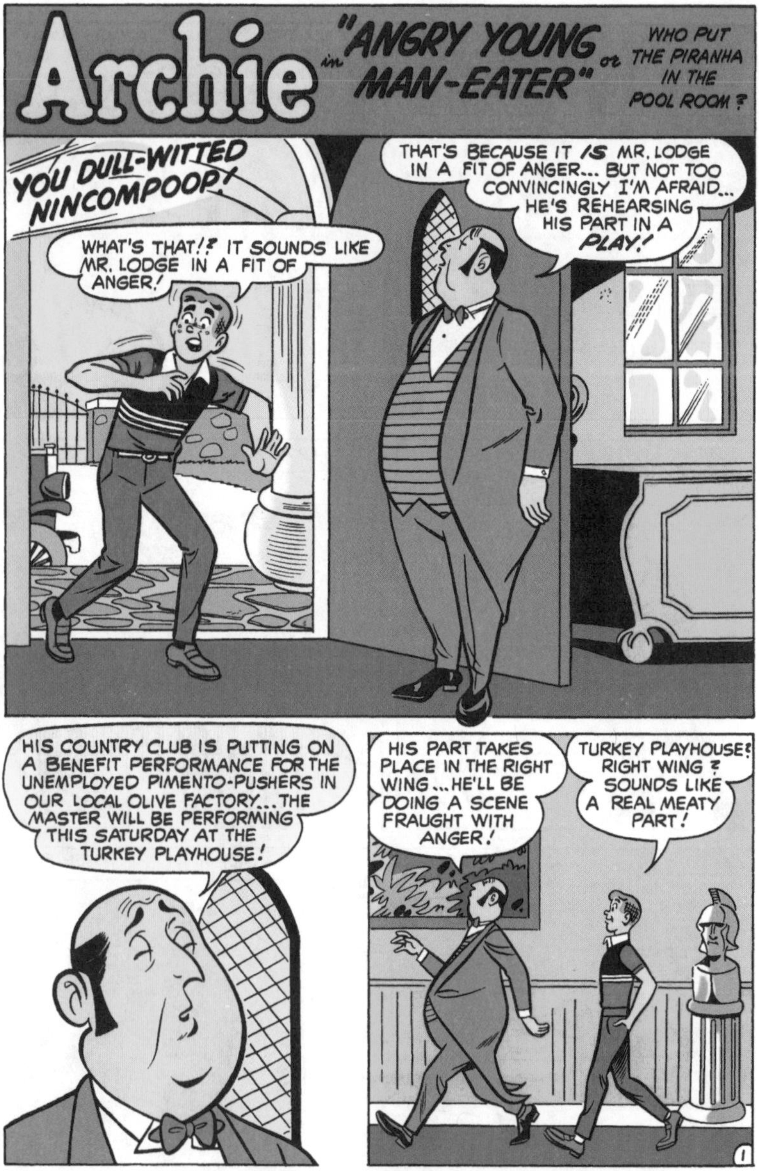
Archie
in "ANGRY YOUNG MAN-EATER" or WHO PUT THE PIRANHA IN THE POOL ROOM?
YOU DULL-WITTED NINCOMPOOP!
WHAT'S THAT!? IT SOUNDS LIKE MR. LODGE IN A FIT OF ANGER!
THAT'S BECAUSE IT IS MR. LODGE IN A FIT OF ANGER... BUT NOT TOO CONVINCINGLY I'M AFRAID... HE'S REHEARSING HIS PART IN A PLAY!
HIS COUNTRY CLUB IS PUTTING ON A BENEFIT PERFORMANCE FOR THE UNEMPLOYED PIMENTO-PUSHERS IN OUR LOCAL OLIVE FACTORY... THE MASTER WILL BE PERFORMING THIS SATURDAY AT THE TURKEY PLAYHOUSE!
HIS PART TAKES PLACE IN THE RIGHT WING... HE'LL BE DOING A SCENE FRAUGHT WITH ANGER!
TURKEY PLAYHOUSE? RIGHT WING? SOUNDS LIKE A REAL MEATY PART!
1

Story & Pencils: Bob Bolling

Inks: Rudy Lapick Letters: Bill Yoshida Colors: Barry Grossman

Originally printed in EVERYTHING'S ARCHIE #3, AUGUST 1969

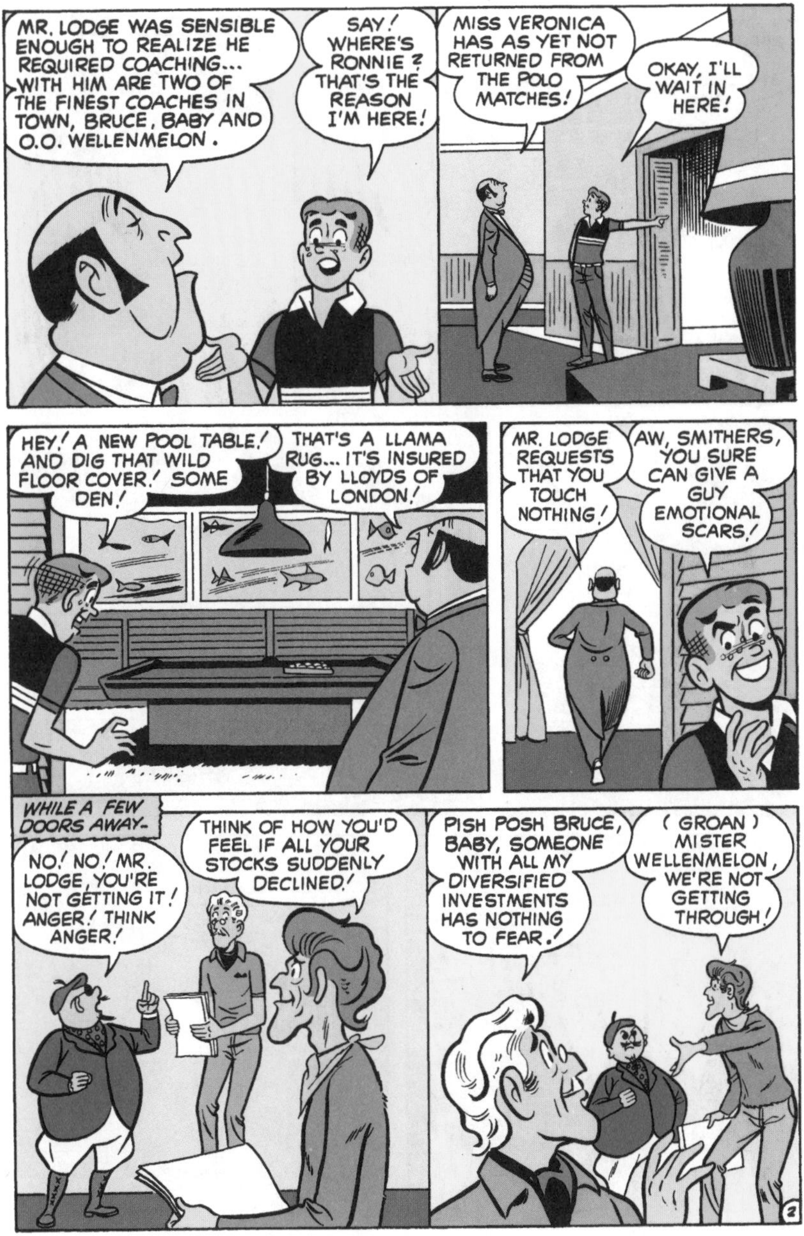
MR. LODGE WAS SENSIBLE ENOUGH TO REALIZE HE REQUIRED COACHING... WITH HIM ARE TWO OF THE FINEST COACHES IN TOWN, BRUCE, BABY AND O.O. WELLENMELON.
SAY! WHERE'S RONNIE? THAT'S THE REASON I'M HERE!
MISS VERONICA HAS AS YET NOT RETURNED FROM THE POLO MATCHES!
OKAY, I'LL WAIT IN HERE!
HEY! A NEW POOL TABLE! AND DIG THAT WILD FLOOR COVER! SOME DEN!
THAT'S A LLAMA RUG... IT'S INSURED BY LLOYDS OF LONDON!
MR. LODGE REQUESTS THAT YOU TOUCH NOTHING!
AW, SMITHERS, YOU SURE CAN GIVE A GUY EMOTIONAL SCARS!
WHILE A FEW DOORS AWAY-
NO! NO! MR. LODGE, YOU'RE NOT GETTING IT! ANGER! THINK ANGER!
THINK OF HOW YOU'D FEEL IF ALL YOUR STOCKS SUDDENLY DECLINED!
PISH POSH BRUCE, BABY, SOMEONE WITH ALL MY DIVERSIFIED INVESTMENTS HAS NOTHING TO FEAR!
(GROAN) MISTER WELLENMELON, WE'RE NOT GETTING THROUGH!
2

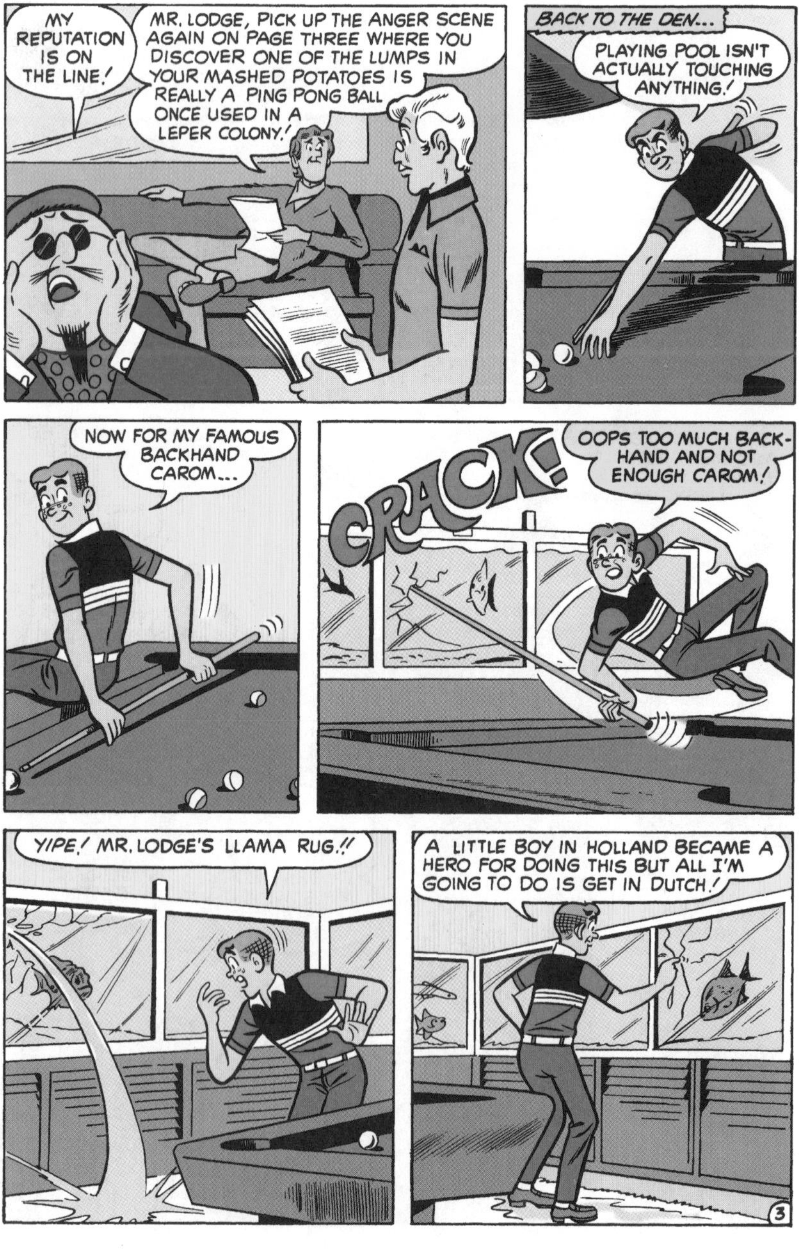
MY REPUTATION IS ON THE LINE!
MR. LODGE, PICK UP THE ANGER SCENE AGAIN ON PAGE THREE WHERE YOU DISCOVER ONE OF THE LUMPS IN YOUR MASHED POTATOES IS REALLY A PING PONG BALL ONCE USED IN A LEPER COLONY!
BACK TO THE DEN...
PLAYING POOL ISN'T ACTUALLY TOUCHING ANYTHING!
NOW FOR MY FAMOUS BACKHAND CAROM...
CRACK!
OOPS TOO MUCH BACK-HAND AND NOT ENOUGH CAROM!
YIPE! MR. LODGE'S LLAMA RUG!!
A LITTLE BOY IN HOLLAND BECAME A HERO FOR DOING THIS BUT ALL I'M GOING TO DO IS GET IN DUTCH!
3

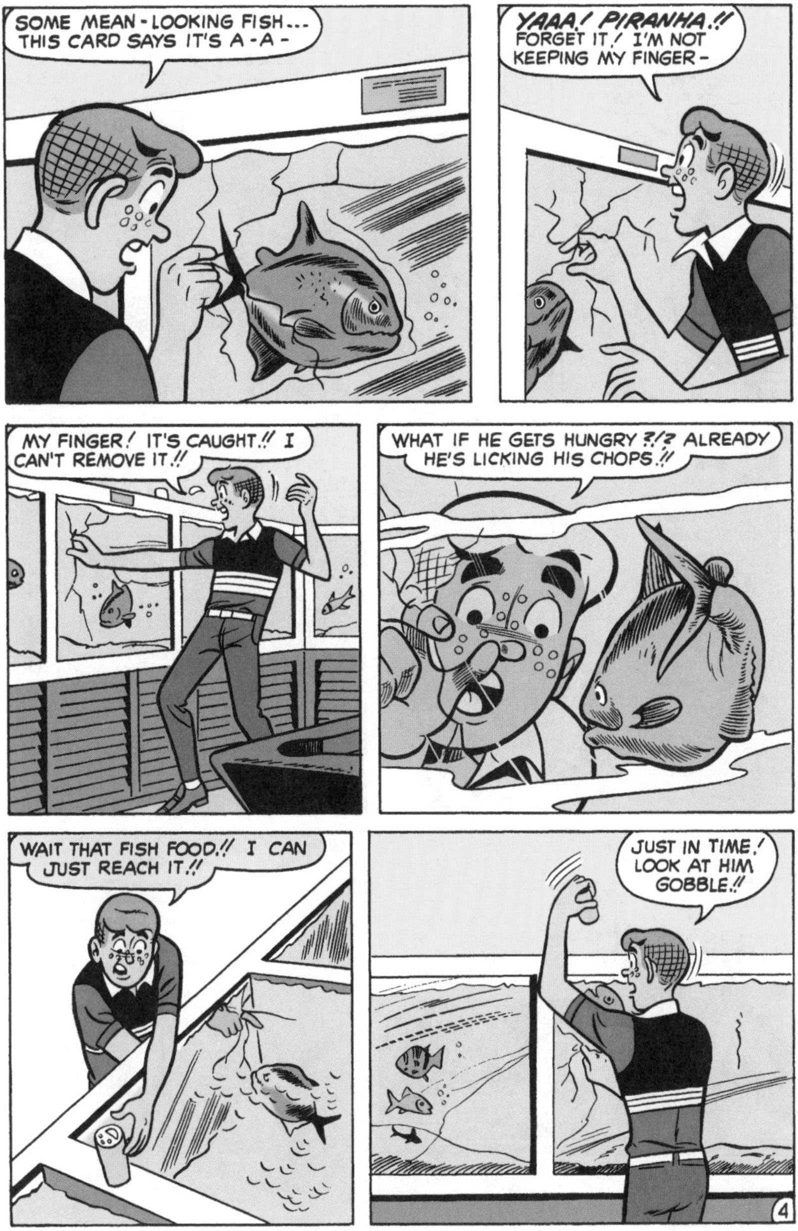
SOME MEAN-LOOKING FISH... THIS CARD SAYS IT'S A-A-
YAAA! PIRANHA.!! FORGET IT.! I'M NOT KEEPING MY FINGER-
MY FINGER! IT'S CAUGHT.!! I CAN'T REMOVE IT.!!
WHAT IF HE GETS HUNGRY ?!? ALREADY HE'S LICKING HIS CHOPS.!!
WAIT THAT FISH FOOD.!! I CAN JUST REACH IT.!!
JUST IN TIME.! LOOK AT HIM GOBBLE.!!
4

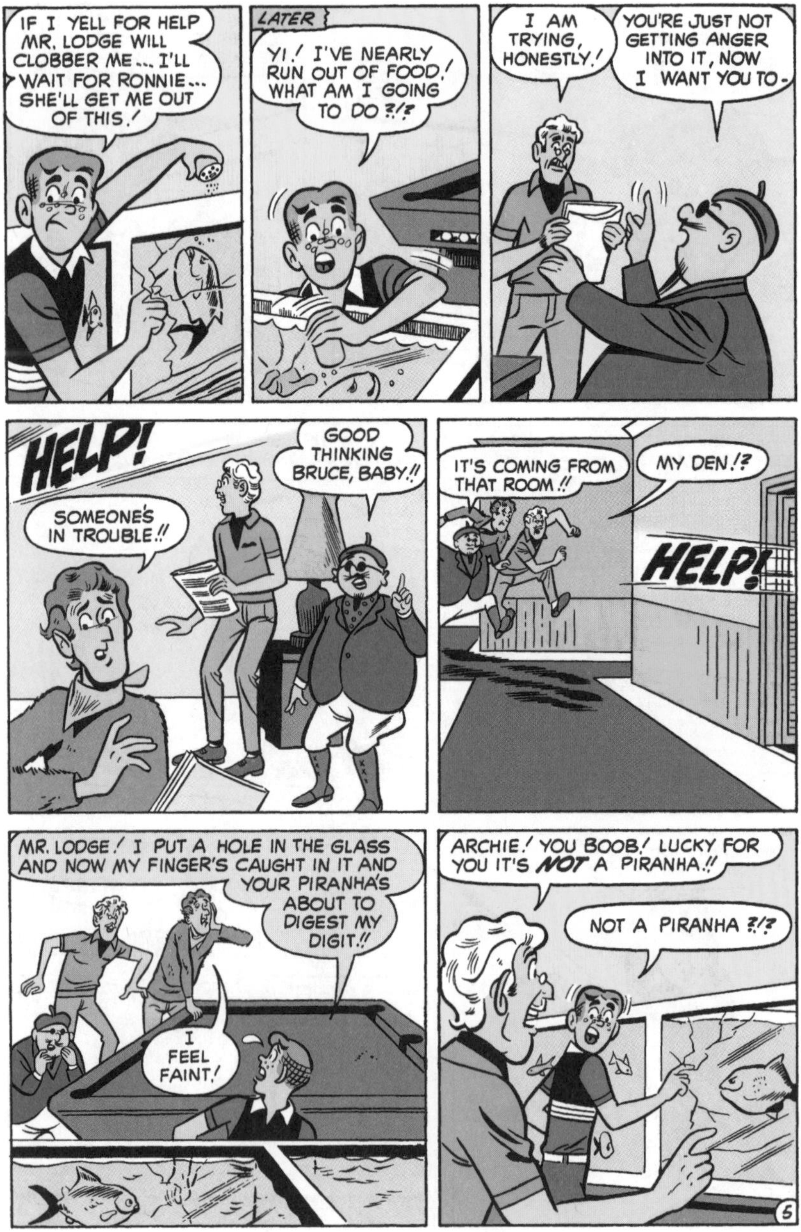
IF I YELL FOR HELP MR. LODGE WILL CLOBBER ME... I'LL WAIT FOR RONNIE... SHE'LL GET ME OUT OF THIS!
LATER
YI! I'VE NEARLY RUN OUT OF FOOD! WHAT AM I GOING TO DO ?!?
I AM TRYING, HONESTLY!
YOU'RE JUST NOT GETTING ANGER INTO IT, NOW I WANT YOU TO-
HELP!
SOMEONE'S IN TROUBLE!!
GOOD THINKING BRUCE, BABY!!
IT'S COMING FROM THAT ROOM!!
MY DEN!?
HELP!
MR. LODGE! I PUT A HOLE IN THE GLASS AND NOW MY FINGER'S CAUGHT IN IT AND YOUR PIRANHA'S ABOUT TO DIGEST MY DIGIT!!
I FEEL FAINT!
ARCHIE! YOU BOOB! LUCKY FOR YOU IT'S NOT A PIRANHA!!
NOT A PIRANHA ?!?
5

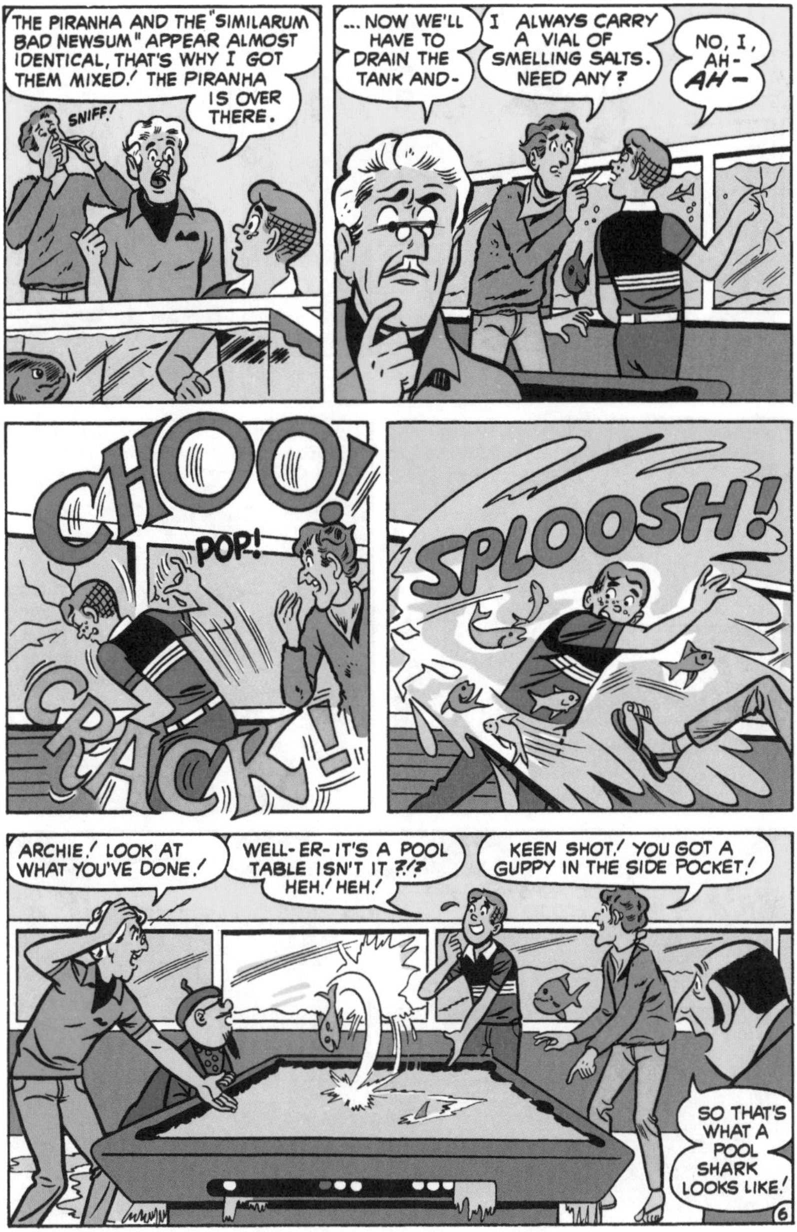
THE PIRANHA AND THE "SIMILARUM BAD NEWSUM" APPEAR ALMOST IDENTICAL, THAT'S WHY I GOT THEM MIXED! THE PIRANHA IS OVER THERE.
SNIFF!
...NOW WE'LL HAVE TO DRAIN THE TANK AND-
I ALWAYS CARRY A VIAL OF SMELLING SALTS. NEED ANY?
NO, I, AH- AH—
CHOO!
POP!
CRACK!
SPLOOSH!
ARCHIE! LOOK AT WHAT YOU'VE DONE!
WELL-ER-IT'S A POOL TABLE ISN'T IT ?!?
HEH! HEH!
KEEN SHOT! YOU GOT A GUPPY IN THE SIDE POCKET!
SO THAT'S WHAT A POOL SHARK LOOKS LIKE!
6

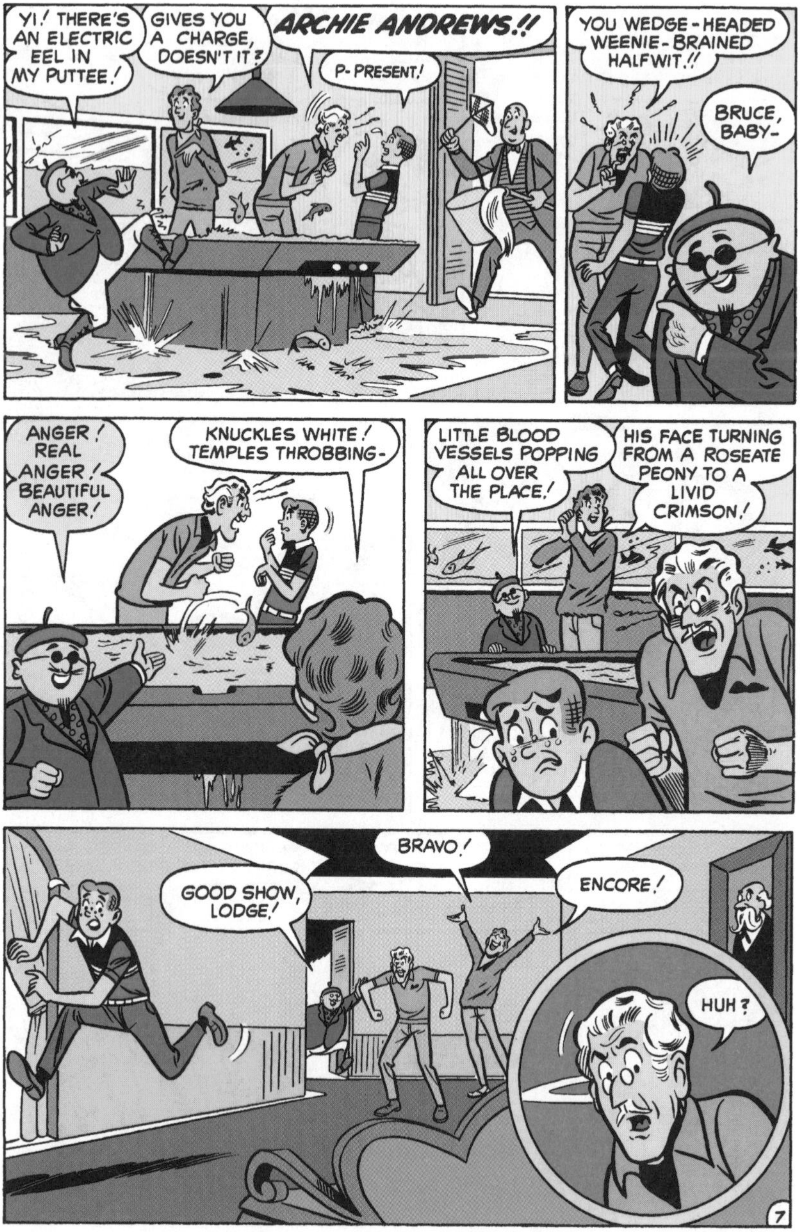
YI! THERE'S AN ELECTRIC EEL IN MY PUTTEE!
GIVES YOU A CHARGE, DOESN'T IT?
ARCHIE ANDREWS!!
P-PRESENT!
YOU WEDGE-HEADED WEENIE-BRAINED HALFWIT!!
BRUCE, BABY-
ANGER! REAL ANGER! BEAUTIFUL ANGER!
KNUCKLES WHITE! TEMPLES THROBBING-
LITTLE BLOOD VESSELS POPPING ALL OVER THE PLACE!
HIS FACE TURNING FROM A ROSEATE PEONY TO A LIVID CRIMSON!
GOOD SHOW, LODGE!
BRAVO!
ENCORE!
HUH?
7

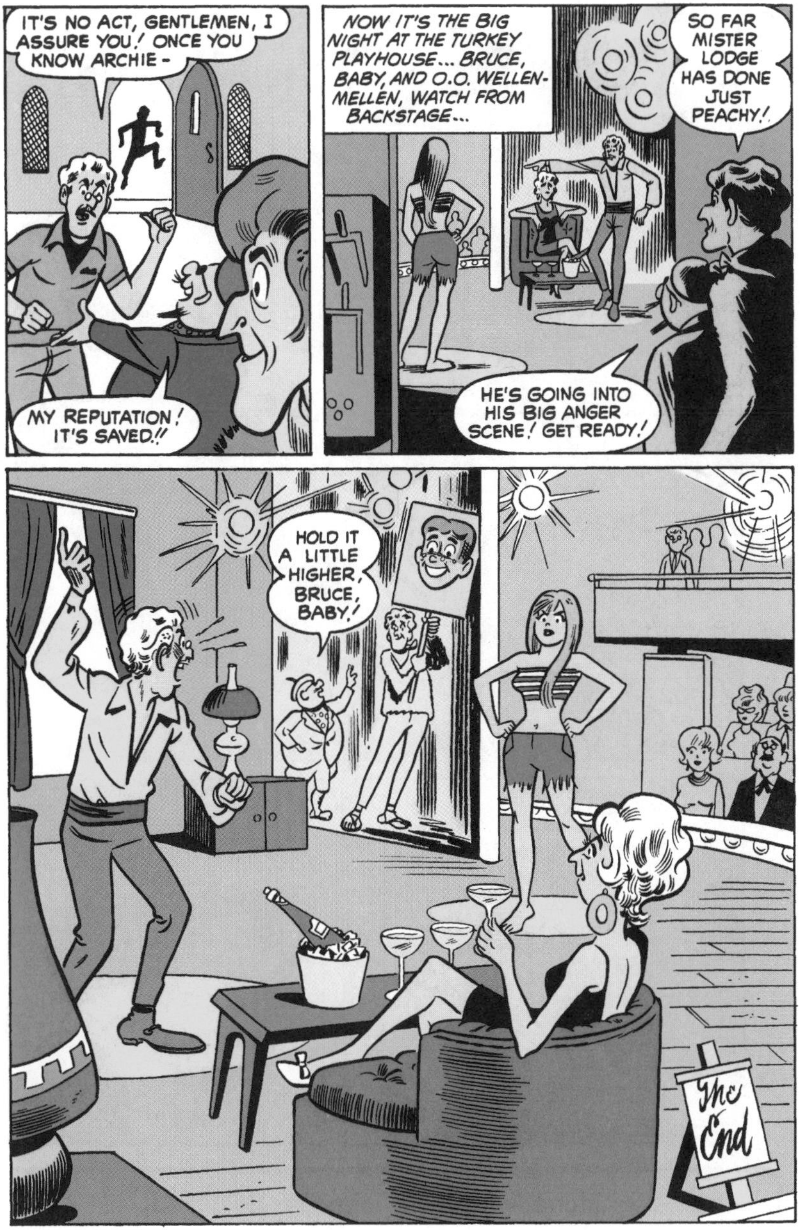
IT'S NO ACT, GENTLEMEN, I ASSURE YOU! ONCE YOU KNOW ARCHIE -
MY REPUTATION! IT'S SAVED!!
NOW IT'S THE BIG NIGHT AT THE TURKEY PLAYHOUSE... BRUCE, BABY, AND O.O. WELLEN-MELLEN, WATCH FROM BACKSTAGE...
SO FAR MISTER LODGE HAS DONE JUST PEACHY!
HE'S GOING INTO HIS BIG ANGER SCENE! GET READY!
HOLD IT A LITTLE HIGHER, BRUCE, BABY!
The End

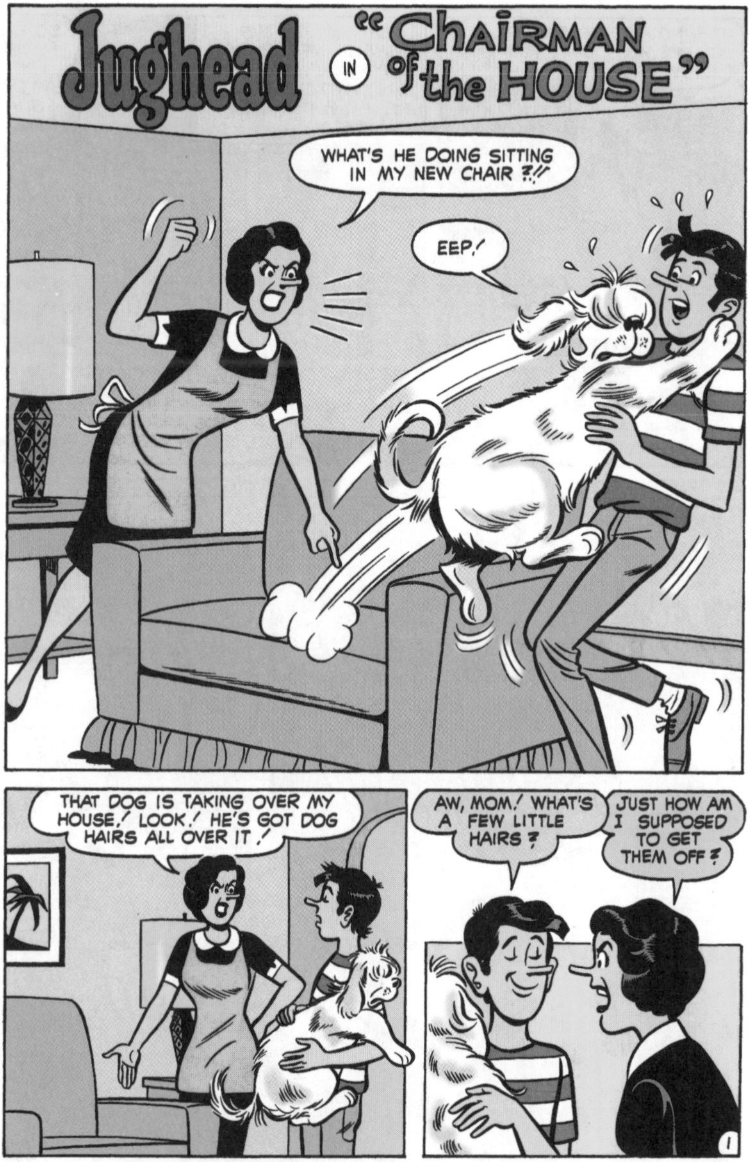
Jughead IN "CHAIRMAN of the HOUSE"
WHAT'S HE DOING SITTING IN MY NEW CHAIR ?!!
EEP!
THAT DOG IS TAKING OVER MY HOUSE! LOOK! HE'S GOT DOG HAIRS ALL OVER IT!
AW, MOM! WHAT'S A FEW LITTLE HAIRS ?
JUST HOW AM I SUPPOSED TO GET THEM OFF ?
1

Story: Frank Doyle Pencils: Bill Vigoda
Inks: Mario Acquaviva Letters: Bill Yoshida

Originally printed in EVERYTHING'S ARCHIE #4, SEPTEMBER 1969

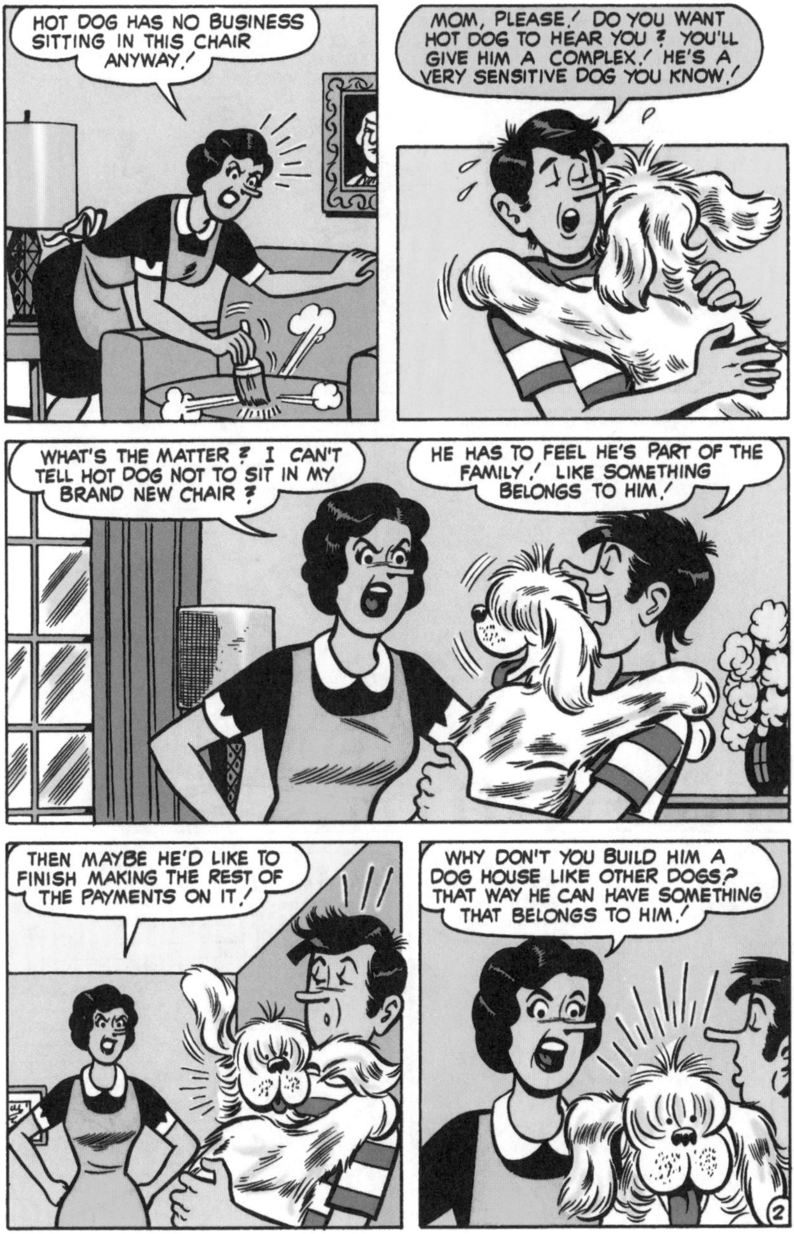
HOT DOG HAS NO BUSINESS SITTING IN THIS CHAIR ANYWAY!
MOM, PLEASE! DO YOU WANT HOT DOG TO HEAR YOU? YOU'LL GIVE HIM A COMPLEX! HE'S A VERY SENSITIVE DOG YOU KNOW!
WHAT'S THE MATTER? I CAN'T TELL HOT DOG NOT TO SIT IN MY BRAND NEW CHAIR?
HE HAS TO FEEL HE'S PART OF THE FAMILY! LIKE SOMETHING BELONGS TO HIM!
THEN MAYBE HE'D LIKE TO FINISH MAKING THE REST OF THE PAYMENTS ON IT!
WHY DON'T YOU BUILD HIM A DOG HOUSE LIKE OTHER DOGS? THAT WAY HE CAN HAVE SOMETHING THAT BELONGS TO HIM!
2

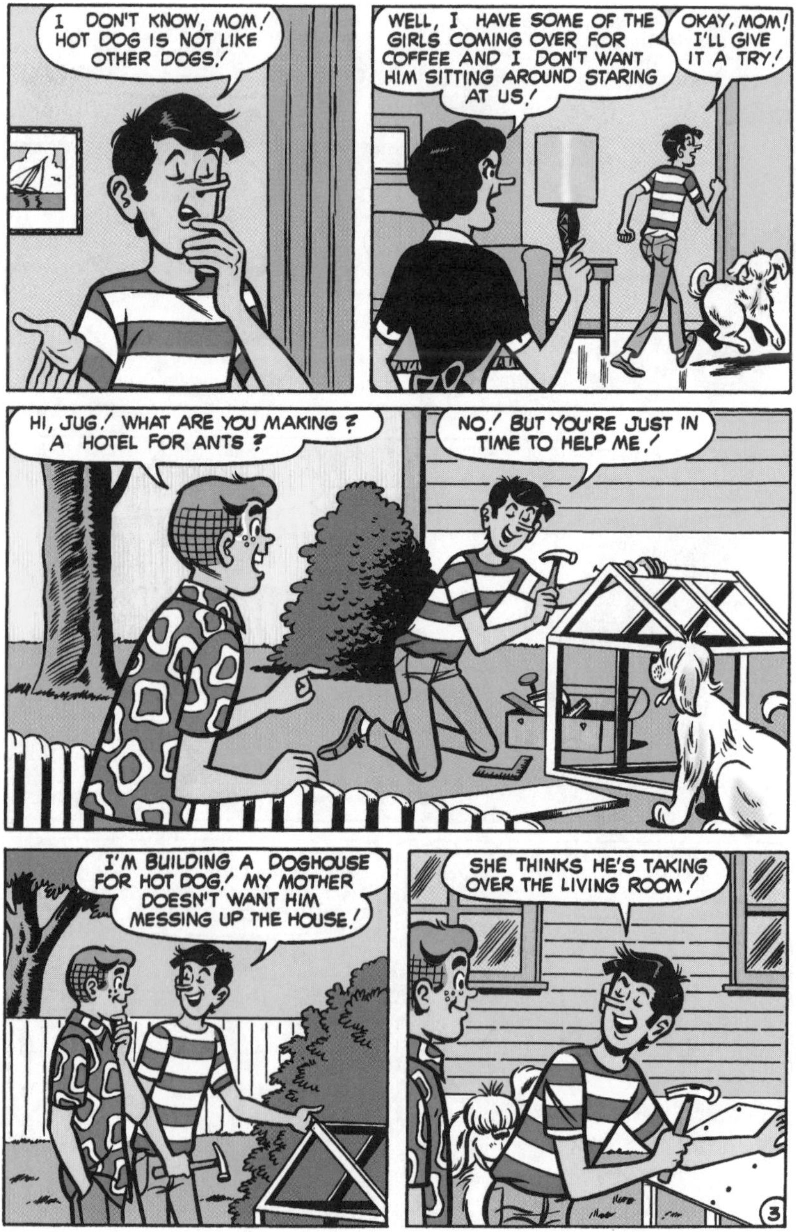
I DON'T KNOW, MOM! HOT DOG IS NOT LIKE OTHER DOGS!
WELL, I HAVE SOME OF THE GIRLS COMING OVER FOR COFFEE AND I DON'T WANT HIM SITTING AROUND STARING AT US!
OKAY, MOM! I'LL GIVE IT A TRY!
HI, JUG! WHAT ARE YOU MAKING? A HOTEL FOR ANTS?
NO! BUT YOU'RE JUST IN TIME TO HELP ME!
I'M BUILDING A DOGHOUSE FOR HOT DOG! MY MOTHER DOESN'T WANT HIM MESSING UP THE HOUSE!
SHE THINKS HE'S TAKING OVER THE LIVING ROOM!
3

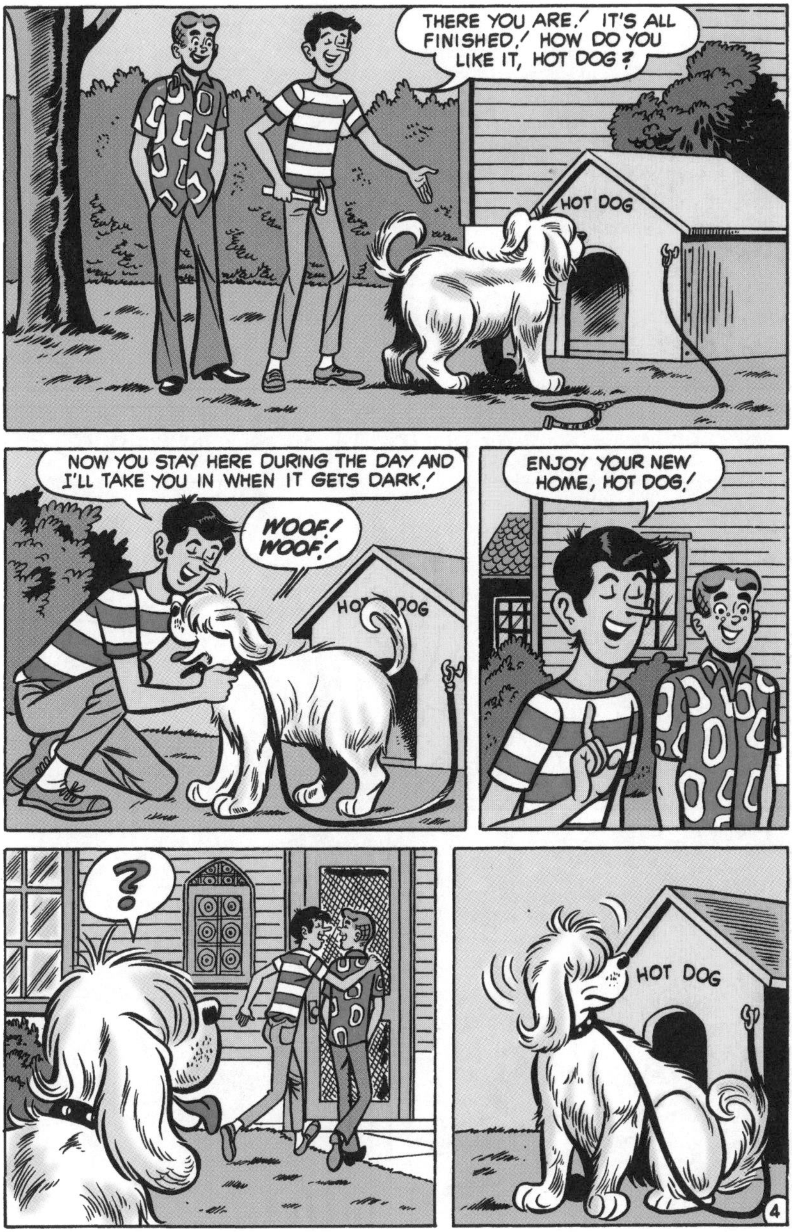
THERE YOU ARE! IT'S ALL FINISHED! HOW DO YOU LIKE IT, HOT DOG?
HOT DOG
NOW YOU STAY HERE DURING THE DAY AND I'LL TAKE YOU IN WHEN IT GETS DARK!
WOOF! WOOF!
ENJOY YOUR NEW HOME, HOT DOG!
?
HOT DOG
4

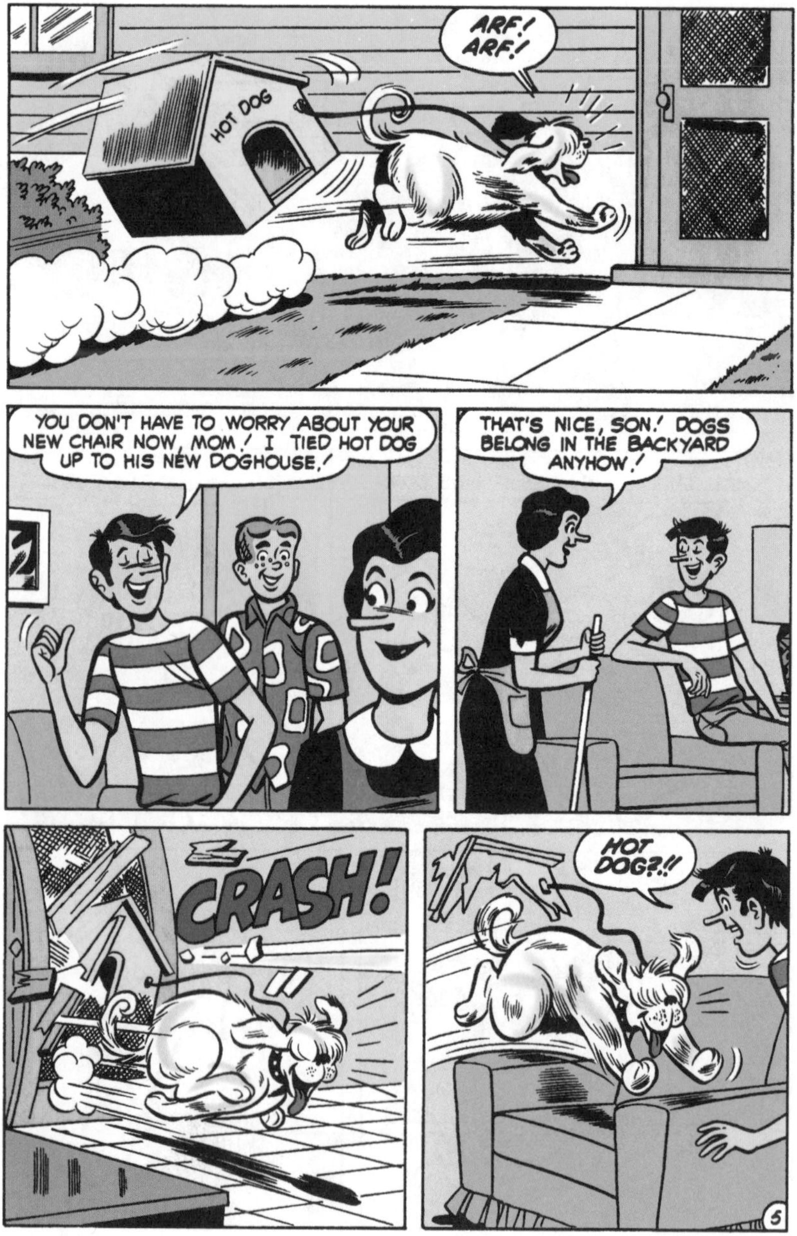
ARF! ARF!
HOT DOG
YOU DON'T HAVE TO WORRY ABOUT YOUR NEW CHAIR NOW, MOM! I TIED HOT DOG UP TO HIS NEW DOGHOUSE!
THAT'S NICE, SON! DOGS BELONG IN THE BACKYARD ANYHOW!
CRASH!
HOT DOG?!!
5

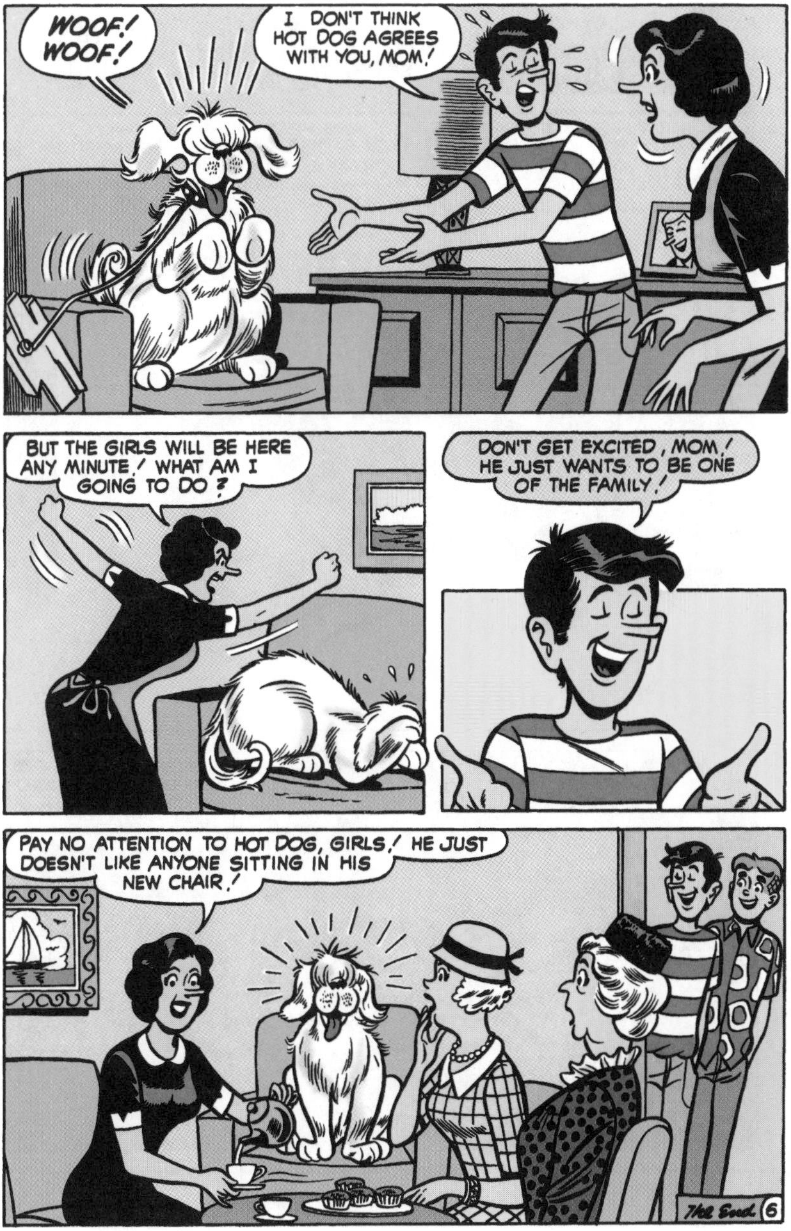
WOOF! WOOF!
I DON'T THINK HOT DOG AGREES WITH YOU, MOM!
BUT THE GIRLS WILL BE HERE ANY MINUTE! WHAT AM I GOING TO DO?
DON'T GET EXCITED, MOM! HE JUST WANTS TO BE ONE OF THE FAMILY!
PAY NO ATTENTION TO HOT DOG, GIRLS! HE JUST DOESN'T LIKE ANYONE SITTING IN HIS NEW CHAIR!
THE END 6

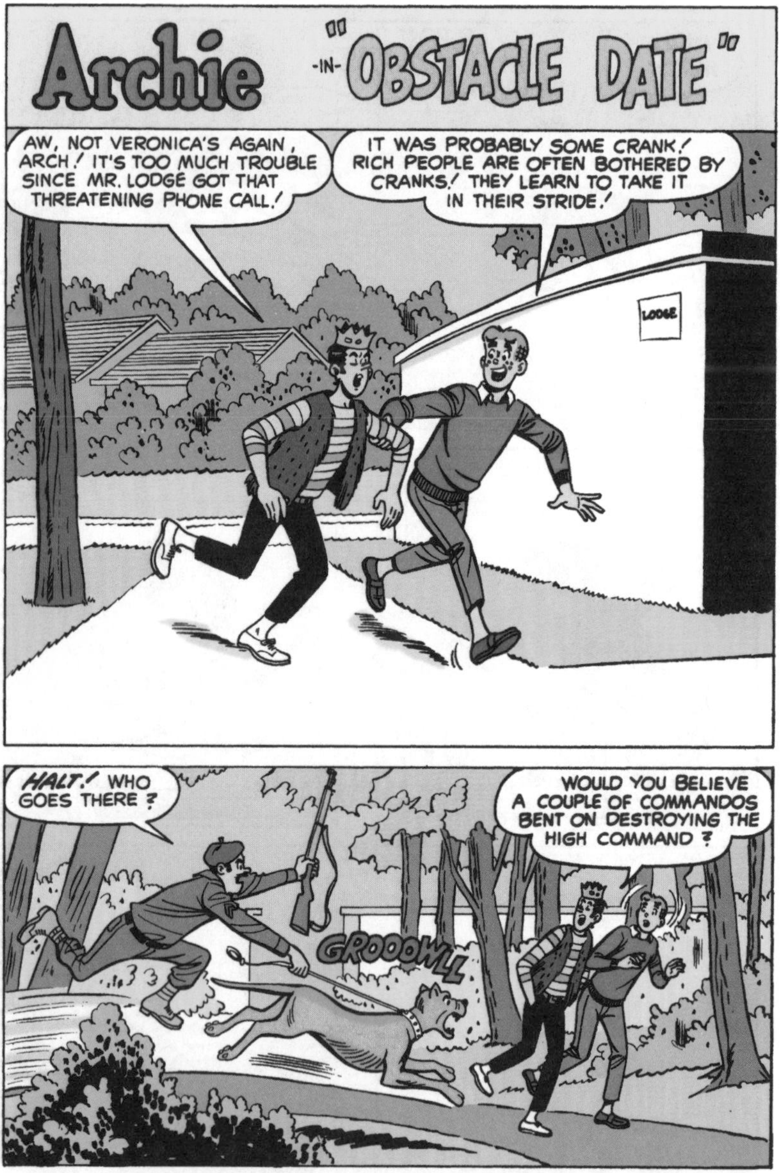
Archie -IN- "OBSTACLE DATE"
AW, NOT VERONICA'S AGAIN, ARCH! IT'S TOO MUCH TROUBLE SINCE MR. LODGE GOT THAT THREATENING PHONE CALL!
IT WAS PROBABLY SOME CRANK! RICH PEOPLE ARE OFTEN BOTHERED BY CRANKS! THEY LEARN TO TAKE IT IN THEIR STRIDE!
LODGE
HALT! WHO GOES THERE?
WOULD YOU BELIEVE A COUPLE OF COMMANDOS BENT ON DESTROYING THE HIGH COMMAND?
GROOOWLL

Story & Pencils: Al Hartley

Inks: Jon D'Agostino Letters: Bill Yoshida

Originally printed in EVERYTHING'S ARCHIE #4, SEPTEMBER 1969

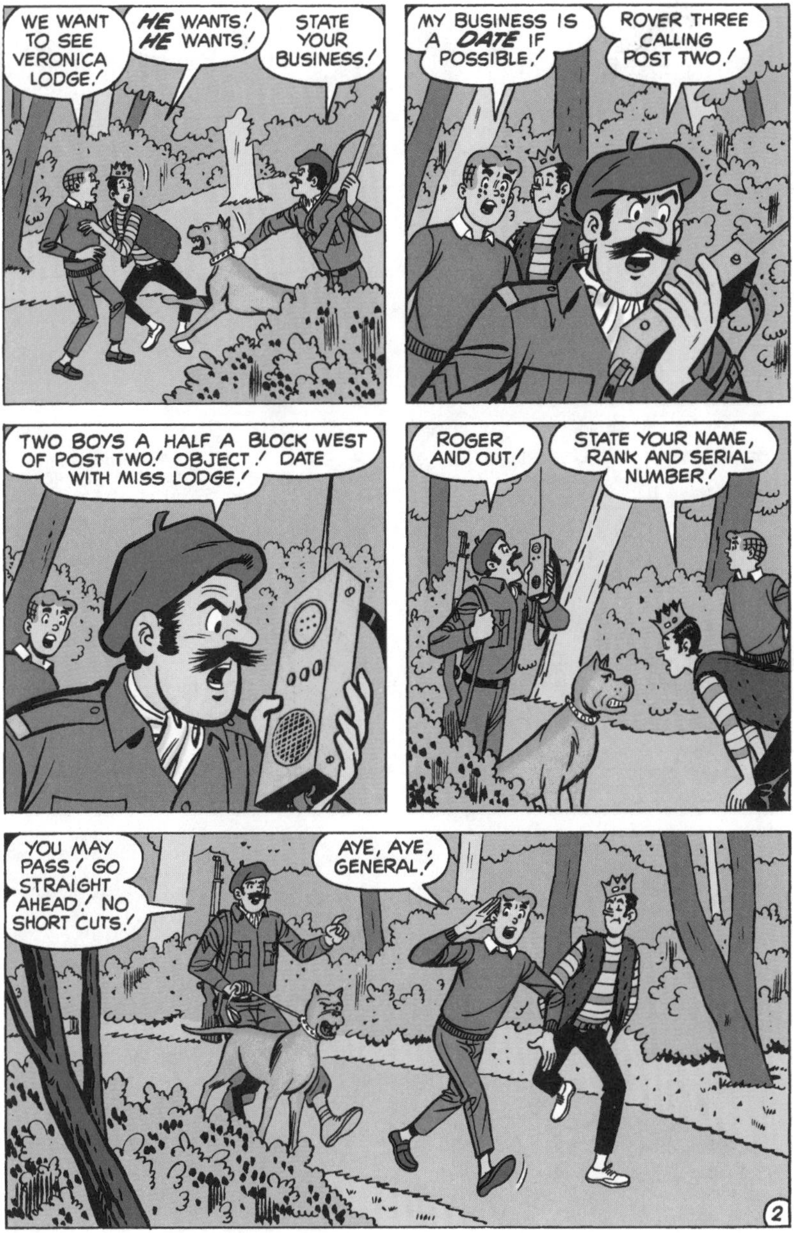
WE WANT TO SEE VERONICA LODGE!
HE WANTS! *HE* WANTS!
STATE YOUR BUSINESS!
MY BUSINESS IS A *DATE* IF POSSIBLE!
ROVER THREE CALLING POST TWO!
TWO BOYS A HALF A BLOCK WEST OF POST TWO! OBJECT! DATE WITH MISS LODGE!
ROGER AND OUT!
STATE YOUR NAME, RANK AND SERIAL NUMBER!
YOU MAY PASS! GO STRAIGHT AHEAD! NO SHORT CUTS!
AYE, AYE, GENERAL!
2

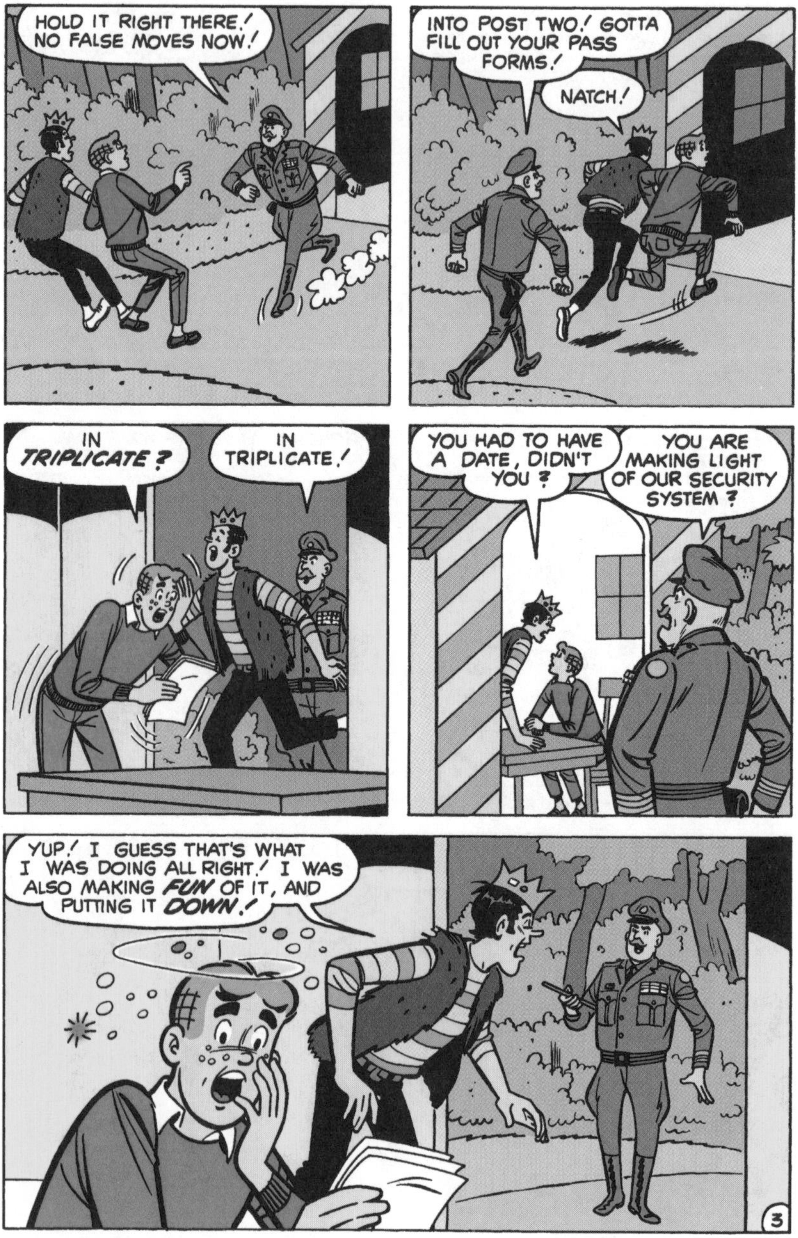
HOLD IT RIGHT THERE! NO FALSE MOVES NOW!
INTO POST TWO! GOTTA FILL OUT YOUR PASS FORMS!
NATCH!
IN *TRIPLICATE?*
IN TRIPLICATE!
YOU HAD TO HAVE A DATE, DIDN'T YOU?
YOU ARE MAKING LIGHT OF OUR SECURITY SYSTEM?
YUP! I GUESS THAT'S WHAT I WAS DOING ALL RIGHT! I WAS ALSO MAKING *FUN* OF IT, AND PUTTING IT *DOWN*!
3

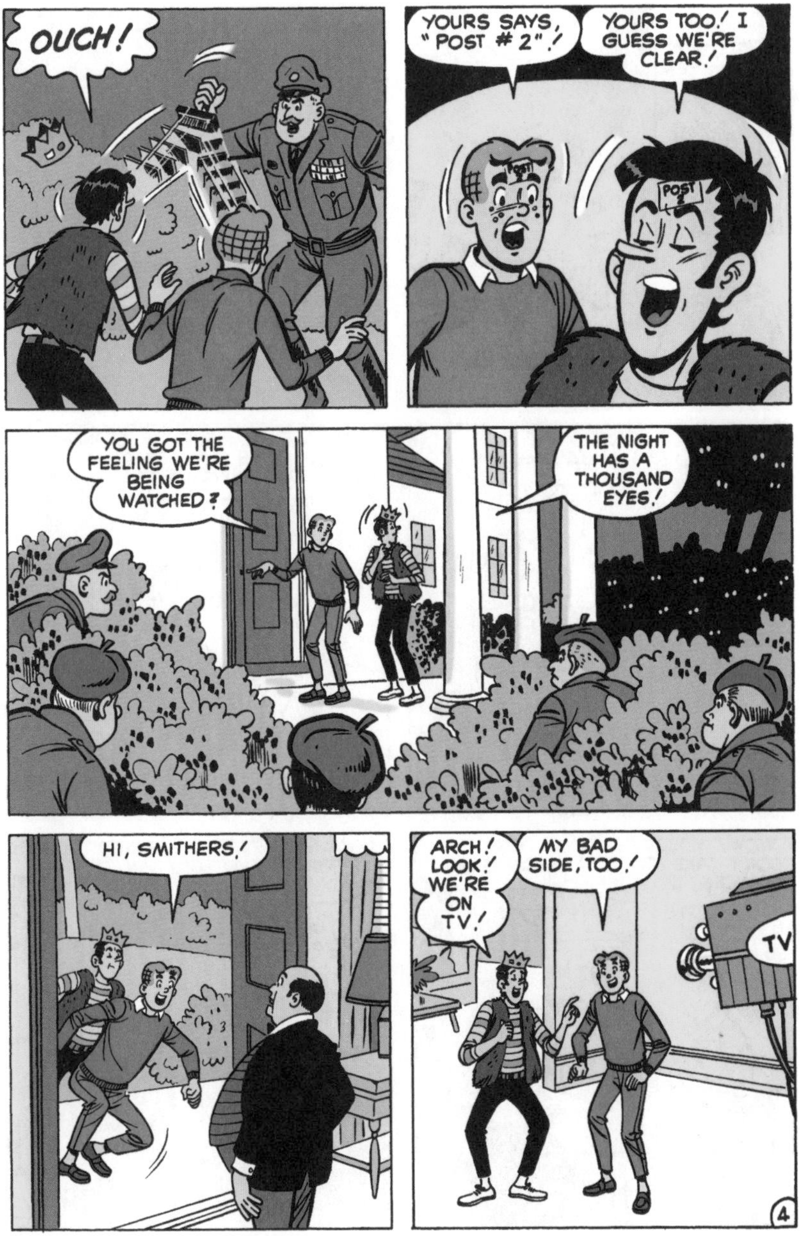
OUCH!
YOURS SAYS, "POST # 2"!
YOURS TOO! I GUESS WE'RE CLEAR!
POST 2
POST 2
YOU GOT THE FEELING WE'RE BEING WATCHED?
THE NIGHT HAS A THOUSAND EYES!
HI, SMITHERS!
ARCH! LOOK! WE'RE ON TV!
MY BAD SIDE, TOO!
TV
4

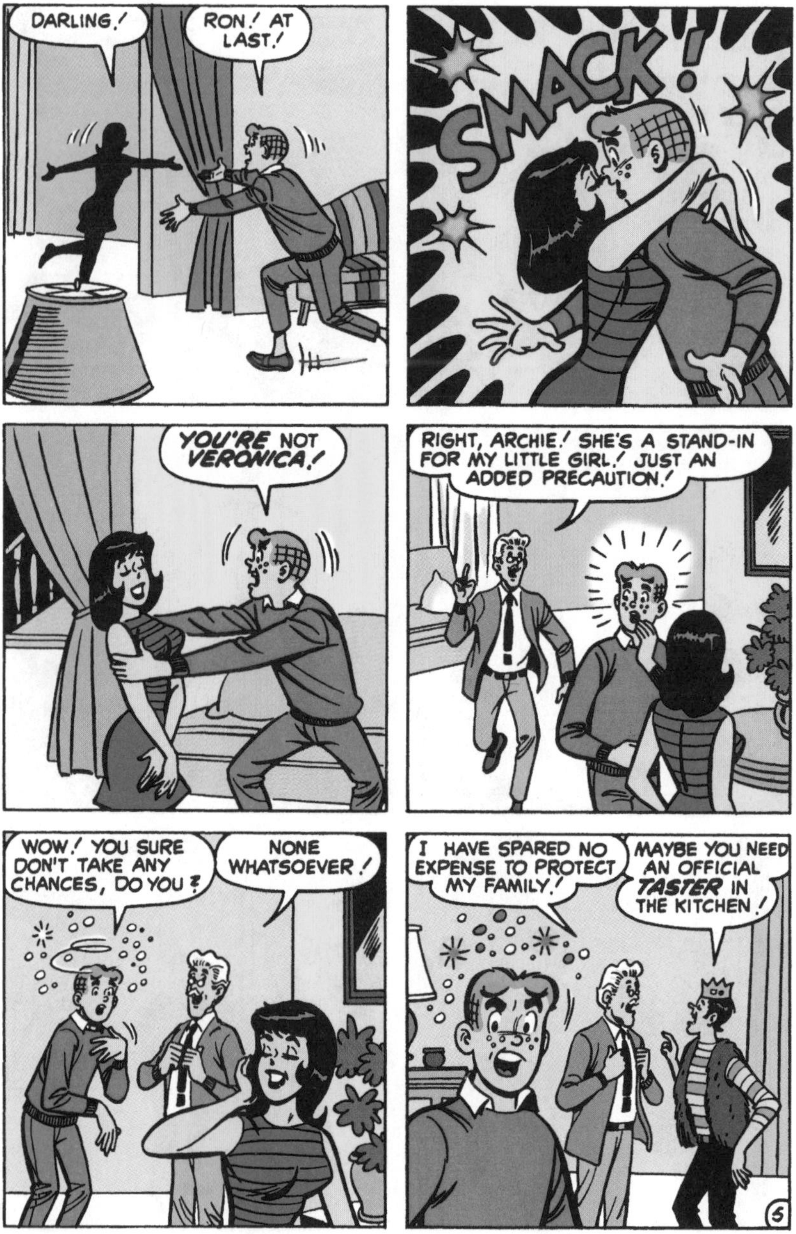
DARLING!
RON! AT LAST!
SMACK!
YOU'RE NOT VERONICA!
RIGHT, ARCHIE! SHE'S A STAND-IN FOR MY LITTLE GIRL! JUST AN ADDED PRECAUTION!
WOW! YOU SURE DON'T TAKE ANY CHANCES, DO YOU?
NONE WHATSOEVER!
I HAVE SPARED NO EXPENSE TO PROTECT MY FAMILY!
MAYBE YOU NEED AN OFFICIAL TASTER IN THE KITCHEN!
5

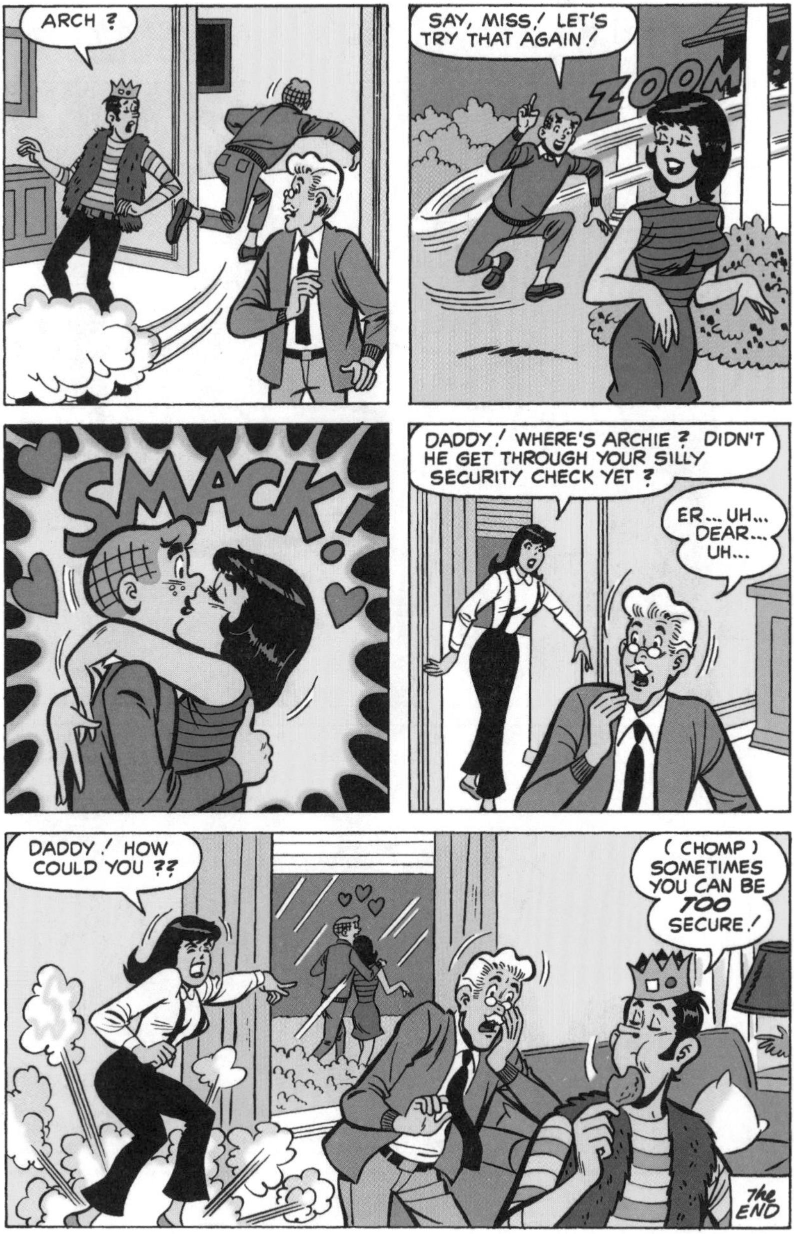
ARCH ?
SAY, MISS! LET'S TRY THAT AGAIN!
ZOOM!
SMACK!
DADDY! WHERE'S ARCHIE ? DIDN'T HE GET THROUGH YOUR SILLY SECURITY CHECK YET ?
ER... UH... DEAR... UH...
DADDY! HOW COULD YOU ??
(CHOMP) SOMETIMES YOU CAN BE TOO SECURE!
The END

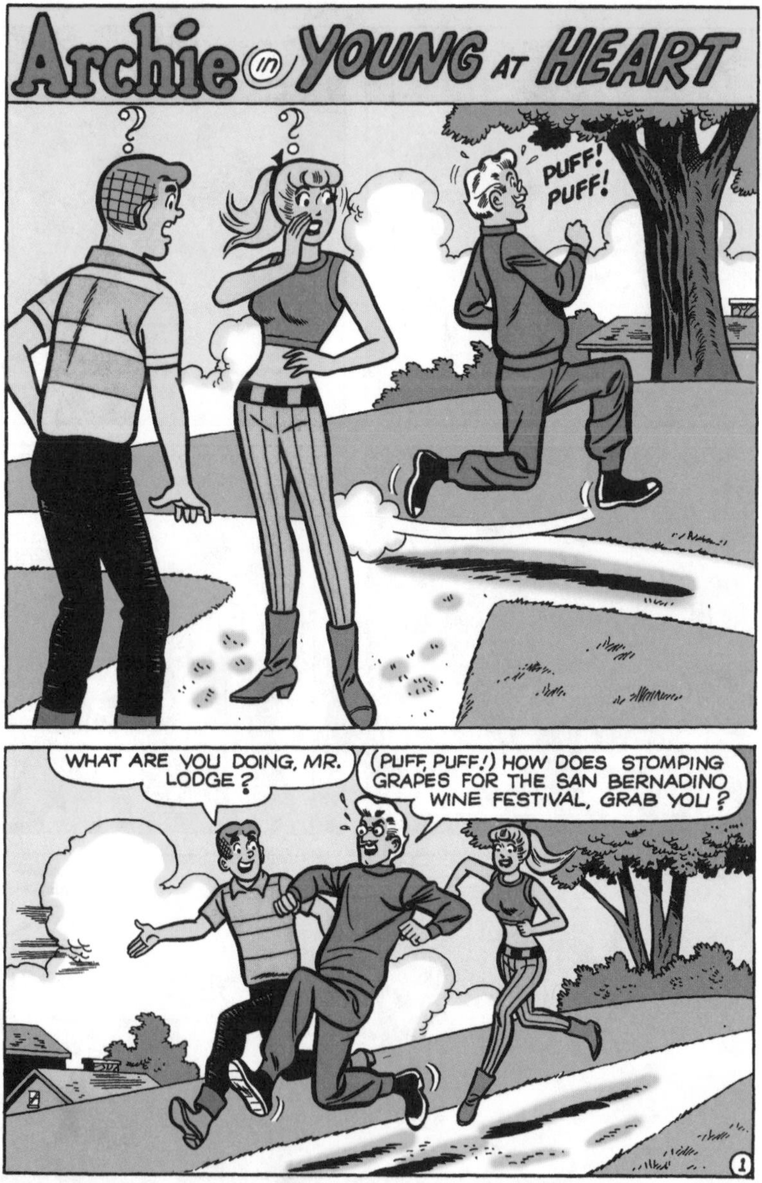
Archie in YOUNG AT HEART
PUFF! PUFF!
WHAT ARE YOU DOING, MR. LODGE?
(PUFF, PUFF!) HOW DOES STOMPING GRAPES FOR THE SAN BERNADINO WINE FESTIVAL, GRAB YOU?
1

Story & Pencils: Bob White

Inks: Rudy Lapick Letters: Bill Yoshida

Originally printed in EVERYTHING'S ARCHIE #4, SEPTEMBER 1969

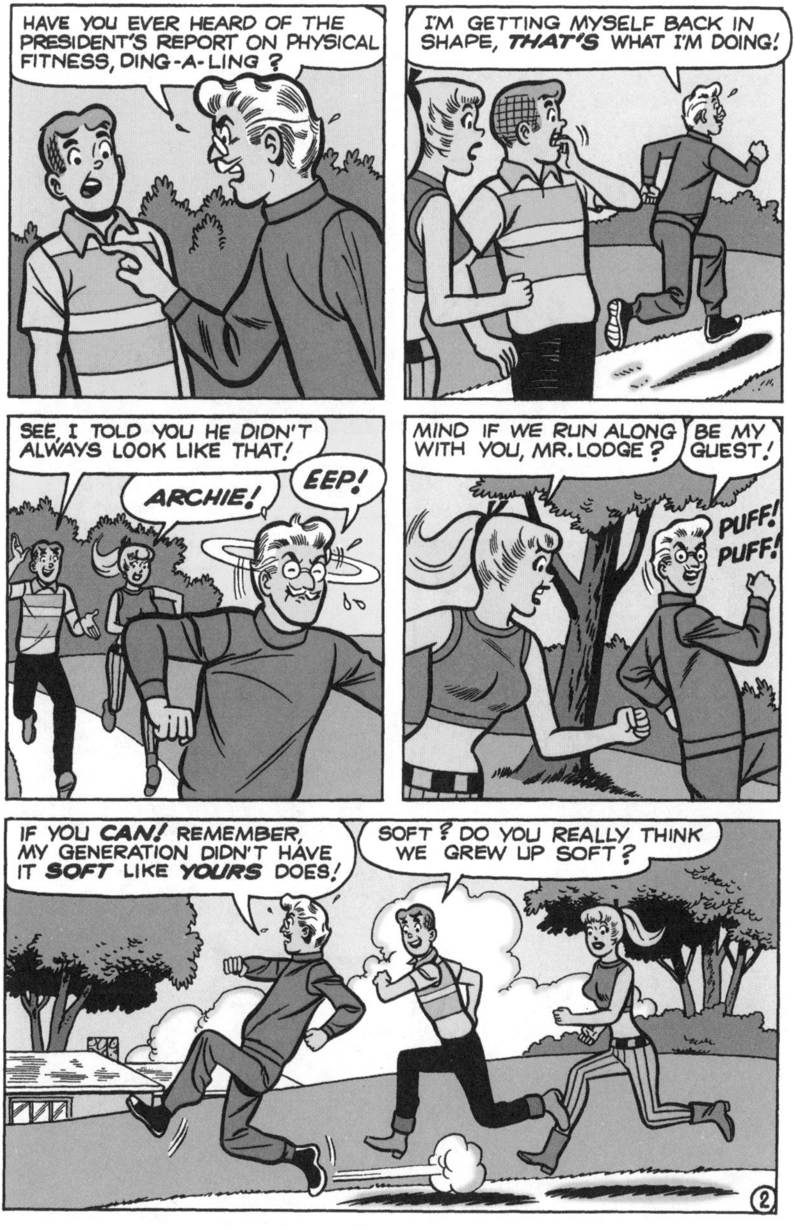
HAVE YOU EVER HEARD OF THE PRESIDENT'S REPORT ON PHYSICAL FITNESS, DING-A-LING ?
I'M GETTING MYSELF BACK IN SHAPE, THAT'S WHAT I'M DOING!
SEE, I TOLD YOU HE DIDN'T ALWAYS LOOK LIKE THAT!
ARCHIE!
EEP!
MIND IF WE RUN ALONG WITH YOU, MR. LODGE ?
BE MY GUEST!
PUFF! PUFF!
IF YOU CAN! REMEMBER, MY GENERATION DIDN'T HAVE IT SOFT LIKE YOURS DOES!
SOFT ? DO YOU REALLY THINK WE GREW UP SOFT ?
2

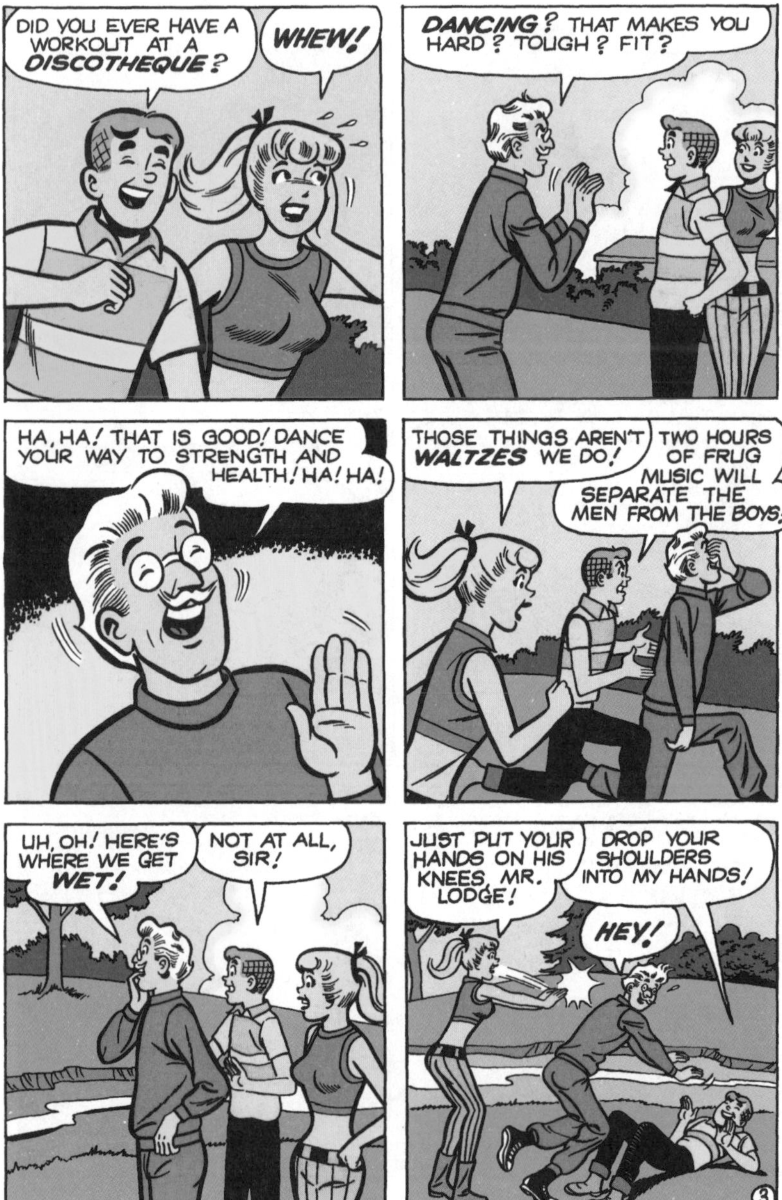
DID YOU EVER HAVE A WORKOUT AT A DISCOTHEQUE?
WHEW!
DANCING? THAT MAKES YOU HARD? TOUGH? FIT?
HA, HA! THAT IS GOOD! DANCE YOUR WAY TO STRENGTH AND HEALTH! HA! HA!
THOSE THINGS AREN'T WALTZES WE DO!
TWO HOURS OF FRUG MUSIC WILL SEPARATE THE MEN FROM THE BOYS!
UH, OH! HERE'S WHERE WE GET WET!
NOT AT ALL, SIR!
JUST PUT YOUR HANDS ON HIS KNEES, MR. LODGE!
DROP YOUR SHOULDERS INTO MY HANDS!
HEY!
3

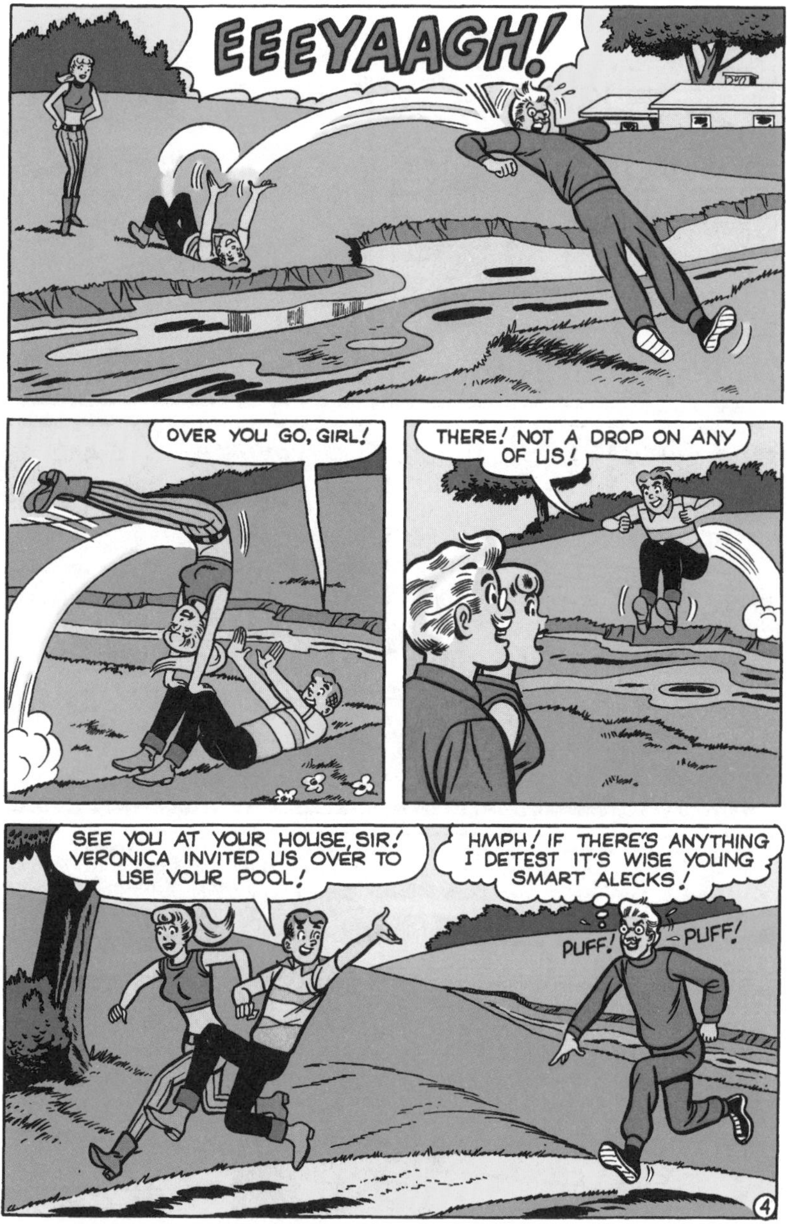
EEEYAAGH!
OVER YOU GO, GIRL!
THERE! NOT A DROP ON ANY OF US!
SEE YOU AT YOUR HOUSE, SIR! VERONICA INVITED US OVER TO USE YOUR POOL!
HMPH! IF THERE'S ANYTHING I DETEST IT'S WISE YOUNG SMART ALECKS!
PUFF!
PUFF!
4

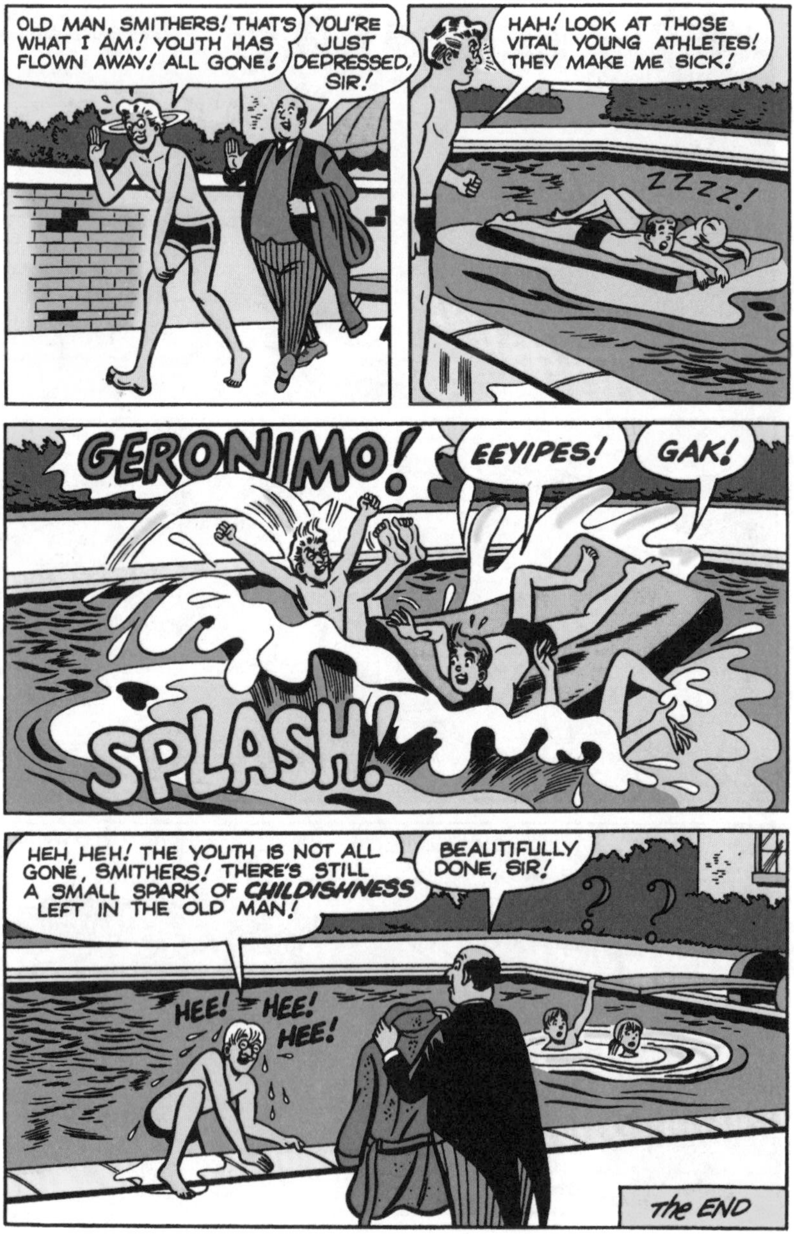
OLD MAN, SMITHERS! THAT'S WHAT I AM! YOUTH HAS FLOWN AWAY! ALL GONE!
YOU'RE JUST DEPRESSED, SIR!
HAH! LOOK AT THOSE VITAL YOUNG ATHLETES! THEY MAKE ME SICK!
ZZZZZ!
GERONIMO!
EEYIPES!
GAK!
SPLASH!
HEH, HEH! THE YOUTH IS NOT ALL GONE, SMITHERS! THERE'S STILL A SMALL SPARK OF CHILDISHNESS LEFT IN THE OLD MAN!
BEAUTIFULLY DONE, SIR!
HEE! HEE! HEE!
The END

Archie in The Literary Lion

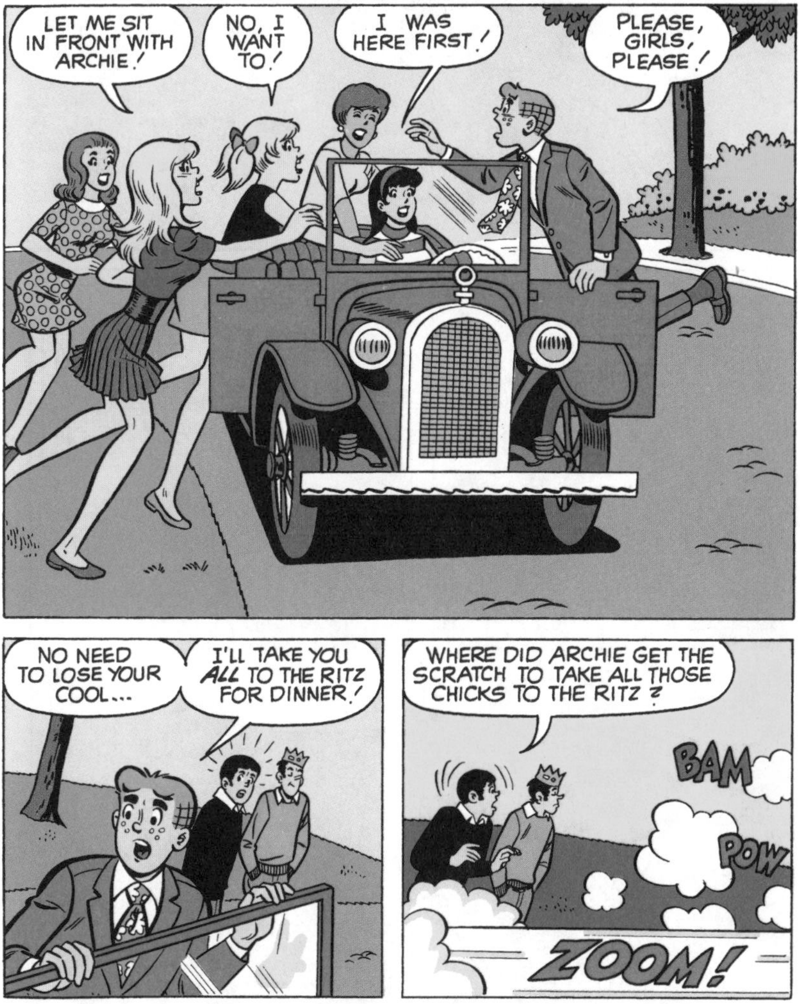
LET ME SIT IN FRONT WITH ARCHIE!
NO, I WANT TO!
I WAS HERE FIRST!
PLEASE, GIRLS, PLEASE!
NO NEED TO LOSE YOUR COOL...
I'LL TAKE YOU ALL TO THE RITZ FOR DINNER!
WHERE DID ARCHIE GET THE SCRATCH TO TAKE ALL THOSE CHICKS TO THE RITZ?
BAM
POW
ZOOM!

Story & Pencils: Al Hartley
Inks: Jon D'Agostino Letters: Bill Yoshida

Originally printed in EVERYTHING'S ARCHIE #9, AUGUST 1970

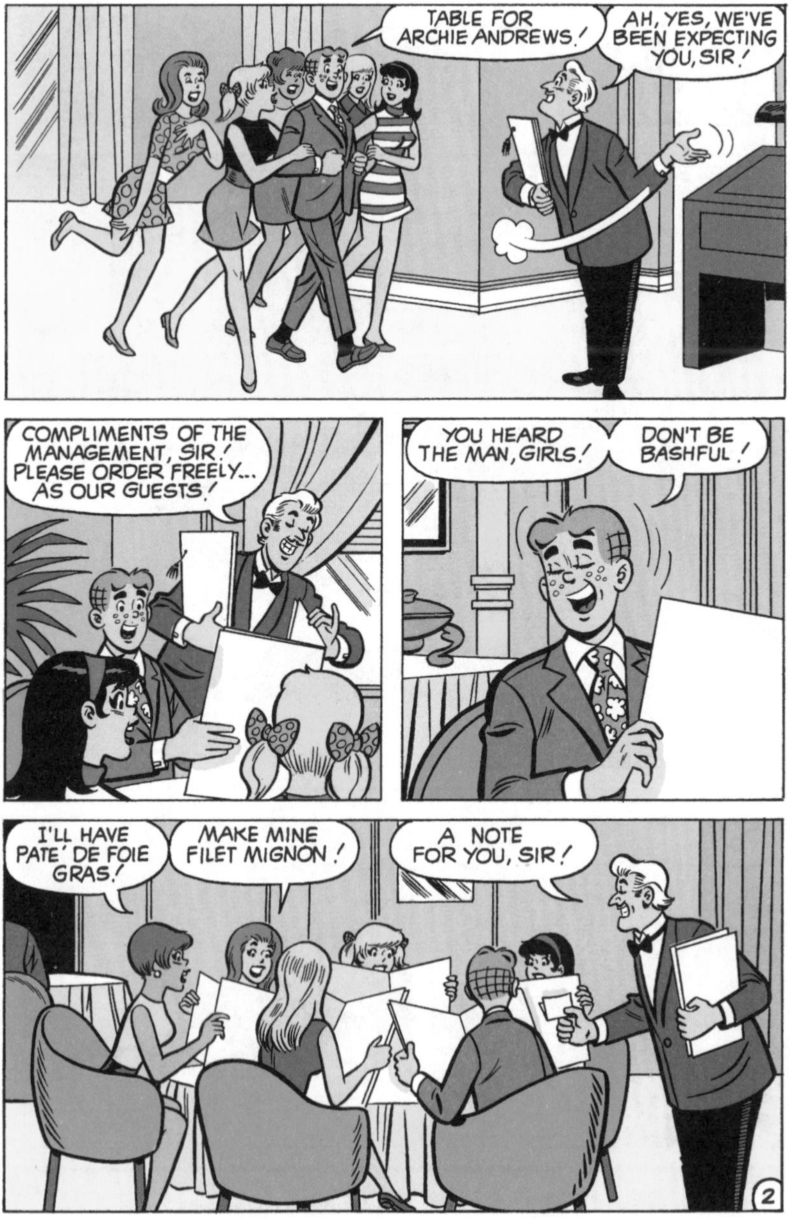
TABLE FOR ARCHIE ANDREWS!
AH, YES, WE'VE BEEN EXPECTING YOU, SIR!
COMPLIMENTS OF THE MANAGEMENT, SIR! PLEASE ORDER FREELY... AS OUR GUESTS!
YOU HEARD THE MAN, GIRLS!
DON'T BE BASHFUL!
I'LL HAVE PATE' DE FOIE GRAS!
MAKE MINE FILET MIGNON!
A NOTE FOR YOU, SIR!
2

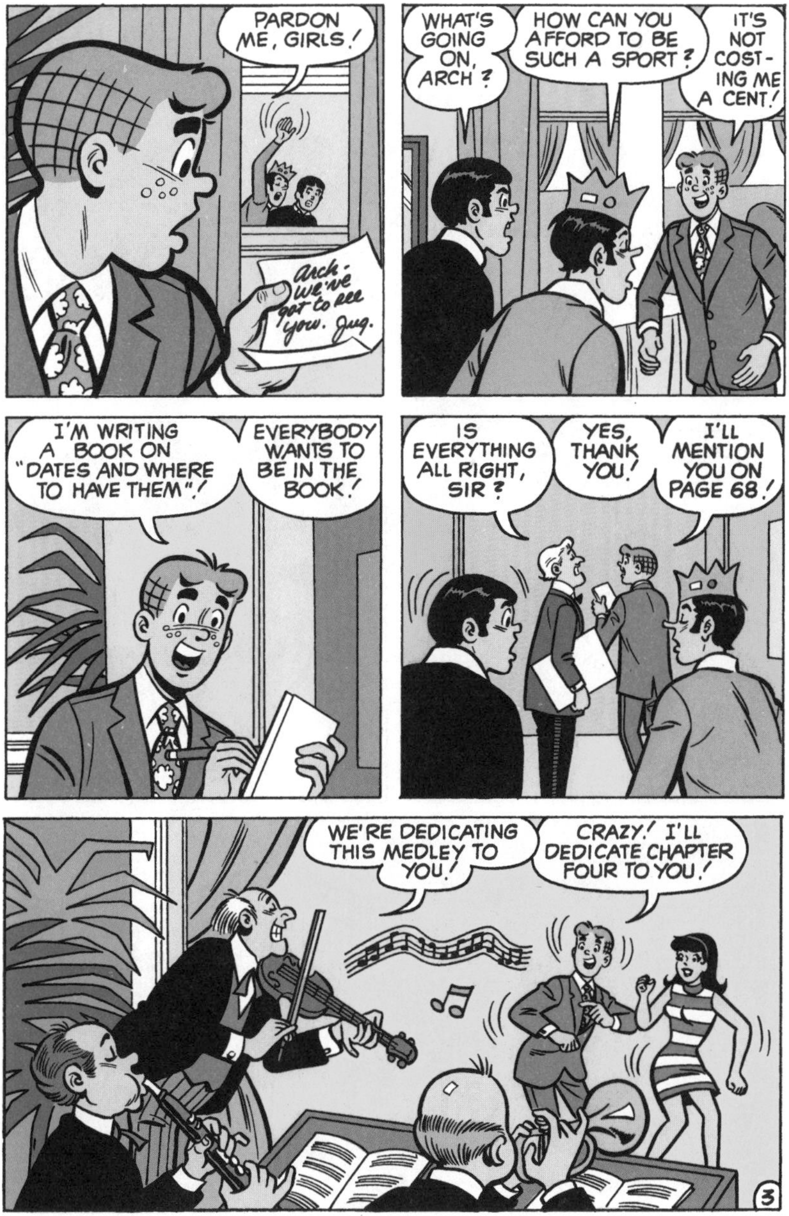
PARDON ME, GIRLS!
arch - we've got to see you. Jug.
WHAT'S GOING ON, ARCH?
HOW CAN YOU AFFORD TO BE SUCH A SPORT?
IT'S NOT COSTING ME A CENT!
I'M WRITING A BOOK ON "DATES AND WHERE TO HAVE THEM"!
EVERYBODY WANTS TO BE IN THE BOOK!
IS EVERYTHING ALL RIGHT, SIR?
YES, THANK YOU!
I'LL MENTION YOU ON PAGE 68!
WE'RE DEDICATING THIS MEDLEY TO YOU!
CRAZY! I'LL DEDICATE CHAPTER FOUR TO YOU!
3

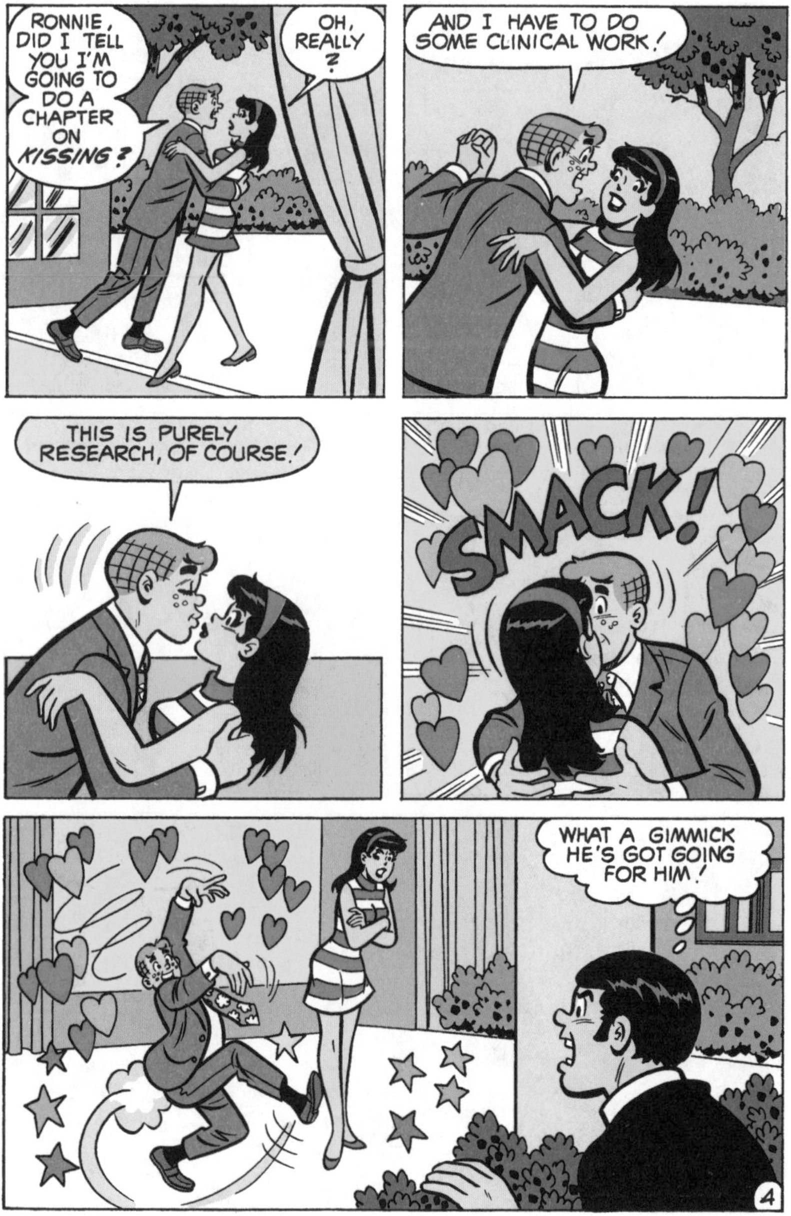
RONNIE, DID I TELL YOU I'M GOING TO DO A CHAPTER ON KISSING?
OH, REALLY?
AND I HAVE TO DO SOME CLINICAL WORK!
THIS IS PURELY RESEARCH, OF COURSE!
SMACK!
WHAT A GIMMICK HE'S GOT GOING FOR HIM!
4

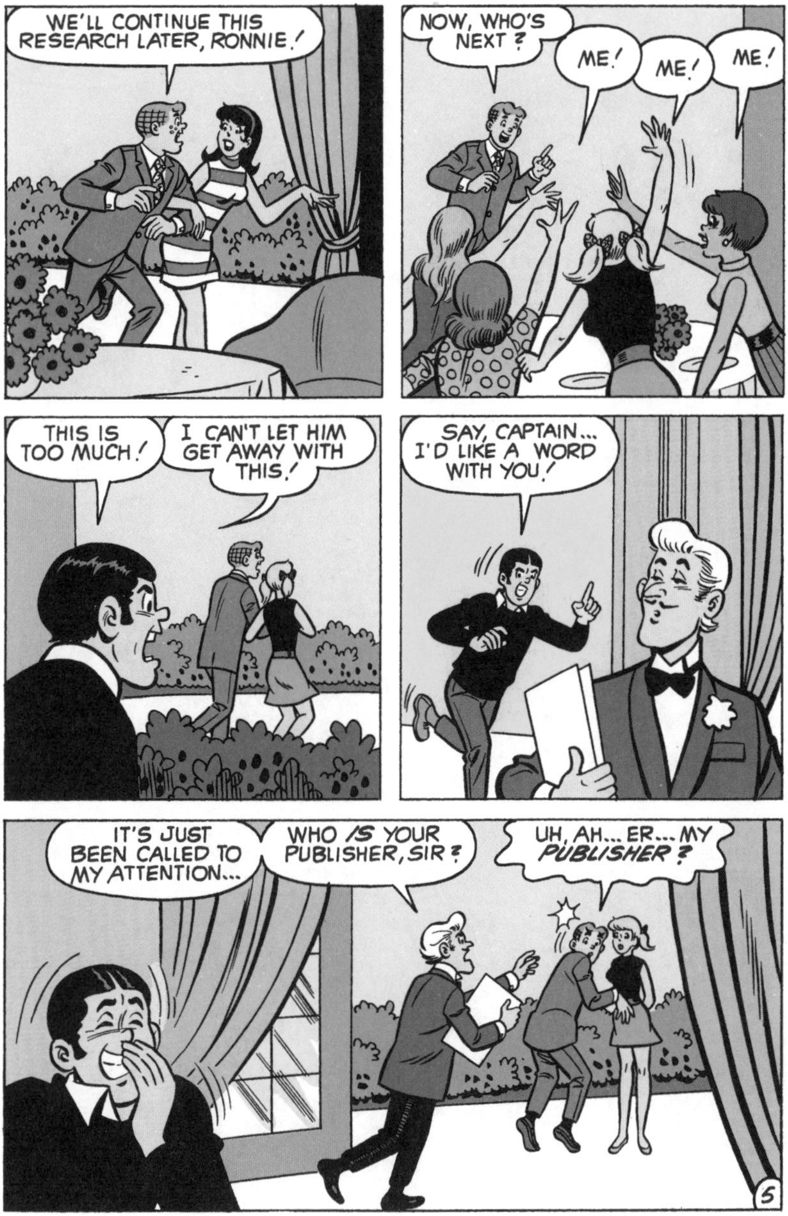
WE'LL CONTINUE THIS RESEARCH LATER, RONNIE!
NOW, WHO'S NEXT?
ME!
ME!
ME!
THIS IS TOO MUCH!
I CAN'T LET HIM GET AWAY WITH THIS!
SAY, CAPTAIN... I'D LIKE A WORD WITH YOU!
IT'S JUST BEEN CALLED TO MY ATTENTION...
WHO *IS* YOUR PUBLISHER, SIR?
UH, AH... ER... MY *PUBLISHER*?
5

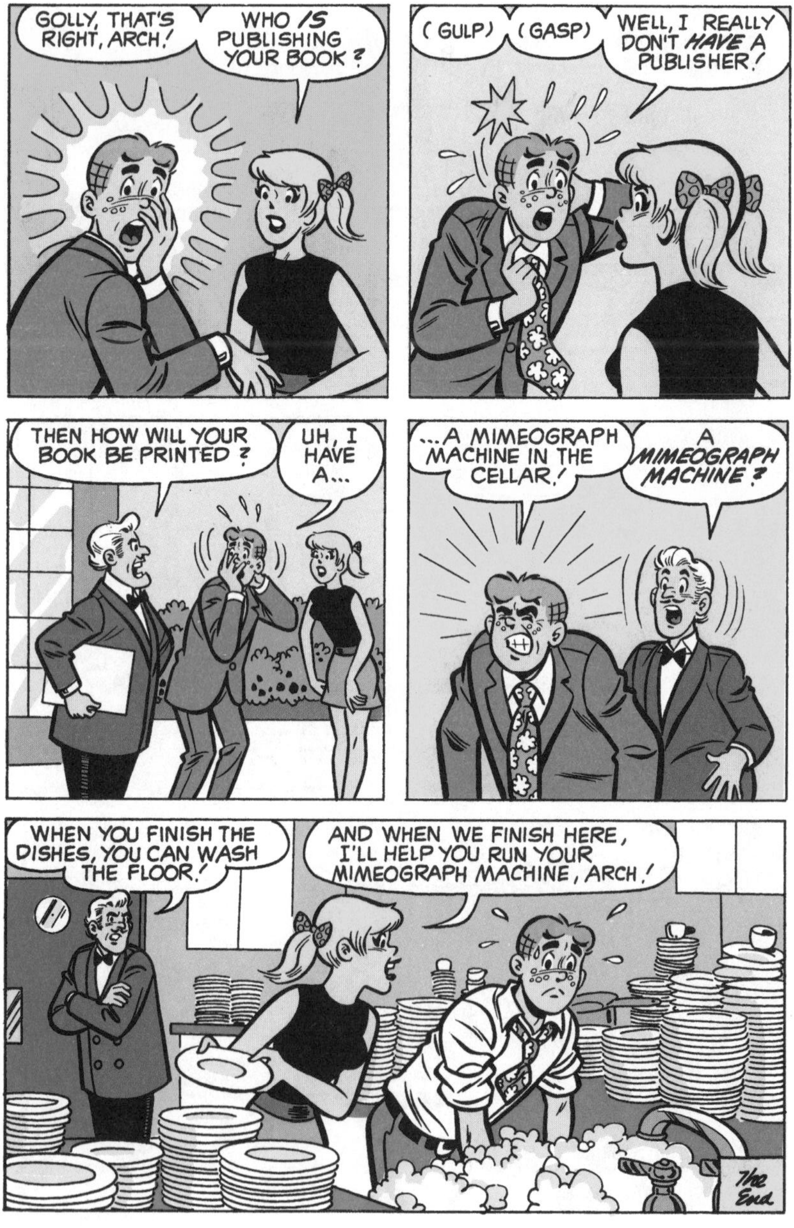
GOLLY, THAT'S RIGHT, ARCH!
WHO IS PUBLISHING YOUR BOOK?
(GULP)
(GASP)
WELL, I REALLY DON'T HAVE A PUBLISHER!
THEN HOW WILL YOUR BOOK BE PRINTED?
UH, I HAVE A...
...A MIMEOGRAPH MACHINE IN THE CELLAR!
A MIMEOGRAPH MACHINE?
WHEN YOU FINISH THE DISHES, YOU CAN WASH THE FLOOR!
AND WHEN WE FINISH HERE, I'LL HELP YOU RUN YOUR MIMEOGRAPH MACHINE, ARCH!
End

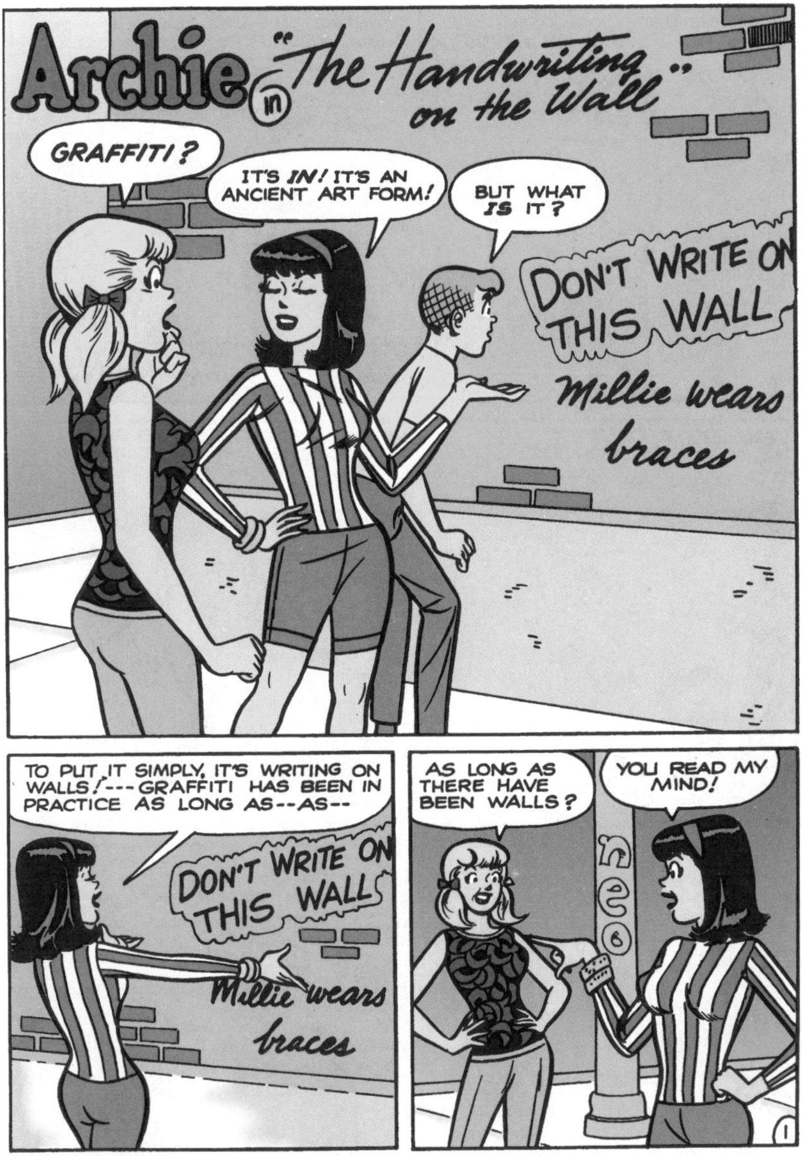
Archie in "The Handwriting on the Wall"
GRAFFITI?
IT'S IN! IT'S AN ANCIENT ART FORM!
BUT WHAT IS IT?
DON'T WRITE ON THIS WALL
Millie wears braces
TO PUT IT SIMPLY, IT'S WRITING ON WALLS!---GRAFFITI HAS BEEN IN PRACTICE AS LONG AS--AS--
DON'T WRITE ON THIS WALL
Millie wears braces
AS LONG AS THERE HAVE BEEN WALLS?
YOU READ MY MIND!

Story: Frank Doyle Pencils: Harry Lucey
Inks: Mario Acquaviva

Originally printed in EVERYTHING'S ARCHIE #10, OCTOBER 1970

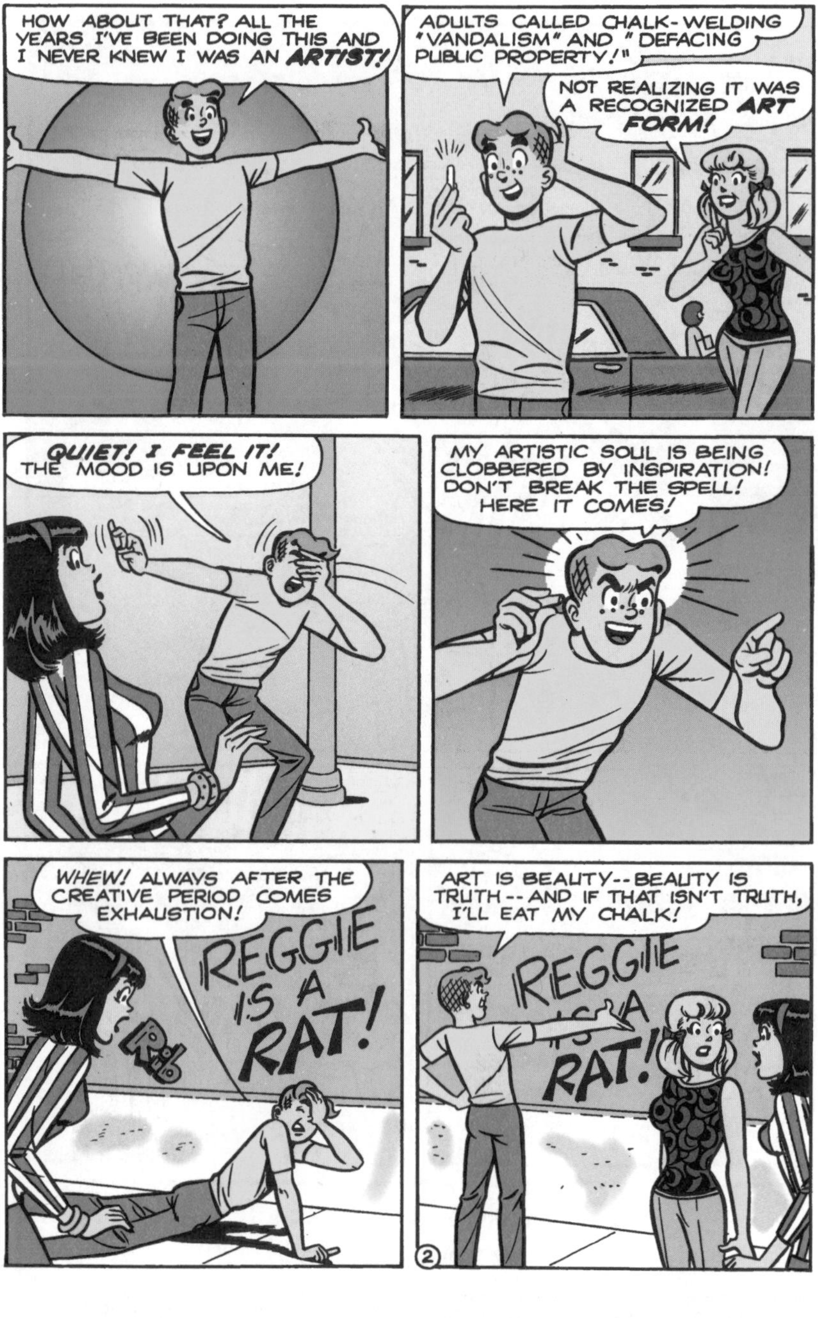
HOW ABOUT THAT? ALL THE YEARS I'VE BEEN DOING THIS AND I NEVER KNEW I WAS AN ARTIST!
ADULTS CALLED CHALK-WELDING "VANDALISM" AND "DEFACING PUBLIC PROPERTY!"
NOT REALIZING IT WAS A RECOGNIZED ART FORM!
QUIET! I FEEL IT! THE MOOD IS UPON ME!
MY ARTISTIC SOUL IS BEING CLOBBERED BY INSPIRATION! DON'T BREAK THE SPELL! HERE IT COMES!
WHEW! ALWAYS AFTER THE CREATIVE PERIOD COMES EXHAUSTION!
REGGIE IS A RAT!
ART IS BEAUTY--BEAUTY IS TRUTH--AND IF THAT ISN'T TRUTH, I'LL EAT MY CHALK!
REGGIE IS A RAT!
2

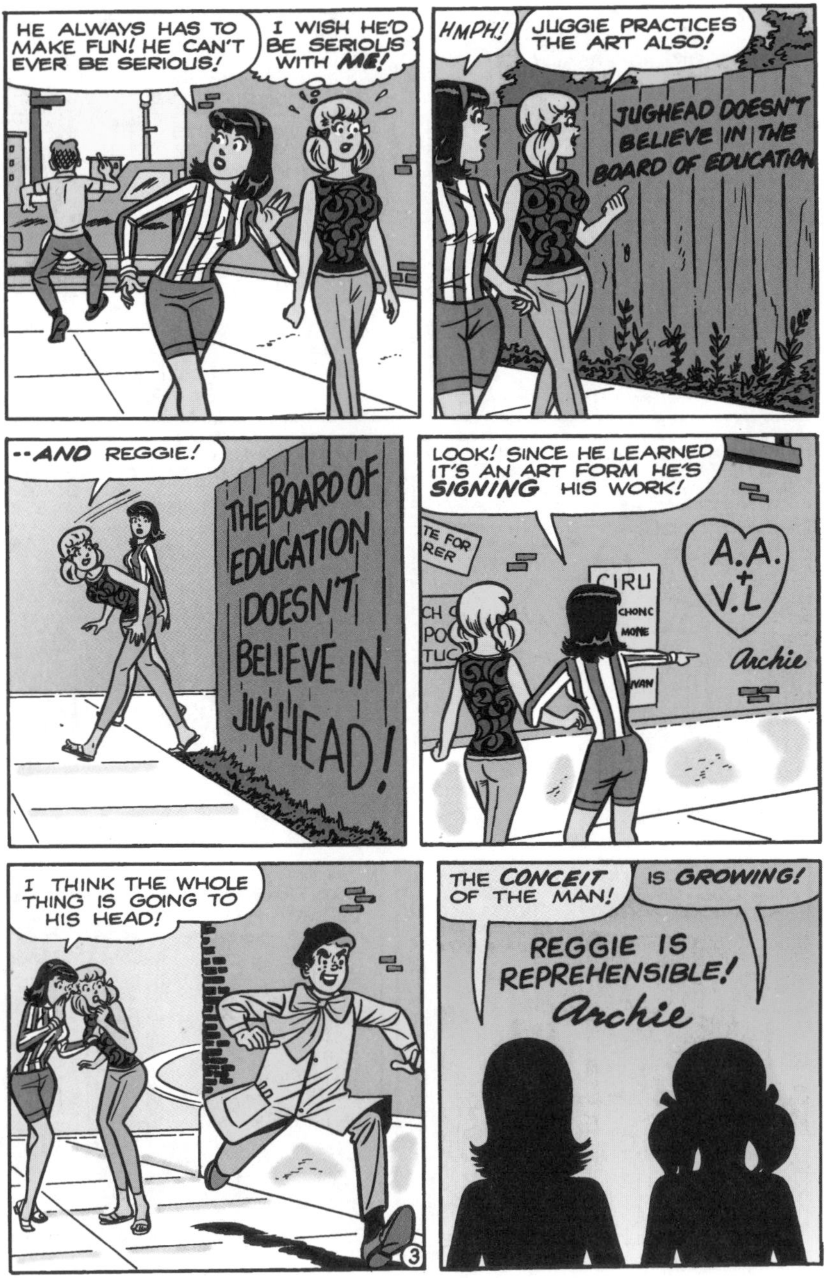
HE ALWAYS HAS TO MAKE FUN! HE CAN'T EVER BE SERIOUS!
I WISH HE'D BE SERIOUS WITH ME!
HMPH!
JUGGIE PRACTICES THE ART ALSO!
JUGHEAD DOESN'T BELIEVE IN THE BOARD OF EDUCATION
--AND REGGIE!
THE BOARD OF EDUCATION DOESN'T BELIEVE IN JUGHEAD!
LOOK! SINCE HE LEARNED IT'S AN ART FORM HE'S SIGNING HIS WORK!
A.A. + V.L
Archie
I THINK THE WHOLE THING IS GOING TO HIS HEAD!
THE CONCEIT OF THE MAN!
IS GROWING!
REGGIE IS REPREHENSIBLE!
Archie

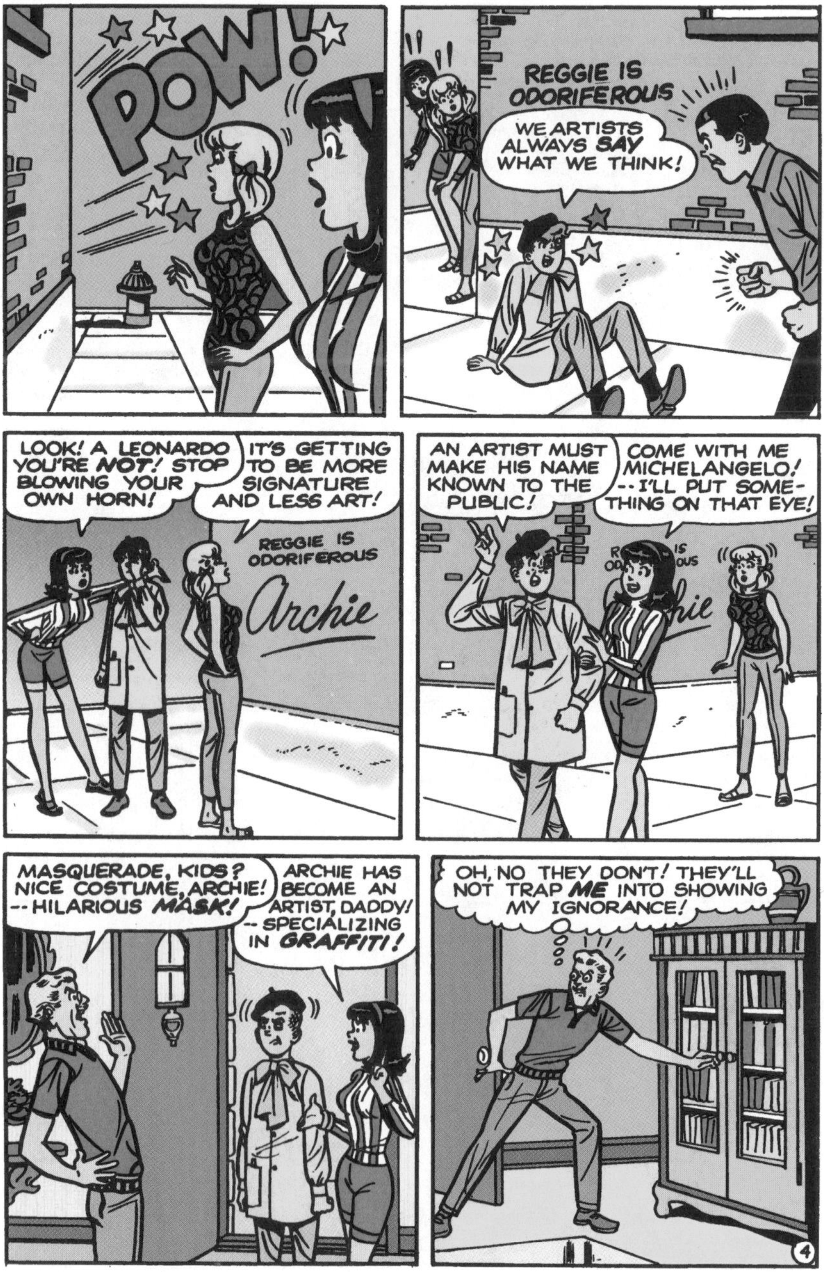
POW!
REGGIE IS ODORIFEROUS
WE ARTISTS ALWAYS SAY WHAT WE THINK!
LOOK! A LEONARDO YOU'RE NOT! STOP BLOWING YOUR OWN HORN!
IT'S GETTING TO BE MORE SIGNATURE AND LESS ART!
REGGIE IS ODORIFEROUS
Archie
AN ARTIST MUST MAKE HIS NAME KNOWN TO THE PUBLIC!
COME WITH ME MICHELANGELO! -- I'LL PUT SOMETHING ON THAT EYE!
MASQUERADE, KIDS? NICE COSTUME, ARCHIE! -- HILARIOUS MASK!
ARCHIE HAS BECOME AN ARTIST, DADDY! -- SPECIALIZING IN GRAFFITI!
OH, NO THEY DON'T! THEY'LL NOT TRAP ME INTO SHOWING MY IGNORANCE!
4

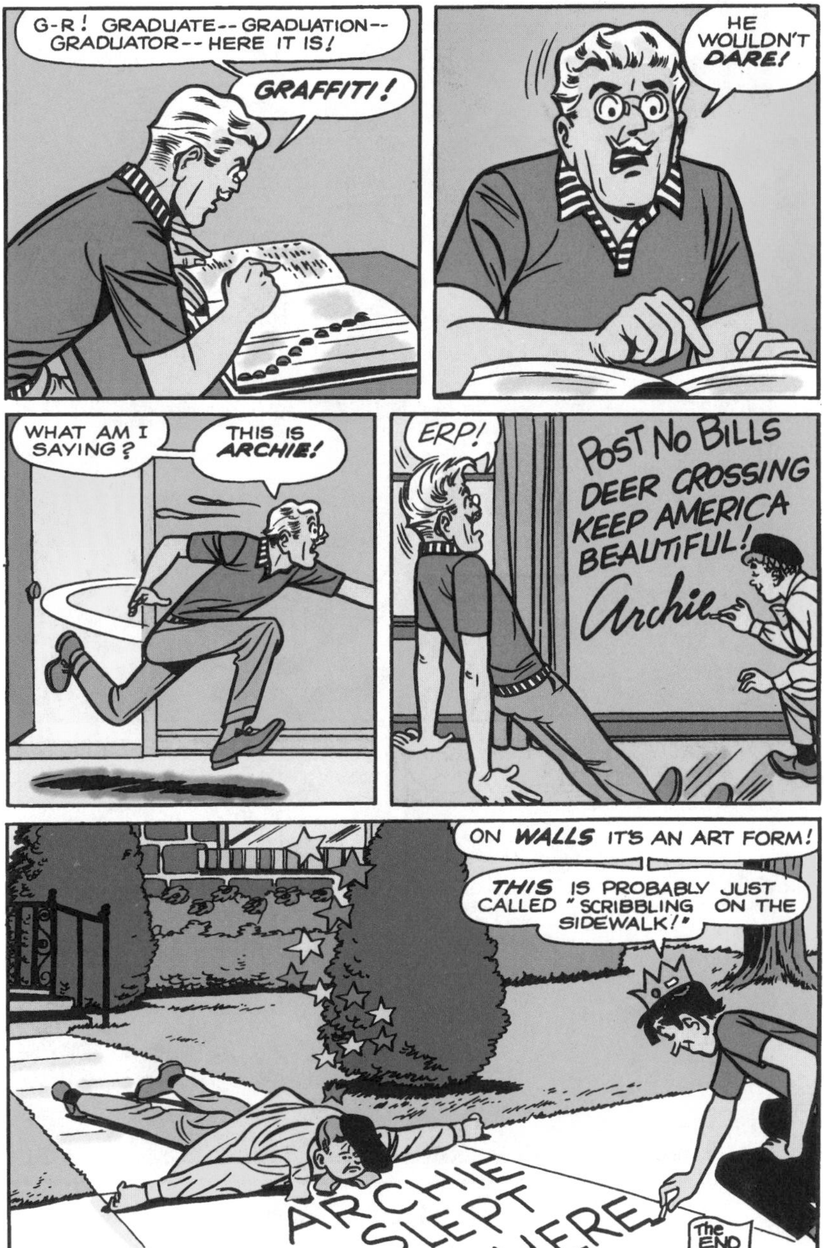
G-R! GRADUATE--GRADUATION--GRADUATOR--HERE IT IS!
GRAFFITI!
HE WOULDN'T DARE!
WHAT AM I SAYING?
THIS IS ARCHIE!
ERP!
POST NO BILLS
DEER CROSSING
KEEP AMERICA BEAUTIFUL!
Archie
ON WALLS IT'S AN ART FORM!
THIS IS PROBABLY JUST CALLED "SCRIBBLING ON THE SIDEWALK!"
ARCHIE SLEPT HERE
The END

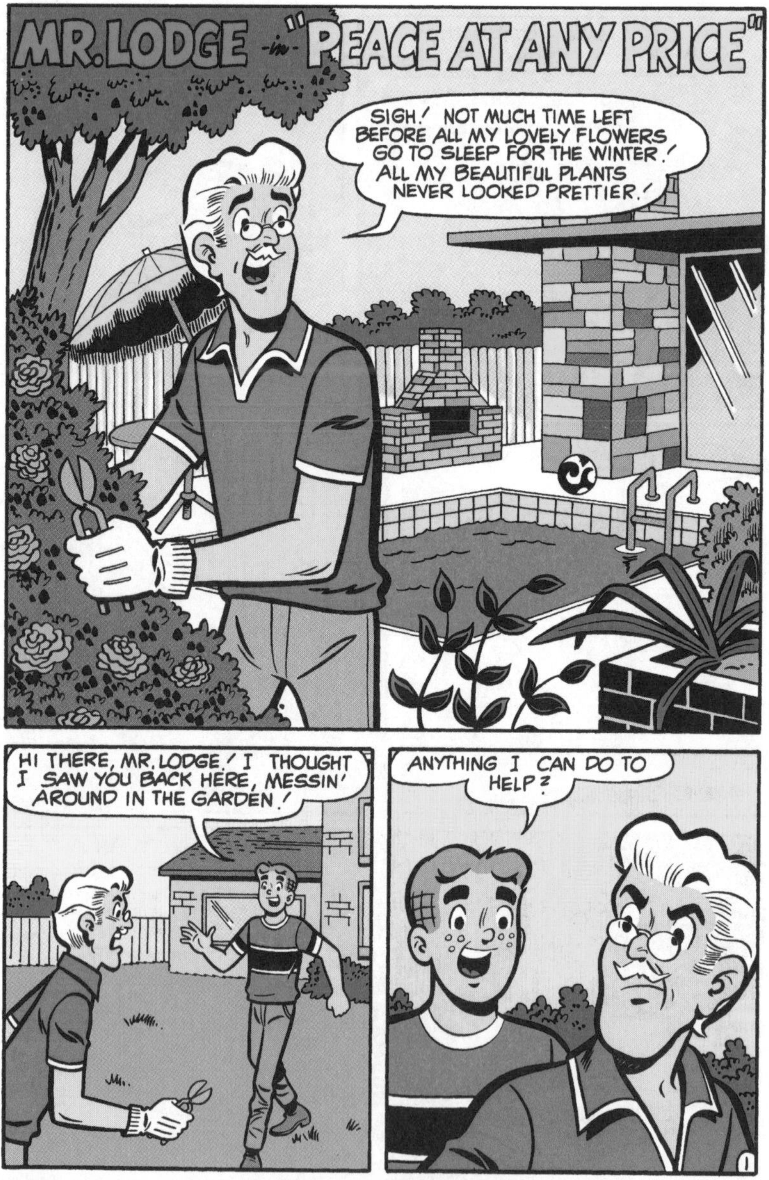
MR. LODGE -in- "PEACE AT ANY PRICE"
SIGH! NOT MUCH TIME LEFT BEFORE ALL MY LOVELY FLOWERS GO TO SLEEP FOR THE WINTER! ALL MY BEAUTIFUL PLANTS NEVER LOOKED PRETTIER!
HI THERE, MR. LODGE! I THOUGHT I SAW YOU BACK HERE, MESSIN' AROUND IN THE GARDEN!
ANYTHING I CAN DO TO HELP?
1

Story & Pencils: Gus LeMoine
Inks: Jon D'Agostino Letters: Bill Yoshida

Originally printed in EVERYTHING'S ARCHIE #11, DECEMBER 1970

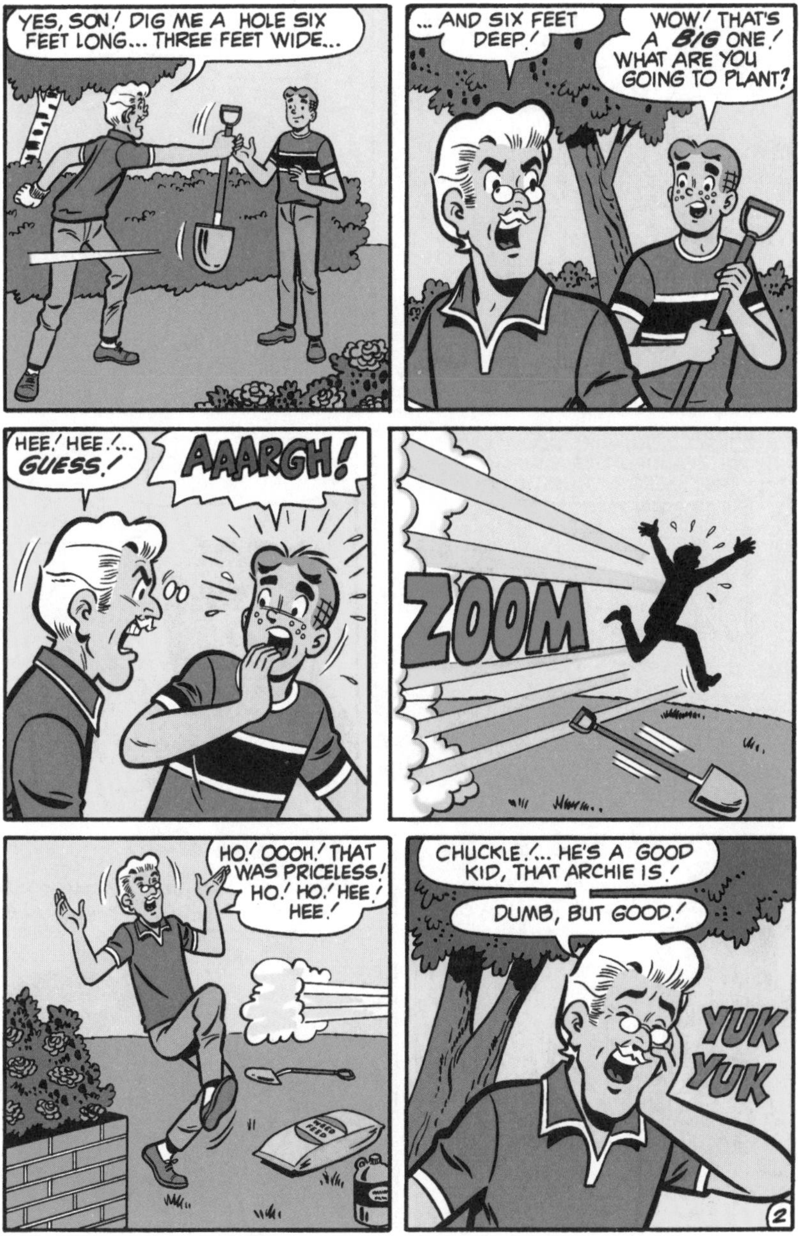
YES, SON! DIG ME A HOLE SIX FEET LONG... THREE FEET WIDE...
... AND SIX FEET DEEP!
WOW! THAT'S A BIG ONE! WHAT ARE YOU GOING TO PLANT?
HEE! HEE!... GUESS!
AAARGH!
ZOOM
HO! OOOH! THAT WAS PRICELESS! HO! HO! HEE! HEE!
WEED FEED
CHUCKLE!... HE'S A GOOD KID, THAT ARCHIE IS!
DUMB, BUT GOOD!
YUK YUK
2

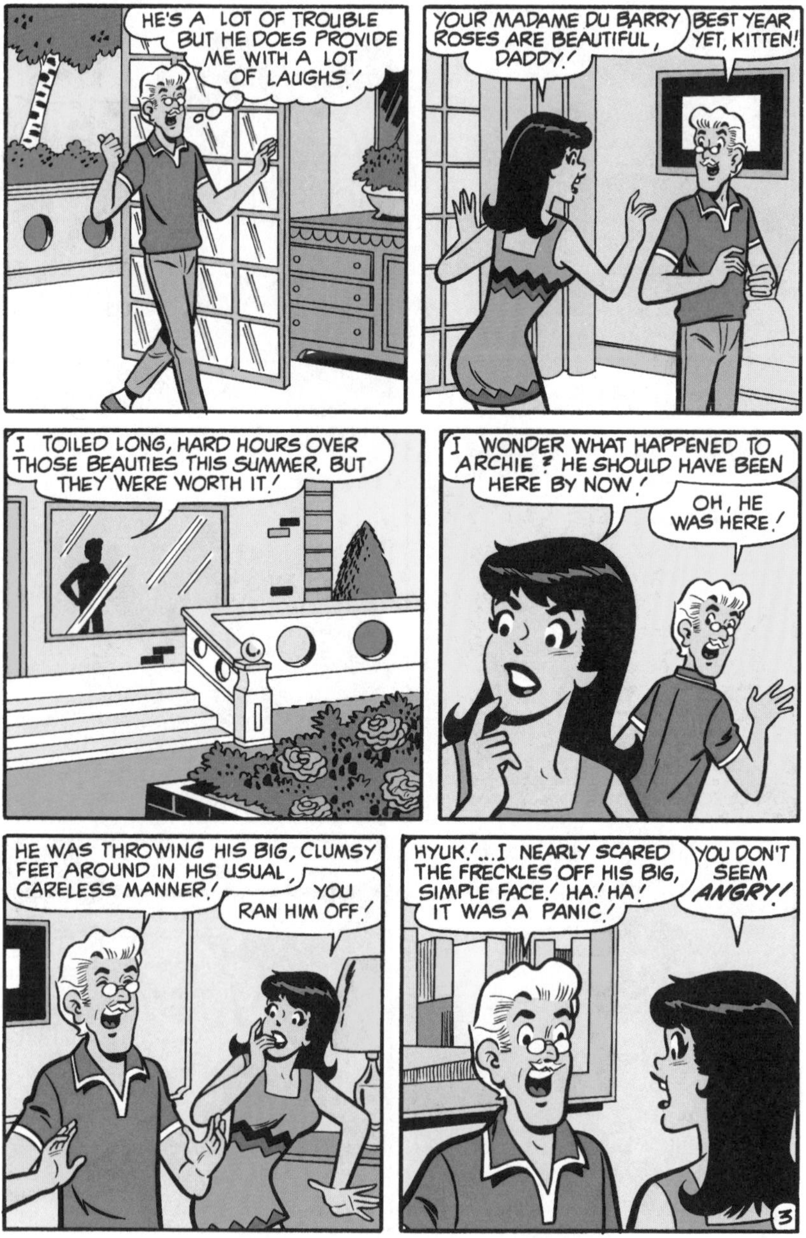
HE'S A LOT OF TROUBLE BUT HE DOES PROVIDE ME WITH A LOT OF LAUGHS!
YOUR MADAME DU BARRY ROSES ARE BEAUTIFUL, DADDY!
BEST YEAR YET, KITTEN!
I TOILED LONG, HARD HOURS OVER THOSE BEAUTIES THIS SUMMER, BUT THEY WERE WORTH IT!
I WONDER WHAT HAPPENED TO ARCHIE? HE SHOULD HAVE BEEN HERE BY NOW!
OH, HE WAS HERE!
HE WAS THROWING HIS BIG, CLUMSY FEET AROUND IN HIS USUAL CARELESS MANNER!
YOU RAN HIM OFF!
HYUK!...I NEARLY SCARED THE FRECKLES OFF HIS BIG, SIMPLE FACE! HA! HA! IT WAS A PANIC!
YOU DON'T SEEM ANGRY!
3

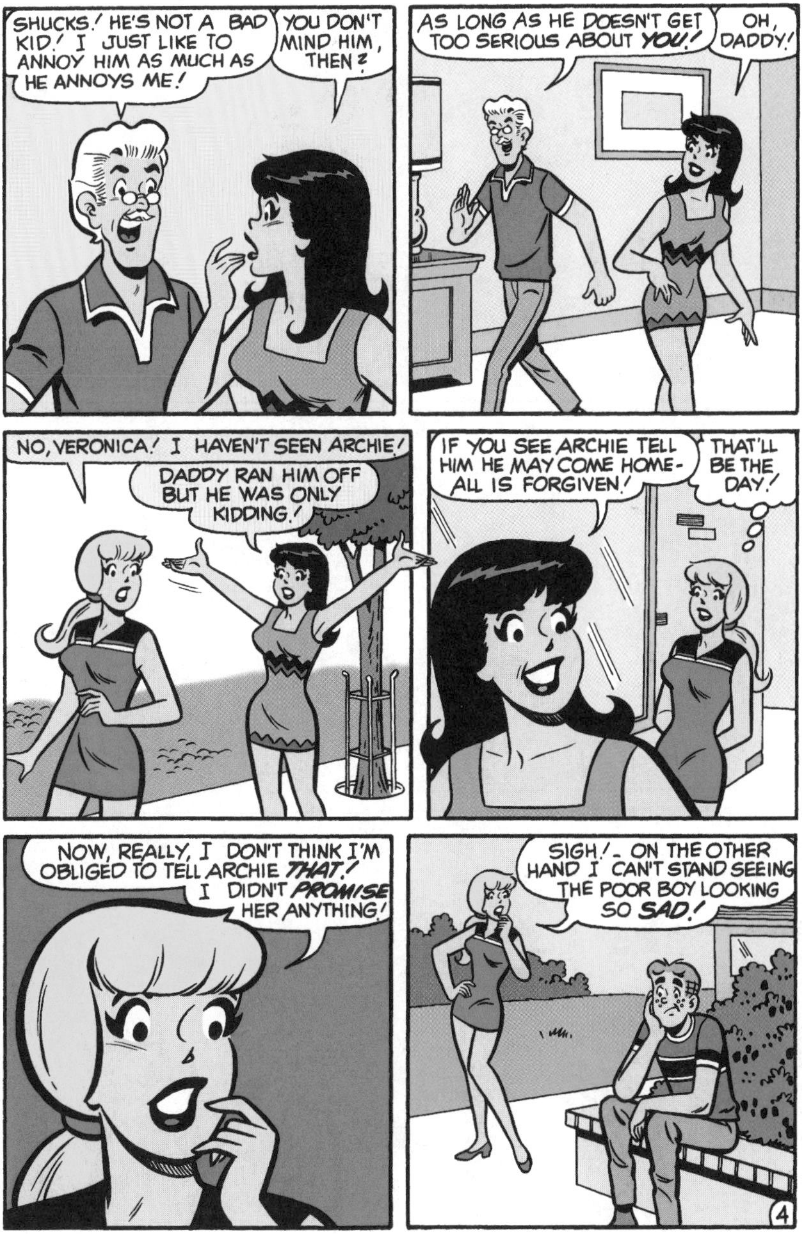
SHUCKS! HE'S NOT A BAD KID! I JUST LIKE TO ANNOY HIM AS MUCH AS HE ANNOYS ME!
YOU DON'T MIND HIM, THEN?
AS LONG AS HE DOESN'T GET TOO SERIOUS ABOUT YOU!
OH, DADDY!
NO, VERONICA! I HAVEN'T SEEN ARCHIE!
DADDY RAN HIM OFF BUT HE WAS ONLY KIDDING!
IF YOU SEE ARCHIE TELL HIM HE MAY COME HOME- ALL IS FORGIVEN!
THAT'LL BE THE DAY!
NOW, REALLY, I DON'T THINK I'M OBLIGED TO TELL ARCHIE THAT! I DIDN'T PROMISE HER ANYTHING!
SIGH! - ON THE OTHER HAND I CAN'T STAND SEEING THE POOR BOY LOOKING SO SAD!
4

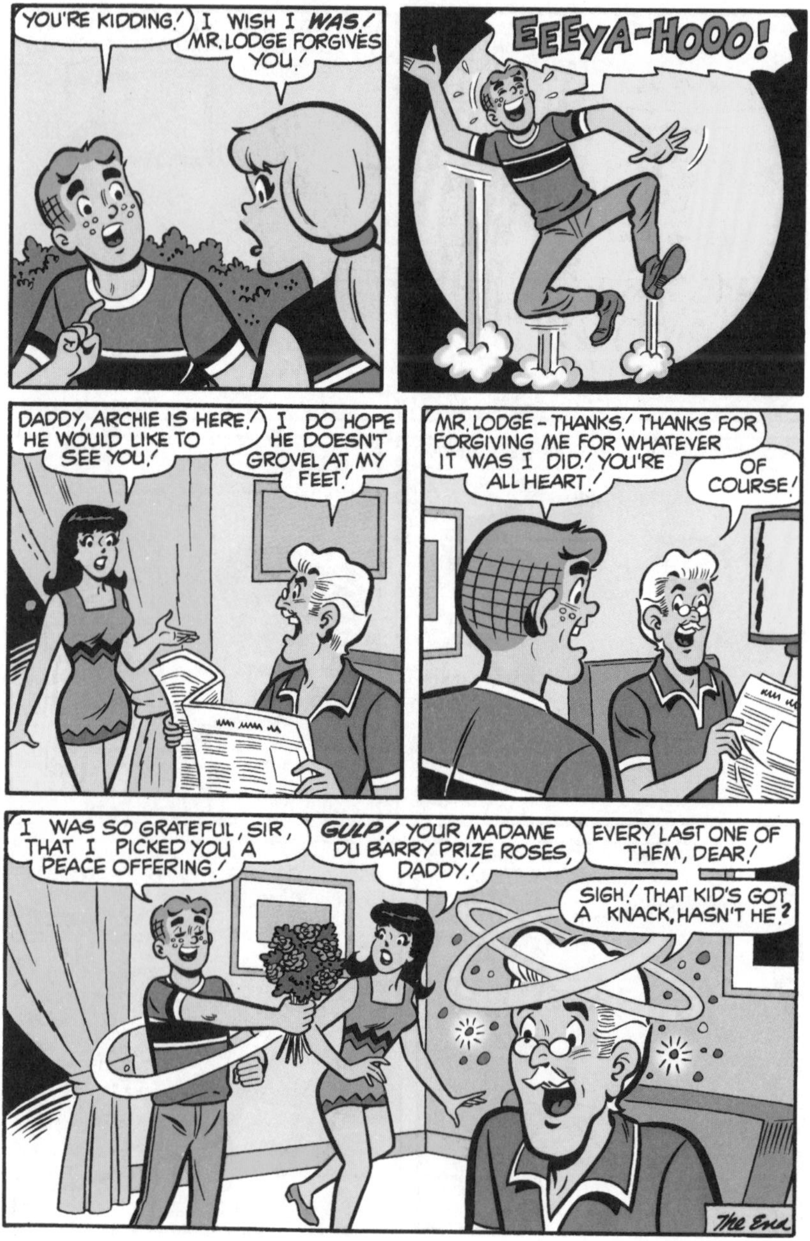
YOU'RE KIDDING!
I WISH I WAS! MR. LODGE FORGIVES YOU!
EEEYA-HOOO!
DADDY, ARCHIE IS HERE! HE WOULD LIKE TO SEE YOU!
I DO HOPE HE DOESN'T GROVEL AT MY FEET!
MR. LODGE – THANKS! THANKS FOR FORGIVING ME FOR WHATEVER IT WAS I DID! YOU'RE ALL HEART!
OF COURSE!
I WAS SO GRATEFUL, SIR, THAT I PICKED YOU A PEACE OFFERING!
GULP! YOUR MADAME DU BARRY PRIZE ROSES, DADDY!
EVERY LAST ONE OF THEM, DEAR!
SIGH! THAT KID'S GOT A KNACK, HASN'T HE?
The End

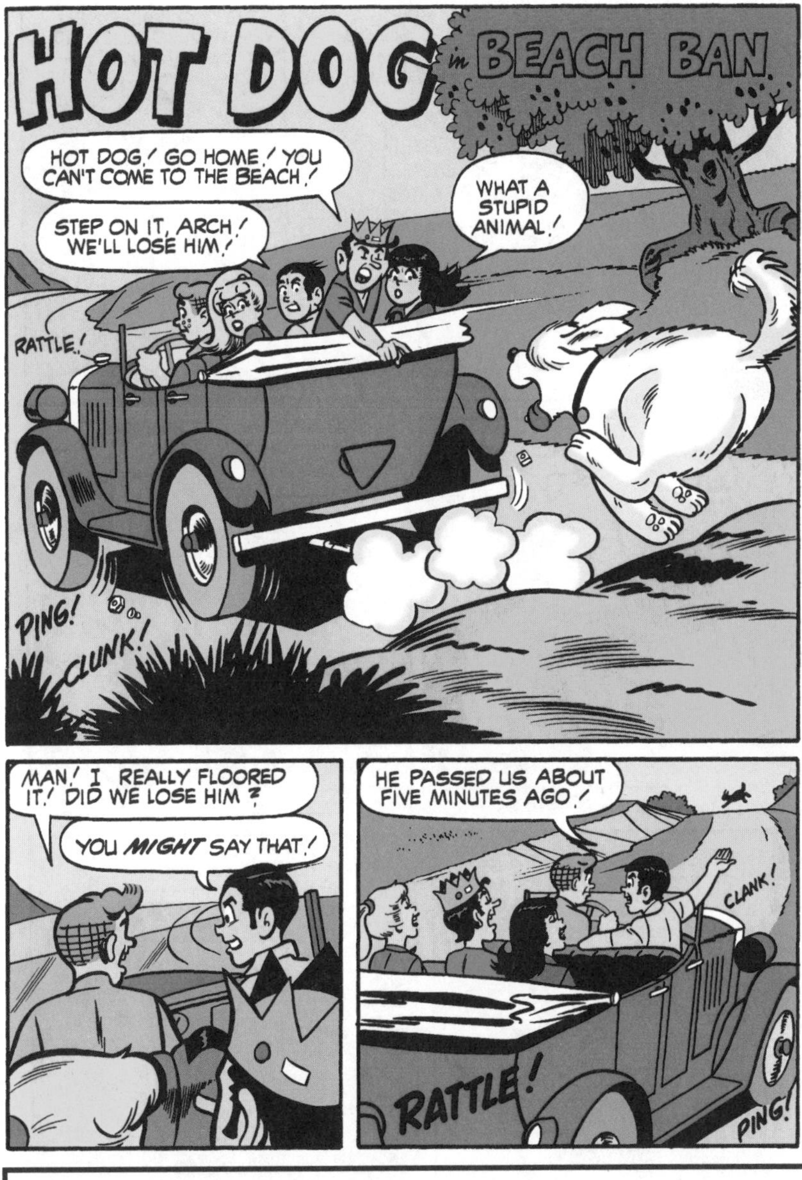
HOT DOG in BEACH BAN
HOT DOG! GO HOME! YOU CAN'T COME TO THE BEACH!
STEP ON IT, ARCH! WE'LL LOSE HIM!
WHAT A STUPID ANIMAL!
RATTLE!
PING!
CLUNK!
MAN! I REALLY FLOORED IT! DID WE LOSE HIM?
YOU *MIGHT* SAY THAT!
HE PASSED US ABOUT FIVE MINUTES AGO!
CLANK!
RATTLE!
PING!

Story: George Gladir **Pencils:** Bob Bolling
Inks: Jon D'Agostino **Letters:** Bill Yoshida

Originally printed in EVERYTHING'S ARCHIE #11, DECEMBER 1970

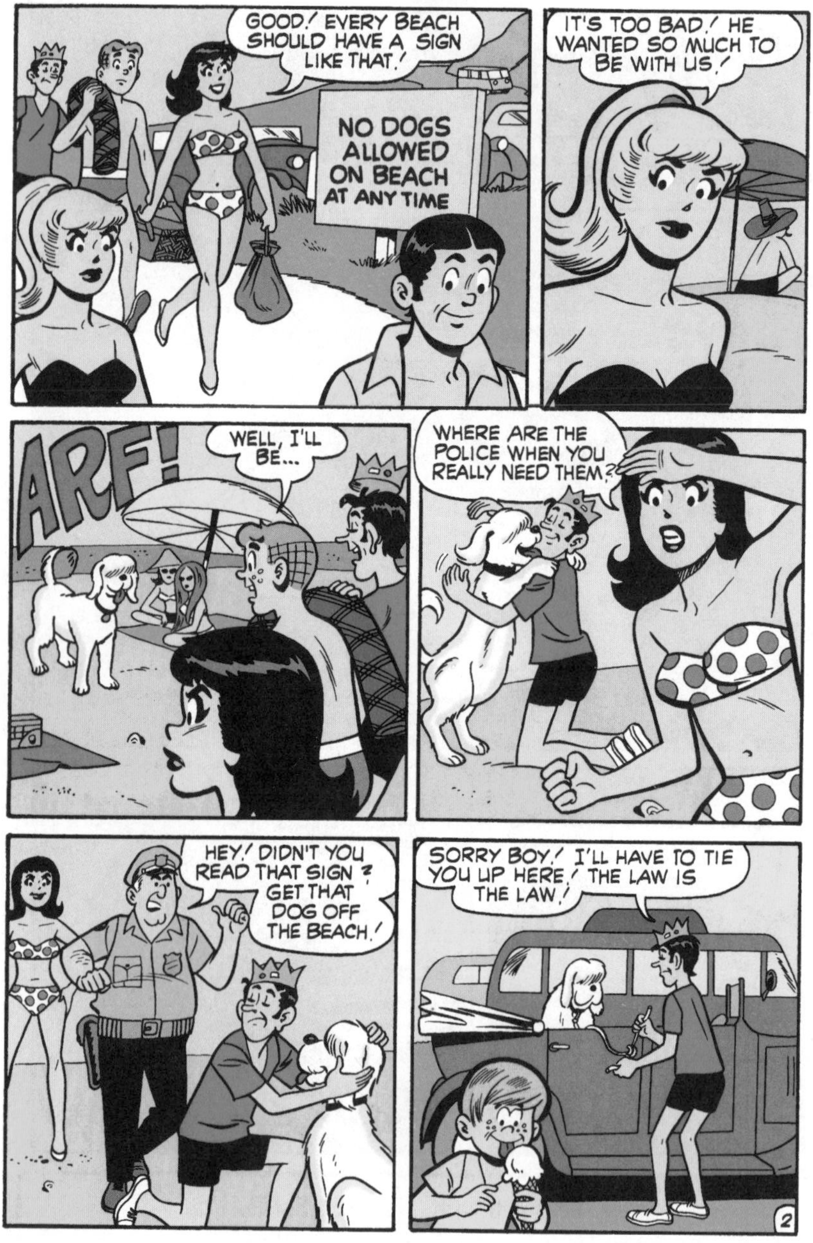
GOOD! EVERY BEACH SHOULD HAVE A SIGN LIKE THAT!
NO DOGS ALLOWED ON BEACH AT ANY TIME
IT'S TOO BAD! HE WANTED SO MUCH TO BE WITH US!
ARF!
WELL, I'LL BE...
WHERE ARE THE POLICE WHEN YOU REALLY NEED THEM?
HEY! DIDN'T YOU READ THAT SIGN? GET THAT DOG OFF THE BEACH!
SORRY BOY! I'LL HAVE TO TIE YOU UP HERE! THE LAW IS THE LAW!
2

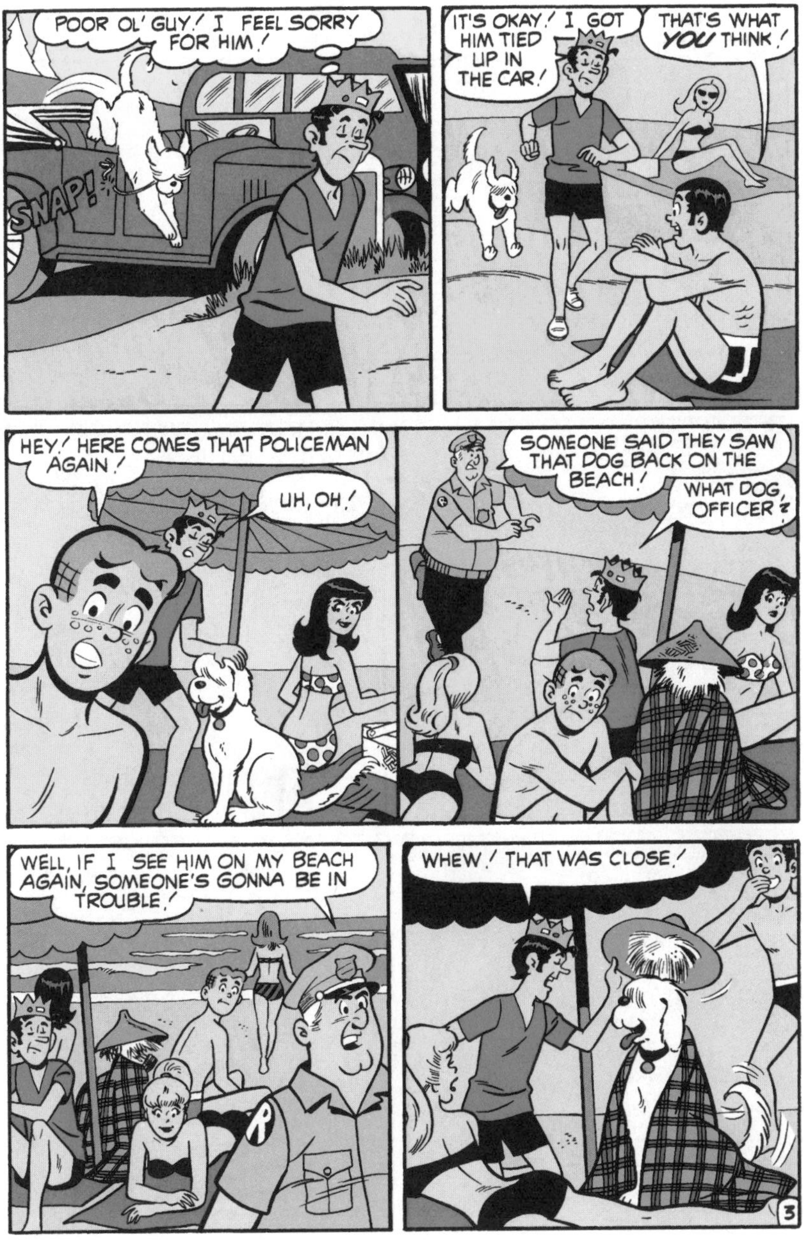

POOR OL' GUY! I FEEL SORRY FOR HIM!
SNAP!
IT'S OKAY! I GOT HIM TIED UP IN THE CAR!
THAT'S WHAT *YOU* THINK!
HEY! HERE COMES THAT POLICEMAN AGAIN!
UH, OH!
SOMEONE SAID THEY SAW THAT DOG BACK ON THE BEACH!
WHAT DOG, OFFICER?
WELL, IF I SEE HIM ON MY BEACH AGAIN, SOMEONE'S GONNA BE IN TROUBLE!
WHEW! THAT WAS CLOSE!
3

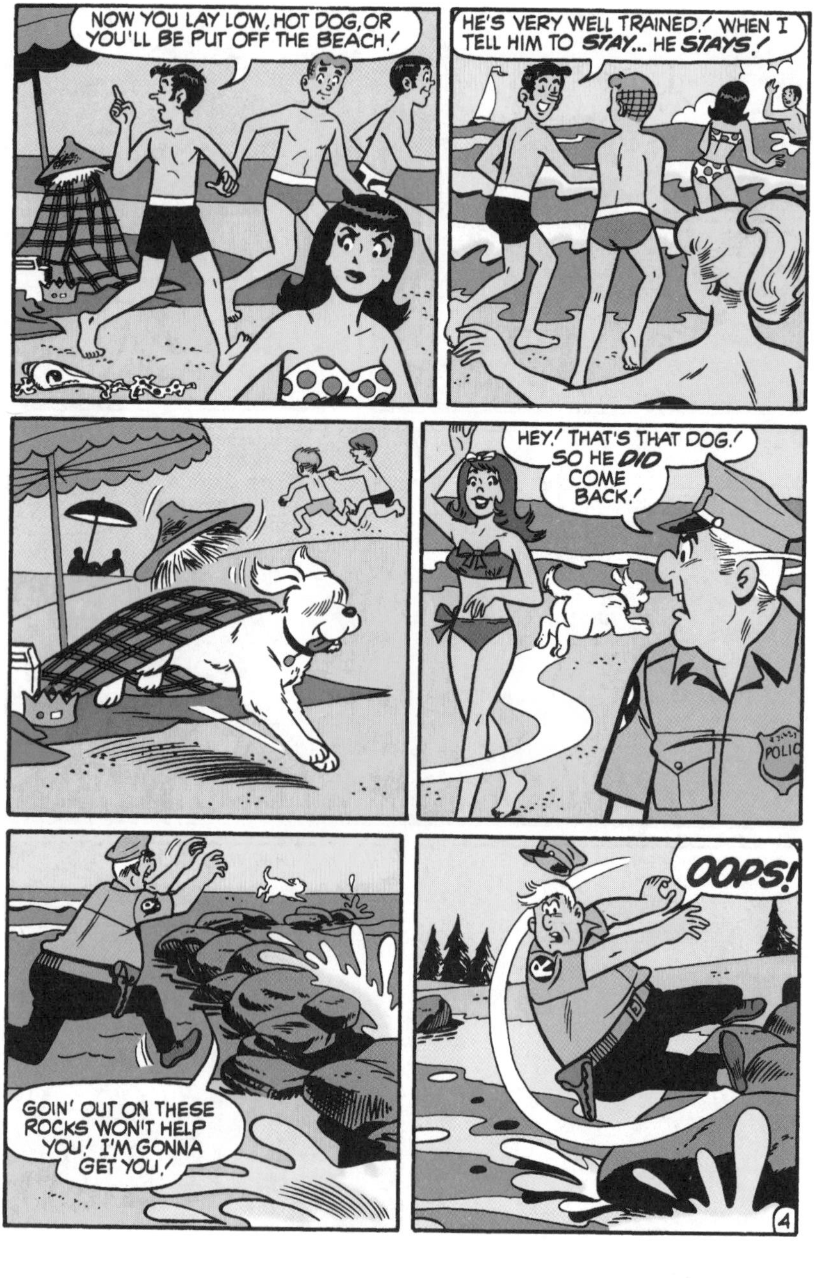
NOW YOU LAY LOW, HOT DOG, OR YOU'LL BE PUT OFF THE BEACH!
HE'S VERY WELL TRAINED! WHEN I TELL HIM TO STAY... HE STAYS!
HEY! THAT'S THAT DOG! SO HE DID COME BACK!
POLIC
GOIN' OUT ON THESE ROCKS WON'T HELP YOU! I'M GONNA GET YOU!
OOPS!
4

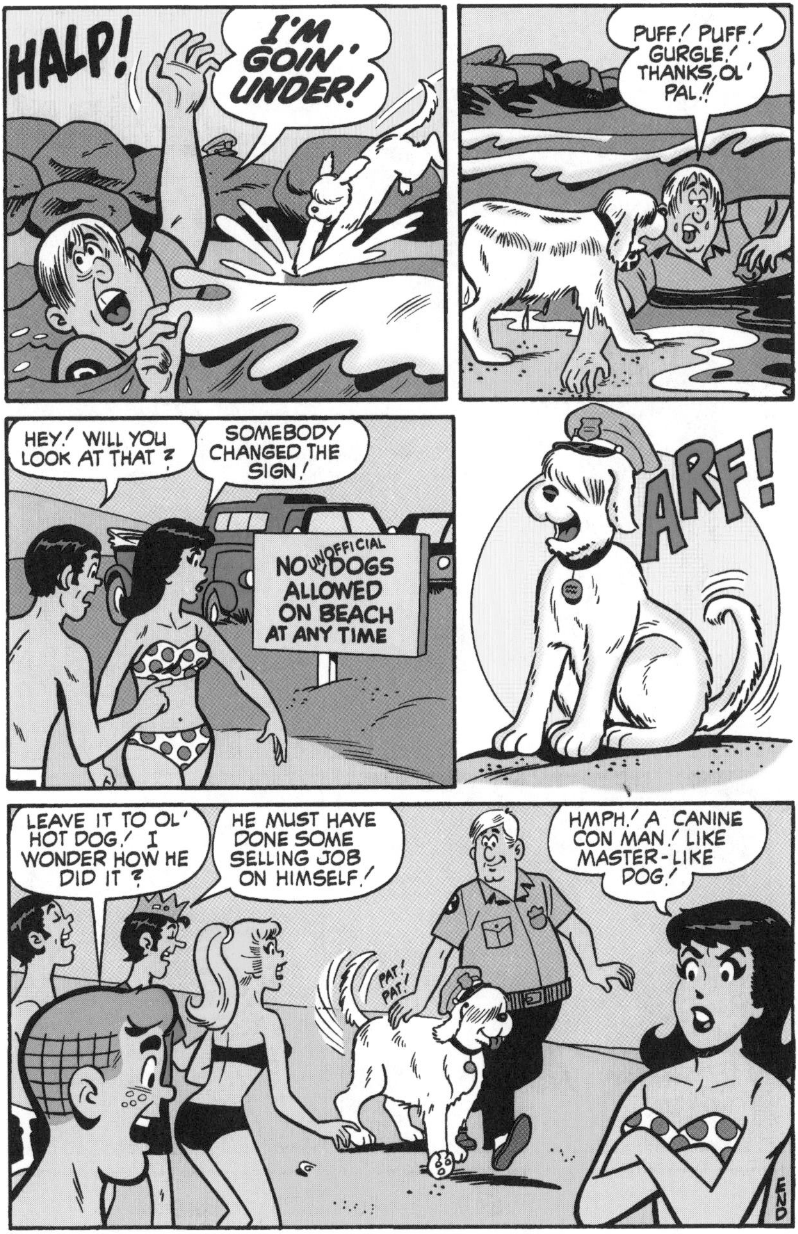
HALP!
I'M GOIN' UNDER!
PUFF! PUFF! GURGLE! THANKS, OL' PAL!!
HEY! WILL YOU LOOK AT THAT?
SOMEBODY CHANGED THE SIGN!
NO UNOFFICIAL DOGS ALLOWED ON BEACH AT ANY TIME
ARF!
LEAVE IT TO OL' HOT DOG! I WONDER HOW HE DID IT?
HE MUST HAVE DONE SOME SELLING JOB ON HIMSELF!
PAT! PAT!
HMPH! A CANINE CON MAN! LIKE MASTER-LIKE DOG!
END

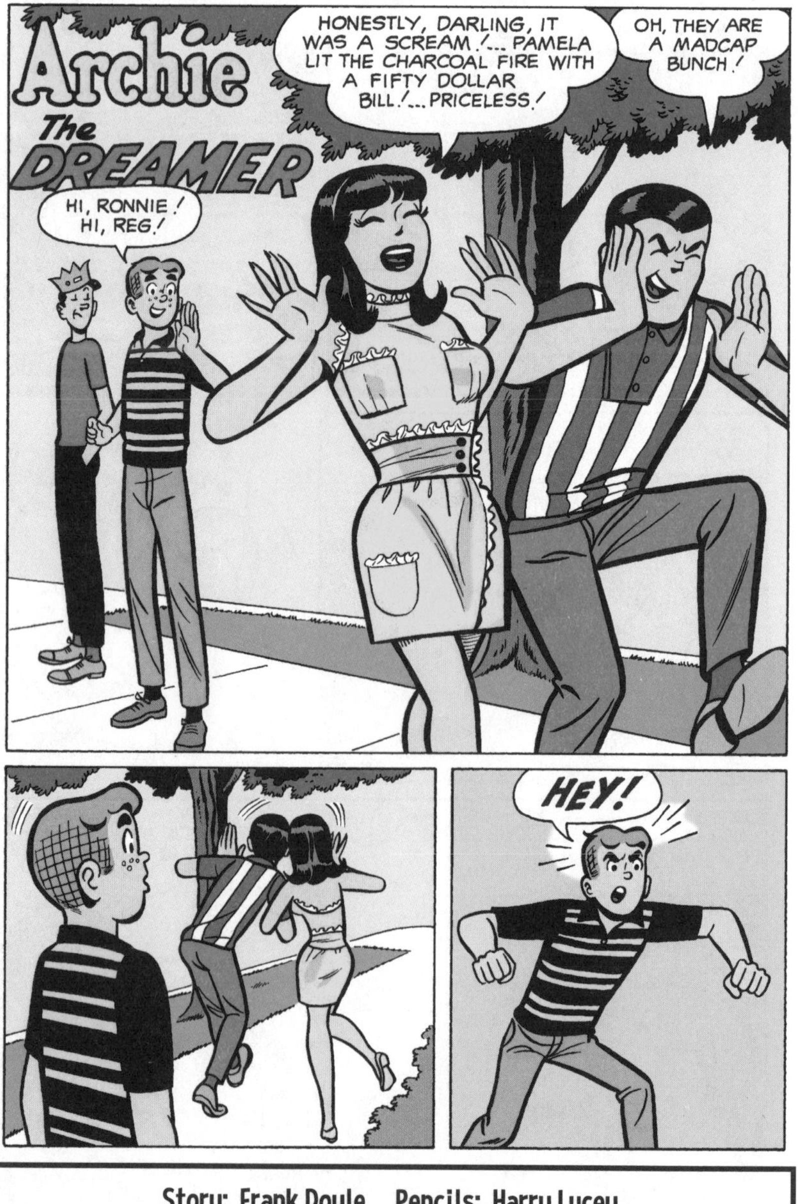
Archie
The DREAMER
HI, RONNIE! HI, REG!
HONESTLY, DARLING, IT WAS A SCREAM!... PAMELA LIT THE CHARCOAL FIRE WITH A FIFTY DOLLAR BILL!... PRICELESS!
OH, THEY ARE A MADCAP BUNCH!
HEY!

Story: Frank Doyle Pencils: Harry Lucey
Inks: Rudy Lapick Letters: Bill Yoshida

Originally printed in EVERYTHING'S ARCHIE #11, DECEMBER 1970

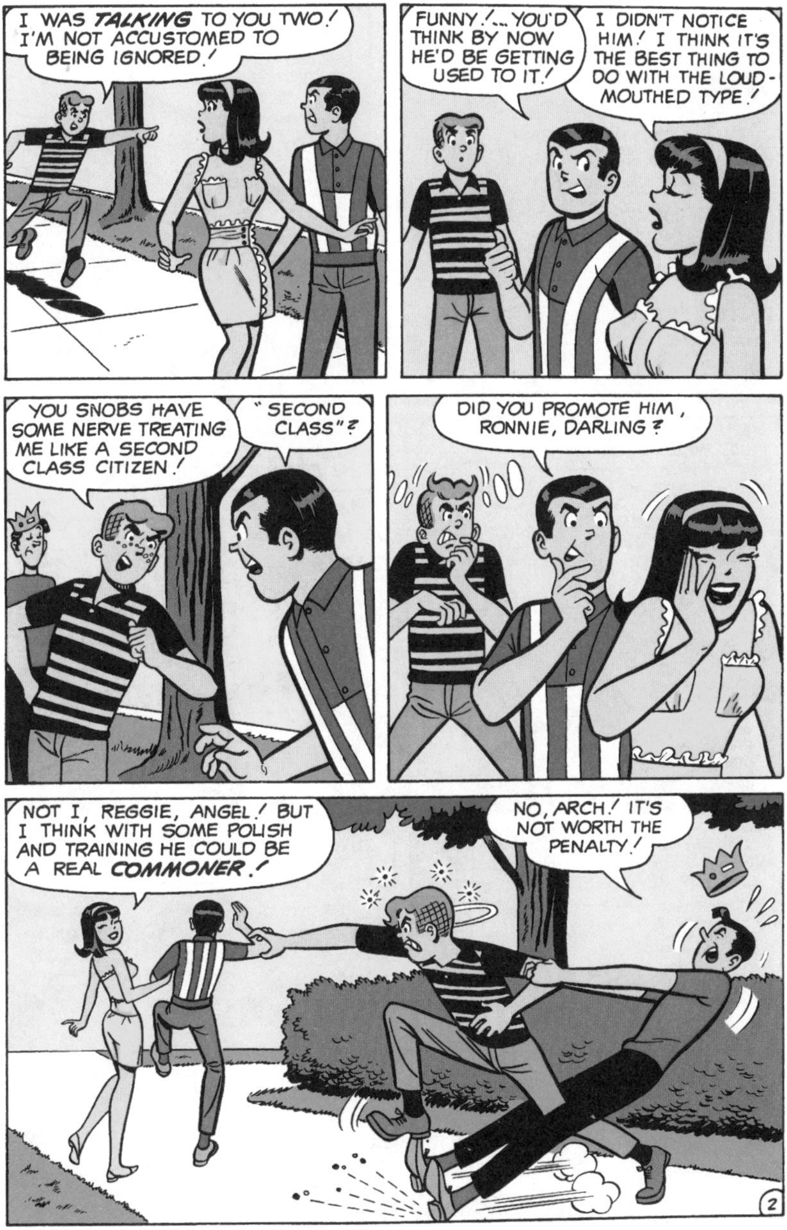
I WAS TALKING TO YOU TWO! I'M NOT ACCUSTOMED TO BEING IGNORED!
FUNNY!... YOU'D THINK BY NOW HE'D BE GETTING USED TO IT!
I DIDN'T NOTICE HIM! I THINK IT'S THE BEST THING TO DO WITH THE LOUD-MOUTHED TYPE!
YOU SNOBS HAVE SOME NERVE TREATING ME LIKE A SECOND CLASS CITIZEN!
"SECOND CLASS"?
DID YOU PROMOTE HIM, RONNIE, DARLING?
NOT I, REGGIE, ANGEL! BUT I THINK WITH SOME POLISH AND TRAINING HE COULD BE A REAL COMMONER!
NO, ARCH! IT'S NOT WORTH THE PENALTY!
2

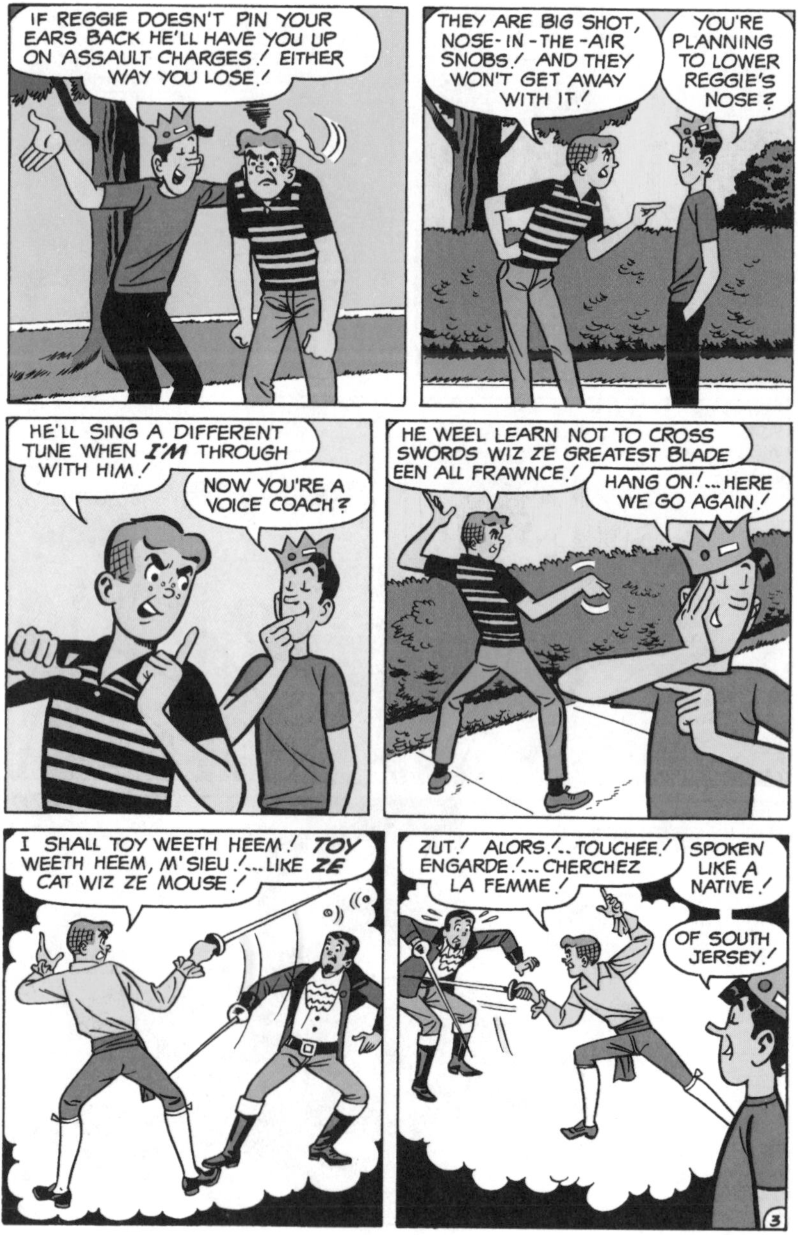
IF REGGIE DOESN'T PIN YOUR EARS BACK HE'LL HAVE YOU UP ON ASSAULT CHARGES! EITHER WAY YOU LOSE!
THEY ARE BIG SHOT, NOSE-IN-THE-AIR SNOBS! AND THEY WON'T GET AWAY WITH IT!
YOU'RE PLANNING TO LOWER REGGIE'S NOSE?
HE'LL SING A DIFFERENT TUNE WHEN I'M THROUGH WITH HIM!
NOW YOU'RE A VOICE COACH?
HE WEEL LEARN NOT TO CROSS SWORDS WIZ ZE GREATEST BLADE EEN ALL FRAWNCE!
HANG ON!...HERE WE GO AGAIN!
I SHALL TOY WEETH HEEM! TOY WEETH HEEM, M'SIEU!...LIKE ZE CAT WIZ ZE MOUSE!
ZUT! ALORS!..TOUCHEE! ENGARDE!...CHERCHEZ LA FEMME!
SPOKEN LIKE A NATIVE!
OF SOUTH JERSEY!
3

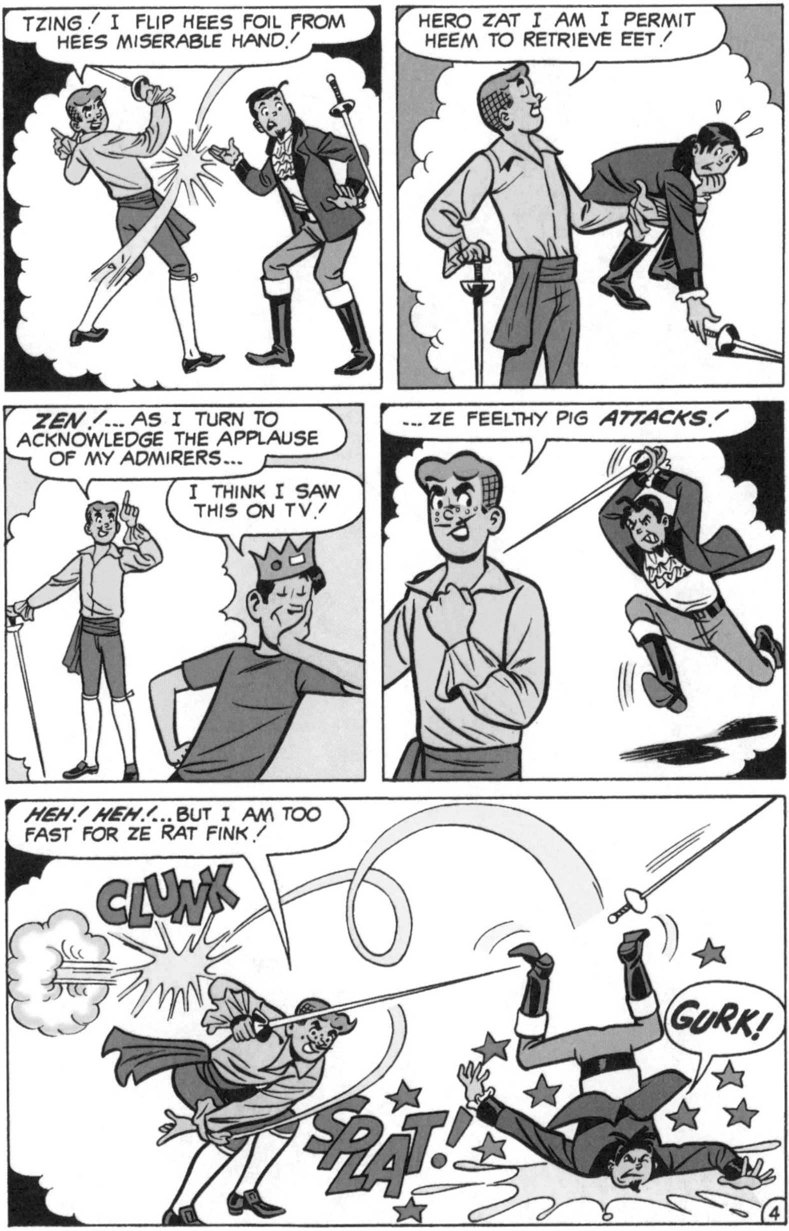
TZING.! I FLIP HEES FOIL FROM HEES MISERABLE HAND.!
HERO ZAT I AM I PERMIT HEEM TO RETRIEVE EET.!
ZEN.!... AS I TURN TO ACKNOWLEDGE THE APPLAUSE OF MY ADMIRERS...
I THINK I SAW THIS ON TV.!
...ZE FEELTHY PIG ATTACKS.!
HEH.! HEH.!...BUT I AM TOO FAST FOR ZE RAT FINK.!
CLUNK
GURK!
SPLAT!
4

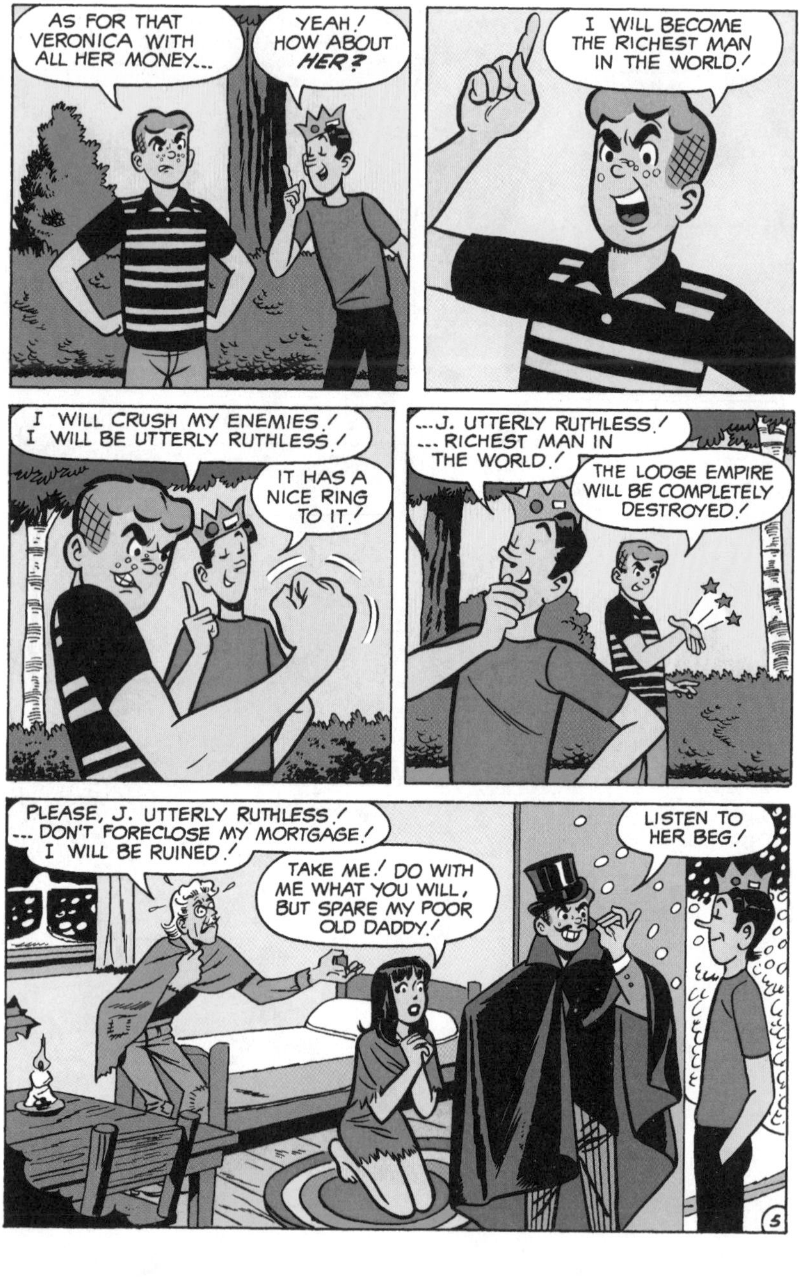
AS FOR THAT VERONICA WITH ALL HER MONEY...
YEAH! HOW ABOUT *HER?*
I WILL BECOME THE RICHEST MAN IN THE WORLD!
I WILL CRUSH MY ENEMIES! I WILL BE UTTERLY RUTHLESS!
IT HAS A NICE RING TO IT!
...J. UTTERLY RUTHLESS! ...RICHEST MAN IN THE WORLD!
THE LODGE EMPIRE WILL BE COMPLETELY DESTROYED!
PLEASE, J. UTTERLY RUTHLESS! ... DON'T FORECLOSE MY MORTGAGE! I WILL BE RUINED!
TAKE ME! DO WITH ME WHAT YOU WILL, BUT SPARE MY POOR OLD DADDY!
LISTEN TO HER BEG!
5

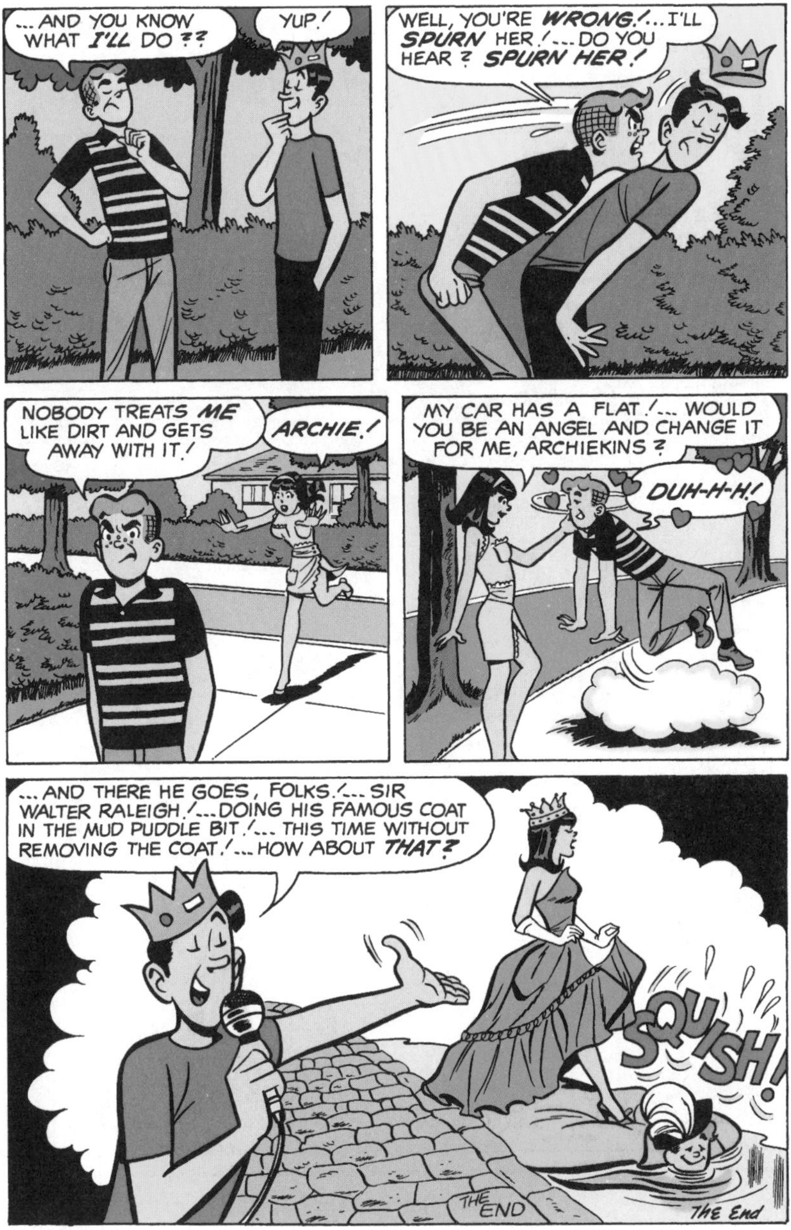

...AND YOU KNOW WHAT I'LL DO ??
YUP!
WELL, YOU'RE WRONG!...I'LL SPURN HER!...DO YOU HEAR? SPURN HER!
NOBODY TREATS ME LIKE DIRT AND GETS AWAY WITH IT!
ARCHIE!
MY CAR HAS A FLAT!... WOULD YOU BE AN ANGEL AND CHANGE IT FOR ME, ARCHIEKINS?
DUH-H-H!
...AND THERE HE GOES, FOLKS!... SIR WALTER RALEIGH!...DOING HIS FAMOUS COAT IN THE MUD PUDDLE BIT!... THIS TIME WITHOUT REMOVING THE COAT!...HOW ABOUT THAT?
SQUISH!
THE END
The End

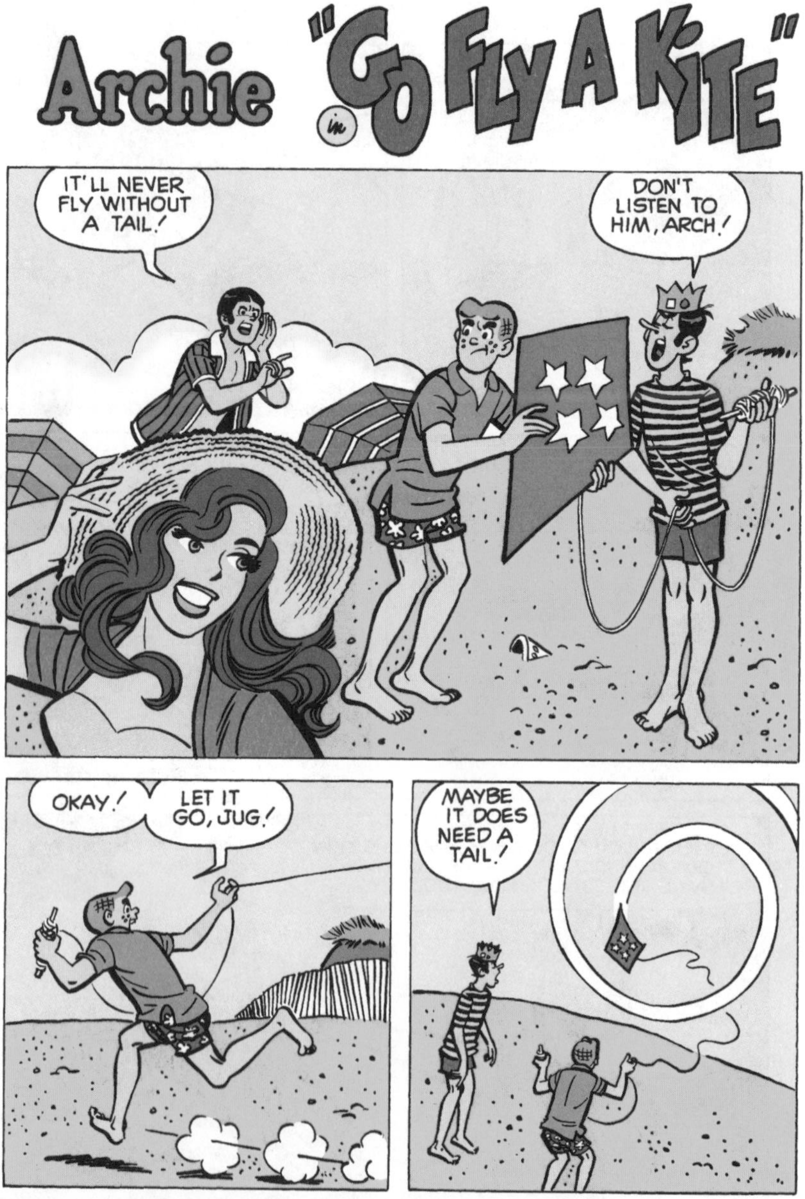

Archie in "GO FLY A KITE"
IT'LL NEVER FLY WITHOUT A TAIL!
DON'T LISTEN TO HIM, ARCH!
OKAY!
LET IT GO, JUG!
MAYBE IT DOES NEED A TAIL!

Story & Art: Al Hartley
Letters: Bill Yoshida

Originally printed in EVERYTHING'S ARCHIE #11, DECEMBER 1970

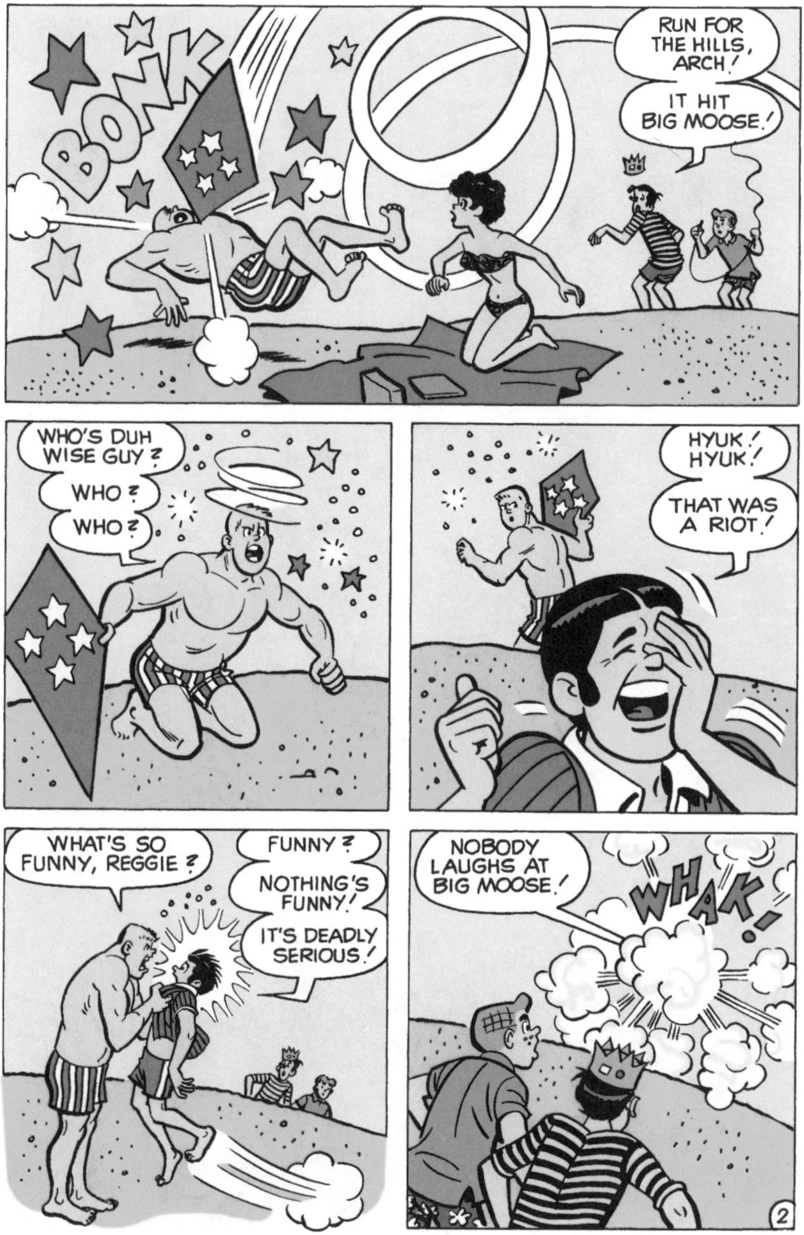
BONK
RUN FOR THE HILLS, ARCH!
IT HIT BIG MOOSE!
WHO'S DUH WISE GUY?
WHO?
WHO?
HYUK! HYUK!
THAT WAS A RIOT!
WHAT'S SO FUNNY, REGGIE?
FUNNY?
NOTHING'S FUNNY!
IT'S DEADLY SERIOUS!
NOBODY LAUGHS AT BIG MOOSE!
WHAK!
2

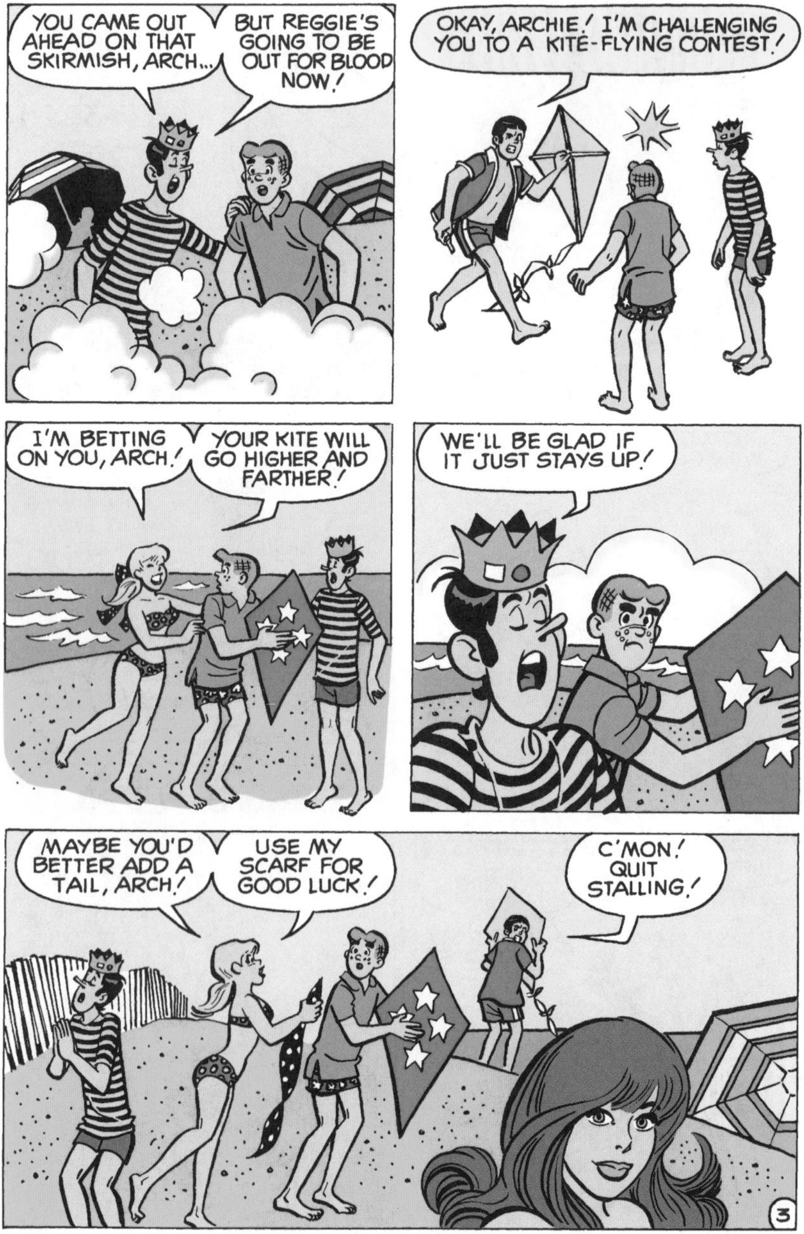
YOU CAME OUT AHEAD ON THAT SKIRMISH, ARCH...
BUT REGGIE'S GOING TO BE OUT FOR BLOOD NOW!
OKAY, ARCHIE! I'M CHALLENGING YOU TO A KITE-FLYING CONTEST!
I'M BETTING ON YOU, ARCH!
YOUR KITE WILL GO HIGHER AND FARTHER!
WE'LL BE GLAD IF IT JUST STAYS UP!
MAYBE YOU'D BETTER ADD A TAIL, ARCH!
USE MY SCARF FOR GOOD LUCK!
C'MON! QUIT STALLING!
3

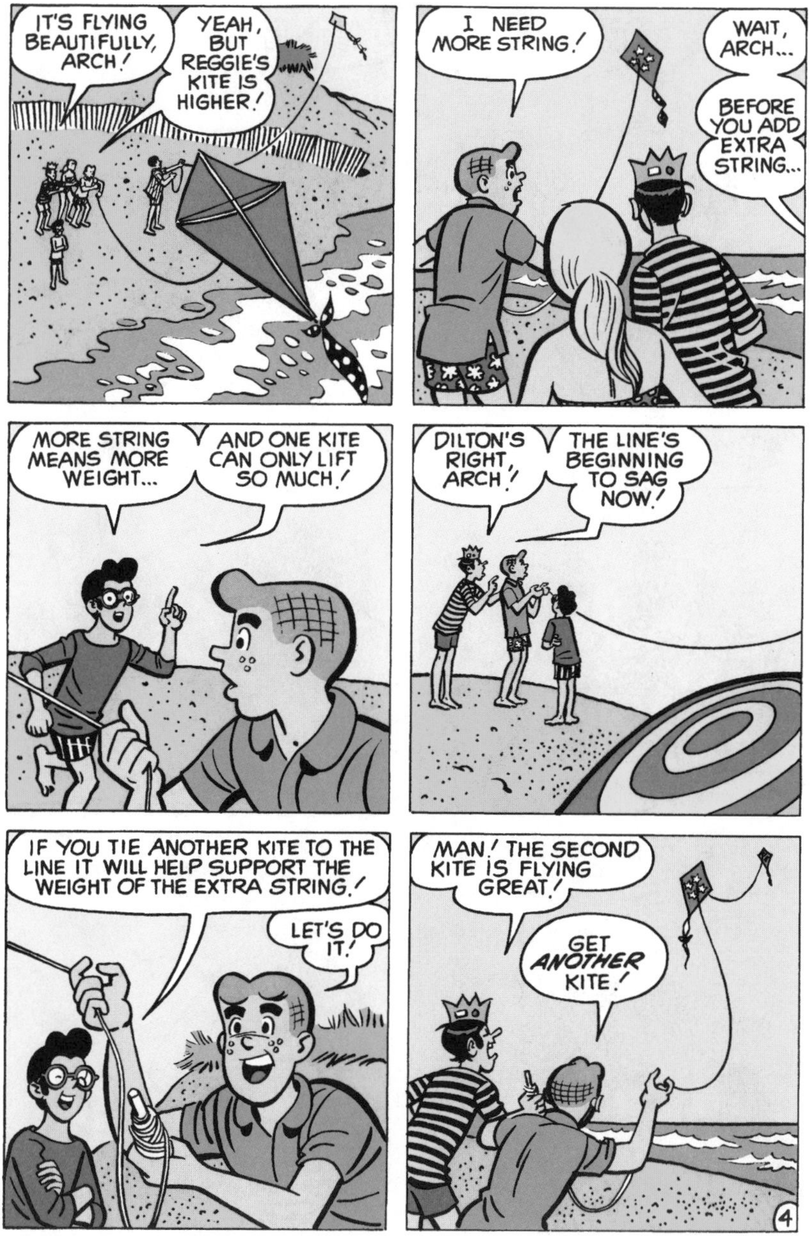
IT'S FLYING BEAUTIFULLY, ARCH!
YEAH, BUT REGGIE'S KITE IS HIGHER!
I NEED MORE STRING!
WAIT, ARCH...
BEFORE YOU ADD EXTRA STRING...
MORE STRING MEANS MORE WEIGHT...
AND ONE KITE CAN ONLY LIFT SO MUCH!
DILTON'S RIGHT, ARCH!
THE LINE'S BEGINNING TO SAG NOW!
IF YOU TIE ANOTHER KITE TO THE LINE IT WILL HELP SUPPORT THE WEIGHT OF THE EXTRA STRING!
LET'S DO IT!
MAN! THE SECOND KITE IS FLYING GREAT!
GET *ANOTHER* KITE!
4

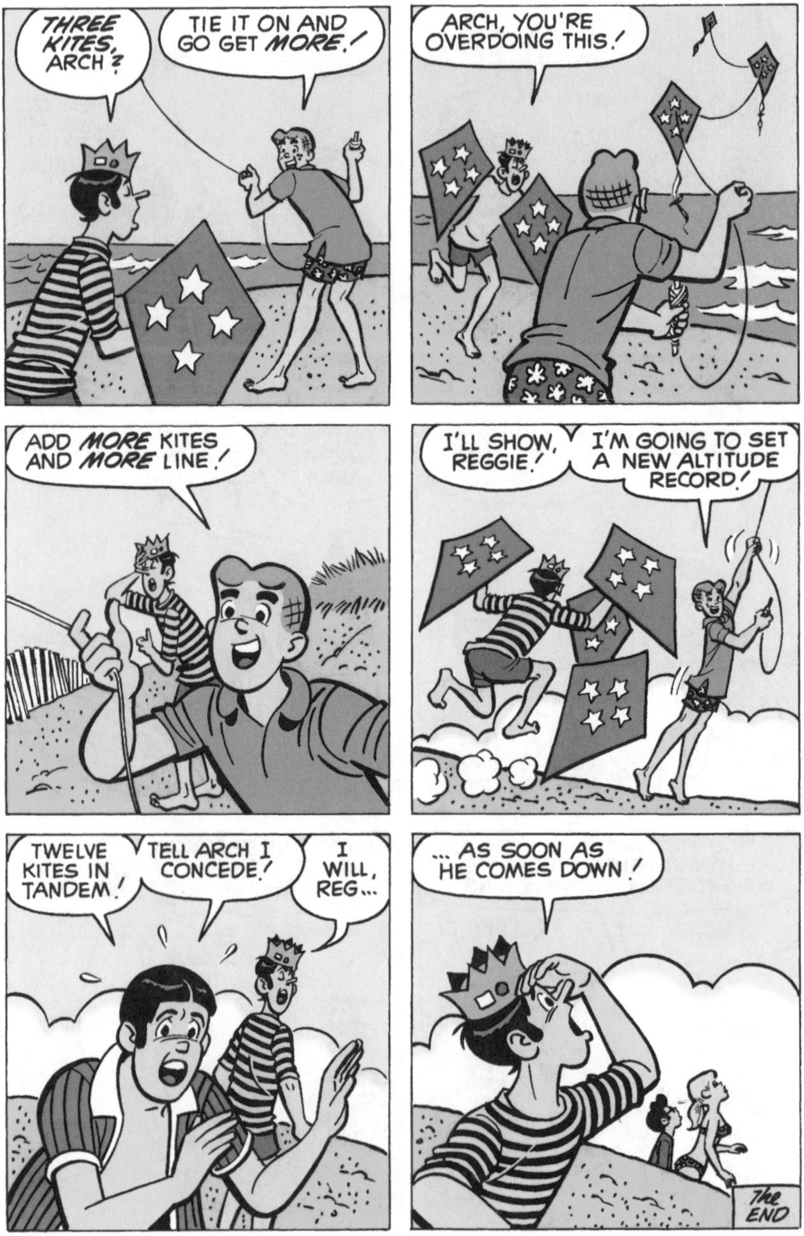
THREE KITES, ARCH?
TIE IT ON AND GO GET MORE.!
ARCH, YOU'RE OVERDOING THIS.!
ADD MORE KITES AND MORE LINE.!
I'LL SHOW, REGGIE.!
I'M GOING TO SET A NEW ALTITUDE RECORD.!
TWELVE KITES IN TANDEM!
TELL ARCH I CONCEDE!
I WILL, REG...
... AS SOON AS HE COMES DOWN!
The END

Archie "OUT OF SIGHT"

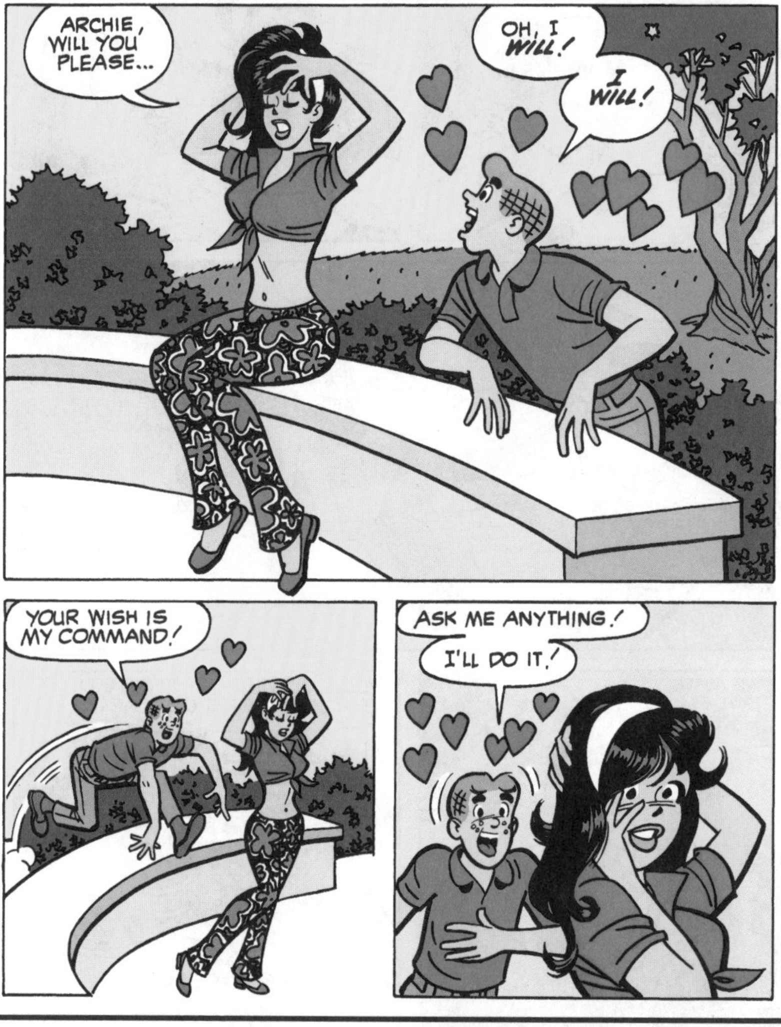
ARCHIE, WILL YOU PLEASE...
OH, I WILL!
I WILL!
YOUR WISH IS MY COMMAND!
ASK ME ANYTHING!
I'LL DO IT!

Story & Art: Al Hartley
Letters: Bill Yoshida

Originally printed in EVERYTHING'S ARCHIE #11, DECEMBER 1970

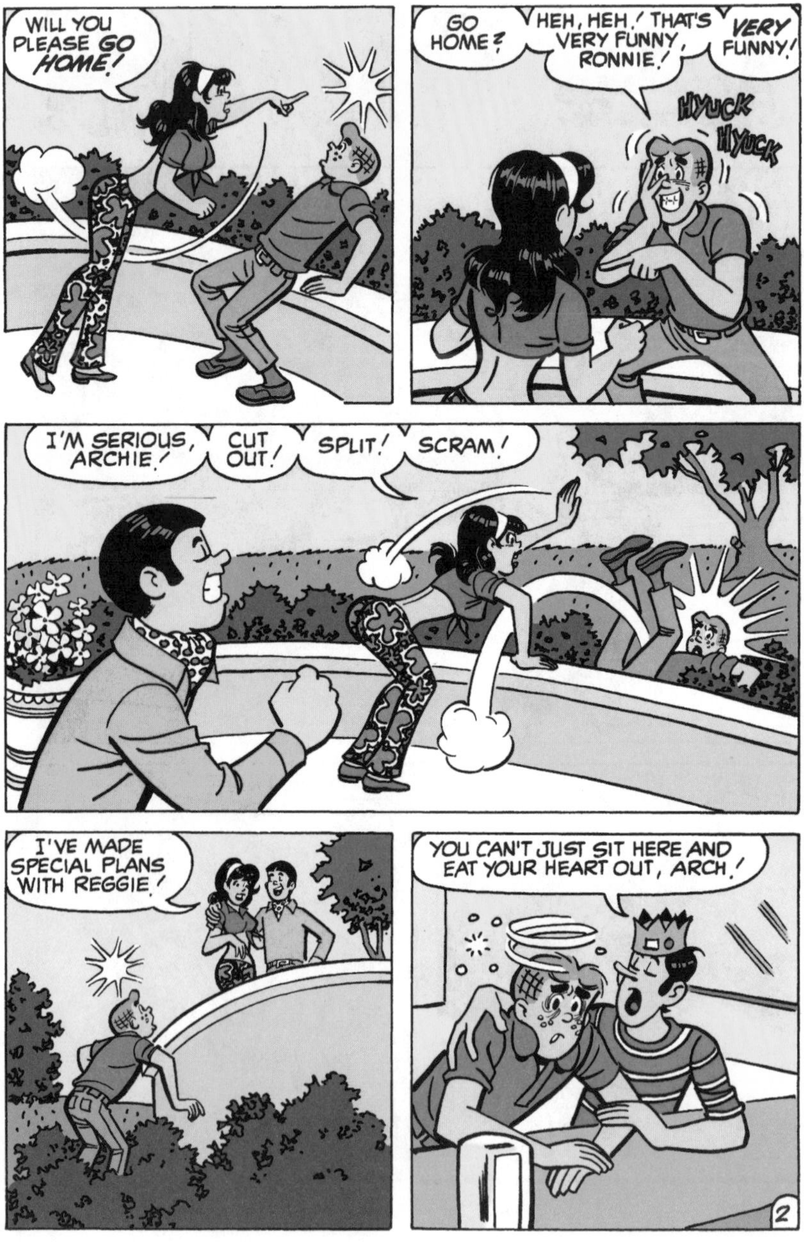

WILL YOU PLEASE GO HOME!
GO HOME?
HEH, HEH! THAT'S VERY FUNNY, RONNIE!
VERY FUNNY!
HYUCK
HYUCK
I'M SERIOUS, ARCHIE!
CUT OUT!
SPLIT!
SCRAM!
I'VE MADE SPECIAL PLANS WITH REGGIE!
YOU CAN'T JUST SIT HERE AND EAT YOUR HEART OUT, ARCH!
2

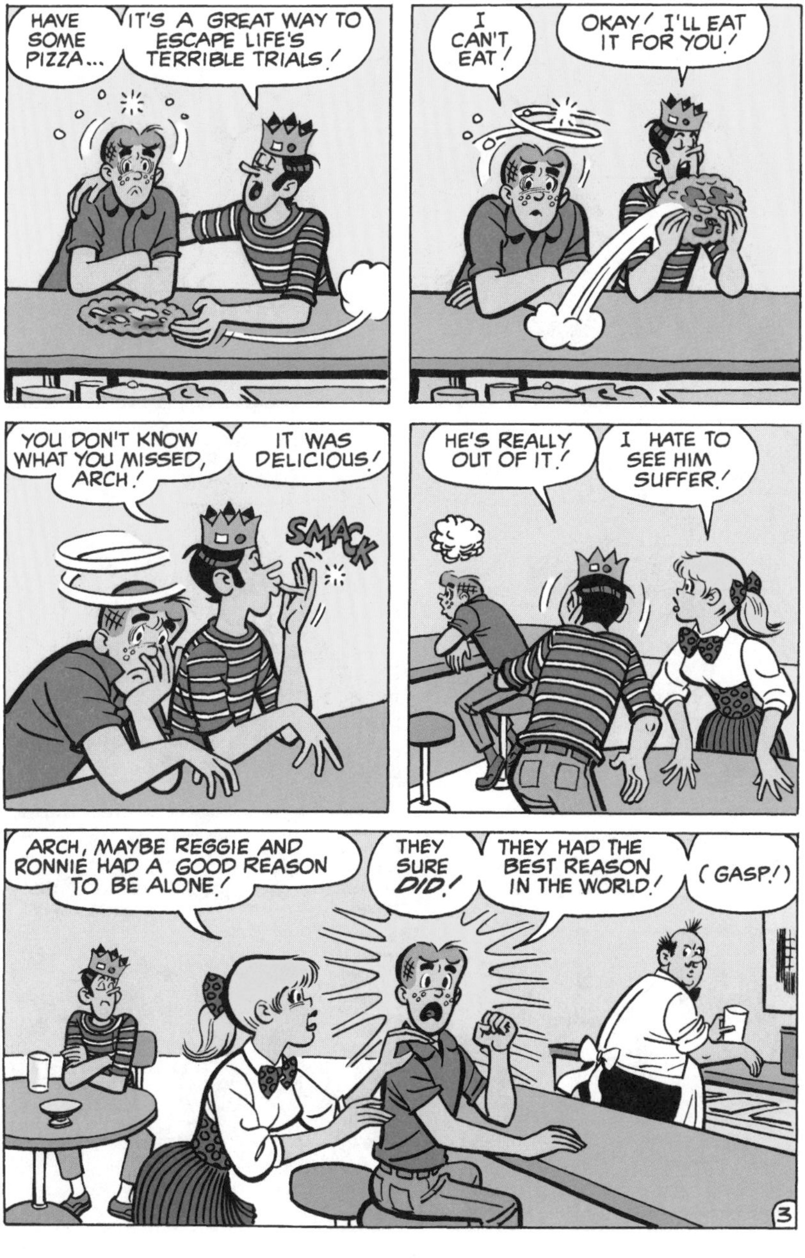
HAVE SOME PIZZA...
IT'S A GREAT WAY TO ESCAPE LIFE'S TERRIBLE TRIALS!
I CAN'T EAT!
OKAY! I'LL EAT IT FOR YOU!
YOU DON'T KNOW WHAT YOU MISSED, ARCH!
IT WAS DELICIOUS!
SMACK
HE'S REALLY OUT OF IT!
I HATE TO SEE HIM SUFFER!
ARCH, MAYBE REGGIE AND RONNIE HAD A GOOD REASON TO BE ALONE!
THEY SURE *DID!*
THEY HAD THE BEST REASON IN THE WORLD!
(GASP!)
3

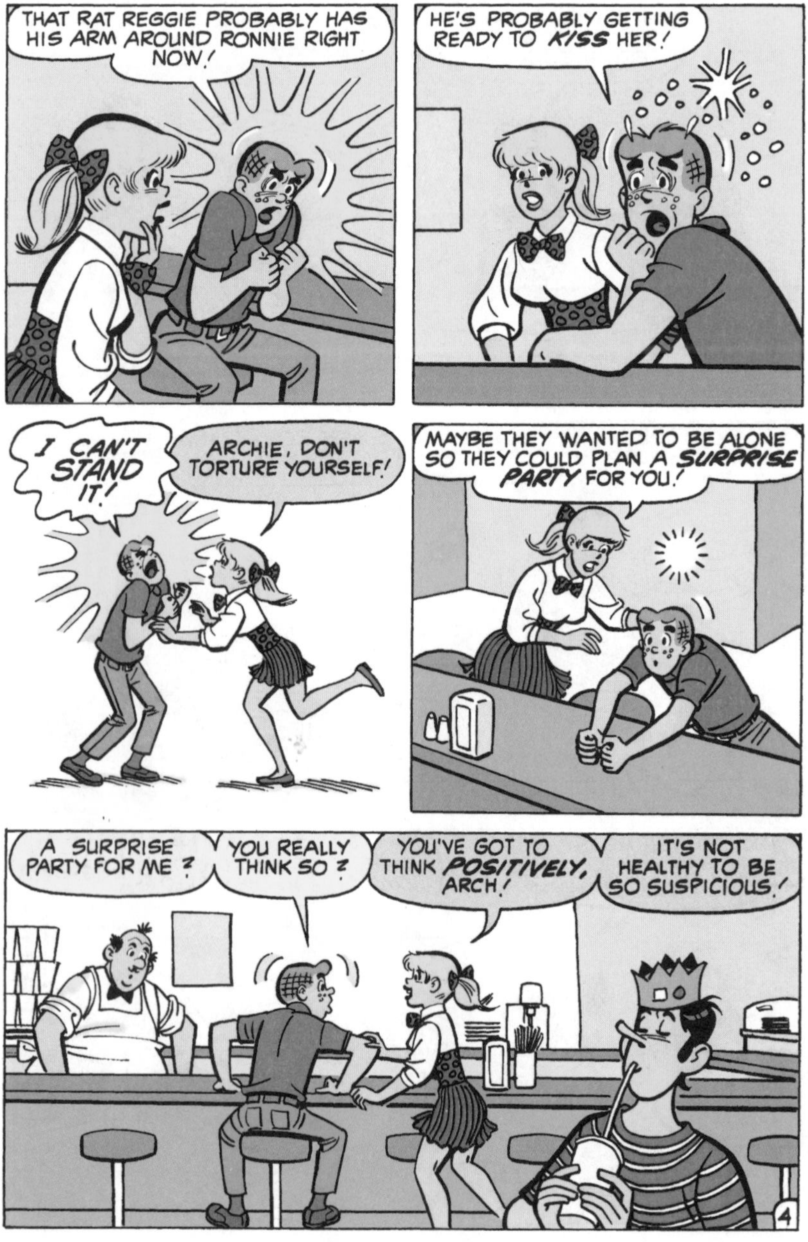
THAT RAT REGGIE PROBABLY HAS HIS ARM AROUND RONNIE RIGHT NOW!
HE'S PROBABLY GETTING READY TO KISS HER!
I CAN'T STAND IT!
ARCHIE, DON'T TORTURE YOURSELF!
MAYBE THEY WANTED TO BE ALONE SO THEY COULD PLAN A SURPRISE PARTY FOR YOU!
A SURPRISE PARTY FOR ME?
YOU REALLY THINK SO?
YOU'VE GOT TO THINK POSITIVELY, ARCH!
IT'S NOT HEALTHY TO BE SO SUSPICIOUS!
4

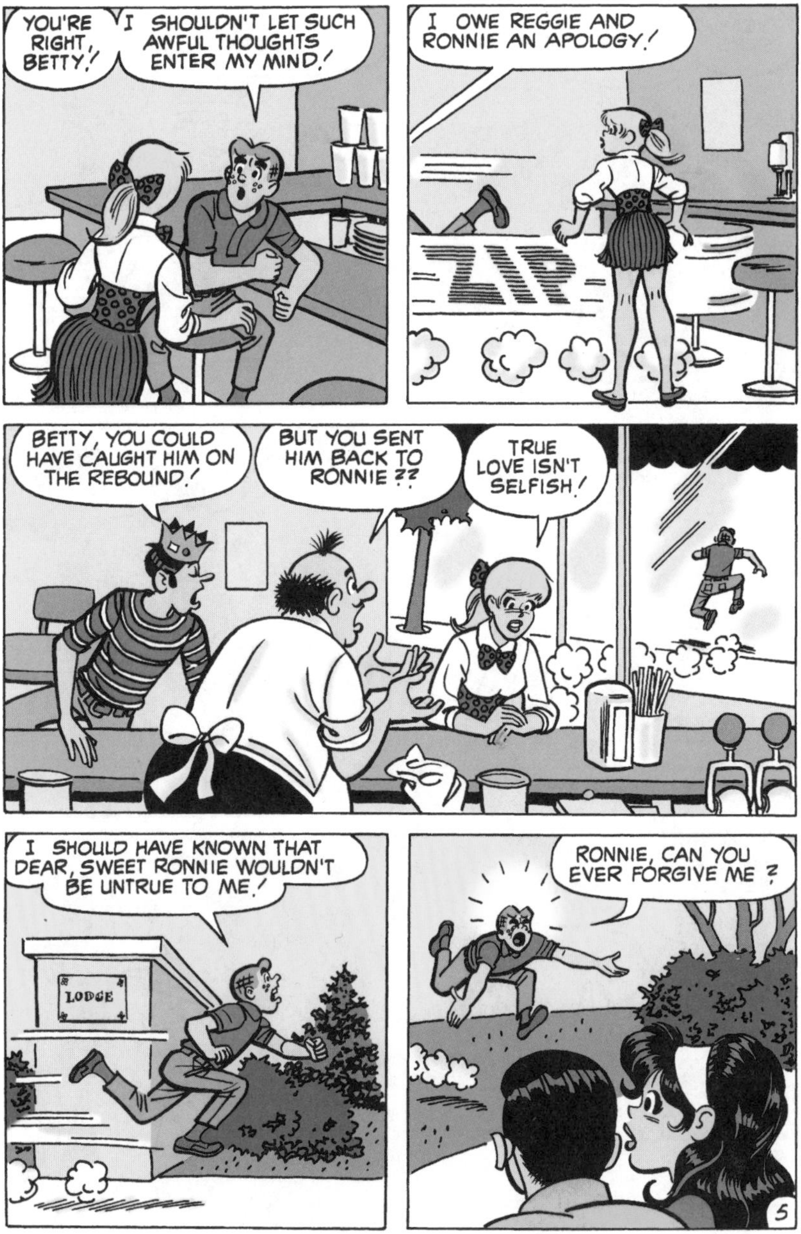
YOU'RE RIGHT, BETTY!
I SHOULDN'T LET SUCH AWFUL THOUGHTS ENTER MY MIND!
I OWE REGGIE AND RONNIE AN APOLOGY!
ZIP
BETTY, YOU COULD HAVE CAUGHT HIM ON THE REBOUND!
BUT YOU SENT HIM BACK TO RONNIE ??
TRUE LOVE ISN'T SELFISH!
I SHOULD HAVE KNOWN THAT DEAR, SWEET RONNIE WOULDN'T BE UNTRUE TO ME!
LODGE
RONNIE, CAN YOU EVER FORGIVE ME ?
5

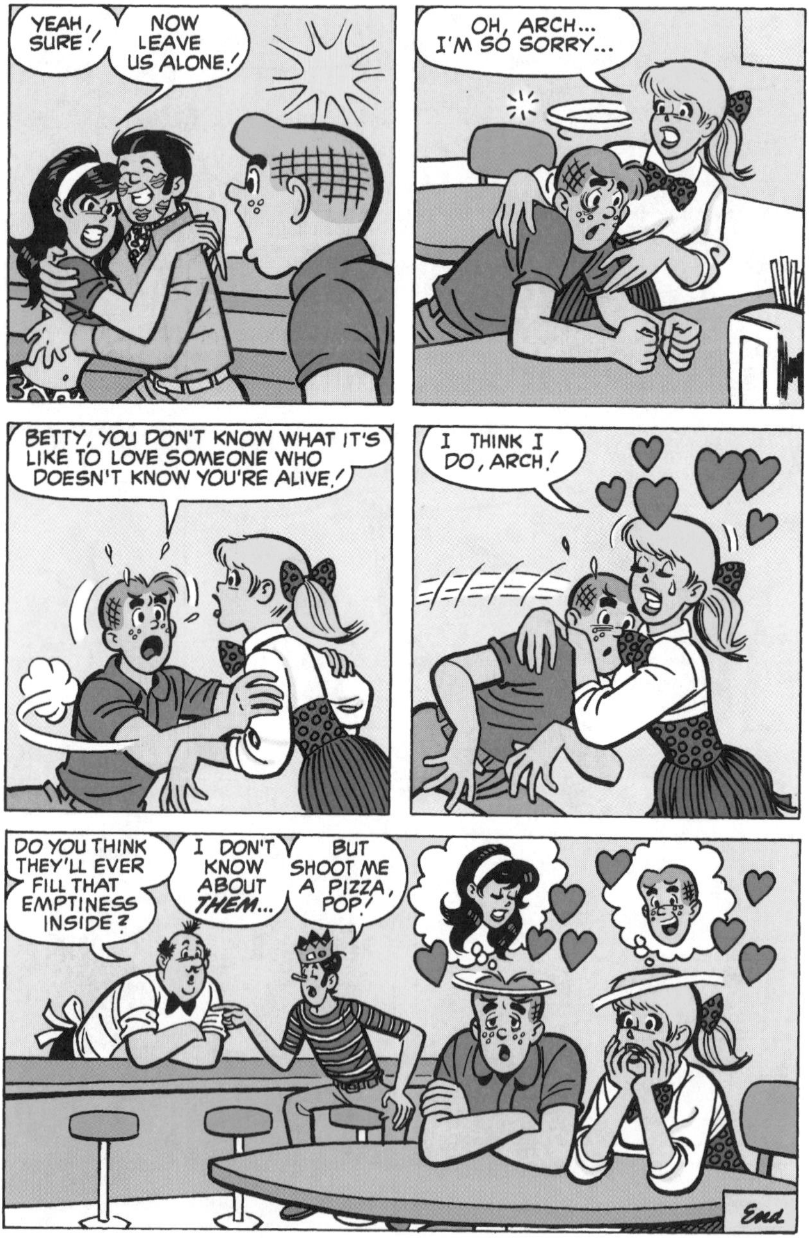
YEAH, SURE!
NOW LEAVE US ALONE!
OH, ARCH... I'M SO SORRY...
BETTY, YOU DON'T KNOW WHAT IT'S LIKE TO LOVE SOMEONE WHO DOESN'T KNOW YOU'RE ALIVE!
I THINK I DO, ARCH!
DO YOU THINK THEY'LL EVER FILL THAT EMPTINESS INSIDE?
I DON'T KNOW ABOUT *THEM*...
BUT SHOOT ME A PIZZA, POP!
End

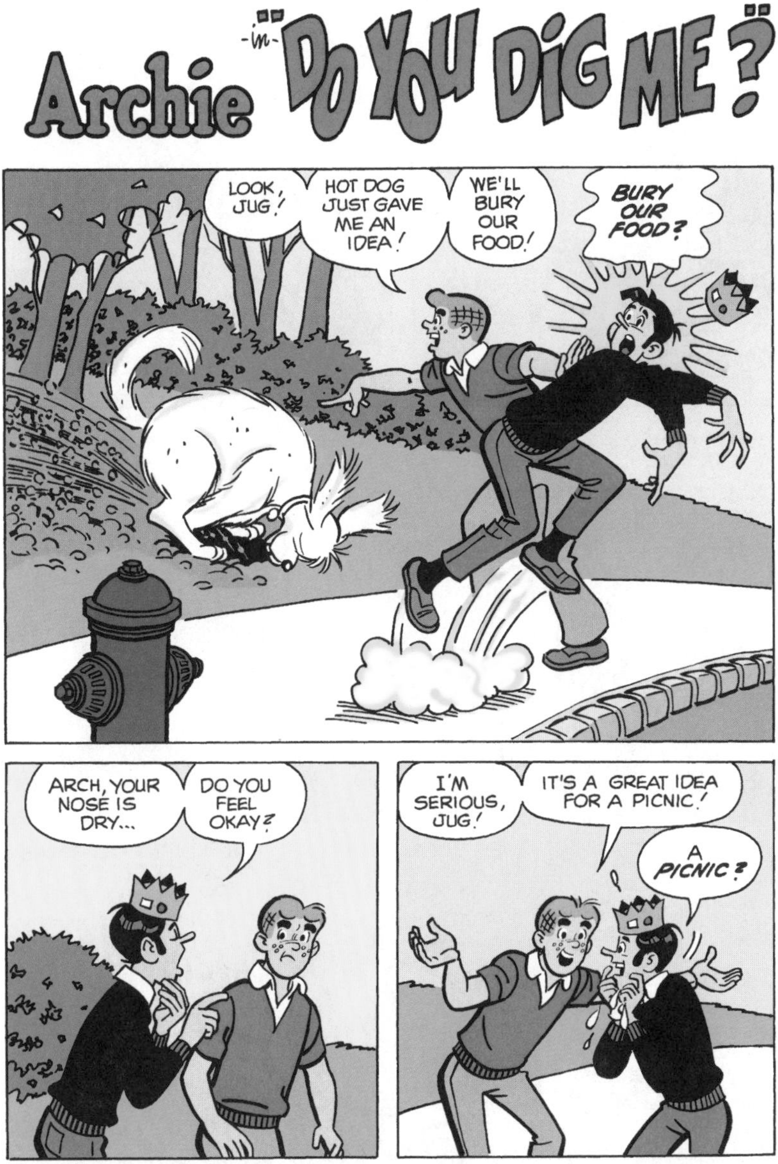

Archie -in- "DO YOU DIG ME?"
LOOK, JUG!
HOT DOG JUST GAVE ME AN IDEA!
WE'LL BURY OUR FOOD!
BURY OUR FOOD?
ARCH, YOUR NOSE IS DRY...
DO YOU FEEL OKAY?
I'M SERIOUS, JUG!
IT'S A GREAT IDEA FOR A PICNIC!
A PICNIC?

Story & Art: Al Hartley
Letters: Bill Yoshida

Originally printed in EVERYTHING'S ARCHIE #12, FEBRUARY 1971

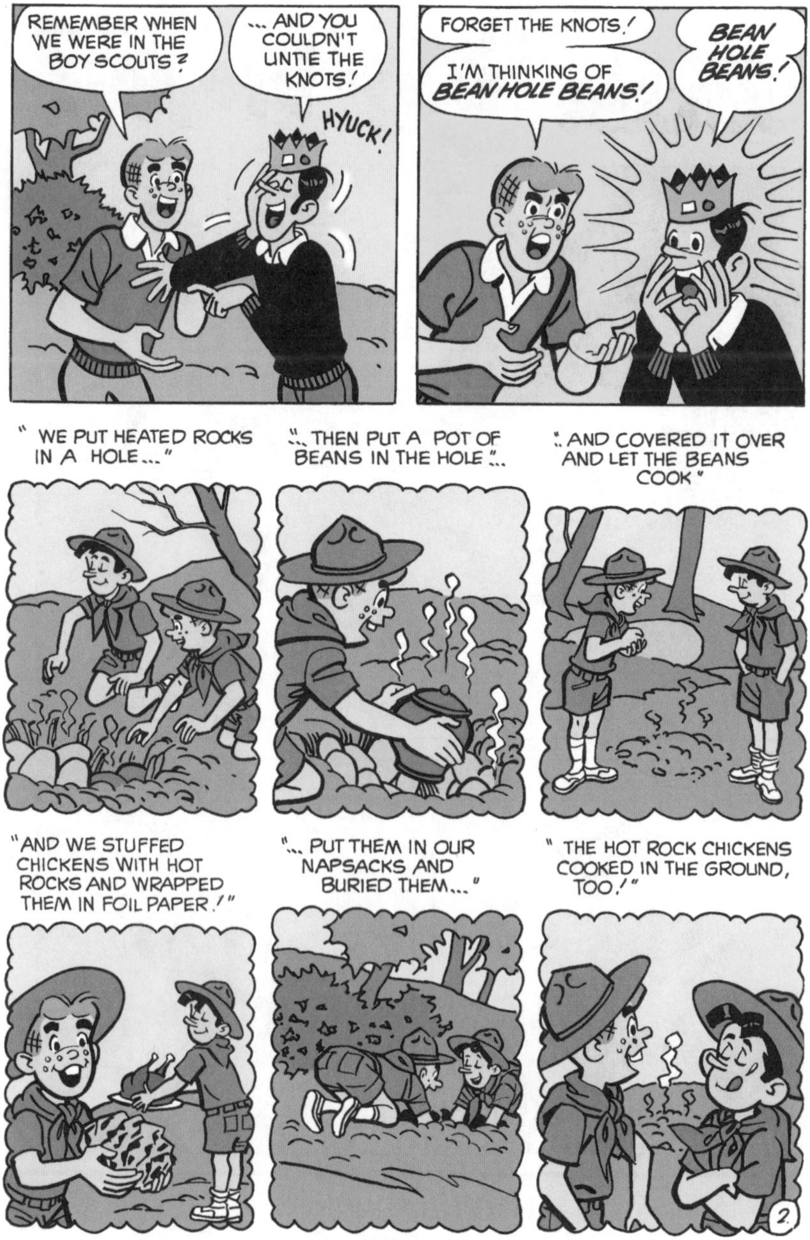
REMEMBER WHEN WE WERE IN THE BOY SCOUTS?
... AND YOU COULDN'T UNTIE THE KNOTS!
HYUCK!
FORGET THE KNOTS!
I'M THINKING OF BEAN HOLE BEANS!
BEAN HOLE BEANS!
" WE PUT HEATED ROCKS IN A HOLE ... "
"... THEN PUT A POT OF BEANS IN THE HOLE "...
"... AND COVERED IT OVER AND LET THE BEANS COOK"
"AND WE STUFFED CHICKENS WITH HOT ROCKS AND WRAPPED THEM IN FOIL PAPER!"
"... PUT THEM IN OUR NAPSACKS AND BURIED THEM... "
" THE HOT ROCK CHICKENS COOKED IN THE GROUND, TOO!"
2

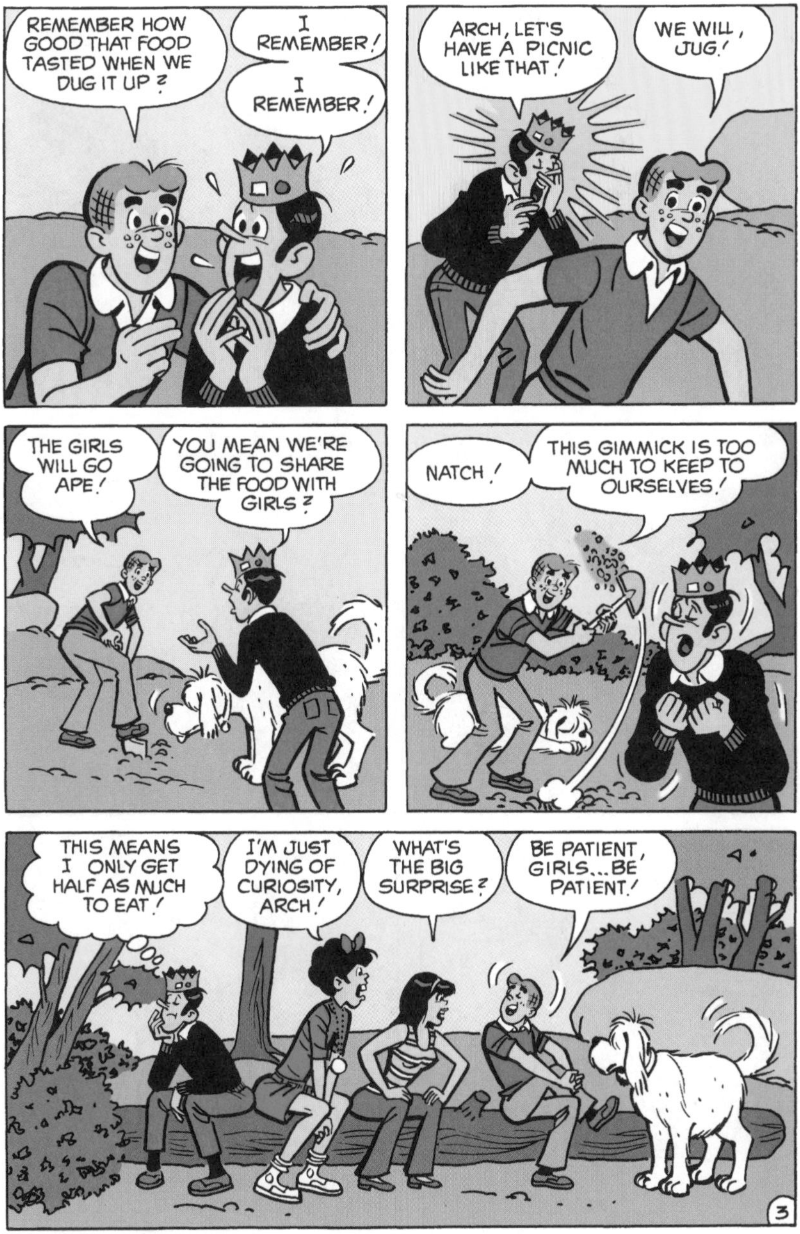
REMEMBER HOW GOOD THAT FOOD TASTED WHEN WE DUG IT UP?
I REMEMBER!
I REMEMBER!
ARCH, LET'S HAVE A PICNIC LIKE THAT!
WE WILL, JUG!
THE GIRLS WILL GO APE!
YOU MEAN WE'RE GOING TO SHARE THE FOOD WITH GIRLS?
NATCH!
THIS GIMMICK IS TOO MUCH TO KEEP TO OURSELVES!
THIS MEANS I ONLY GET HALF AS MUCH TO EAT!
I'M JUST DYING OF CURIOSITY, ARCH!
WHAT'S THE BIG SURPRISE?
BE PATIENT, GIRLS... BE PATIENT!
3

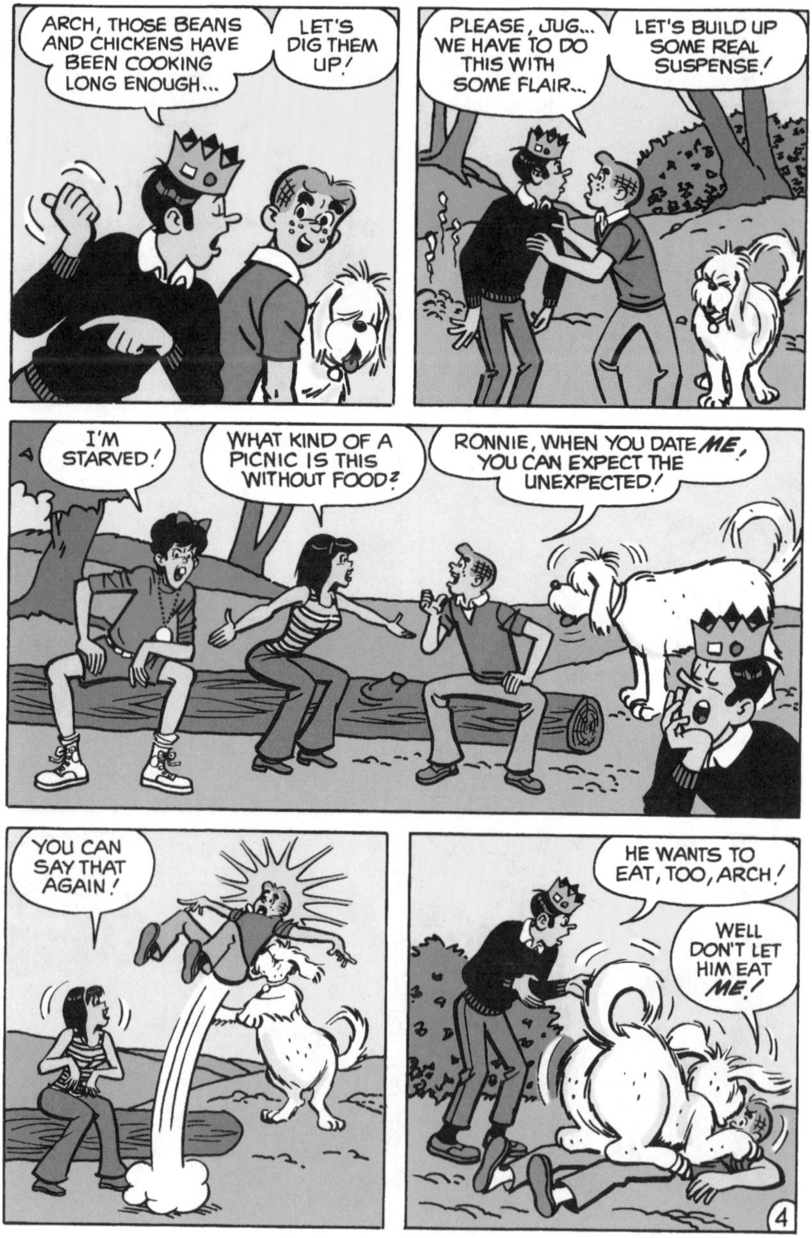
ARCH, THOSE BEANS AND CHICKENS HAVE BEEN COOKING LONG ENOUGH...
LET'S DIG THEM UP!
PLEASE, JUG... WE HAVE TO DO THIS WITH SOME FLAIR...
LET'S BUILD UP SOME REAL SUSPENSE!
I'M STARVED!
WHAT KIND OF A PICNIC IS THIS WITHOUT FOOD?
RONNIE, WHEN YOU DATE *ME*, YOU CAN EXPECT THE UNEXPECTED!
YOU CAN SAY THAT AGAIN!
HE WANTS TO EAT, TOO, ARCH!
WELL DON'T LET HIM EAT *ME*!
4

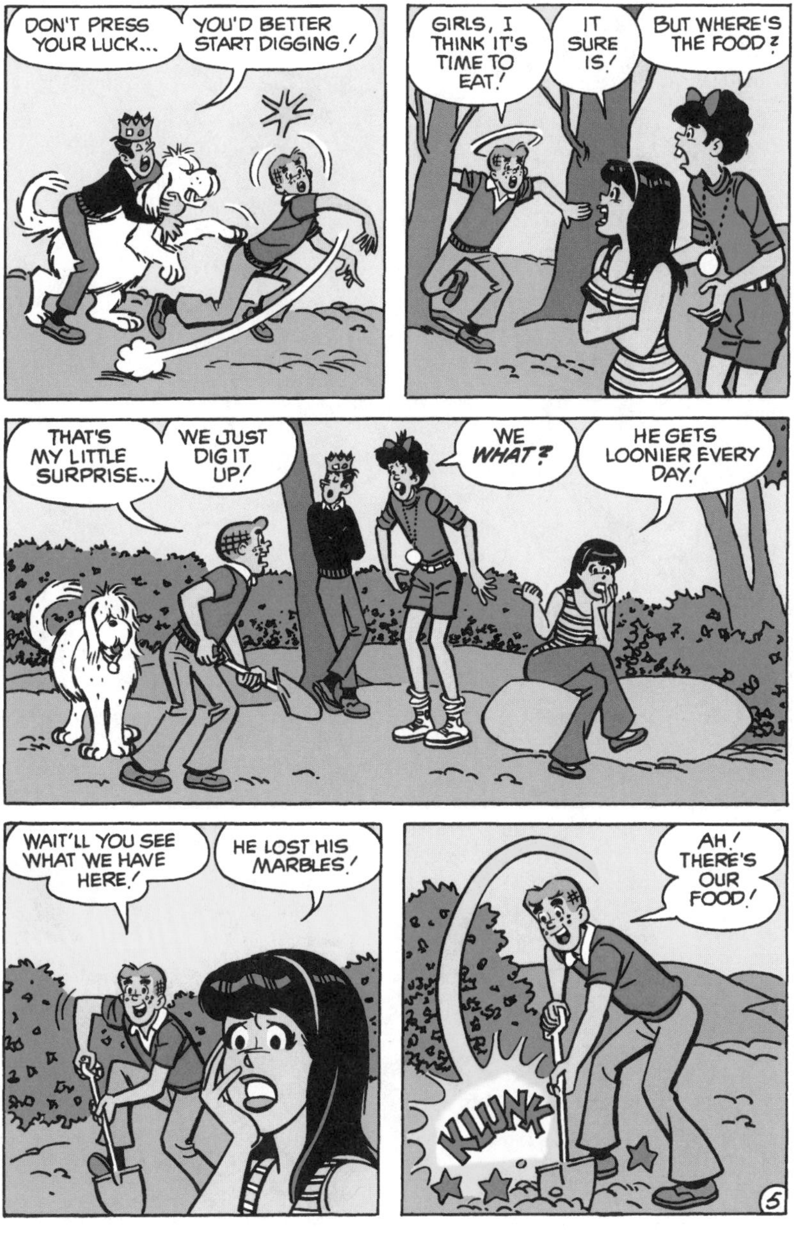
DON'T PRESS YOUR LUCK...
YOU'D BETTER START DIGGING!
GIRLS, I THINK IT'S TIME TO EAT!
IT SURE IS!
BUT WHERE'S THE FOOD?
THAT'S MY LITTLE SURPRISE...
WE JUST DIG IT UP!
WE *WHAT?*
HE GETS LOONIER EVERY DAY!
WAIT'LL YOU SEE WHAT WE HAVE HERE!
HE LOST HIS MARBLES!
AH! THERE'S OUR FOOD!
KLUNK
5

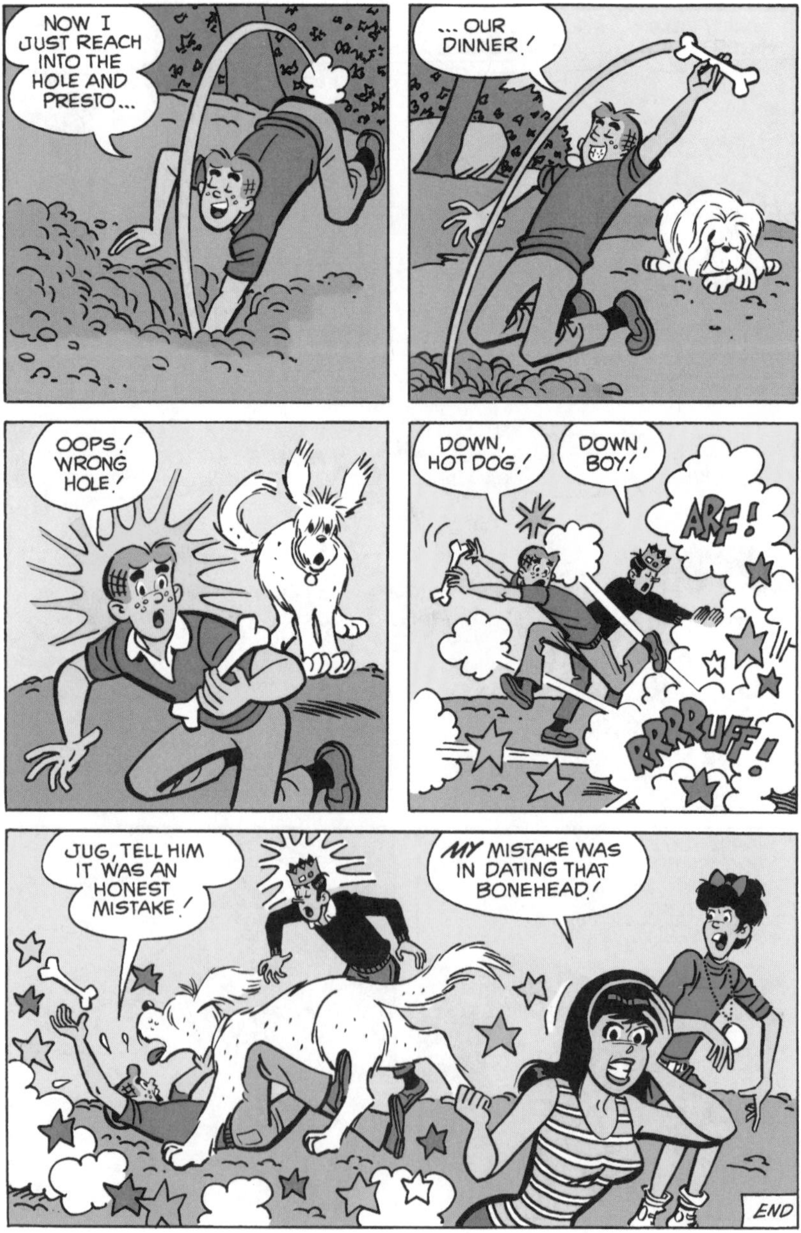
NOW I JUST REACH INTO THE HOLE AND PRESTO...
... OUR DINNER!
OOPS! WRONG HOLE!
DOWN, HOT DOG!
DOWN, BOY!
ARF!
RRRRUFF!
JUG, TELL HIM IT WAS AN HONEST MISTAKE!
MY MISTAKE WAS IN DATING THAT BONEHEAD!
END

Archie -in- "I Saw Him First"

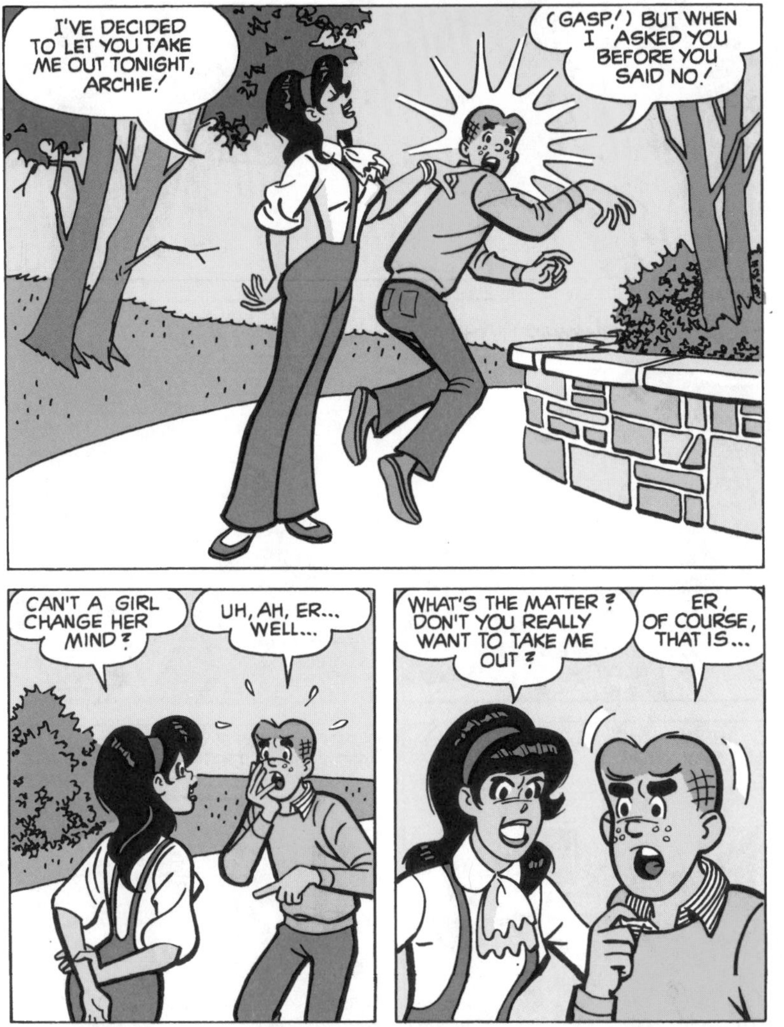
I'VE DECIDED TO LET YOU TAKE ME OUT TONIGHT, ARCHIE!
(GASP!) BUT WHEN I ASKED YOU BEFORE YOU SAID NO!
CAN'T A GIRL CHANGE HER MIND?
UH, AH, ER... WELL...
WHAT'S THE MATTER? DON'T YOU REALLY WANT TO TAKE ME OUT?
ER, OF COURSE, THAT IS...

Story & Pencils: Al Hartley

Inks: Jon D'Agostino   Letters: Bill Yoshida

Originally printed in EVERYTHING'S ARCHIE #12, FEBRUARY 1971

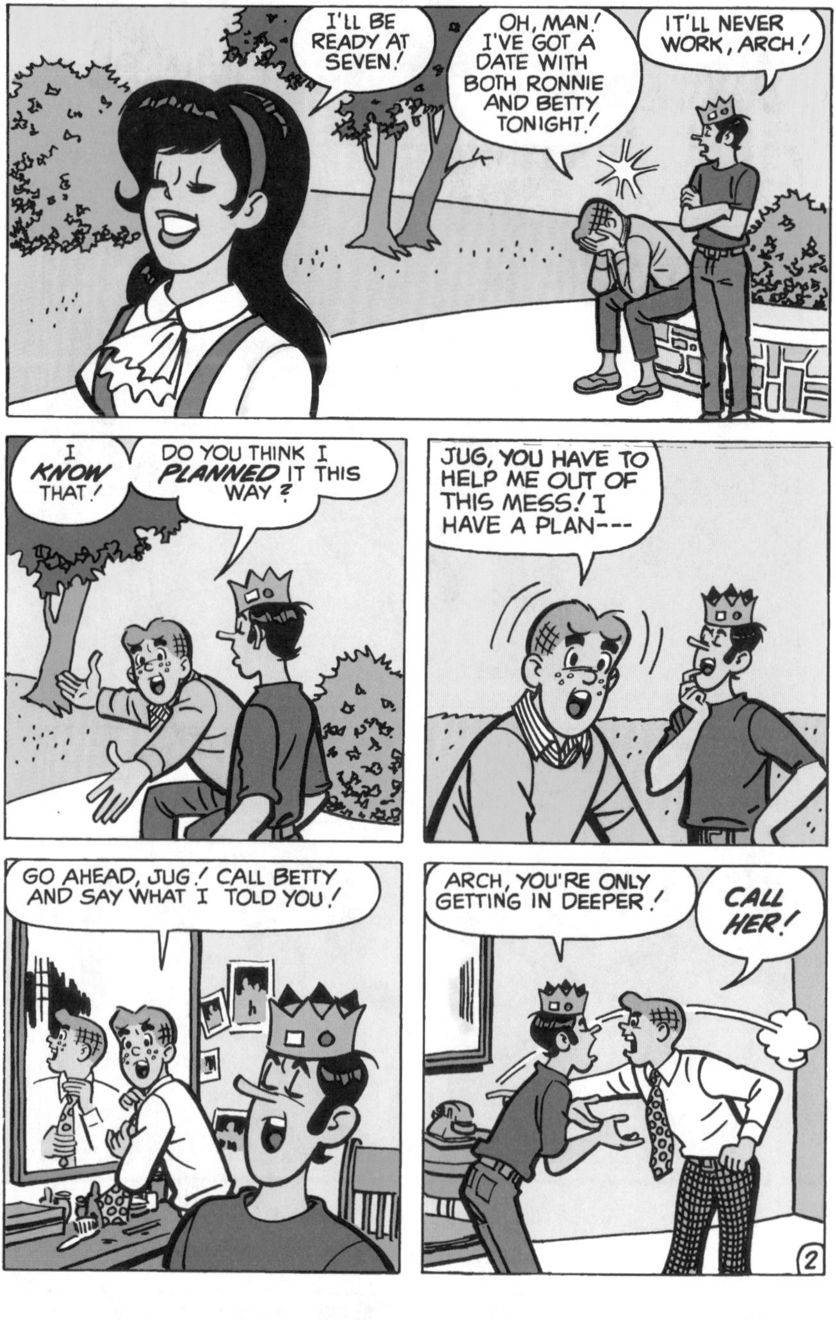
I'LL BE READY AT SEVEN!
OH, MAN! I'VE GOT A DATE WITH BOTH RONNIE AND BETTY TONIGHT!
IT'LL NEVER WORK, ARCH!
I KNOW THAT!
DO YOU THINK I PLANNED IT THIS WAY?
JUG, YOU HAVE TO HELP ME OUT OF THIS MESS! I HAVE A PLAN---
GO AHEAD, JUG! CALL BETTY AND SAY WHAT I TOLD YOU!
ARCH, YOU'RE ONLY GETTING IN DEEPER!
CALL HER!
2

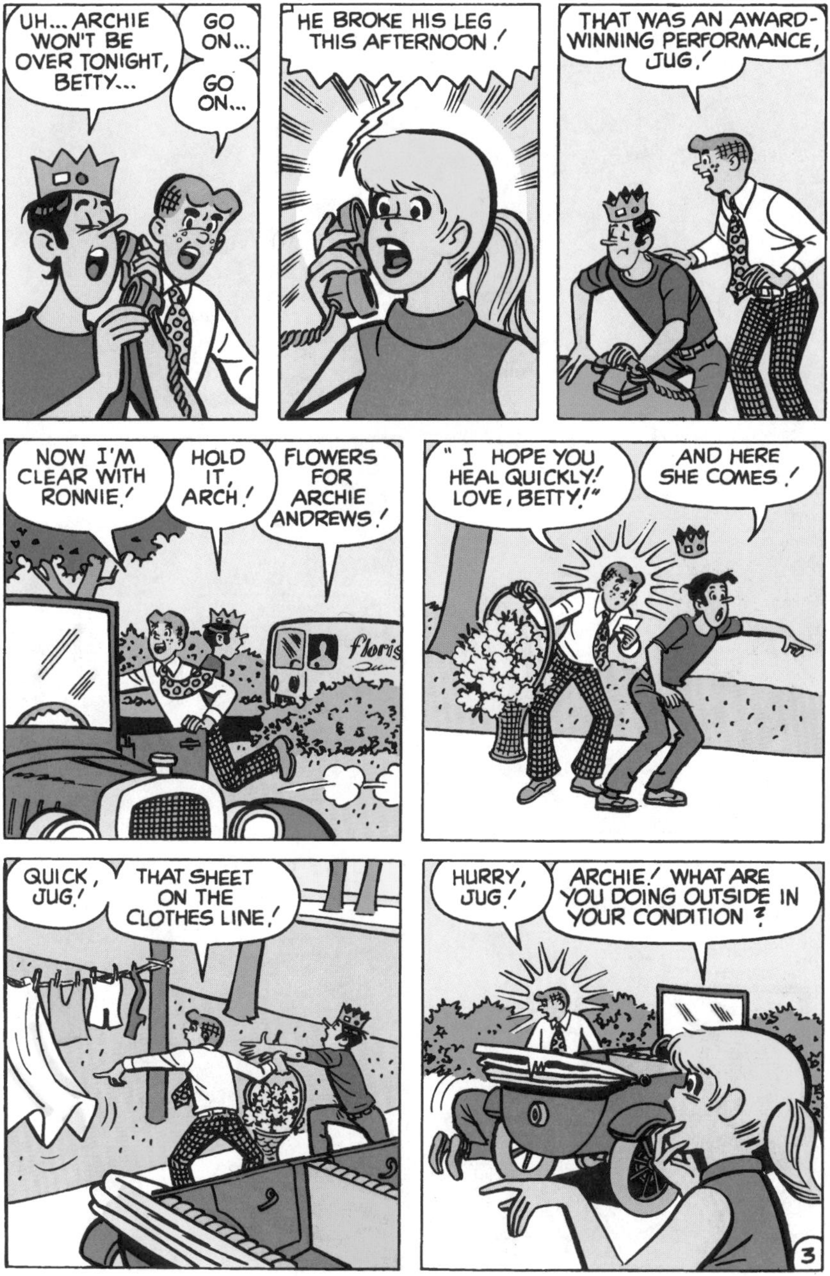
UH... ARCHIE WON'T BE OVER TONIGHT, BETTY...
GO ON...
GO ON...
HE BROKE HIS LEG THIS AFTERNOON!
THAT WAS AN AWARD-WINNING PERFORMANCE, JUG!
NOW I'M CLEAR WITH RONNIE!
HOLD IT, ARCH!
FLOWERS FOR ARCHIE ANDREWS!
floris
"I HOPE YOU HEAL QUICKLY! LOVE, BETTY!"
AND HERE SHE COMES!
QUICK, JUG!
THAT SHEET ON THE CLOTHES LINE!
HURRY, JUG!
ARCHIE! WHAT ARE YOU DOING OUTSIDE IN YOUR CONDITION?
3

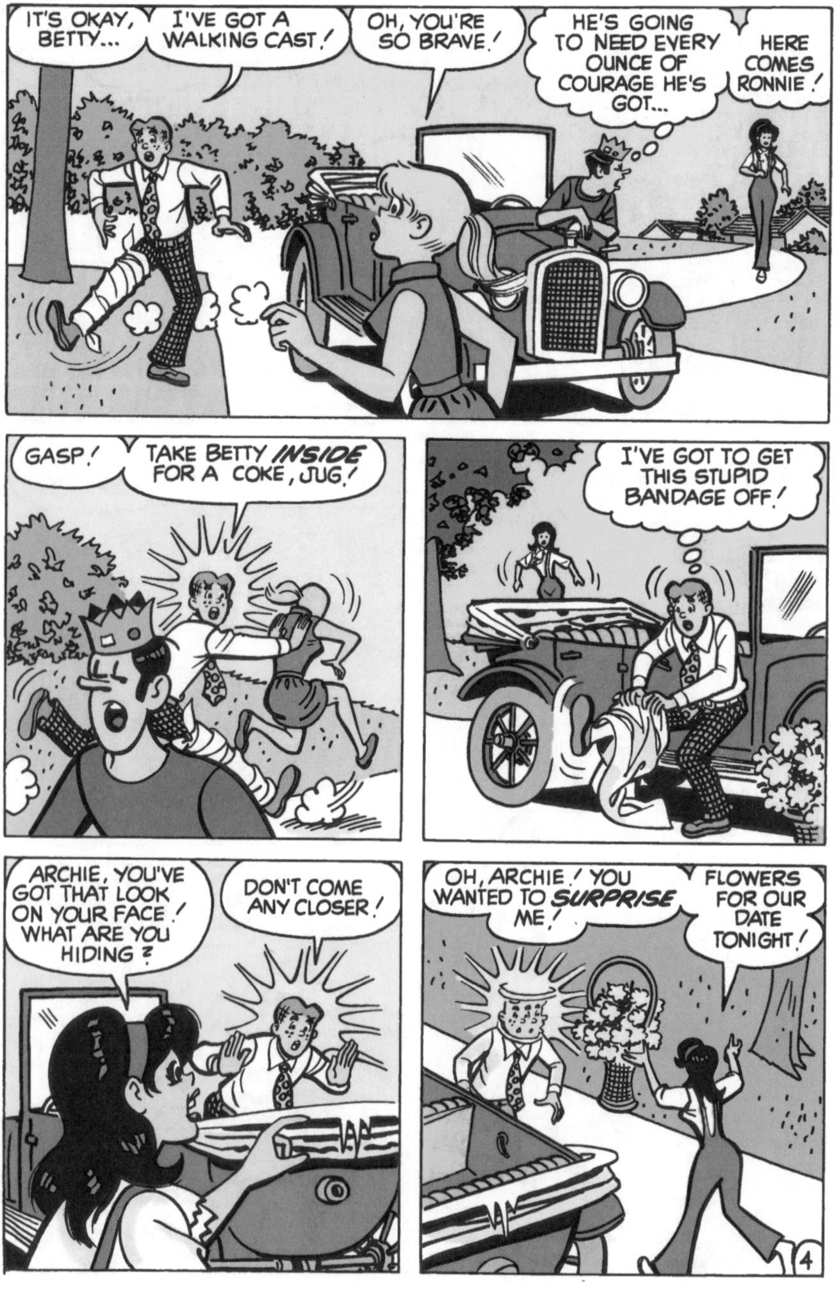
IT'S OKAY, BETTY...
I'VE GOT A WALKING CAST!
OH, YOU'RE SO BRAVE!
HE'S GOING TO NEED EVERY OUNCE OF COURAGE HE'S GOT...
HERE COMES RONNIE!
GASP!
TAKE BETTY *INSIDE* FOR A COKE, JUG!
I'VE GOT TO GET THIS STUPID BANDAGE OFF!
ARCHIE, YOU'VE GOT THAT LOOK ON YOUR FACE! WHAT ARE YOU HIDING?
DON'T COME ANY CLOSER!
OH, ARCHIE! YOU WANTED TO *SURPRISE* ME!
FLOWERS FOR OUR DATE TONIGHT!
4

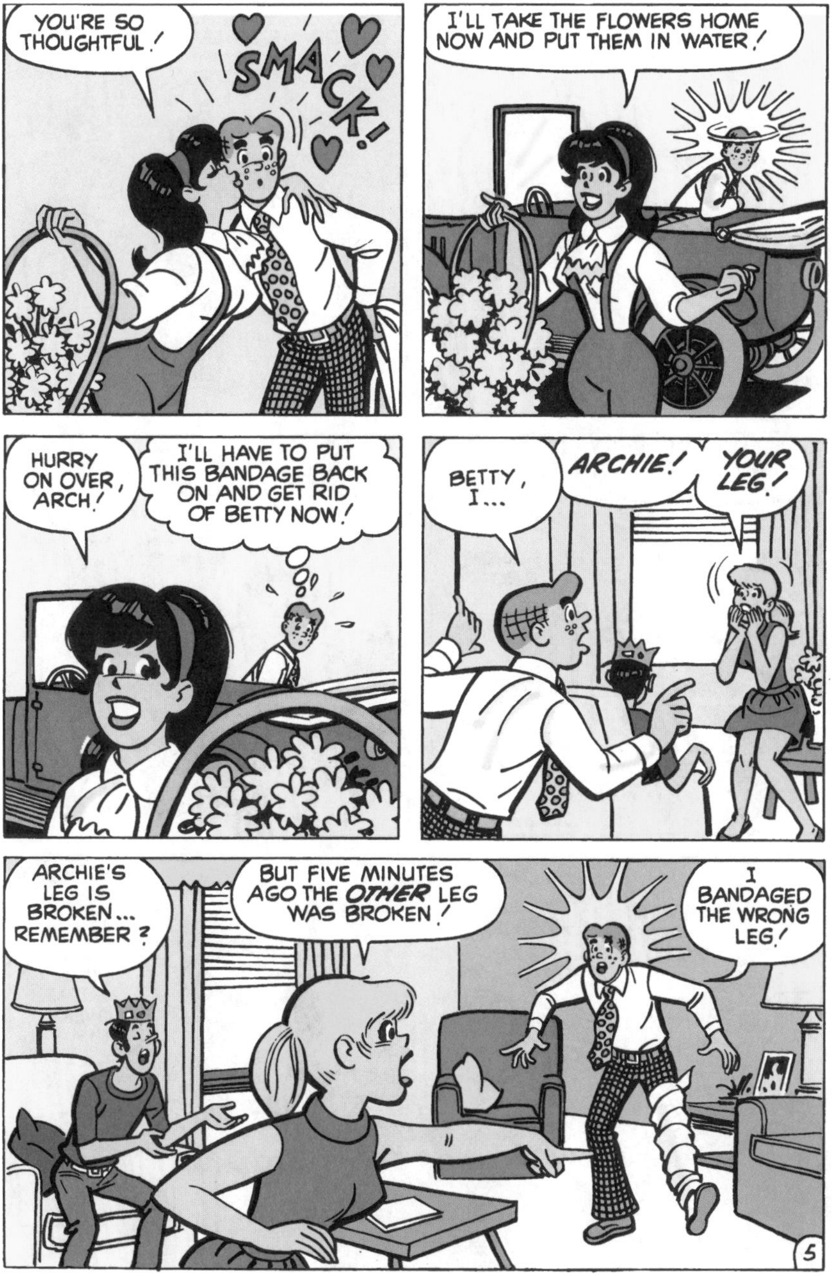
YOU'RE SO THOUGHTFUL!
SMACK!
I'LL TAKE THE FLOWERS HOME NOW AND PUT THEM IN WATER!
HURRY ON OVER, ARCH!
I'LL HAVE TO PUT THIS BANDAGE BACK ON AND GET RID OF BETTY NOW!
BETTY, I...
ARCHIE!
YOUR LEG!
ARCHIE'S LEG IS BROKEN... REMEMBER?
BUT FIVE MINUTES AGO THE OTHER LEG WAS BROKEN!
I BANDAGED THE WRONG LEG!
5

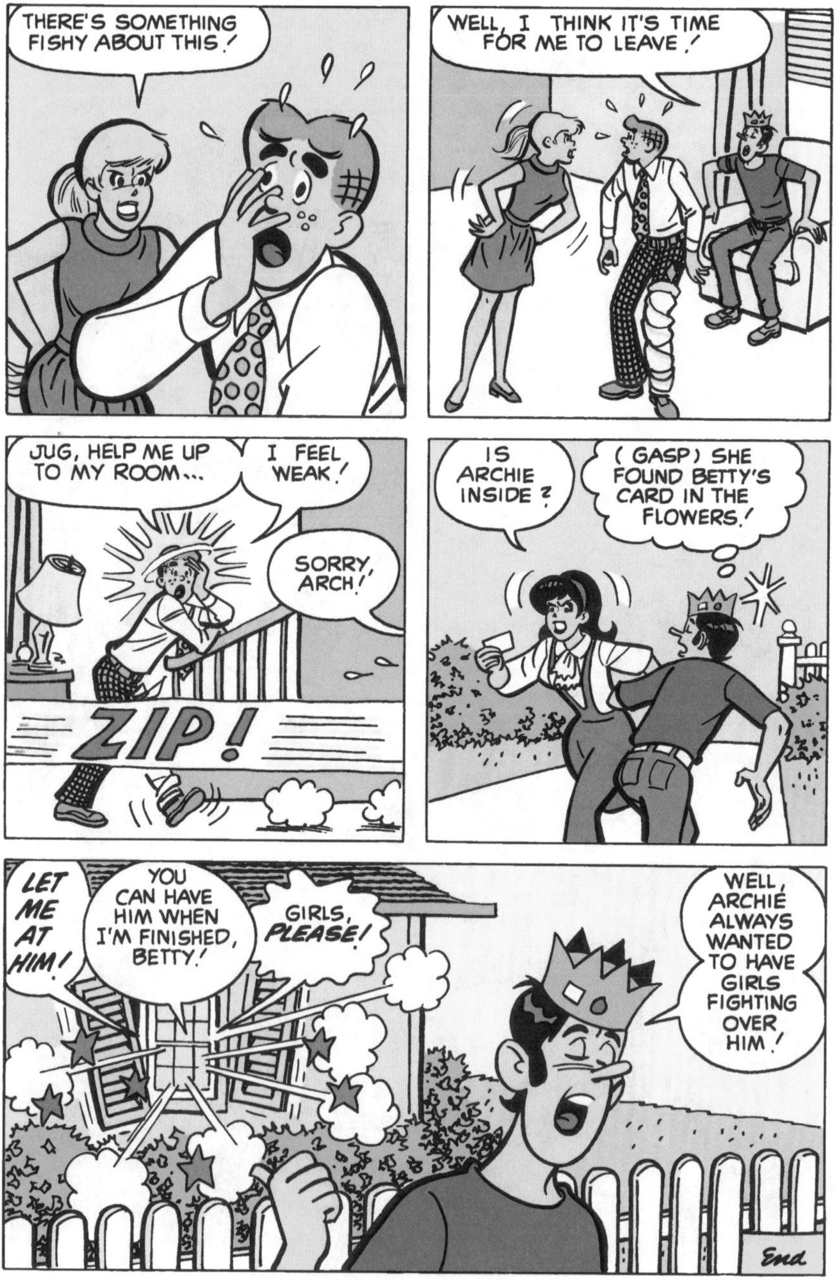
THERE'S SOMETHING FISHY ABOUT THIS!
WELL, I THINK IT'S TIME FOR ME TO LEAVE!
JUG, HELP ME UP TO MY ROOM...
I FEEL WEAK!
SORRY, ARCH!
ZIP!
IS ARCHIE INSIDE?
(GASP) SHE FOUND BETTY'S CARD IN THE FLOWERS!
LET ME AT HIM!
YOU CAN HAVE HIM WHEN I'M FINISHED, BETTY!
GIRLS, PLEASE!
WELL, ARCHIE ALWAYS WANTED TO HAVE GIRLS FIGHTING OVER HIM!
End

Archie "The MONEY GAME!"

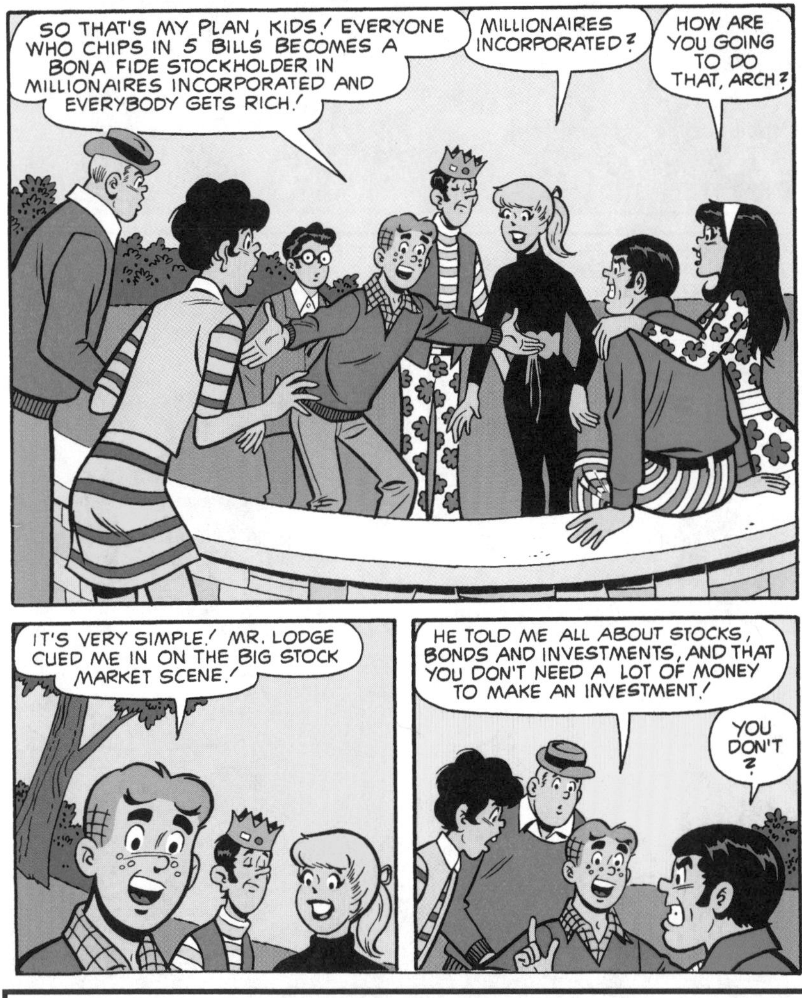
SO THAT'S MY PLAN, KIDS! EVERYONE WHO CHIPS IN 5 BILLS BECOMES A BONA FIDE STOCKHOLDER IN MILLIONAIRES INCORPORATED AND EVERYBODY GETS RICH!
MILLIONAIRES INCORPORATED?
HOW ARE YOU GOING TO DO THAT, ARCH?
IT'S VERY SIMPLE! MR. LODGE CUED ME IN ON THE BIG STOCK MARKET SCENE!
HE TOLD ME ALL ABOUT STOCKS, BONDS AND INVESTMENTS, AND THAT YOU DON'T NEED A LOT OF MONEY TO MAKE AN INVESTMENT!
YOU DON'T?

Story & Pencils: Al Hartley
Inks: Jon D'Agostino   Letters: Bill Yoshida

Originally printed in EVERYTHING'S ARCHIE #13, APRIL 1971

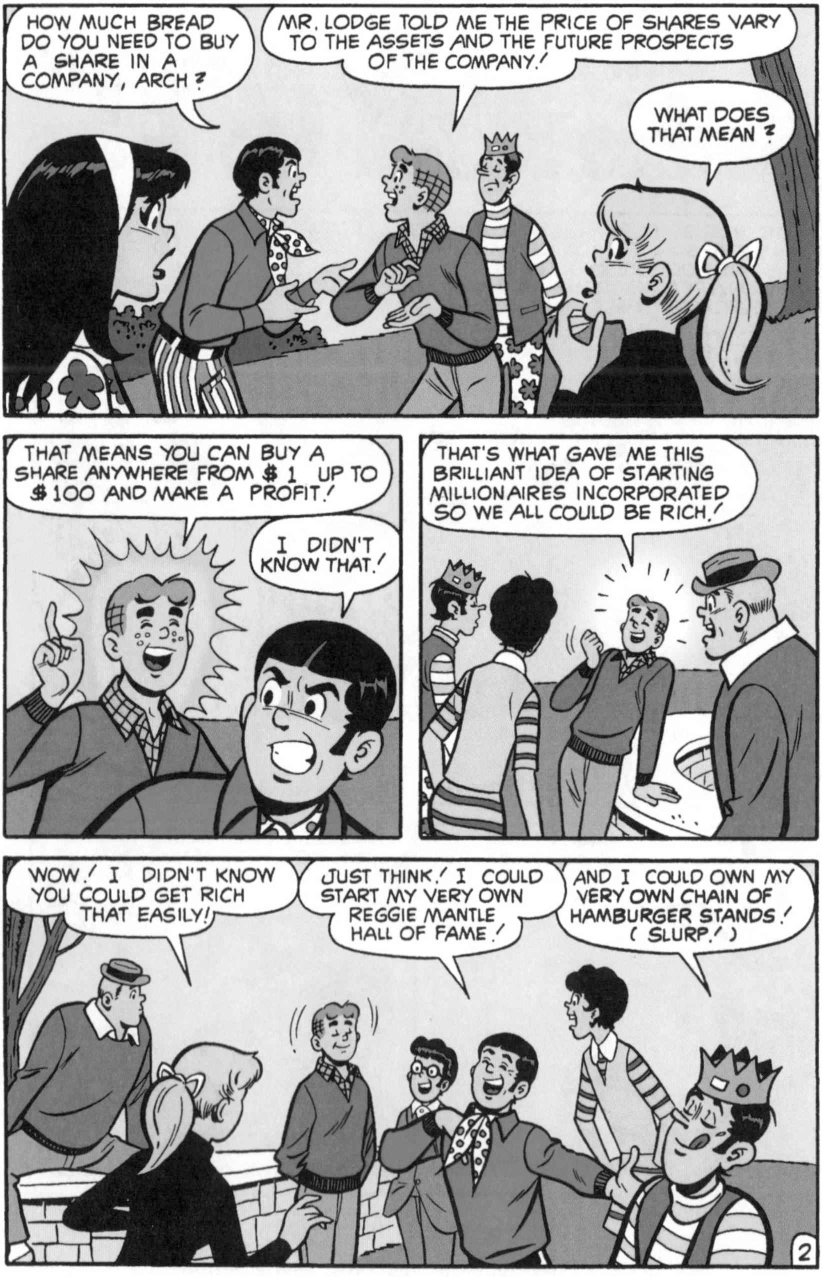
HOW MUCH BREAD DO YOU NEED TO BUY A SHARE IN A COMPANY, ARCH ?
MR. LODGE TOLD ME THE PRICE OF SHARES VARY TO THE ASSETS AND THE FUTURE PROSPECTS OF THE COMPANY!
WHAT DOES THAT MEAN ?
THAT MEANS YOU CAN BUY A SHARE ANYWHERE FROM $ 1 UP TO $ 100 AND MAKE A PROFIT!
I DIDN'T KNOW THAT!
THAT'S WHAT GAVE ME THIS BRILLIANT IDEA OF STARTING MILLIONAIRES INCORPORATED SO WE ALL COULD BE RICH!
WOW! I DIDN'T KNOW YOU COULD GET RICH THAT EASILY!
JUST THINK! I COULD START MY VERY OWN REGGIE MANTLE HALL OF FAME!
AND I COULD OWN MY VERY OWN CHAIN OF HAMBURGER STANDS! (SLURP!)
2

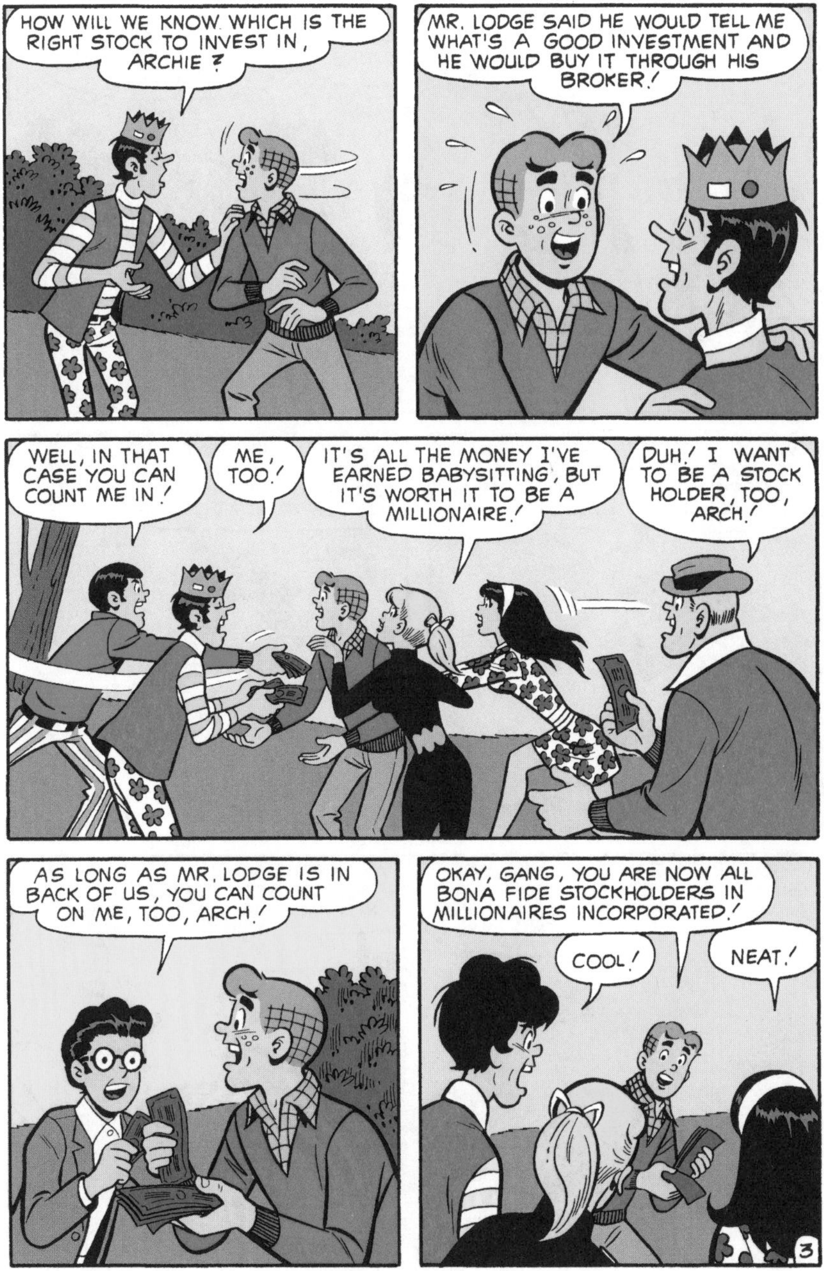
HOW WILL WE KNOW WHICH IS THE RIGHT STOCK TO INVEST IN, ARCHIE?
MR. LODGE SAID HE WOULD TELL ME WHAT'S A GOOD INVESTMENT AND HE WOULD BUY IT THROUGH HIS BROKER!
WELL, IN THAT CASE YOU CAN COUNT ME IN!
ME, TOO!
IT'S ALL THE MONEY I'VE EARNED BABYSITTING, BUT IT'S WORTH IT TO BE A MILLIONAIRE!
DUH! I WANT TO BE A STOCK HOLDER, TOO, ARCH!
AS LONG AS MR. LODGE IS IN BACK OF US, YOU CAN COUNT ON ME, TOO, ARCH!
OKAY, GANG, YOU ARE NOW ALL BONA FIDE STOCKHOLDERS IN MILLIONAIRES INCORPORATED!
COOL!
NEAT!
3

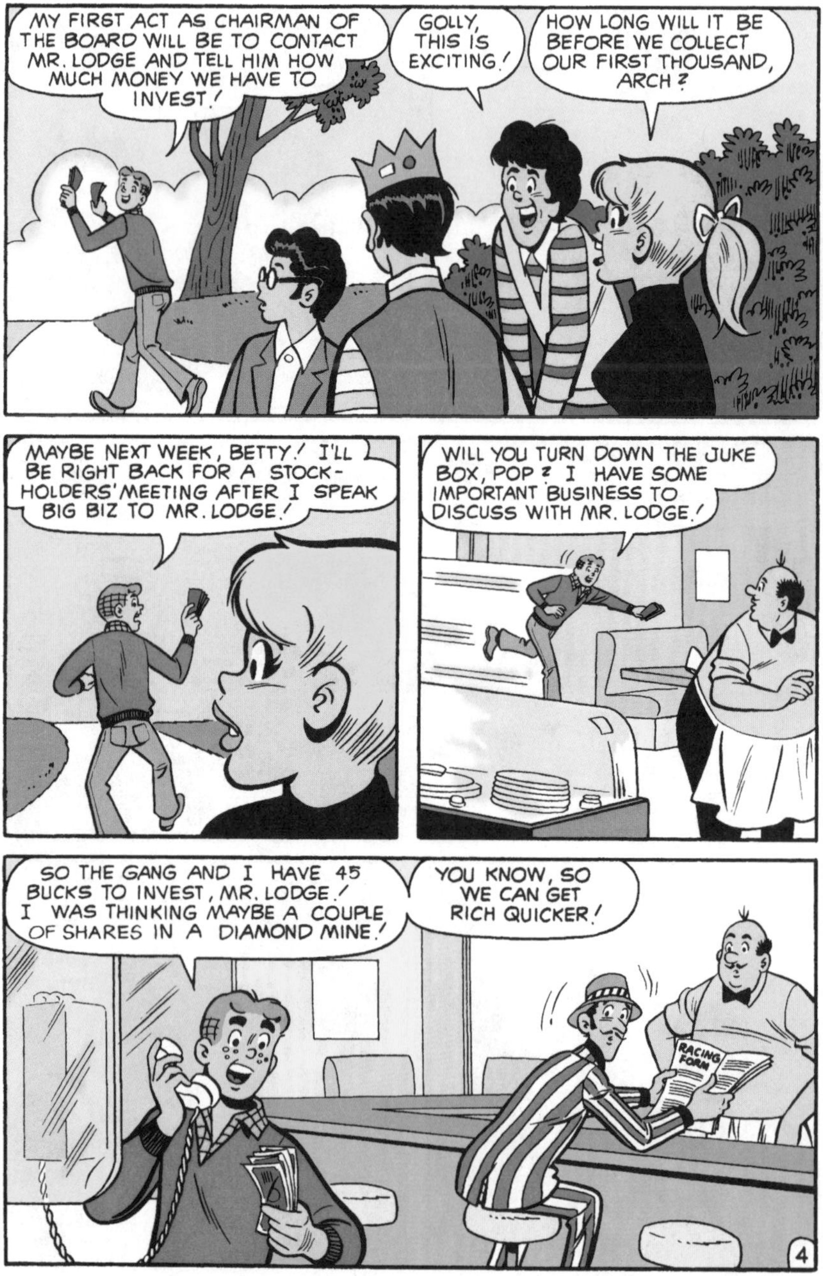
MY FIRST ACT AS CHAIRMAN OF THE BOARD WILL BE TO CONTACT MR. LODGE AND TELL HIM HOW MUCH MONEY WE HAVE TO INVEST!
GOLLY, THIS IS EXCITING!
HOW LONG WILL IT BE BEFORE WE COLLECT OUR FIRST THOUSAND, ARCH?
MAYBE NEXT WEEK, BETTY! I'LL BE RIGHT BACK FOR A STOCK-HOLDERS' MEETING AFTER I SPEAK BIG BIZ TO MR. LODGE!
WILL YOU TURN DOWN THE JUKE BOX, POP? I HAVE SOME IMPORTANT BUSINESS TO DISCUSS WITH MR. LODGE!
SO THE GANG AND I HAVE 45 BUCKS TO INVEST, MR. LODGE! I WAS THINKING MAYBE A COUPLE OF SHARES IN A DIAMOND MINE!
YOU KNOW, SO WE CAN GET RICH QUICKER!
RACING FORM
4

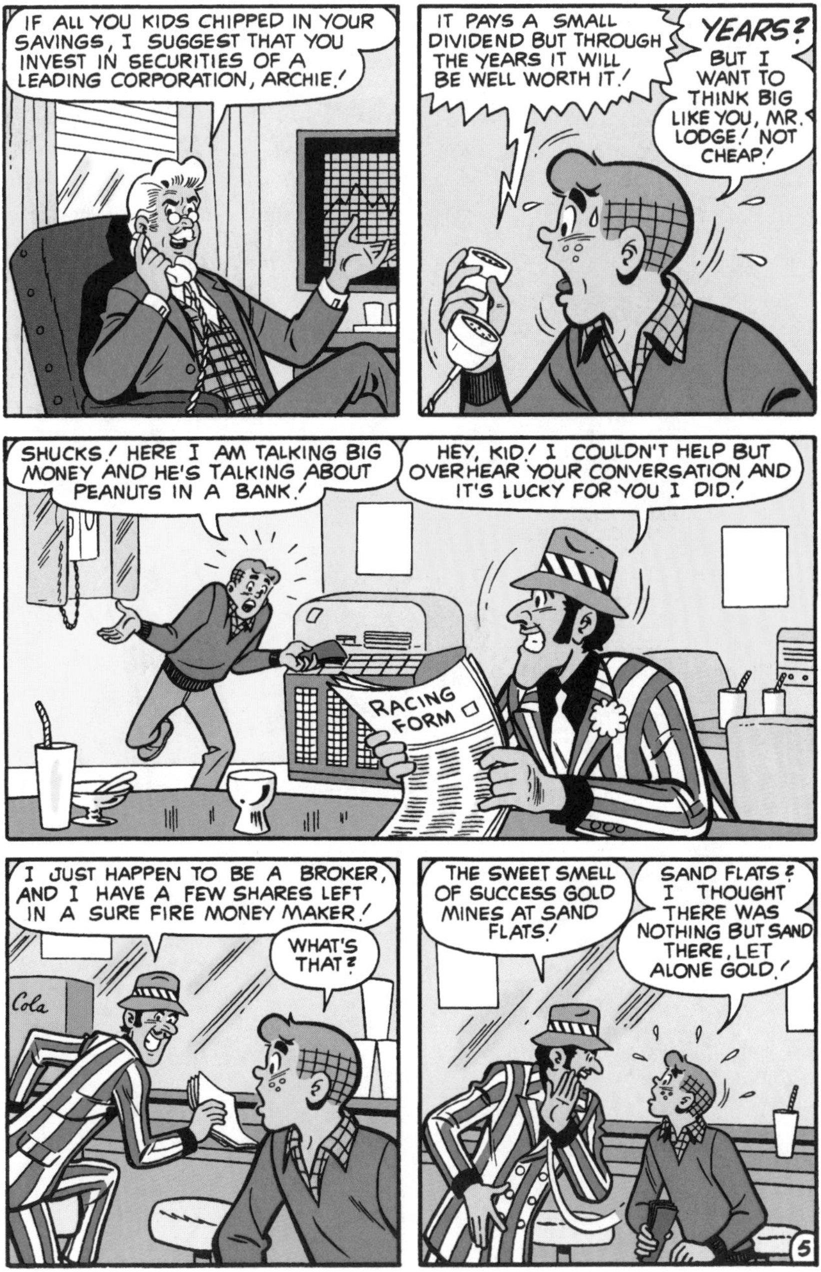
IF ALL YOU KIDS CHIPPED IN YOUR SAVINGS, I SUGGEST THAT YOU INVEST IN SECURITIES OF A LEADING CORPORATION, ARCHIE!
IT PAYS A SMALL DIVIDEND BUT THROUGH THE YEARS IT WILL BE WELL WORTH IT!
YEARS? BUT I WANT TO THINK BIG LIKE YOU, MR. LODGE! NOT CHEAP!
SHUCKS! HERE I AM TALKING BIG MONEY AND HE'S TALKING ABOUT PEANUTS IN A BANK!
HEY, KID! I COULDN'T HELP BUT OVERHEAR YOUR CONVERSATION AND IT'S LUCKY FOR YOU I DID!
RACING FORM
I JUST HAPPEN TO BE A BROKER, AND I HAVE A FEW SHARES LEFT IN A SURE FIRE MONEY MAKER!
WHAT'S THAT?
Cola
THE SWEET SMELL OF SUCCESS GOLD MINES AT SAND FLATS!
SAND FLATS? I THOUGHT THERE WAS NOTHING BUT SAND THERE, LET ALONE GOLD!
5

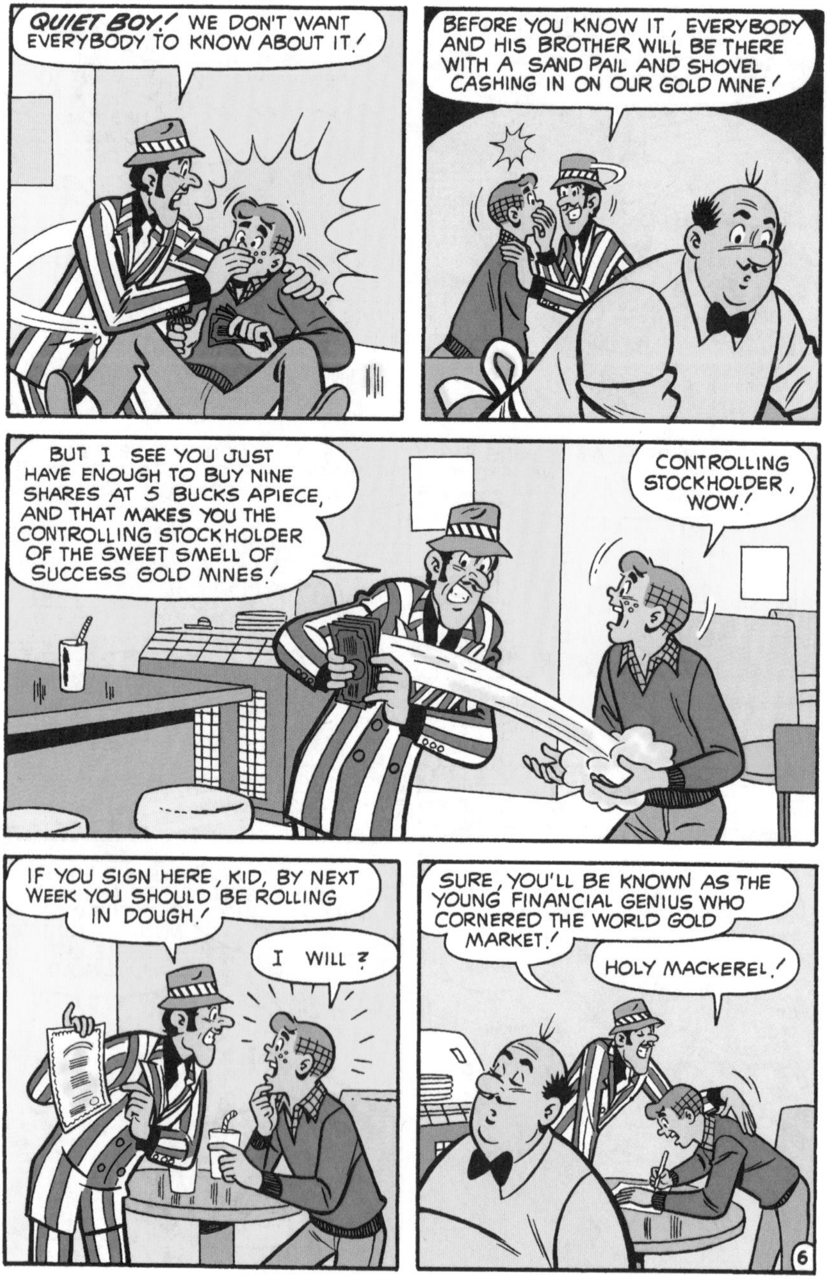
QUIET BOY! WE DON'T WANT EVERYBODY TO KNOW ABOUT IT!
BEFORE YOU KNOW IT, EVERYBODY AND HIS BROTHER WILL BE THERE WITH A SAND PAIL AND SHOVEL CASHING IN ON OUR GOLD MINE!
BUT I SEE YOU JUST HAVE ENOUGH TO BUY NINE SHARES AT 5 BUCKS APIECE, AND THAT MAKES YOU THE CONTROLLING STOCKHOLDER OF THE SWEET SMELL OF SUCCESS GOLD MINES!
CONTROLLING STOCKHOLDER, WOW!
IF YOU SIGN HERE, KID, BY NEXT WEEK YOU SHOULD BE ROLLING IN DOUGH!
I WILL ?
SURE, YOU'LL BE KNOWN AS THE YOUNG FINANCIAL GENIUS WHO CORNERED THE WORLD GOLD MARKET!
HOLY MACKEREL!
6

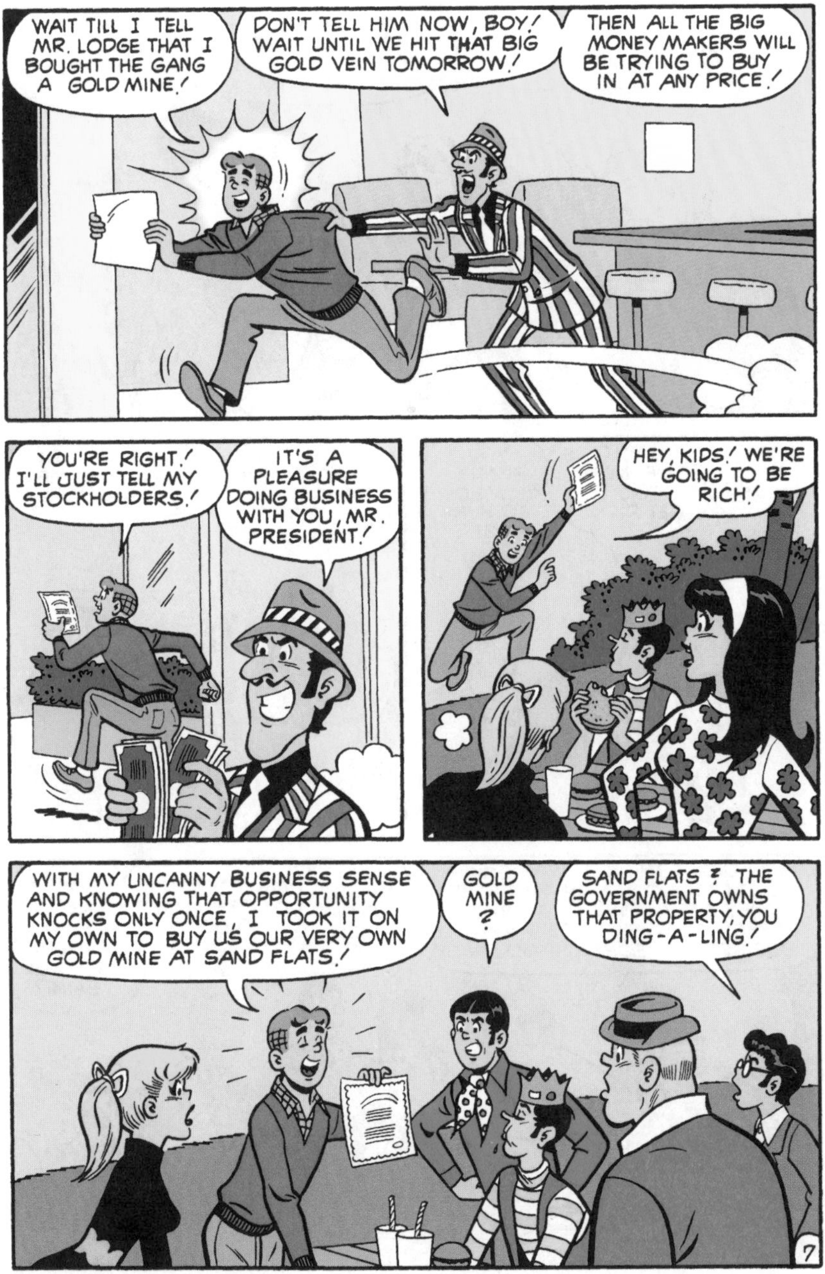
WAIT TILL I TELL MR. LODGE THAT I BOUGHT THE GANG A GOLD MINE!
DON'T TELL HIM NOW, BOY! WAIT UNTIL WE HIT THAT BIG GOLD VEIN TOMORROW!
THEN ALL THE BIG MONEY MAKERS WILL BE TRYING TO BUY IN AT ANY PRICE!
YOU'RE RIGHT! I'LL JUST TELL MY STOCKHOLDERS!
IT'S A PLEASURE DOING BUSINESS WITH YOU, MR. PRESIDENT!
HEY, KIDS! WE'RE GOING TO BE RICH!
WITH MY UNCANNY BUSINESS SENSE AND KNOWING THAT OPPORTUNITY KNOCKS ONLY ONCE, I TOOK IT ON MY OWN TO BUY US OUR VERY OWN GOLD MINE AT SAND FLATS!
GOLD MINE?
SAND FLATS?! THE GOVERNMENT OWNS THAT PROPERTY, YOU DING-A-LING!
7

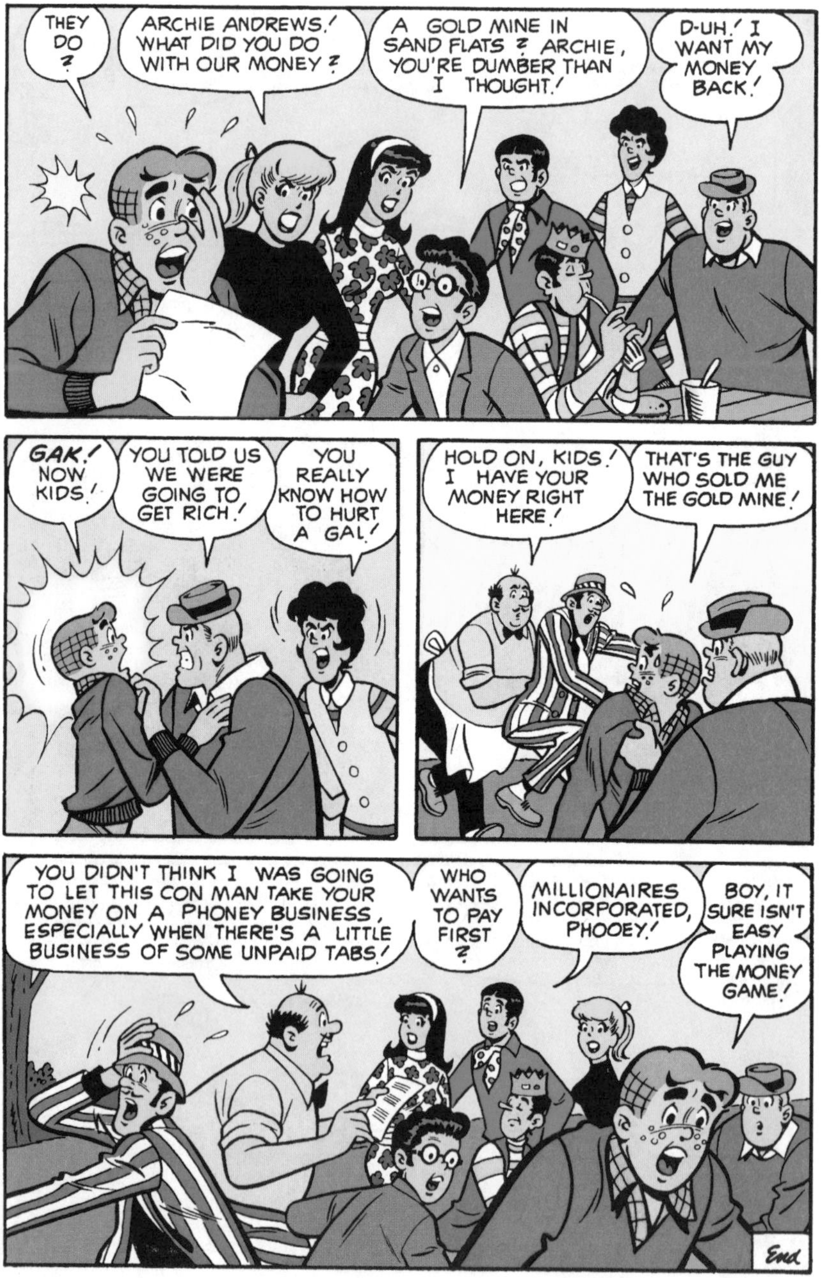
THEY DO ?
ARCHIE ANDREWS! WHAT DID YOU DO WITH OUR MONEY ?
A GOLD MINE IN SAND FLATS ? ARCHIE, YOU'RE DUMBER THAN I THOUGHT!
D-UH! I WANT MY MONEY BACK!
GAK! NOW KIDS!
YOU TOLD US WE WERE GOING TO GET RICH!
YOU REALLY KNOW HOW TO HURT A GAL!
HOLD ON, KIDS! I HAVE YOUR MONEY RIGHT HERE!
THAT'S THE GUY WHO SOLD ME THE GOLD MINE!
YOU DIDN'T THINK I WAS GOING TO LET THIS CON MAN TAKE YOUR MONEY ON A PHONEY BUSINESS, ESPECIALLY WHEN THERE'S A LITTLE BUSINESS OF SOME UNPAID TABS!
WHO WANTS TO PAY FIRST ?
MILLIONAIRES INCORPORATED, PHOOEY!
BOY, IT SURE ISN'T EASY PLAYING THE MONEY GAME!
End

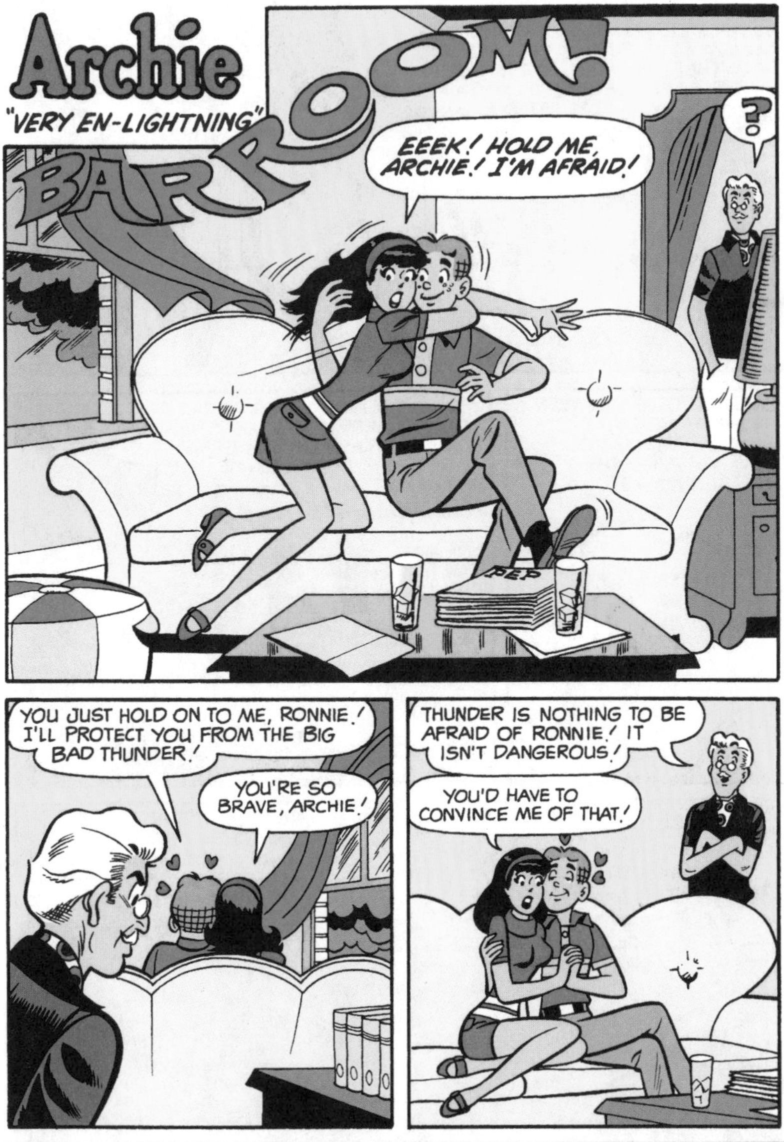
Archie
"VERY EN-LIGHTNING"
BARROOM!
EEEK! HOLD ME, ARCHIE! I'M AFRAID!
?
PEP
YOU JUST HOLD ON TO ME, RONNIE! I'LL PROTECT YOU FROM THE BIG BAD THUNDER!
YOU'RE SO BRAVE, ARCHIE!
THUNDER IS NOTHING TO BE AFRAID OF RONNIE! IT ISN'T DANGEROUS!
YOU'D HAVE TO CONVINCE ME OF THAT!

Story: George Gladir Pencils: Bob Bolling
Inks: Jon D'Agostino Letters: Bill Yoshida

Originally printed in EVERYTHING'S ARCHIE #13, APRIL 1971

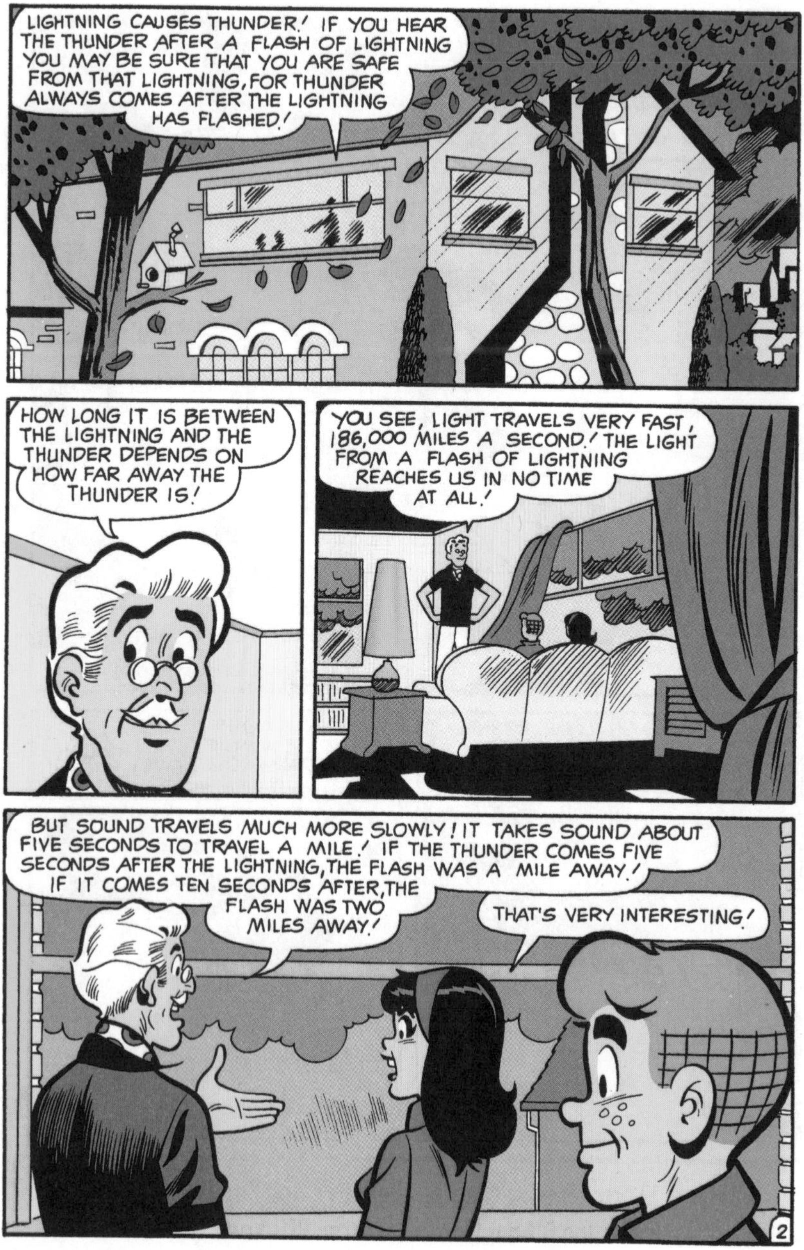
LIGHTNING CAUSES THUNDER! IF YOU HEAR THE THUNDER AFTER A FLASH OF LIGHTNING YOU MAY BE SURE THAT YOU ARE SAFE FROM THAT LIGHTNING, FOR THUNDER ALWAYS COMES AFTER THE LIGHTNING HAS FLASHED!
HOW LONG IT IS BETWEEN THE LIGHTNING AND THE THUNDER DEPENDS ON HOW FAR AWAY THE THUNDER IS!
YOU SEE, LIGHT TRAVELS VERY FAST, 186,000 MILES A SECOND! THE LIGHT FROM A FLASH OF LIGHTNING REACHES US IN NO TIME AT ALL!
BUT SOUND TRAVELS MUCH MORE SLOWLY! IT TAKES SOUND ABOUT FIVE SECONDS TO TRAVEL A MILE! IF THE THUNDER COMES FIVE SECONDS AFTER THE LIGHTNING, THE FLASH WAS A MILE AWAY! IF IT COMES TEN SECONDS AFTER, THE FLASH WAS TWO MILES AWAY!
THAT'S VERY INTERESTING!
2

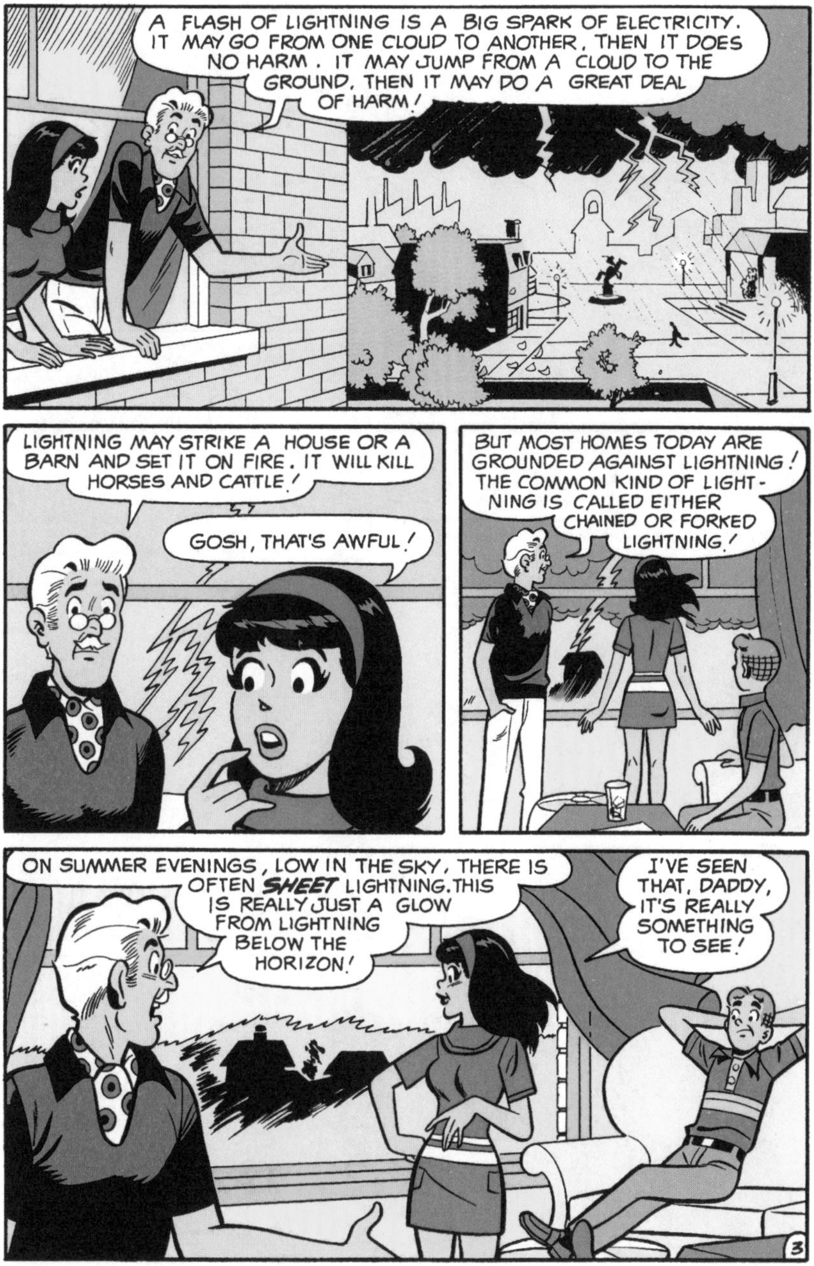
A FLASH OF LIGHTNING IS A BIG SPARK OF ELECTRICITY. IT MAY GO FROM ONE CLOUD TO ANOTHER, THEN IT DOES NO HARM. IT MAY JUMP FROM A CLOUD TO THE GROUND, THEN IT MAY DO A GREAT DEAL OF HARM!
LIGHTNING MAY STRIKE A HOUSE OR A BARN AND SET IT ON FIRE. IT WILL KILL HORSES AND CATTLE!
GOSH, THAT'S AWFUL!
BUT MOST HOMES TODAY ARE GROUNDED AGAINST LIGHTNING! THE COMMON KIND OF LIGHT-NING IS CALLED EITHER CHAINED OR FORKED LIGHTNING!
ON SUMMER EVENINGS, LOW IN THE SKY, THERE IS OFTEN SHEET LIGHTNING. THIS IS REALLY JUST A GLOW FROM LIGHTNING BELOW THE HORIZON!
I'VE SEEN THAT, DADDY, IT'S REALLY SOMETHING TO SEE!
3

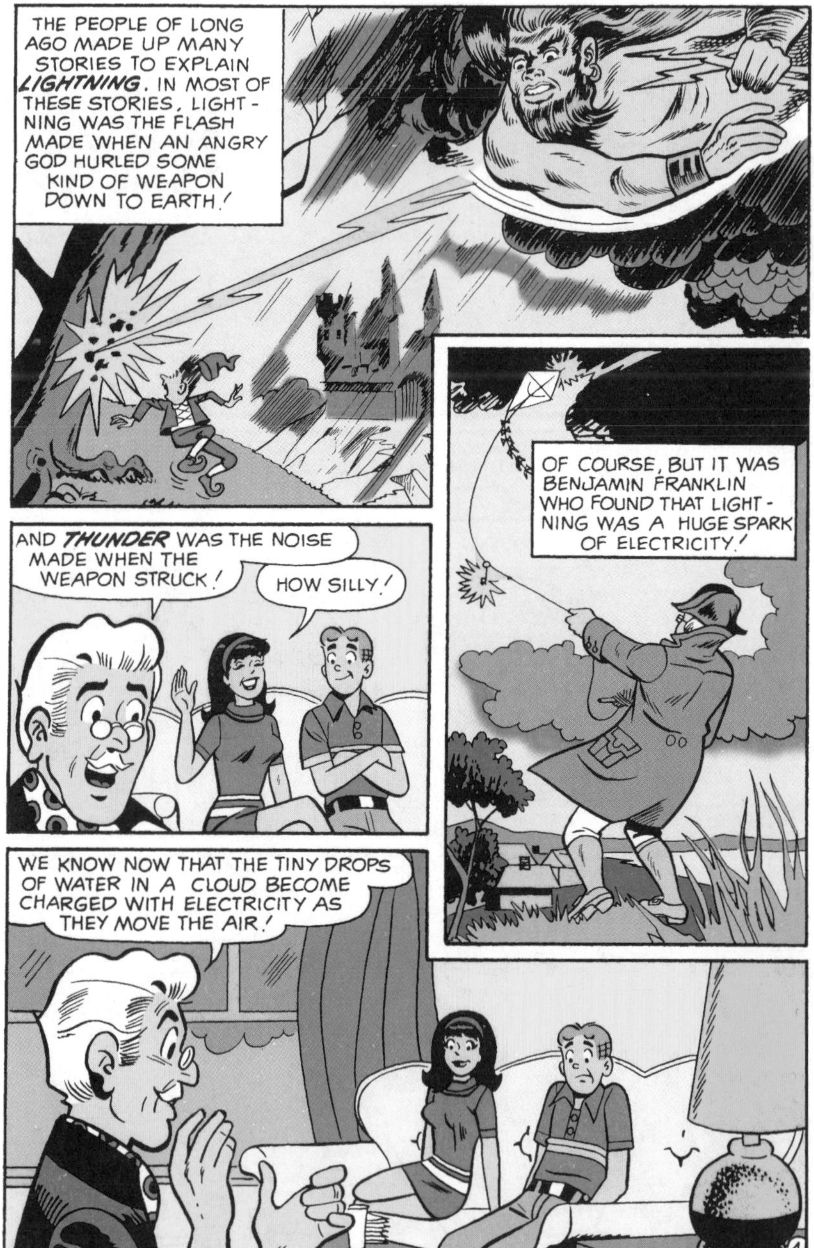
THE PEOPLE OF LONG AGO MADE UP MANY STORIES TO EXPLAIN LIGHTNING. IN MOST OF THESE STORIES, LIGHTNING WAS THE FLASH MADE WHEN AN ANGRY GOD HURLED SOME KIND OF WEAPON DOWN TO EARTH!
AND THUNDER WAS THE NOISE MADE WHEN THE WEAPON STRUCK!
HOW SILLY!
OF COURSE, BUT IT WAS BENJAMIN FRANKLIN WHO FOUND THAT LIGHTNING WAS A HUGE SPARK OF ELECTRICITY!
WE KNOW NOW THAT THE TINY DROPS OF WATER IN A CLOUD BECOME CHARGED WITH ELECTRICITY AS THEY MOVE THE AIR!
4

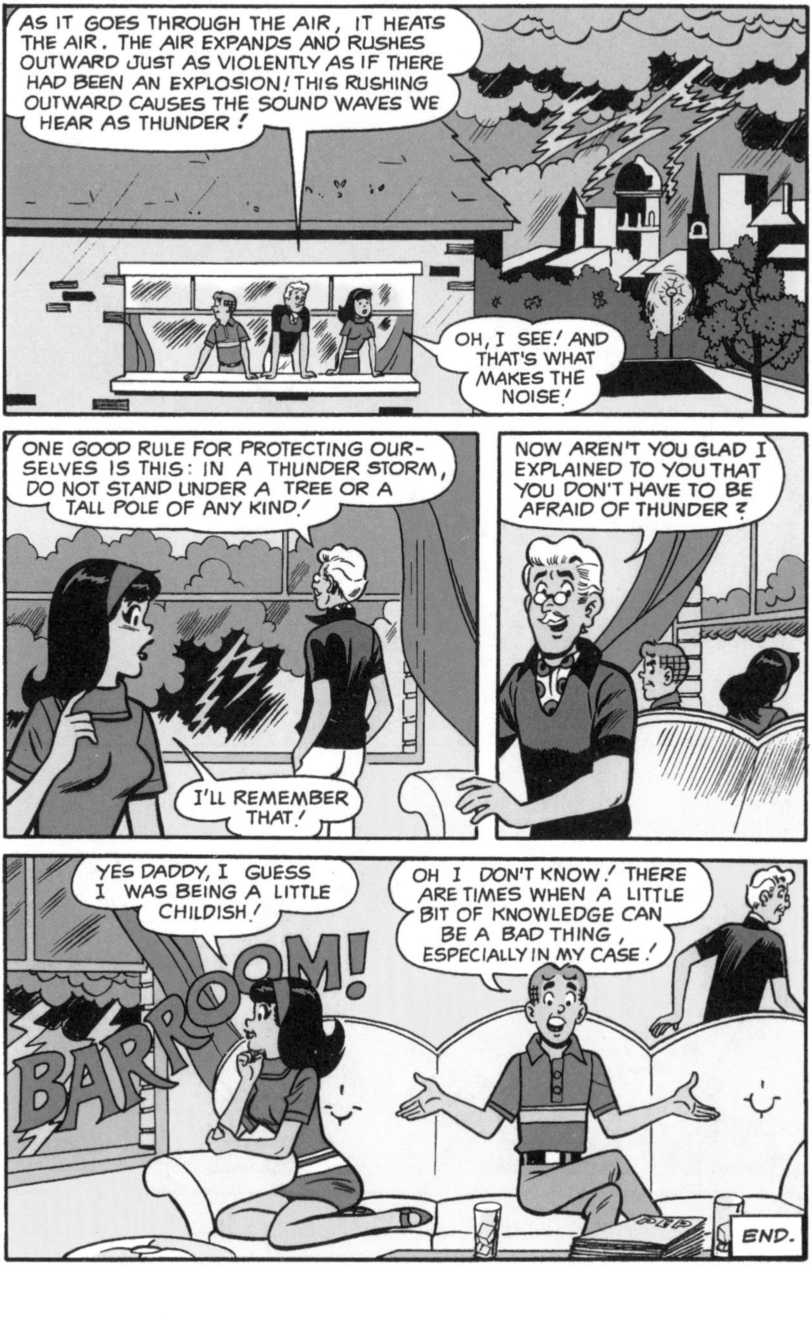
AS IT GOES THROUGH THE AIR, IT HEATS THE AIR. THE AIR EXPANDS AND RUSHES OUTWARD JUST AS VIOLENTLY AS IF THERE HAD BEEN AN EXPLOSION! THIS RUSHING OUTWARD CAUSES THE SOUND WAVES WE HEAR AS THUNDER!
OH, I SEE! AND THAT'S WHAT MAKES THE NOISE!
ONE GOOD RULE FOR PROTECTING OURSELVES IS THIS: IN A THUNDER STORM, DO NOT STAND UNDER A TREE OR A TALL POLE OF ANY KIND!
I'LL REMEMBER THAT!
NOW AREN'T YOU GLAD I EXPLAINED TO YOU THAT YOU DON'T HAVE TO BE AFRAID OF THUNDER?
YES DADDY, I GUESS I WAS BEING A LITTLE CHILDISH!
BARROOM!
OH I DON'T KNOW! THERE ARE TIMES WHEN A LITTLE BIT OF KNOWLEDGE CAN BE A BAD THING, ESPECIALLY IN MY CASE!
PEP
END.

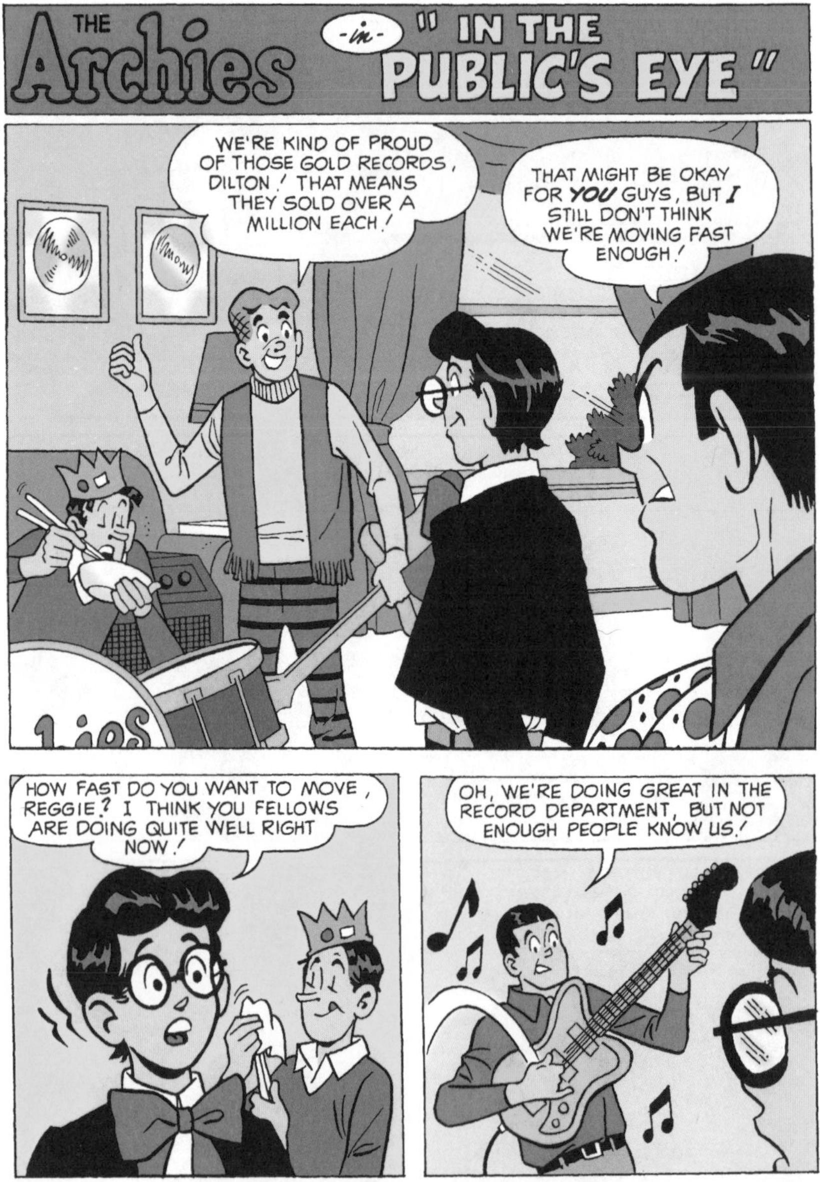
THE Archies -in- " IN THE PUBLIC'S EYE "
WE'RE KIND OF PROUD OF THOSE GOLD RECORDS, DILTON! THAT MEANS THEY SOLD OVER A MILLION EACH!
THAT MIGHT BE OKAY FOR YOU GUYS, BUT I STILL DON'T THINK WE'RE MOVING FAST ENOUGH!
HOW FAST DO YOU WANT TO MOVE, REGGIE? I THINK YOU FELLOWS ARE DOING QUITE WELL RIGHT NOW!
OH, WE'RE DOING GREAT IN THE RECORD DEPARTMENT, BUT NOT ENOUGH PEOPLE KNOW US!

Story: George Gladir **Art: Samm Schwartz**
Letters: Bill Yoshida **Colors: Barry Grossman**

Originally printed in EVERYTHING'S ARCHIE #14, JUNE 1971

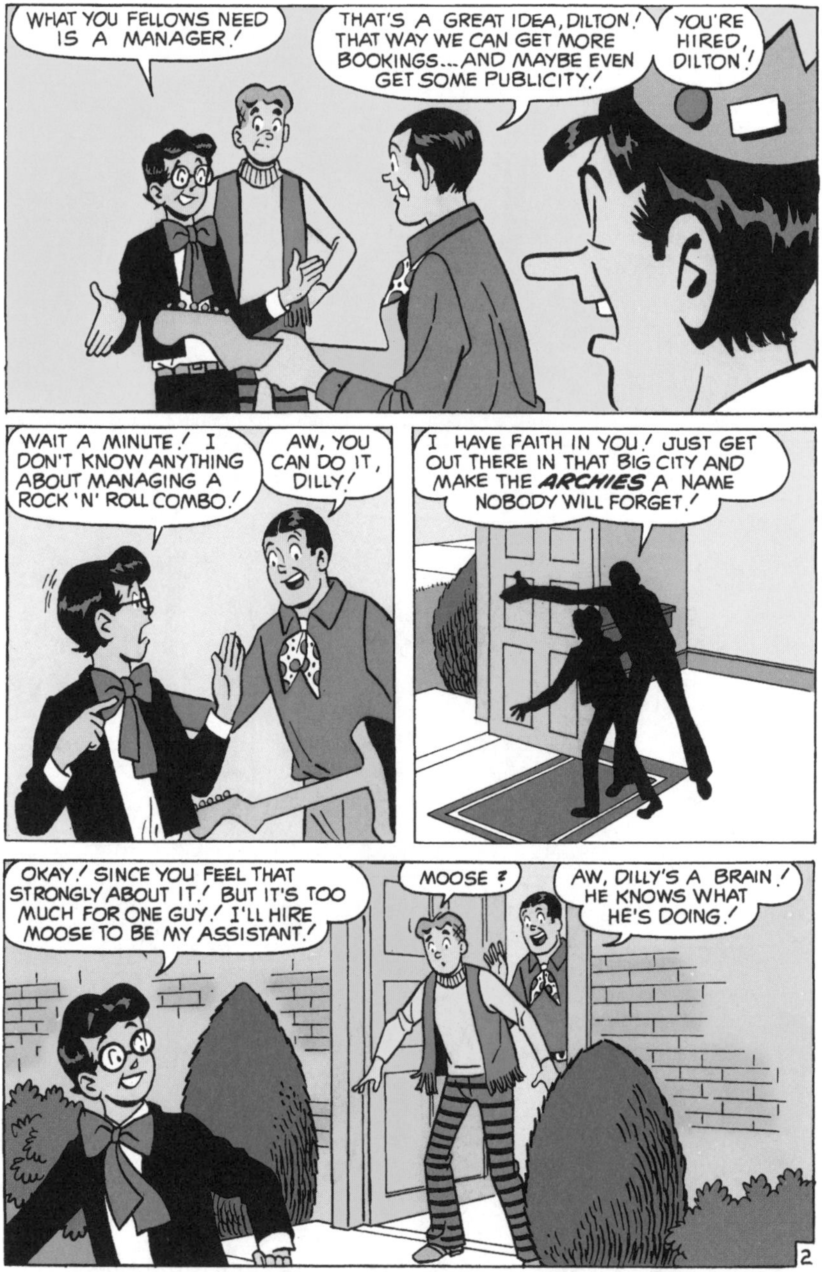
WHAT YOU FELLOWS NEED IS A MANAGER!
THAT'S A GREAT IDEA, DILTON! THAT WAY WE CAN GET MORE BOOKINGS... AND MAYBE EVEN GET SOME PUBLICITY!
YOU'RE HIRED, DILTON!
WAIT A MINUTE! I DON'T KNOW ANYTHING ABOUT MANAGING A ROCK 'N' ROLL COMBO!
AW, YOU CAN DO IT, DILLY!
I HAVE FAITH IN YOU! JUST GET OUT THERE IN THAT BIG CITY AND MAKE THE ARCHIES A NAME NOBODY WILL FORGET!
OKAY! SINCE YOU FEEL THAT STRONGLY ABOUT IT! BUT IT'S TOO MUCH FOR ONE GUY! I'LL HIRE MOOSE TO BE MY ASSISTANT!
MOOSE ?
AW, DILLY'S A BRAIN! HE KNOWS WHAT HE'S DOING!
2

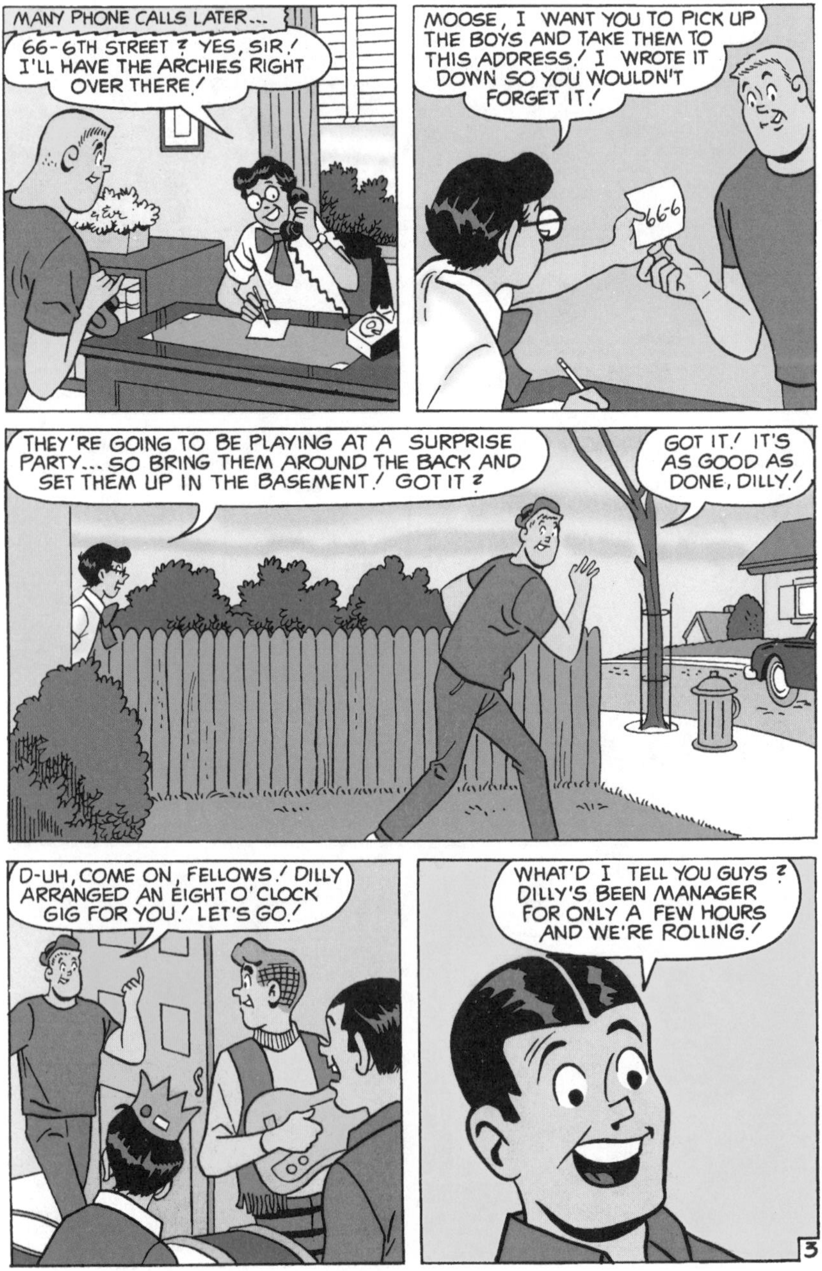
MANY PHONE CALLS LATER...
66-6TH STREET? YES, SIR! I'LL HAVE THE ARCHIES RIGHT OVER THERE!
MOOSE, I WANT YOU TO PICK UP THE BOYS AND TAKE THEM TO THIS ADDRESS! I WROTE IT DOWN SO YOU WOULDN'T FORGET IT!
66-6
THEY'RE GOING TO BE PLAYING AT A SURPRISE PARTY... SO BRING THEM AROUND THE BACK AND SET THEM UP IN THE BASEMENT! GOT IT?
GOT IT! IT'S AS GOOD AS DONE, DILLY!
D-UH, COME ON, FELLOWS! DILLY ARRANGED AN EIGHT O'CLOCK GIG FOR YOU! LET'S GO!
WHAT'D I TELL YOU GUYS? DILLY'S BEEN MANAGER FOR ONLY A FEW HOURS AND WE'RE ROLLING!
3

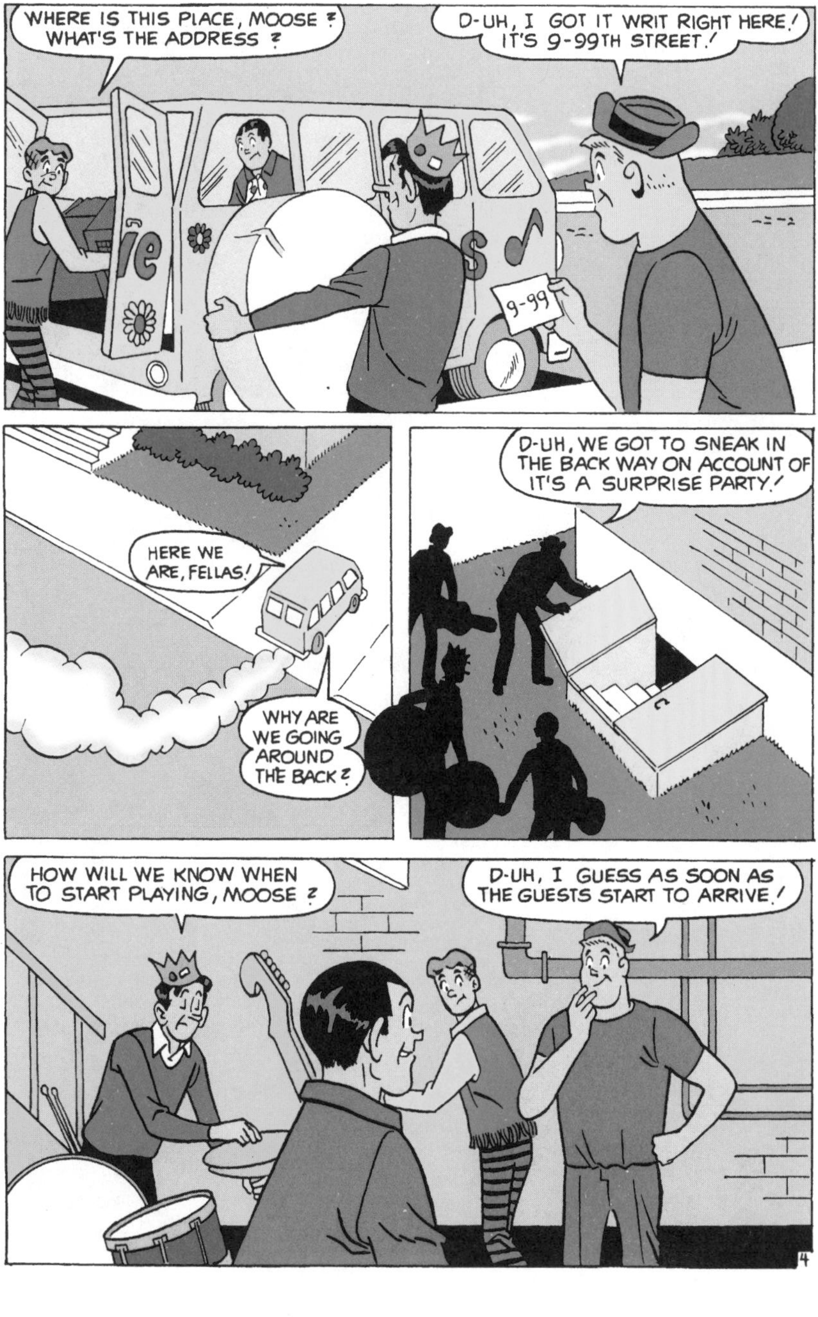
WHERE IS THIS PLACE, MOOSE? WHAT'S THE ADDRESS?
D-UH, I GOT IT WRIT RIGHT HERE! IT'S 9-99TH STREET!
9-99
HERE WE ARE, FELLAS!
WHY ARE WE GOING AROUND THE BACK?
D-UH, WE GOT TO SNEAK IN THE BACK WAY ON ACCOUNT OF IT'S A SURPRISE PARTY!
HOW WILL WE KNOW WHEN TO START PLAYING, MOOSE?
D-UH, I GUESS AS SOON AS THE GUESTS START TO ARRIVE!
4

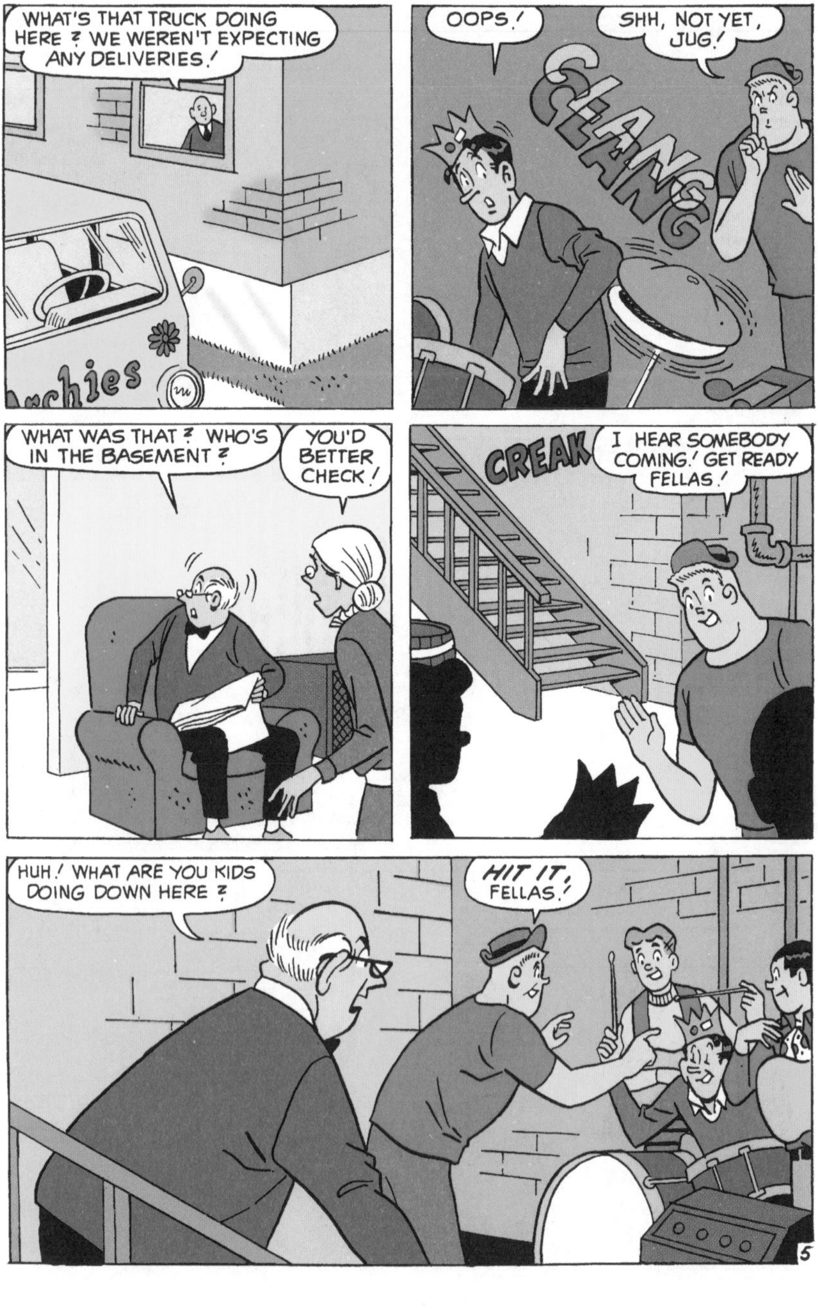
WHAT'S THAT TRUCK DOING HERE? WE WEREN'T EXPECTING ANY DELIVERIES!
Archies
OOPS!
SHH, NOT YET, JUG!
CLANG
CLANG
WHAT WAS THAT? WHO'S IN THE BASEMENT?
YOU'D BETTER CHECK!
CREAK
I HEAR SOMEBODY COMING! GET READY FELLAS!
HUH! WHAT ARE YOU KIDS DOING DOWN HERE?
HIT IT, FELLAS!
5

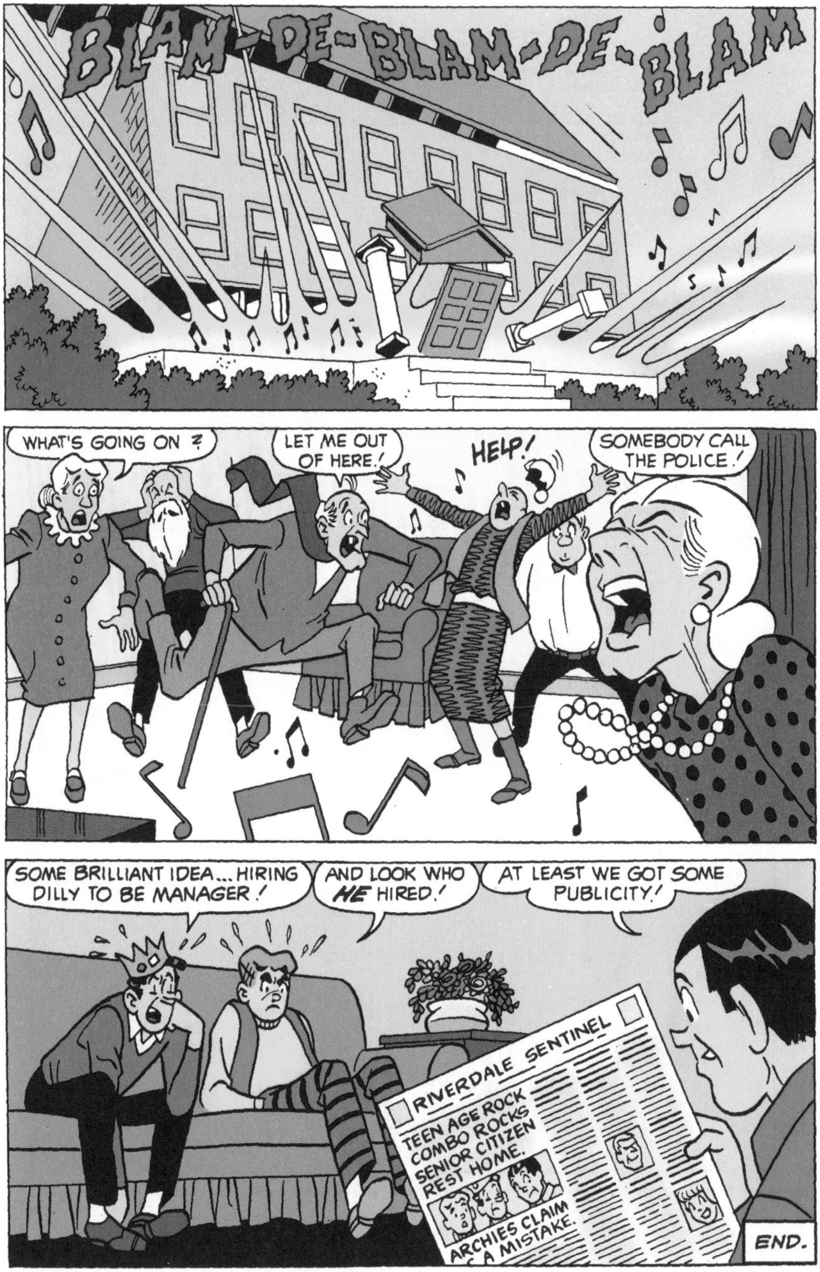
BLAM-DE-BLAM-DE-BLAM
WHAT'S GOING ON ?
LET ME OUT OF HERE!
HELP!
SOMEBODY CALL THE POLICE!
SOME BRILLIANT IDEA... HIRING DILLY TO BE MANAGER!
AND LOOK WHO HE HIRED!
AT LEAST WE GOT SOME PUBLICITY!
RIVERDALE SENTINEL
TEEN AGE ROCK COMBO ROCKS SENIOR CITIZEN REST HOME.
ARCHIES CLAIM A MISTAKE.
END.

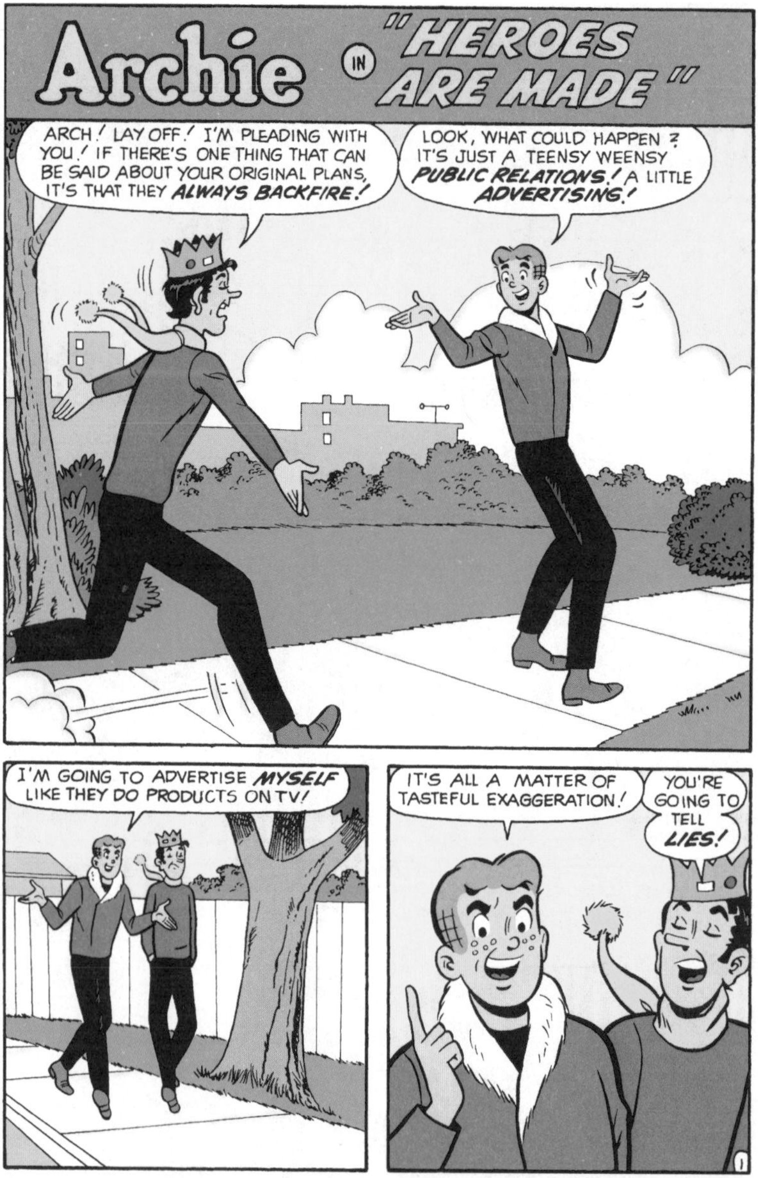
Archie
IN
"HEROES ARE MADE"
ARCH! LAY OFF! I'M PLEADING WITH YOU! IF THERE'S ONE THING THAT CAN BE SAID ABOUT YOUR ORIGINAL PLANS, IT'S THAT THEY ALWAYS BACKFIRE!
LOOK, WHAT COULD HAPPEN? IT'S JUST A TEENSY WEENSY PUBLIC RELATIONS! A LITTLE ADVERTISING!
I'M GOING TO ADVERTISE MYSELF LIKE THEY DO PRODUCTS ON TV!
IT'S ALL A MATTER OF TASTEFUL EXAGGERATION!
YOU'RE GOING TO TELL LIES!
1

Story: Frank Doyle Pencils: Bob White
Inks: Jon D'Agostino Letters: Bill Yoshida Colors: Barry Grossman

Originally printed in EVERYTHING'S ARCHIE #14, JUNE 1971

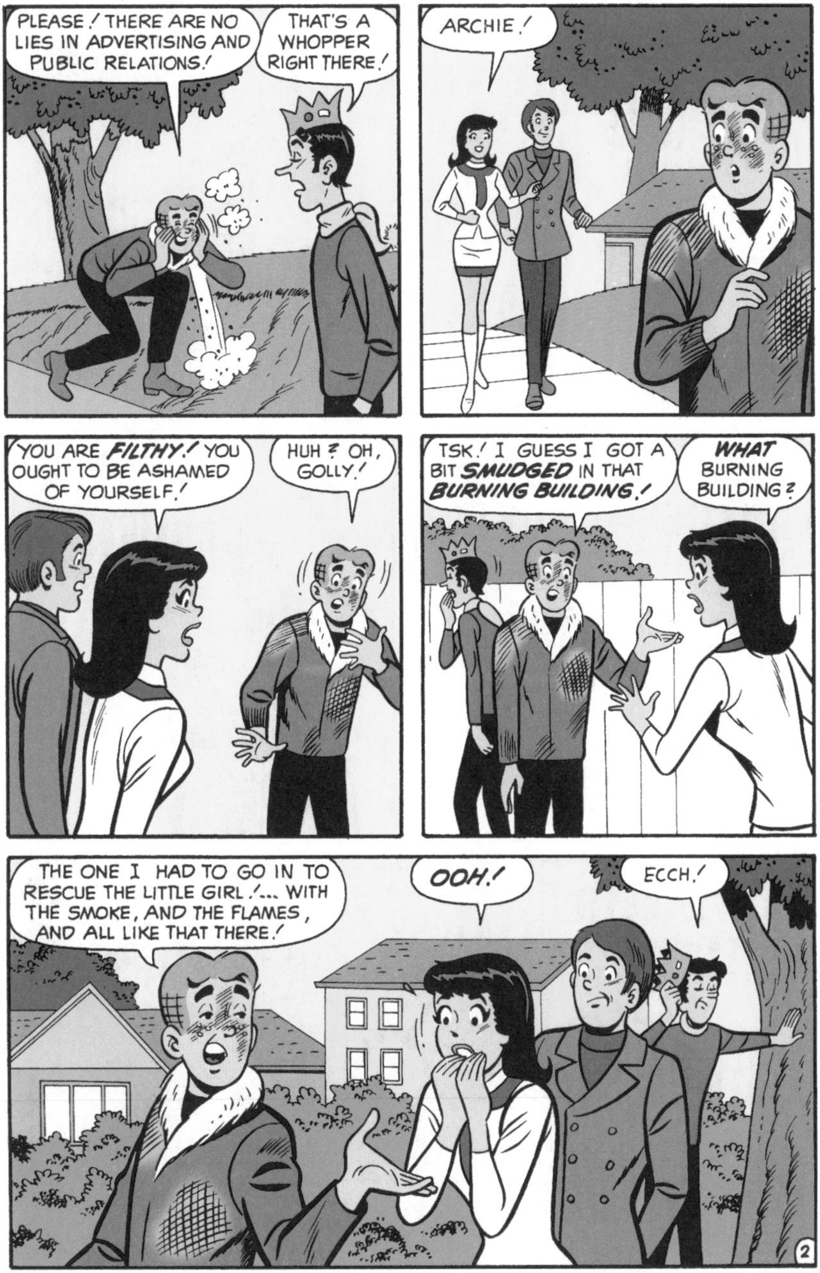
PLEASE! THERE ARE NO LIES IN ADVERTISING AND PUBLIC RELATIONS!
THAT'S A WHOPPER RIGHT THERE!
ARCHIE!
YOU ARE FILTHY! YOU OUGHT TO BE ASHAMED OF YOURSELF!
HUH? OH, GOLLY!
TSK! I GUESS I GOT A BIT SMUDGED IN THAT BURNING BUILDING!
WHAT BURNING BUILDING?
THE ONE I HAD TO GO IN TO RESCUE THE LITTLE GIRL!... WITH THE SMOKE, AND THE FLAMES, AND ALL LIKE THAT THERE!
OOH!
ECCH!
2

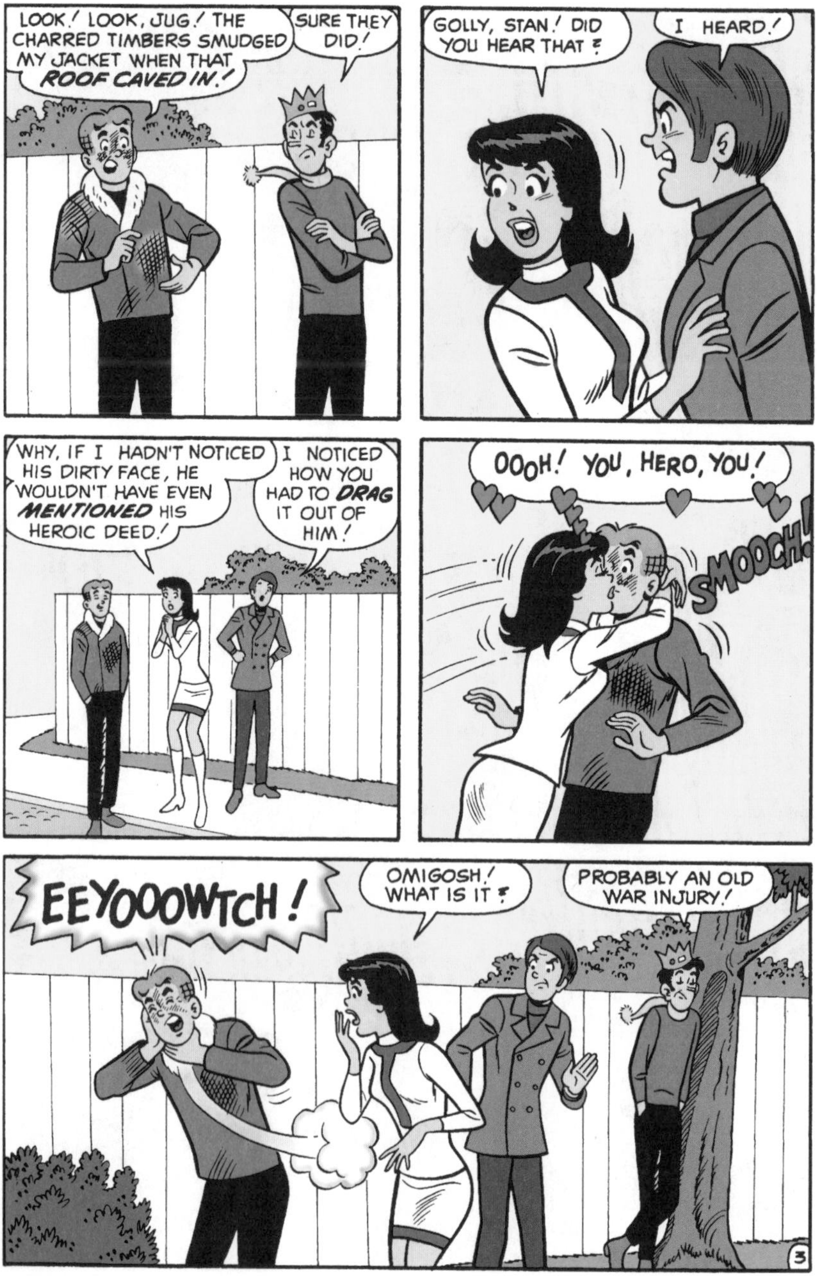
LOOK! LOOK, JUG! THE CHARRED TIMBERS SMUDGED MY JACKET WHEN THAT ROOF CAVED IN!
SURE THEY DID!
GOLLY, STAN! DID YOU HEAR THAT?
I HEARD!
WHY, IF I HADN'T NOTICED HIS DIRTY FACE, HE WOULDN'T HAVE EVEN MENTIONED HIS HEROIC DEED!
I NOTICED HOW YOU HAD TO DRAG IT OUT OF HIM!
OOOH! YOU, HERO, YOU!
SMOOCH!
EEYOOOWTCH!
OMIGOSH! WHAT IS IT?
PROBABLY AN OLD WAR INJURY!
3

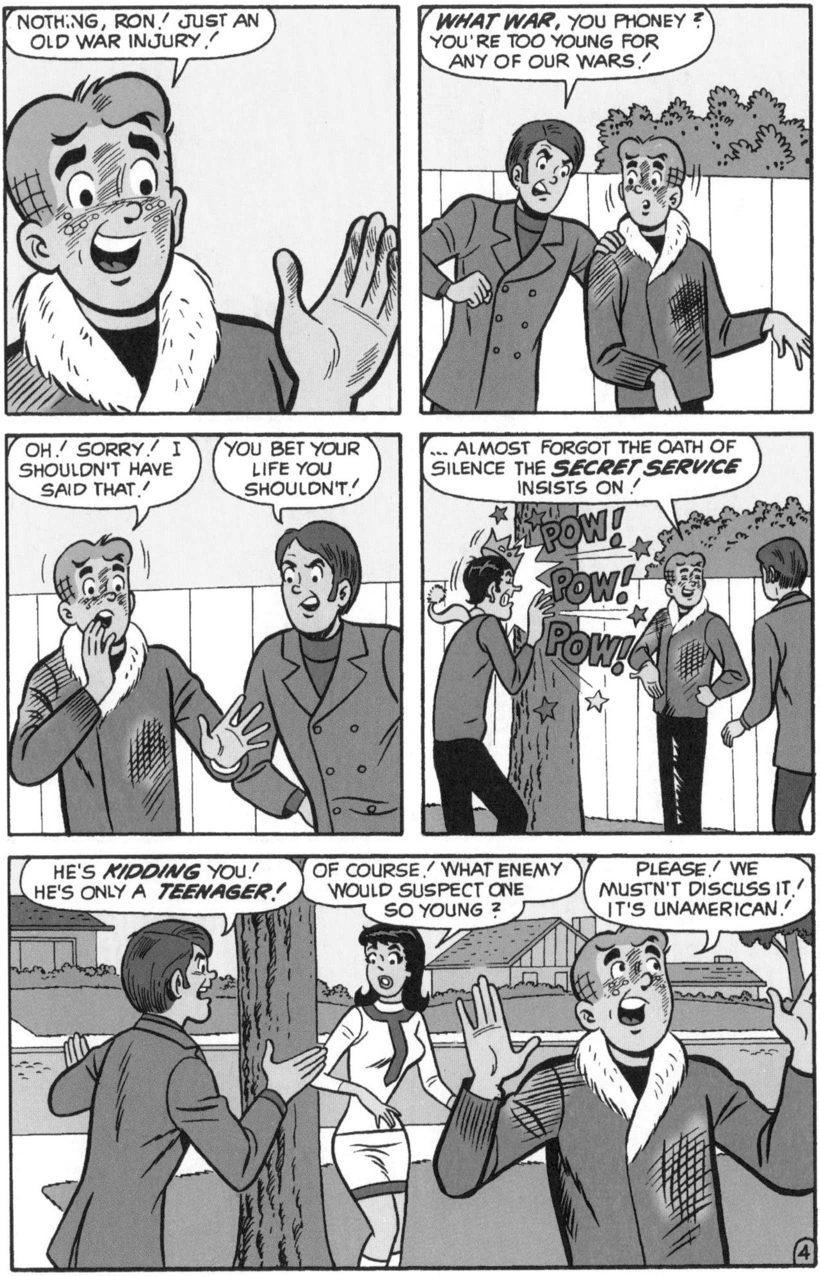
NOTHING, RON! JUST AN OLD WAR INJURY!
WHAT WAR, YOU PHONEY? YOU'RE TOO YOUNG FOR ANY OF OUR WARS!
OH! SORRY! I SHOULDN'T HAVE SAID THAT!
YOU BET YOUR LIFE YOU SHOULDN'T!
... ALMOST FORGOT THE OATH OF SILENCE THE SECRET SERVICE INSISTS ON!
POW!
POW!
POW!
HE'S KIDDING YOU! HE'S ONLY A TEENAGER!
OF COURSE! WHAT ENEMY WOULD SUSPECT ONE SO YOUNG?
PLEASE! WE MUSTN'T DISCUSS IT! IT'S UNAMERICAN!
4

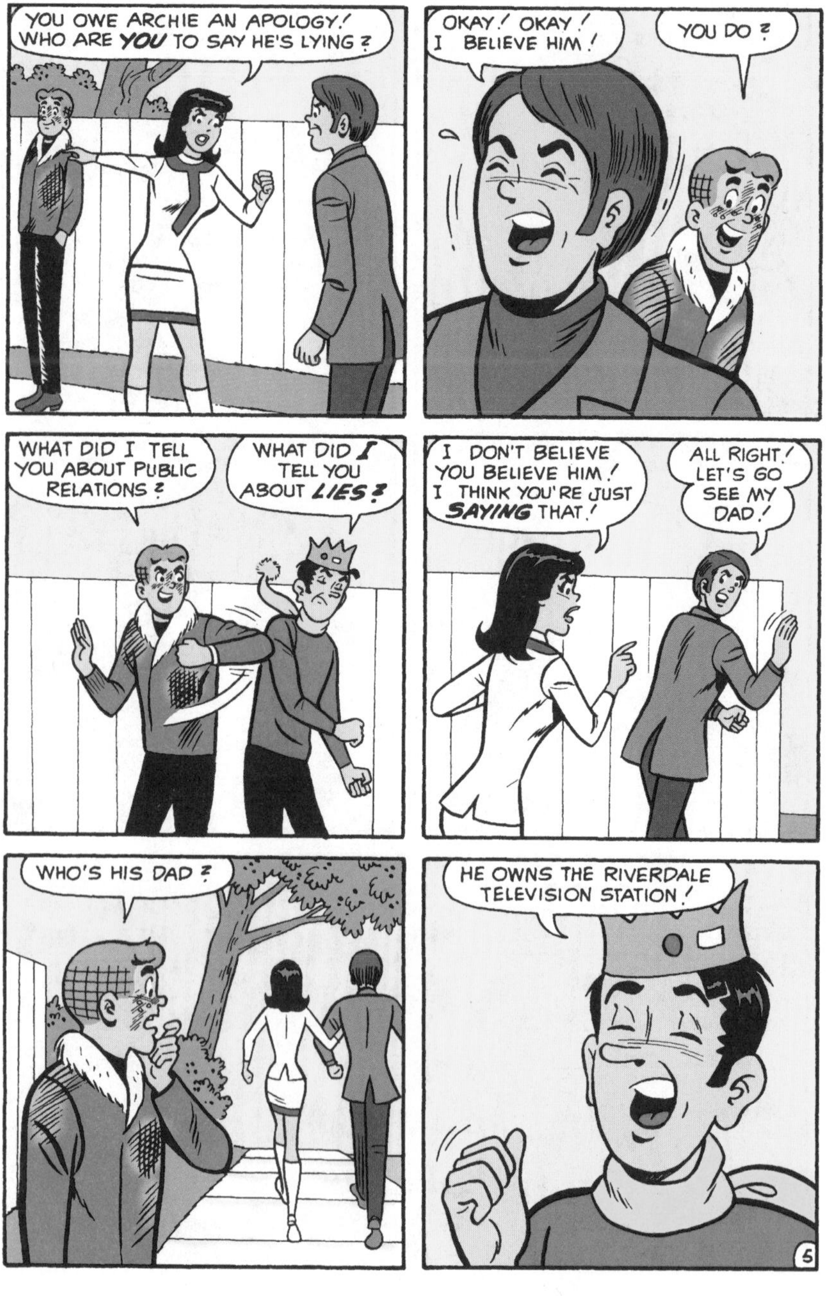
YOU OWE ARCHIE AN APOLOGY! WHO ARE YOU TO SAY HE'S LYING?
OKAY! OKAY! I BELIEVE HIM!
YOU DO?
WHAT DID I TELL YOU ABOUT PUBLIC RELATIONS?
WHAT DID I TELL YOU ABOUT LIES?
I DON'T BELIEVE YOU BELIEVE HIM! I THINK YOU'RE JUST SAYING THAT!
ALL RIGHT! LET'S GO SEE MY DAD!
WHO'S HIS DAD?
HE OWNS THE RIVERDALE TELEVISION STATION!
5

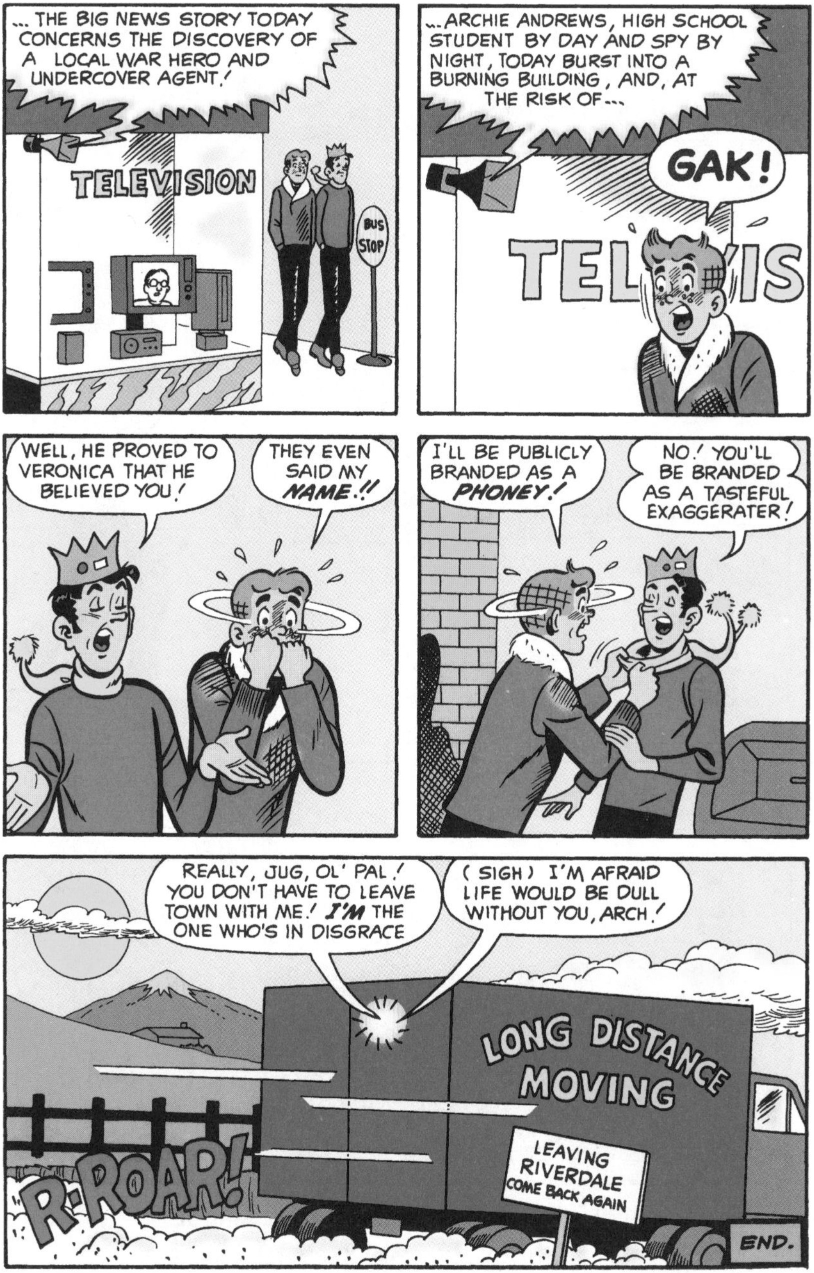
... THE BIG NEWS STORY TODAY CONCERNS THE DISCOVERY OF A LOCAL WAR HERO AND UNDERCOVER AGENT!
TELEVISION
BUS STOP
...ARCHIE ANDREWS, HIGH SCHOOL STUDENT BY DAY AND SPY BY NIGHT, TODAY BURST INTO A BURNING BUILDING, AND, AT THE RISK OF...
GAK!
WELL, HE PROVED TO VERONICA THAT HE BELIEVED YOU!
THEY EVEN SAID MY NAME!!
I'LL BE PUBLICLY BRANDED AS A PHONEY!
NO! YOU'LL BE BRANDED AS A TASTEFUL EXAGGERATER!
REALLY, JUG, OL' PAL! YOU DON'T HAVE TO LEAVE TOWN WITH ME! I'M THE ONE WHO'S IN DISGRACE
(SIGH) I'M AFRAID LIFE WOULD BE DULL WITHOUT YOU, ARCH!
LONG DISTANCE MOVING
LEAVING RIVERDALE COME BACK AGAIN
R-ROAR!
END.

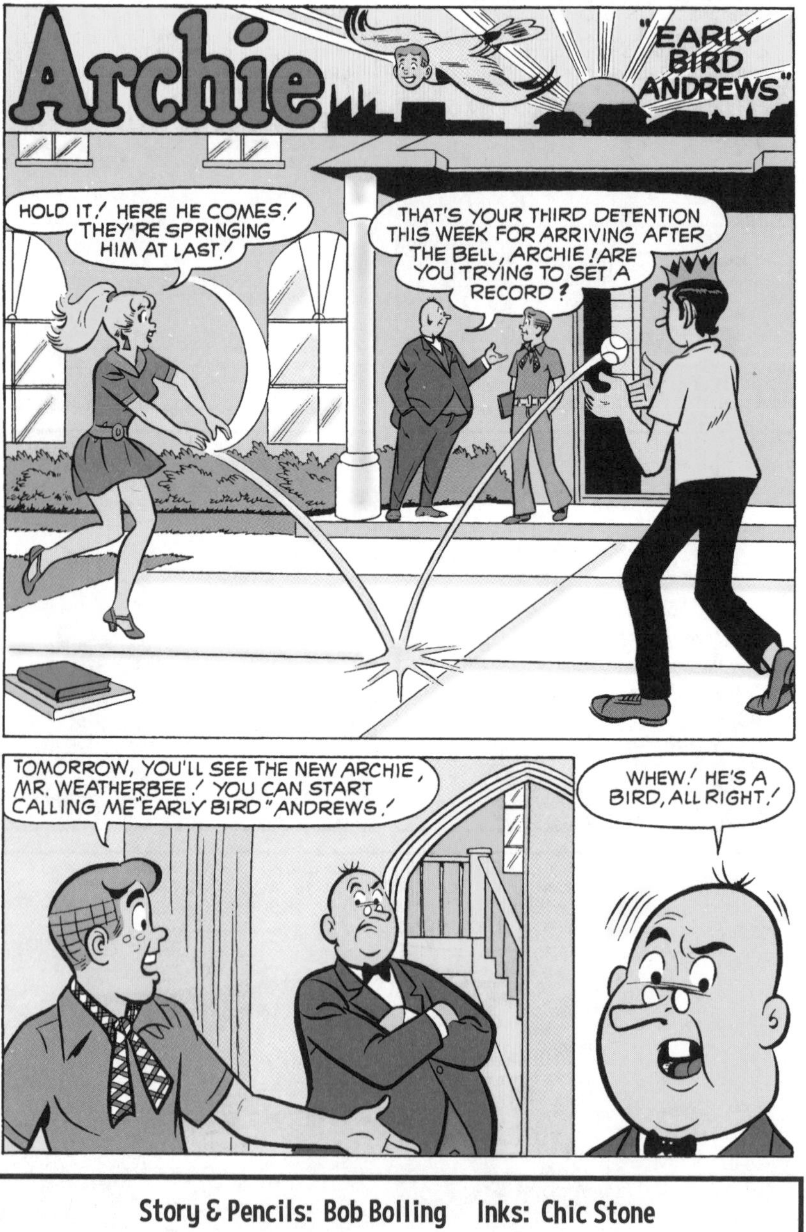
Archie
"EARLY BIRD ANDREWS"
HOLD IT! HERE HE COMES! THEY'RE SPRINGING HIM AT LAST!
THAT'S YOUR THIRD DETENTION THIS WEEK FOR ARRIVING AFTER THE BELL, ARCHIE! ARE YOU TRYING TO SET A RECORD?
TOMORROW, YOU'LL SEE THE NEW ARCHIE, MR. WEATHERBEE! YOU CAN START CALLING ME "EARLY BIRD" ANDREWS!
WHEW! HE'S A BIRD, ALL RIGHT!

Story & Pencils: Bob Bolling Inks: Chic Stone
Letters: Bill Yoshida Colors: Barry Grossman

Originally printed in EVERYTHING'S ARCHIE #14, JUNE 1971

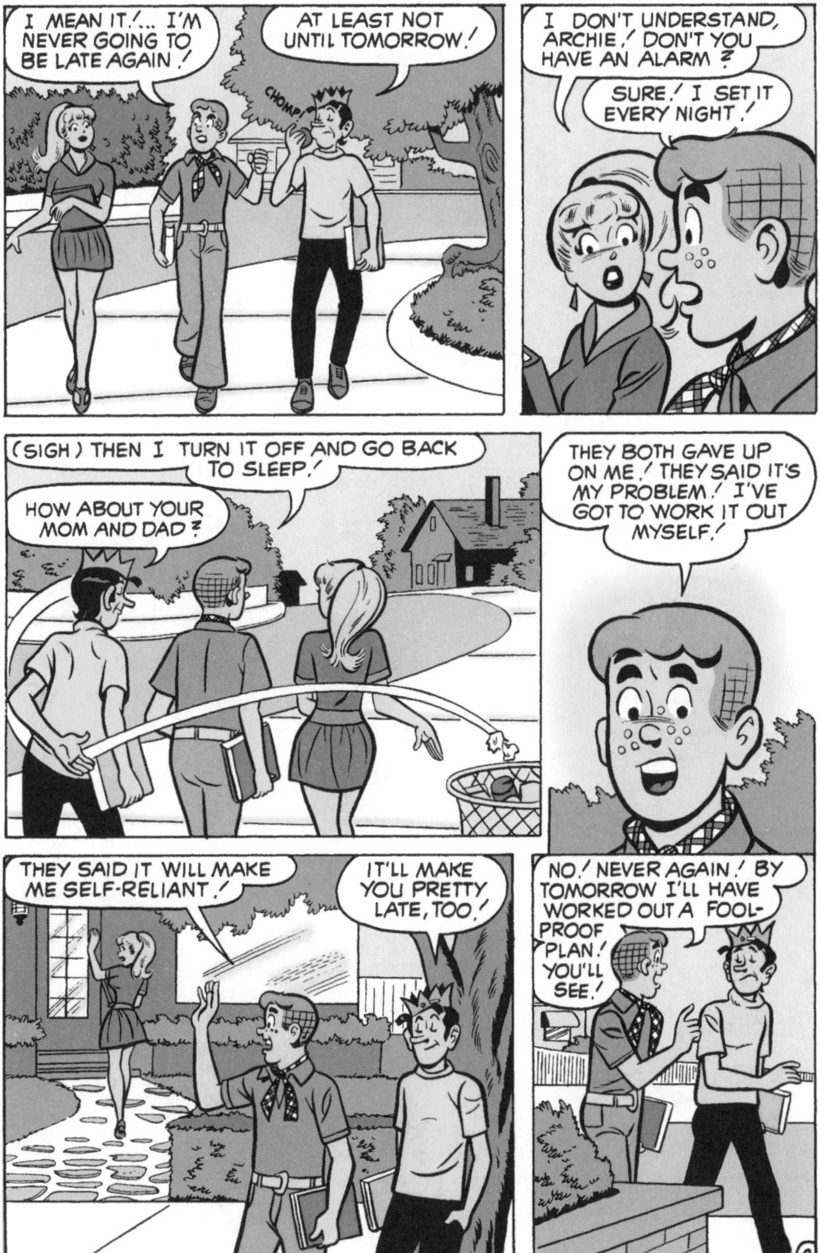
I MEAN IT!... I'M NEVER GOING TO BE LATE AGAIN!
AT LEAST NOT UNTIL TOMORROW!
CHOMP!
I DON'T UNDERSTAND, ARCHIE! DON'T YOU HAVE AN ALARM?
SURE! I SET IT EVERY NIGHT!
(SIGH) THEN I TURN IT OFF AND GO BACK TO SLEEP!
HOW ABOUT YOUR MOM AND DAD?
THEY BOTH GAVE UP ON ME! THEY SAID IT'S MY PROBLEM! I'VE GOT TO WORK IT OUT MYSELF!
THEY SAID IT WILL MAKE ME SELF-RELIANT!
IT'LL MAKE YOU PRETTY LATE, TOO!
NO! NEVER AGAIN! BY TOMORROW I'LL HAVE WORKED OUT A FOOL-PROOF PLAN! YOU'LL SEE!
2

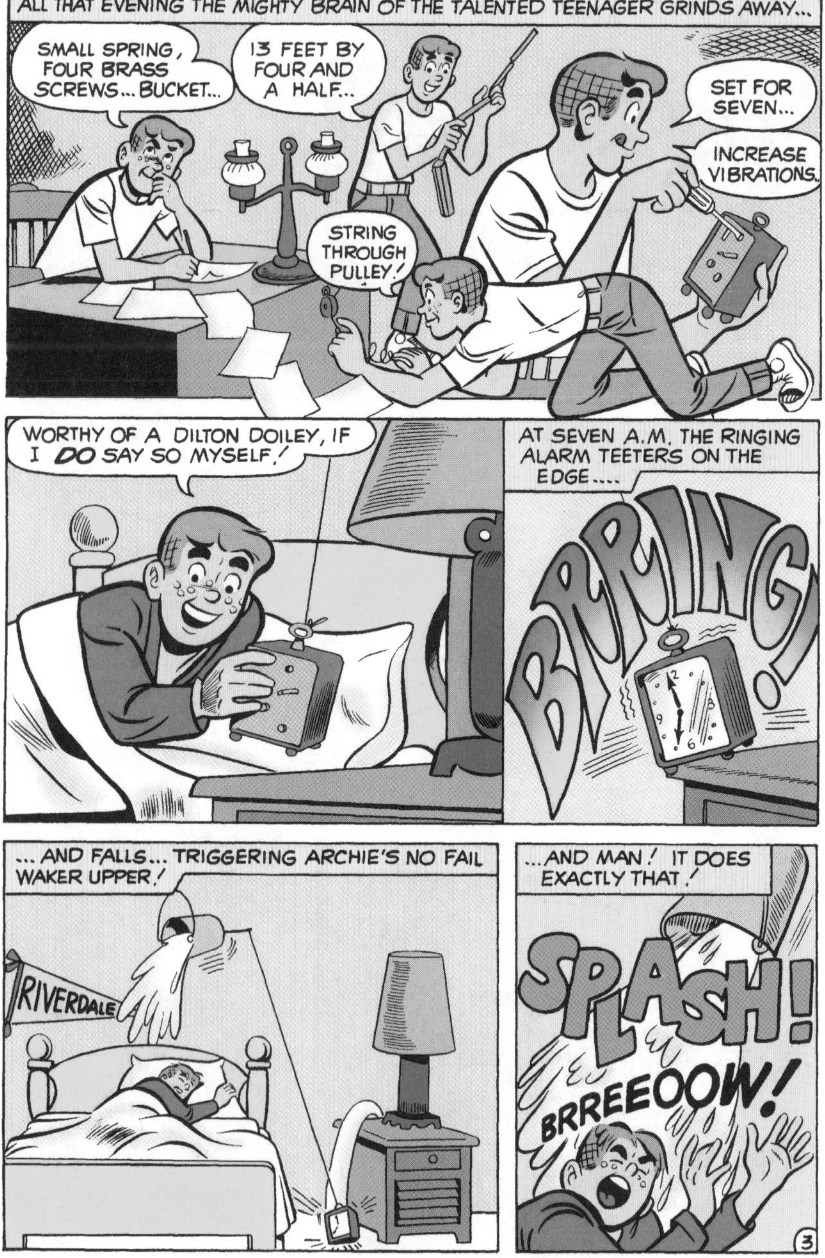
ALL THAT EVENING THE MIGHTY BRAIN OF THE TALENTED TEENAGER GRINDS AWAY...
SMALL SPRING, FOUR BRASS SCREWS... BUCKET...
13 FEET BY FOUR AND A HALF...
SET FOR SEVEN...
INCREASE VIBRATIONS.
STRING THROUGH PULLEY!
WORTHY OF A DILTON DOILEY, IF I DO SAY SO MYSELF!
AT SEVEN A.M. THE RINGING ALARM TEETERS ON THE EDGE....
BRRING!
... AND FALLS... TRIGGERING ARCHIE'S NO FAIL WAKER UPPER!
RIVERDALE
...AND MAN! IT DOES EXACTLY THAT!
SPLASH!
BRREEOOW!
3

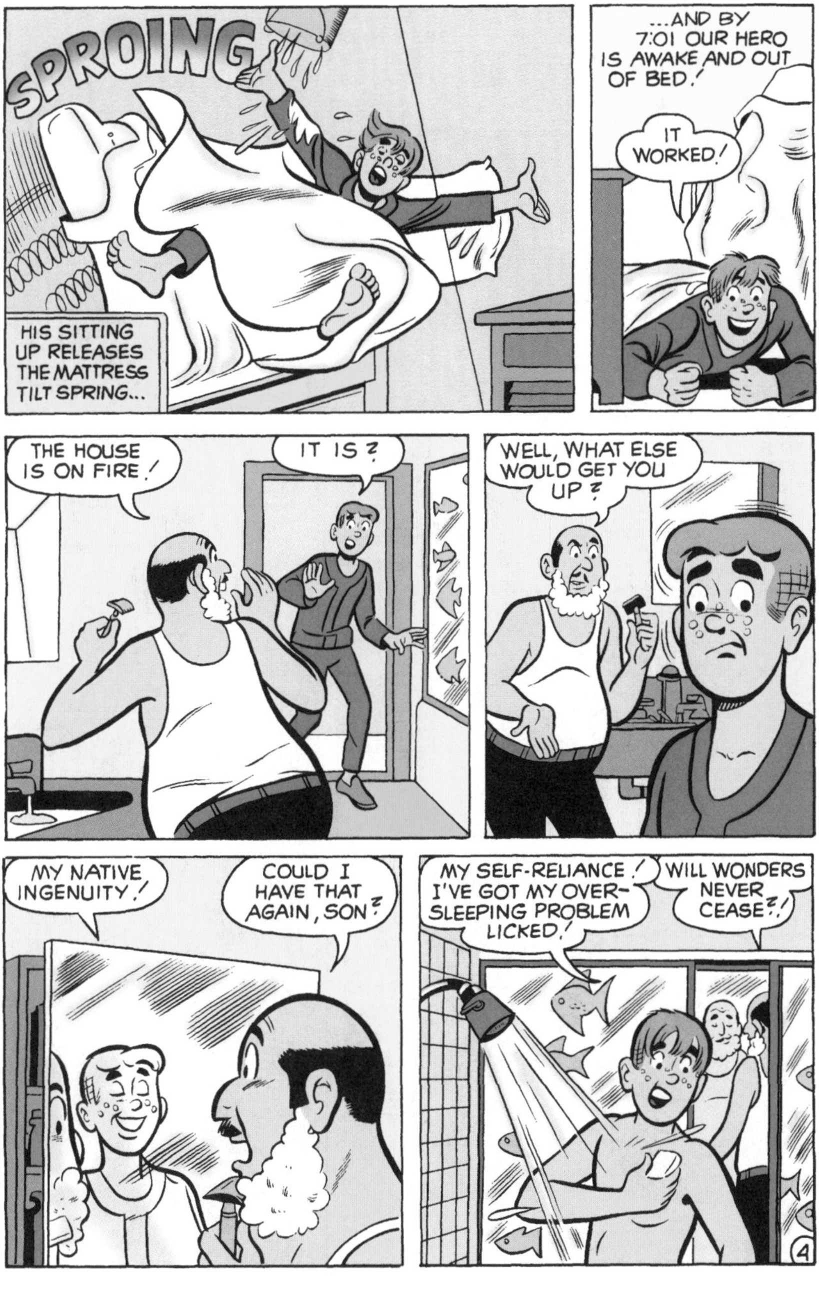
SPROING
HIS SITTING UP RELEASES THE MATTRESS TILT SPRING...
...AND BY 7:01 OUR HERO IS AWAKE AND OUT OF BED!
IT WORKED!
THE HOUSE IS ON FIRE!
IT IS?
WELL, WHAT ELSE WOULD GET YOU UP?
MY NATIVE INGENUITY!
COULD I HAVE THAT AGAIN, SON?
MY SELF-RELIANCE! I'VE GOT MY OVER-SLEEPING PROBLEM LICKED!
WILL WONDERS NEVER CEASE?!
4

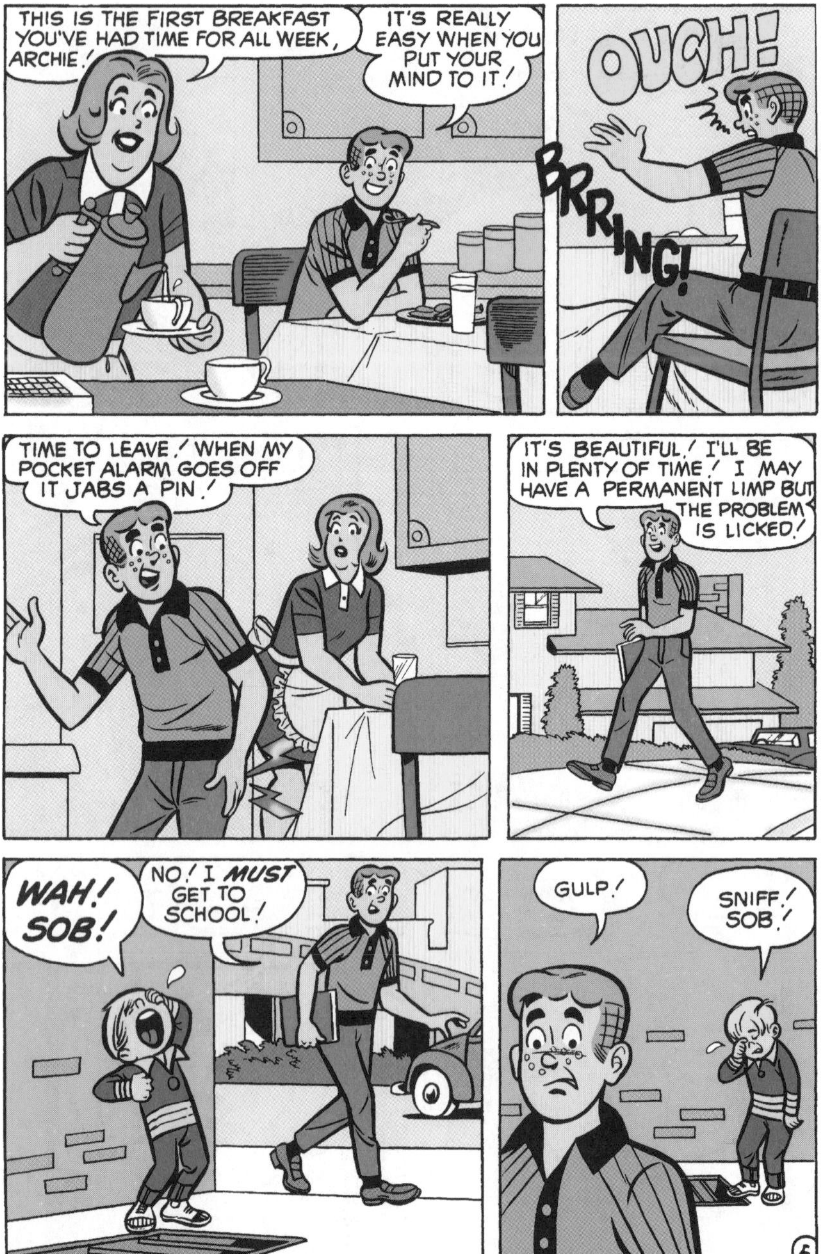
THIS IS THE FIRST BREAKFAST YOU'VE HAD TIME FOR ALL WEEK, ARCHIE!
IT'S REALLY EASY WHEN YOU PUT YOUR MIND TO IT!
OUCH!
BRRING!
TIME TO LEAVE! WHEN MY POCKET ALARM GOES OFF IT JABS A PIN!
IT'S BEAUTIFUL! I'LL BE IN PLENTY OF TIME! I MAY HAVE A PERMANENT LIMP BUT THE PROBLEM IS LICKED!
WAH! SOB!
NO! I MUST GET TO SCHOOL!
GULP!
SNIFF! SOB!
5

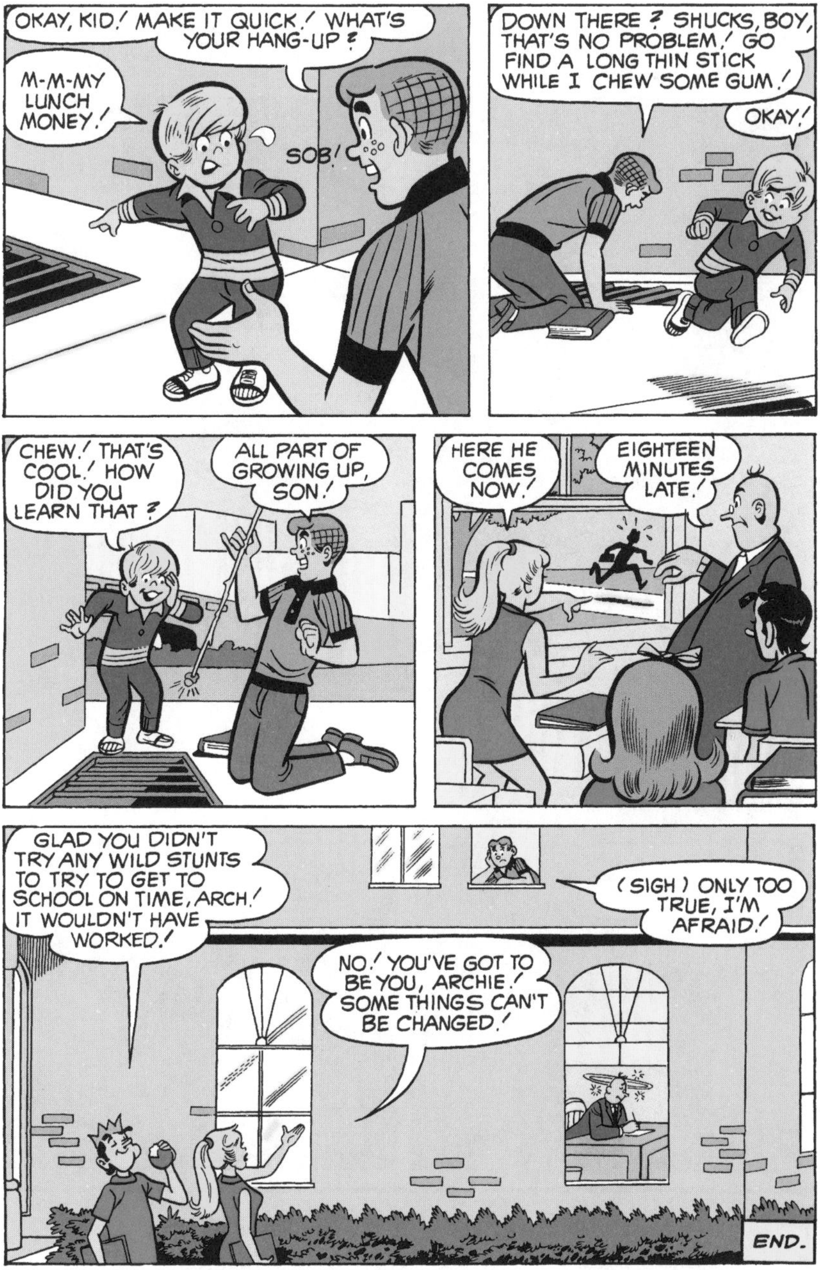
OKAY, KID! MAKE IT QUICK! WHAT'S YOUR HANG-UP?
M-M-MY LUNCH MONEY!
SOB!
DOWN THERE? SHUCKS, BOY, THAT'S NO PROBLEM! GO FIND A LONG THIN STICK WHILE I CHEW SOME GUM!
OKAY!
CHEW! THAT'S COOL! HOW DID YOU LEARN THAT?
ALL PART OF GROWING UP, SON!
HERE HE COMES NOW!
EIGHTEEN MINUTES LATE!
GLAD YOU DIDN'T TRY ANY WILD STUNTS TO TRY TO GET TO SCHOOL ON TIME, ARCH! IT WOULDN'T HAVE WORKED!
(SIGH) ONLY TOO TRUE, I'M AFRAID!
NO! YOU'VE GOT TO BE YOU, ARCHIE! SOME THINGS CAN'T BE CHANGED!
END.

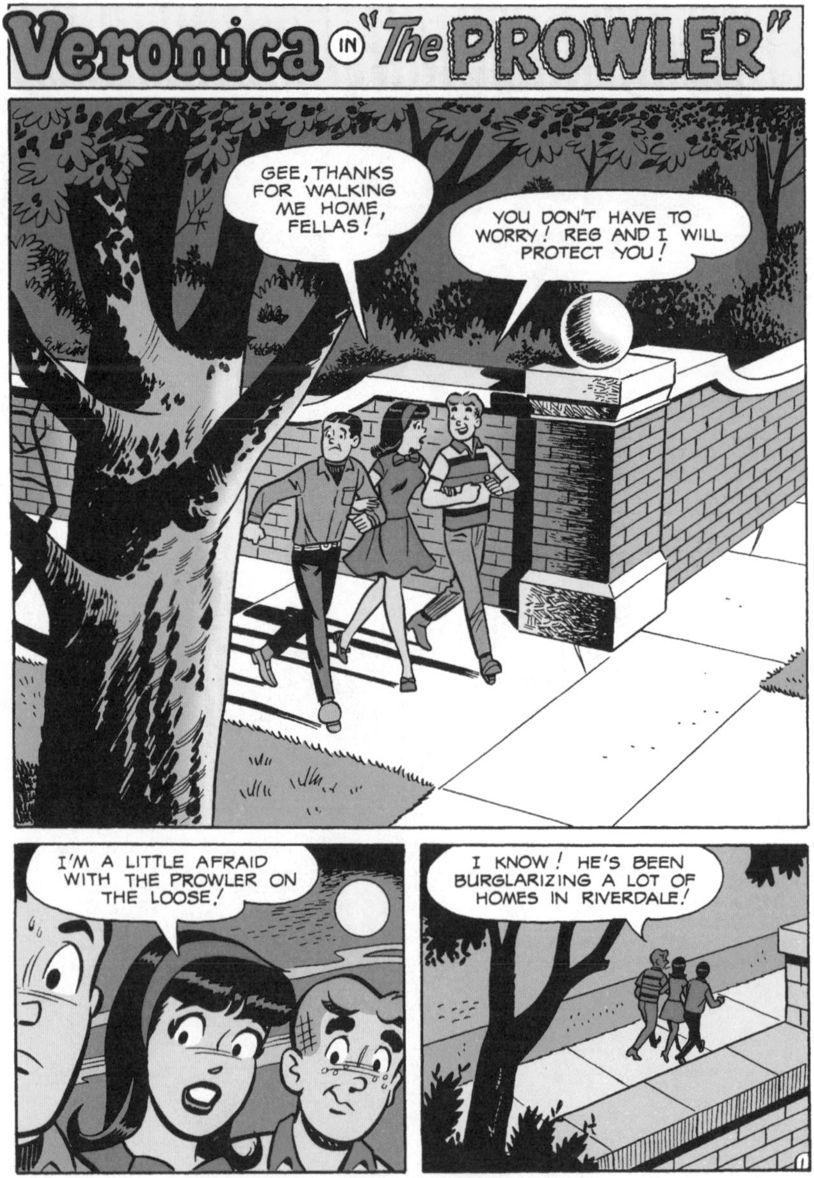
Veronica IN "The PROWLER"
GEE, THANKS FOR WALKING ME HOME, FELLAS!
YOU DON'T HAVE TO WORRY! REG AND I WILL PROTECT YOU!
I'M A LITTLE AFRAID WITH THE PROWLER ON THE LOOSE!
I KNOW! HE'S BEEN BURGLARIZING A LOT OF HOMES IN RIVERDALE!
1

Story: Frank Doyle   Pencils: Dan DeCarlo
Inks: Rudy Lapick   Letters: Bill Yoshida

Originally printed in EVERYTHING'S ARCHIE #14, JUNE 1971

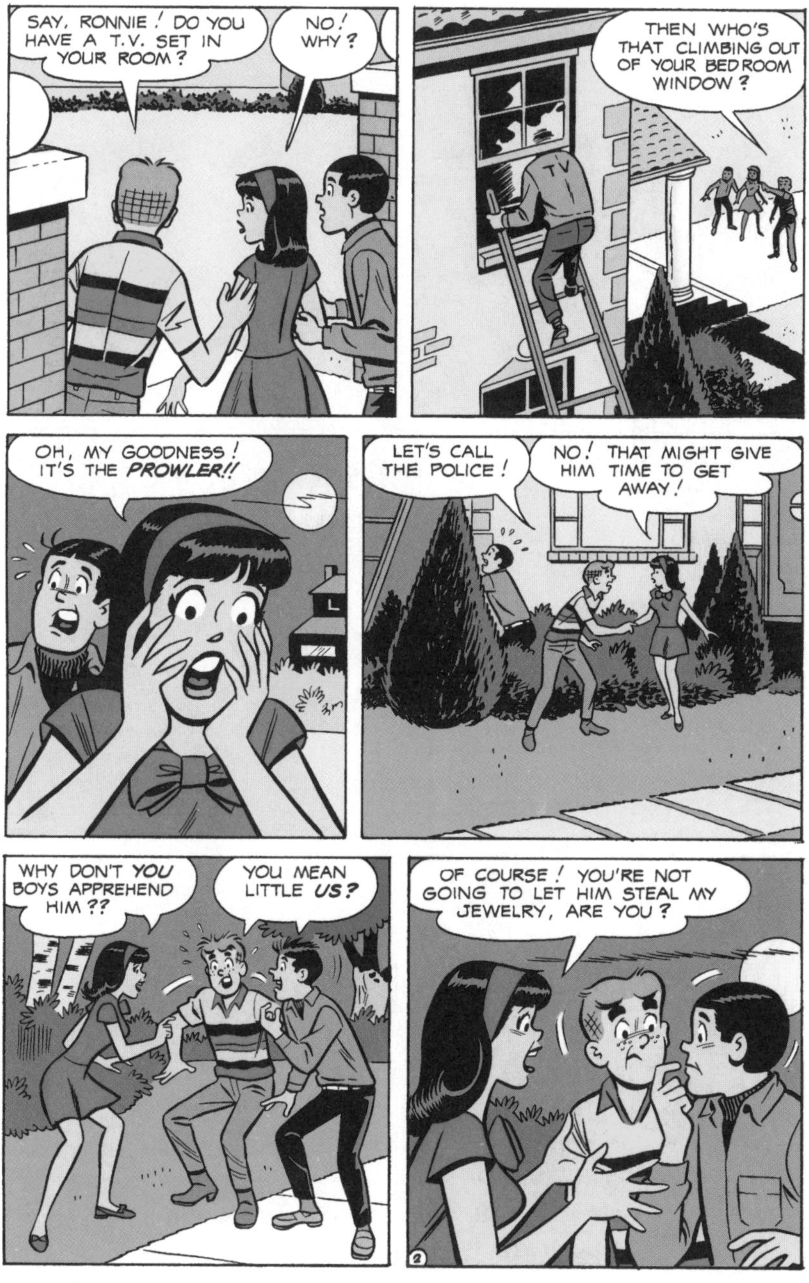
SAY, RONNIE! DO YOU HAVE A T.V. SET IN YOUR ROOM?
NO! WHY?
THEN WHO'S THAT CLIMBING OUT OF YOUR BEDROOM WINDOW?
TV
OH, MY GOODNESS! IT'S THE PROWLER!!
LET'S CALL THE POLICE!
NO! THAT MIGHT GIVE HIM TIME TO GET AWAY!
WHY DON'T YOU BOYS APPREHEND HIM??
YOU MEAN LITTLE US?
OF COURSE! YOU'RE NOT GOING TO LET HIM STEAL MY JEWELRY, ARE YOU?
2

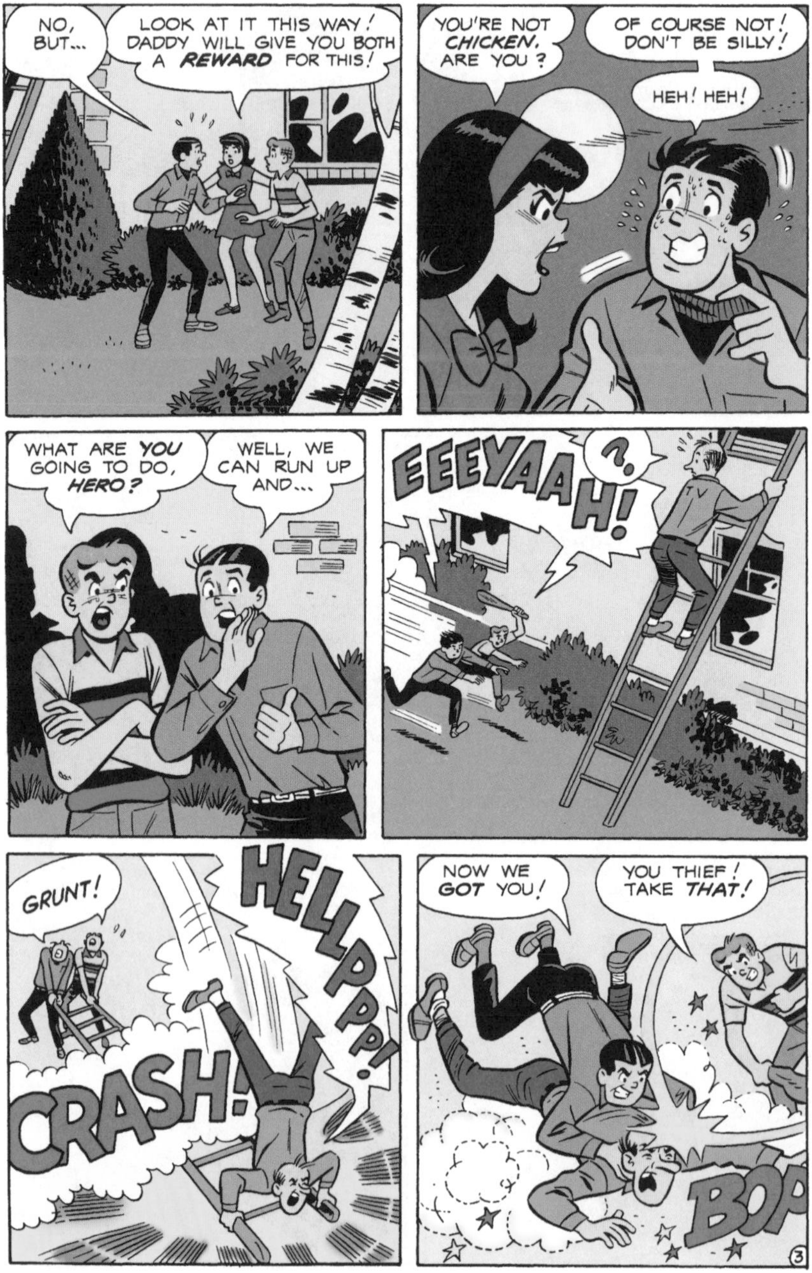
NO, BUT...
LOOK AT IT THIS WAY! DADDY WILL GIVE YOU BOTH A REWARD FOR THIS!
YOU'RE NOT CHICKEN, ARE YOU ?
OF COURSE NOT! DON'T BE SILLY!
HEH! HEH!
WHAT ARE YOU GOING TO DO, HERO?
WELL, WE CAN RUN UP AND...
EEEYAAAH!
?
GRUNT!
HELLPPP!
CRASH!
NOW WE GOT YOU!
YOU THIEF! TAKE THAT!
BOP
3

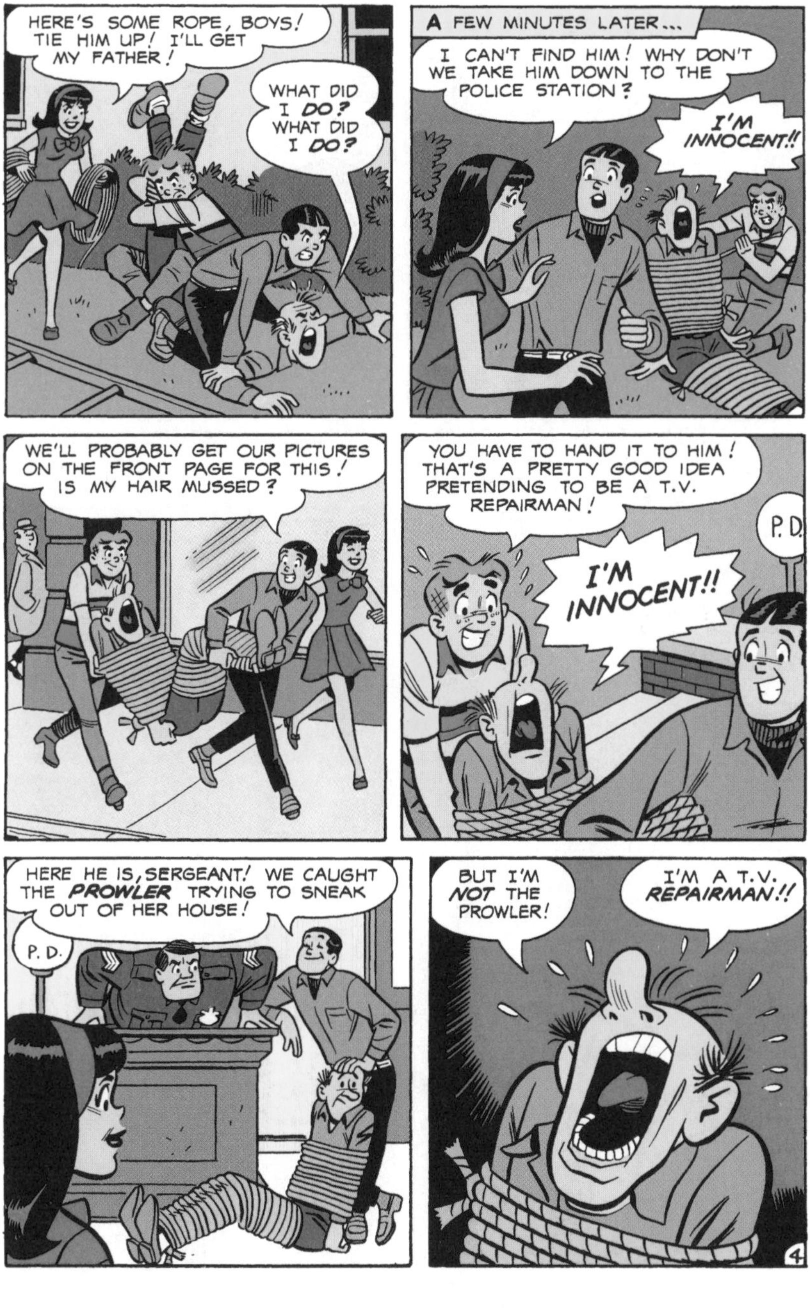
HERE'S SOME ROPE, BOYS! TIE HIM UP! I'LL GET MY FATHER!
WHAT DID I DO? WHAT DID I DO?
A FEW MINUTES LATER...
I CAN'T FIND HIM! WHY DON'T WE TAKE HIM DOWN TO THE POLICE STATION?
I'M INNOCENT!!
WE'LL PROBABLY GET OUR PICTURES ON THE FRONT PAGE FOR THIS! IS MY HAIR MUSSED?
YOU HAVE TO HAND IT TO HIM! THAT'S A PRETTY GOOD IDEA PRETENDING TO BE A T.V. REPAIRMAN!
P. D.
I'M INNOCENT!!
HERE HE IS, SERGEANT! WE CAUGHT THE PROWLER TRYING TO SNEAK OUT OF HER HOUSE!
P. D.
BUT I'M NOT THE PROWLER!
I'M A T.V. REPAIRMAN!!
4

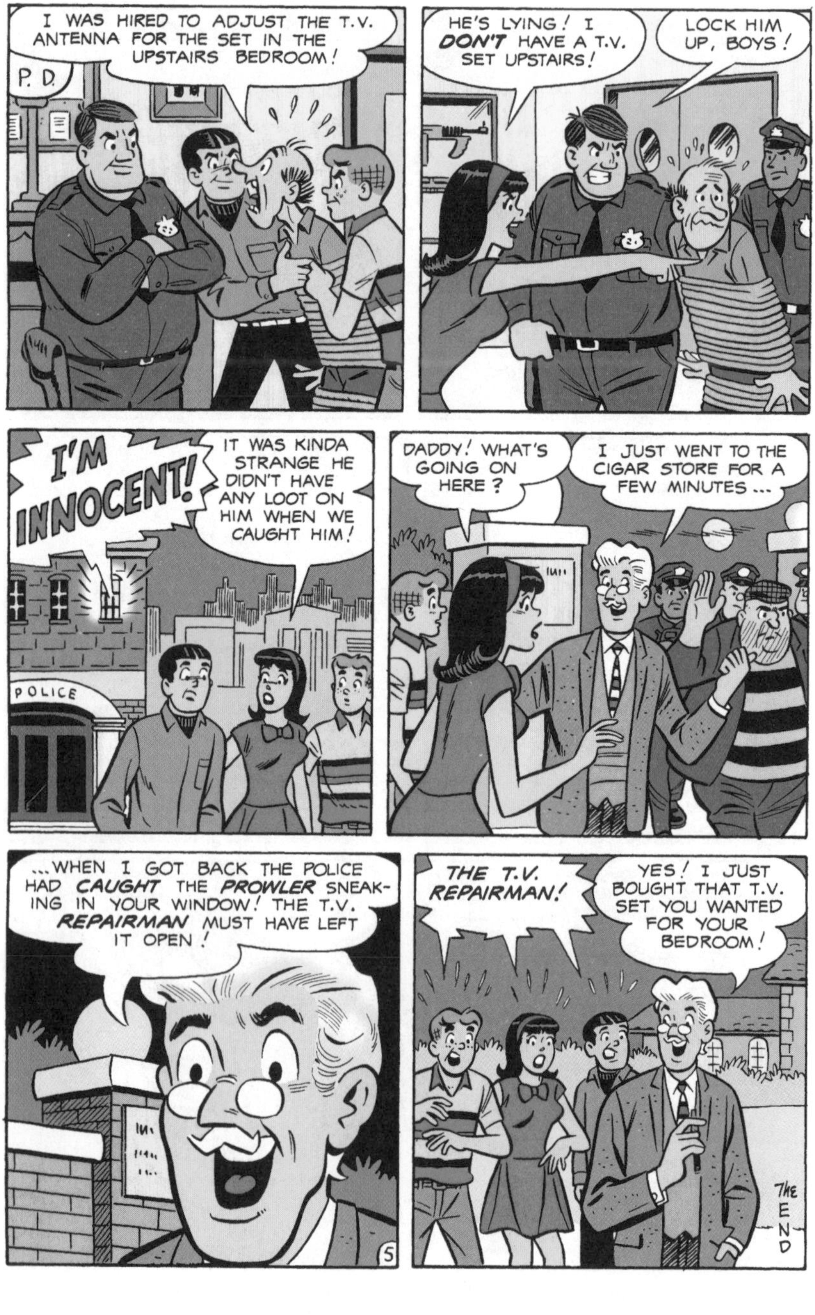
I WAS HIRED TO ADJUST THE T.V. ANTENNA FOR THE SET IN THE UPSTAIRS BEDROOM!
P. D.
HE'S LYING! I DON'T HAVE A T.V. SET UPSTAIRS!
LOCK HIM UP, BOYS!
I'M INNOCENT!
IT WAS KINDA STRANGE HE DIDN'T HAVE ANY LOOT ON HIM WHEN WE CAUGHT HIM!
POLICE
DADDY! WHAT'S GOING ON HERE?
I JUST WENT TO THE CIGAR STORE FOR A FEW MINUTES ...
...WHEN I GOT BACK THE POLICE HAD CAUGHT THE PROWLER SNEAKING IN YOUR WINDOW! THE T.V. REPAIRMAN MUST HAVE LEFT IT OPEN!
5
THE T.V. REPAIRMAN!
YES! I JUST BOUGHT THAT T.V. SET YOU WANTED FOR YOUR BEDROOM!
THE END

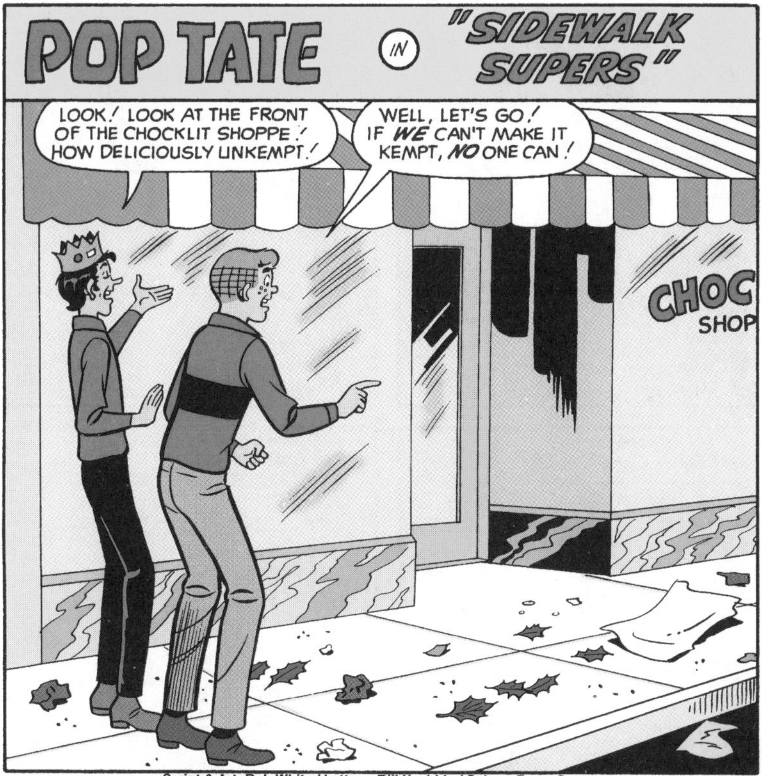
POP TATE IN "SIDEWALK SUPERS"
LOOK! LOOK AT THE FRONT OF THE CHOCKLIT SHOPPE! HOW DELICIOUSLY UNKEMPT!
WELL, LET'S GO! IF *WE* CAN'T MAKE IT KEMPT, *NO* ONE CAN!
CHOC
SHOP

Script & Art: Bob White / Letters: Bill Yoshida / Colors: Barry Grossman

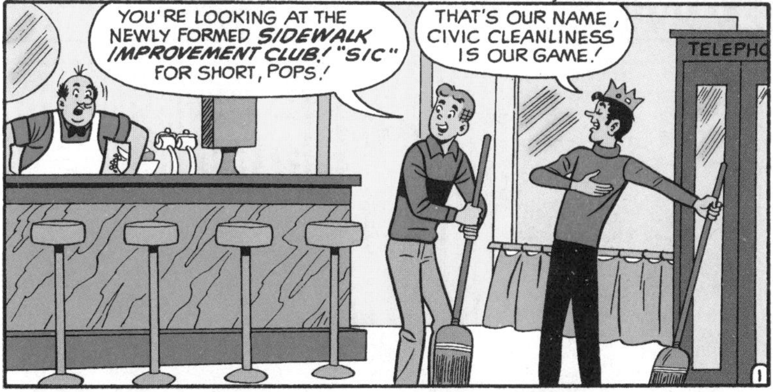
YOU'RE LOOKING AT THE NEWLY FORMED *SIDEWALK IMPROVEMENT CLUB!* "*SIC*" FOR SHORT, POPS!
THAT'S OUR NAME, CIVIC CLEANLINESS IS OUR GAME!
TELEPHO
1

Story & Art: Bob White

Letters: Bill Yoshida Colors: Barry Grossman

Originally printed in EVERYTHING'S ARCHIE #14, JUNE 1971

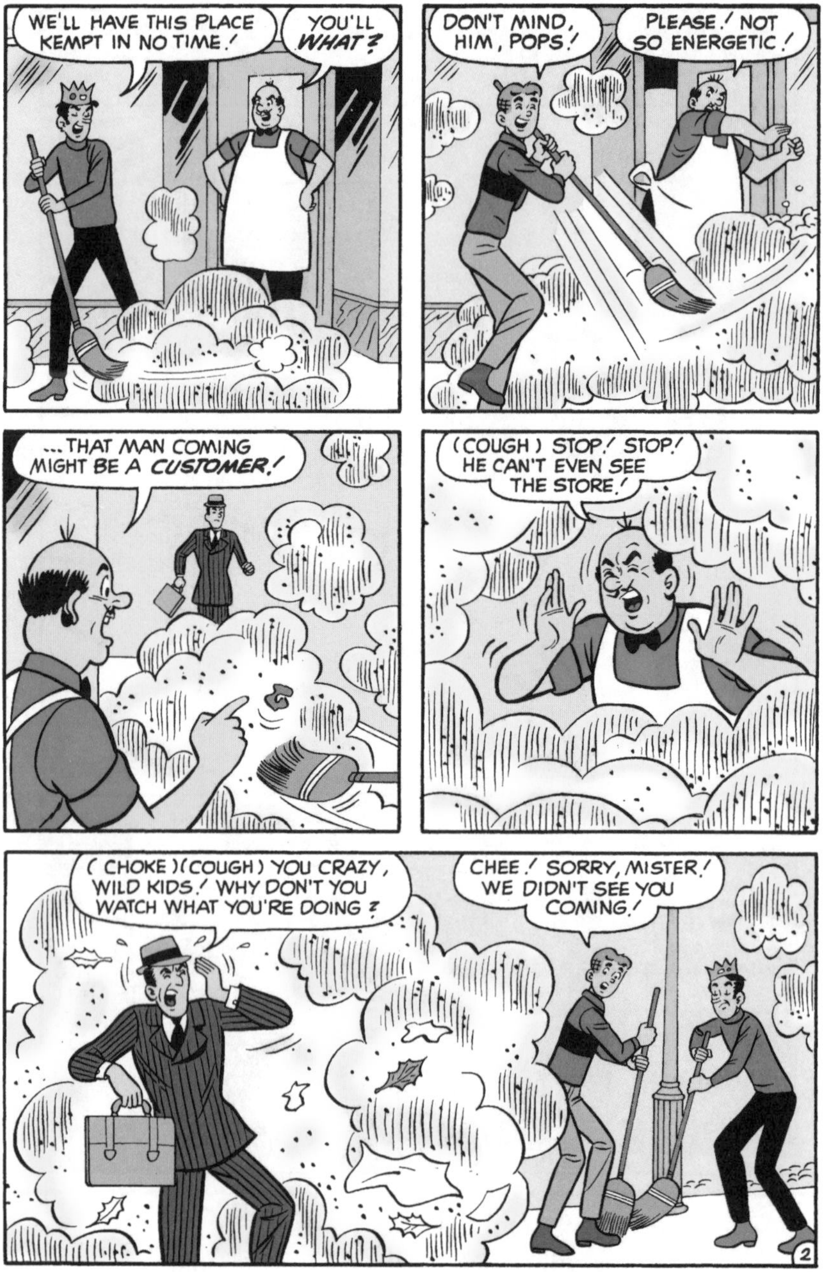
WE'LL HAVE THIS PLACE KEMPT IN NO TIME!
YOU'LL WHAT?
DON'T MIND, HIM, POPS!
PLEASE! NOT SO ENERGETIC!
...THAT MAN COMING MIGHT BE A CUSTOMER!
(COUGH) STOP! STOP! HE CAN'T EVEN SEE THE STORE!
(CHOKE)(COUGH) YOU CRAZY, WILD KIDS! WHY DON'T YOU WATCH WHAT YOU'RE DOING?
CHEE! SORRY, MISTER! WE DIDN'T SEE YOU COMING!
2

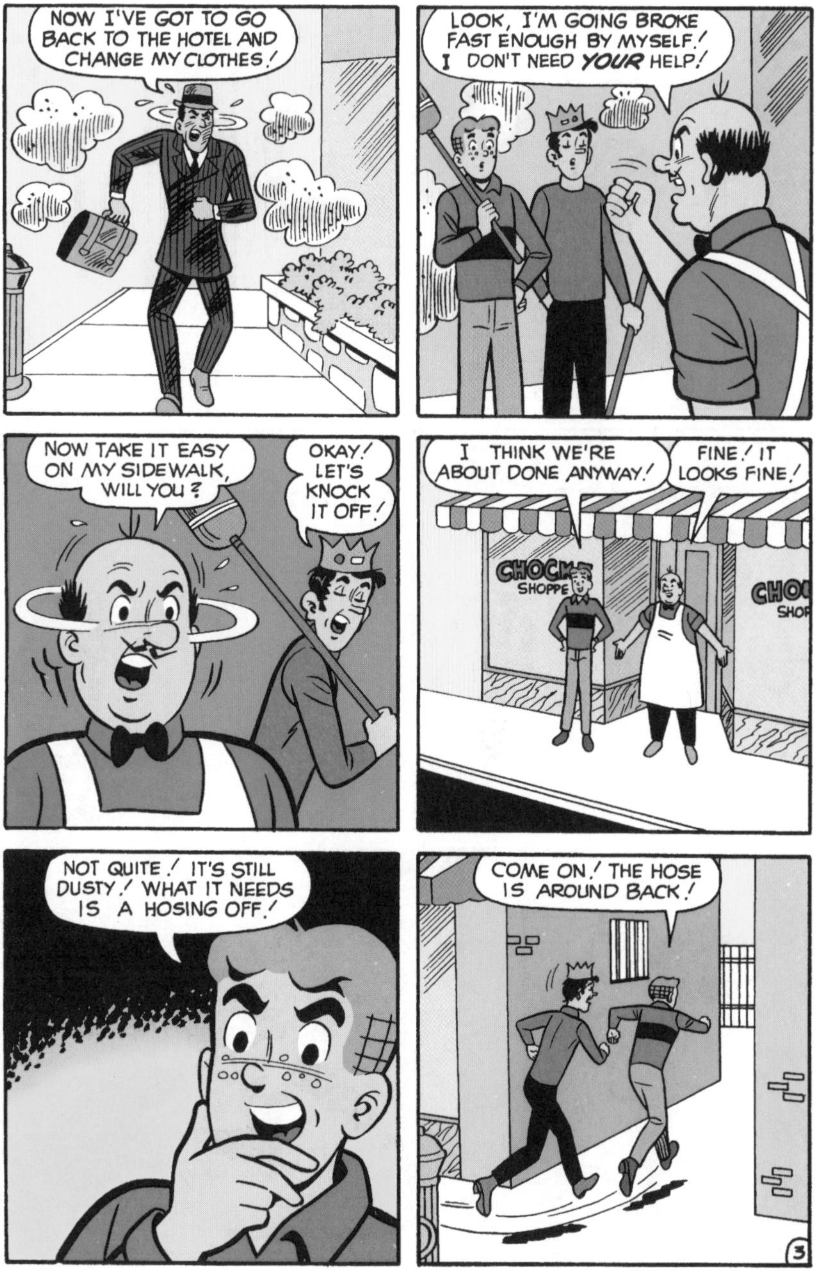
NOW I'VE GOT TO GO BACK TO THE HOTEL AND CHANGE MY CLOTHES!
LOOK, I'M GOING BROKE FAST ENOUGH BY MYSELF! I DON'T NEED YOUR HELP!
NOW TAKE IT EASY ON MY SIDEWALK, WILL YOU?
OKAY! LET'S KNOCK IT OFF!
I THINK WE'RE ABOUT DONE ANYWAY!
FINE! IT LOOKS FINE!
SHOPPE
NOT QUITE! IT'S STILL DUSTY! WHAT IT NEEDS IS A HOSING OFF!
COME ON! THE HOSE IS AROUND BACK!
3

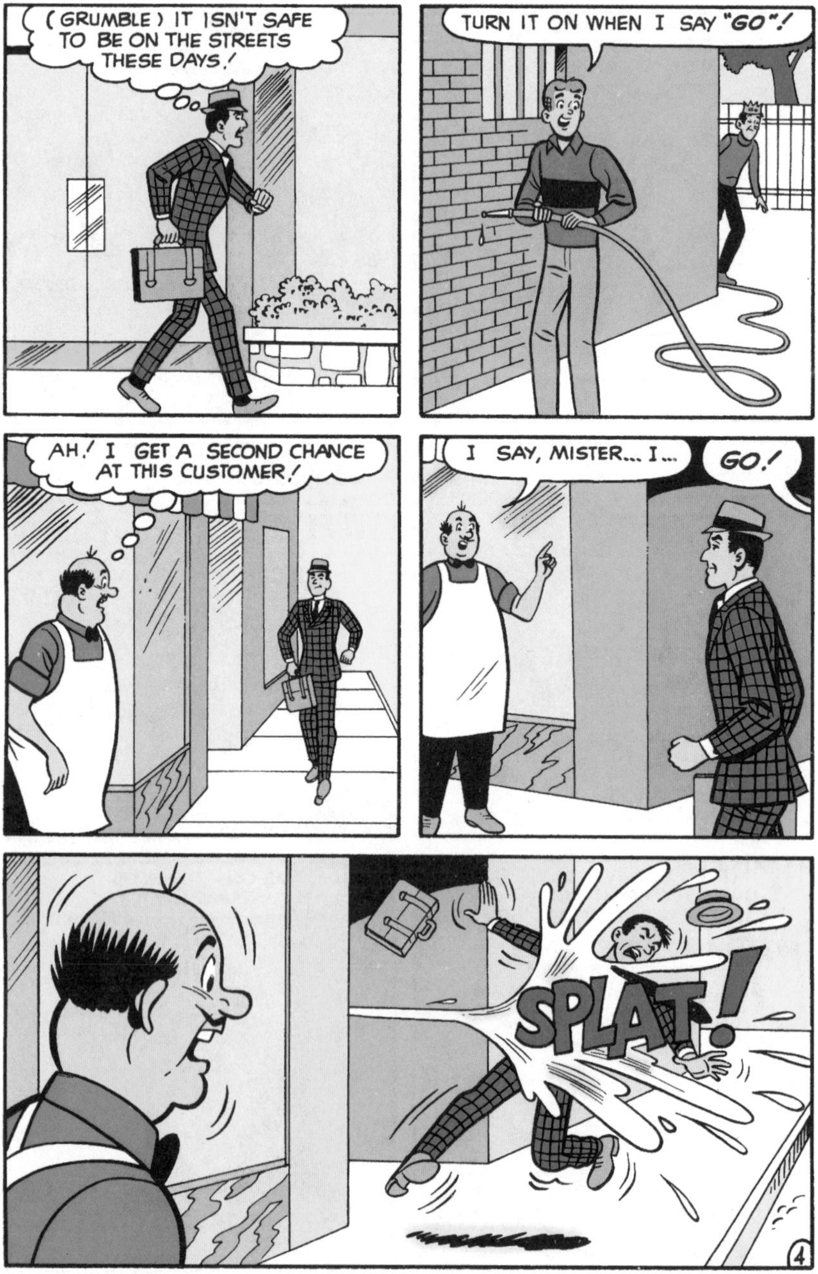
(GRUMBLE) IT ISN'T SAFE TO BE ON THE STREETS THESE DAYS!
TURN IT ON WHEN I SAY "GO"!
AH! I GET A SECOND CHANCE AT THIS CUSTOMER!
I SAY, MISTER... I...
GO!
SPLAT!
4

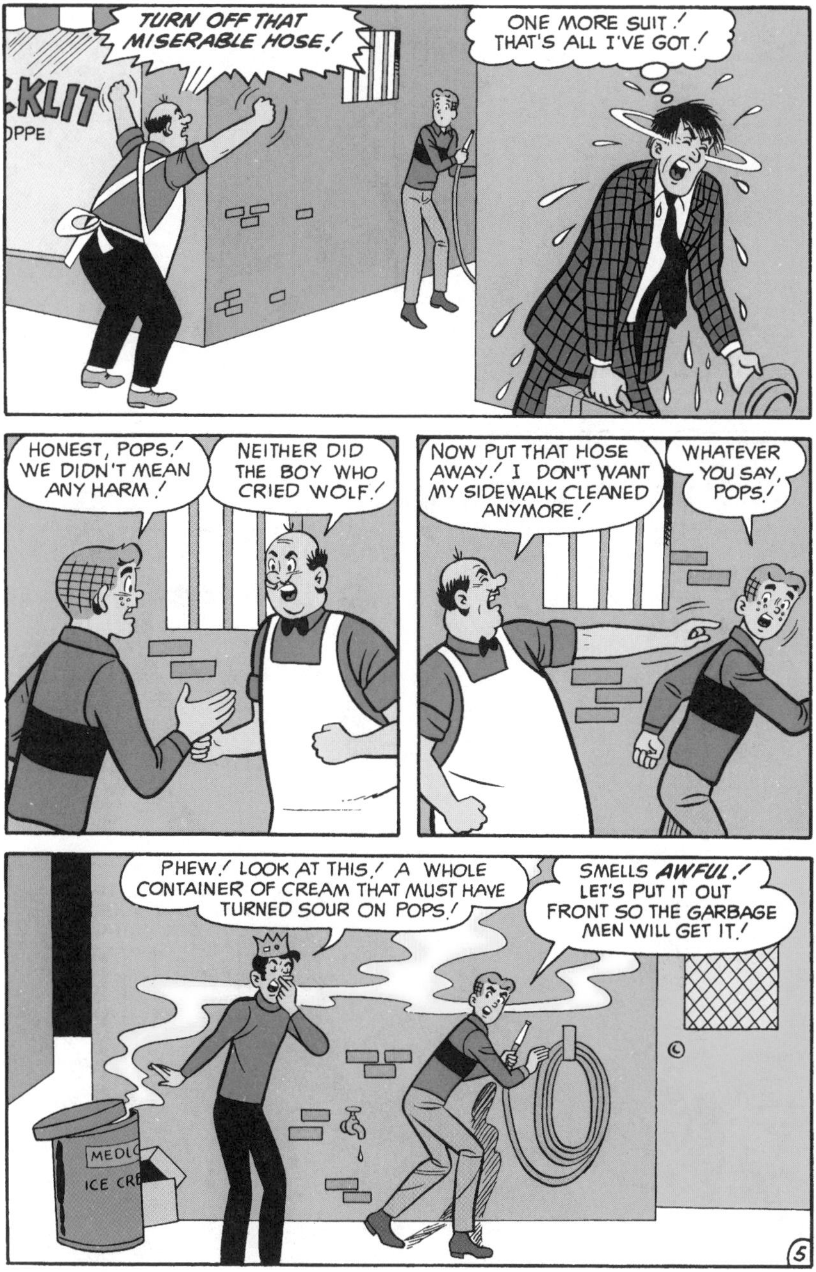
TURN OFF THAT MISERABLE HOSE!
KLIT
OPPE
ONE MORE SUIT! THAT'S ALL I'VE GOT!
HONEST, POPS! WE DIDN'T MEAN ANY HARM!
NEITHER DID THE BOY WHO CRIED WOLF!
NOW PUT THAT HOSE AWAY! I DON'T WANT MY SIDEWALK CLEANED ANYMORE!
WHATEVER YOU SAY, POPS!
PHEW! LOOK AT THIS! A WHOLE CONTAINER OF CREAM THAT MUST HAVE TURNED SOUR ON POPS!
SMELLS AWFUL! LET'S PUT IT OUT FRONT SO THE GARBAGE MEN WILL GET IT!
MEDL
ICE CR
5

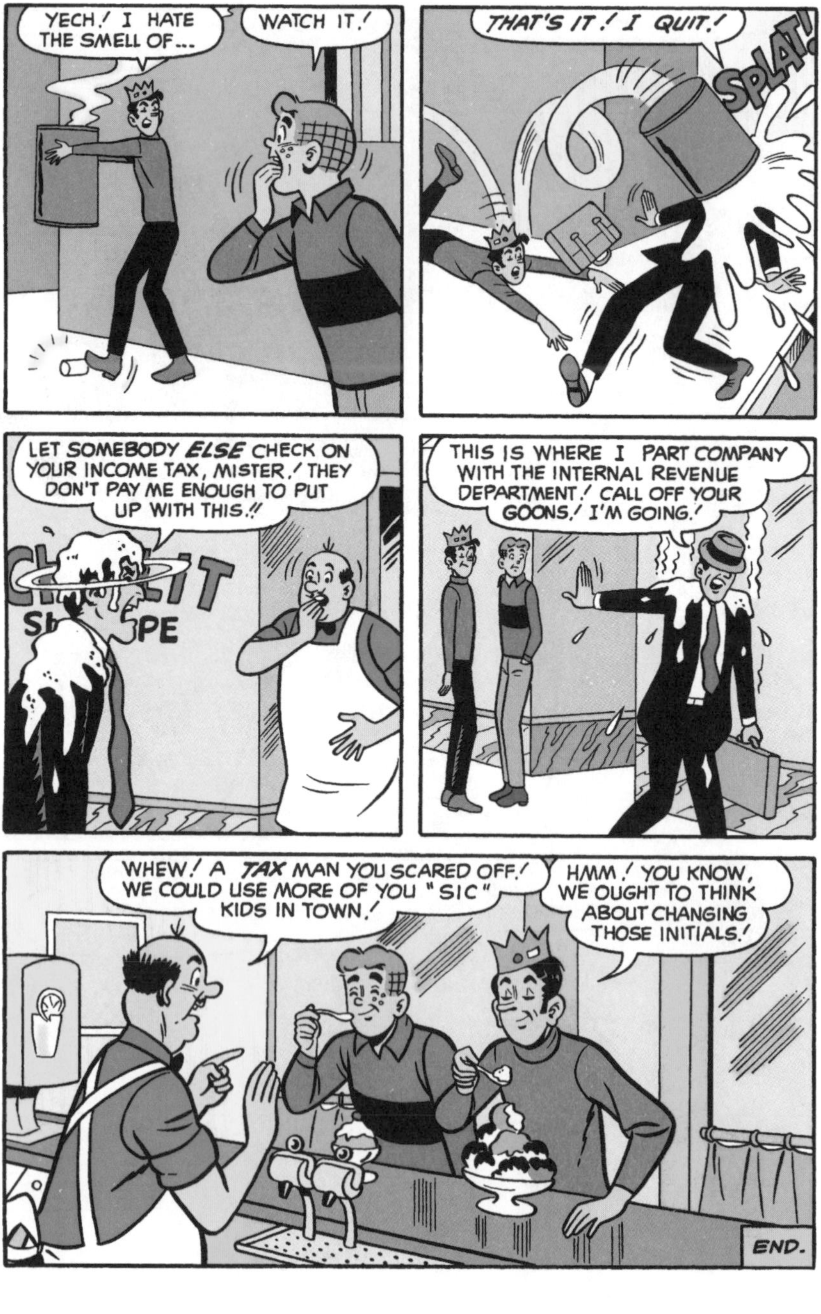
YECH! I HATE THE SMELL OF...
WATCH IT!
THAT'S IT! I QUIT!
SPLAT!
LET SOMEBODY ELSE CHECK ON YOUR INCOME TAX, MISTER! THEY DON'T PAY ME ENOUGH TO PUT UP WITH THIS!!
THIS IS WHERE I PART COMPANY WITH THE INTERNAL REVENUE DEPARTMENT! CALL OFF YOUR GOONS! I'M GOING!
WHEW! A TAX MAN YOU SCARED OFF! WE COULD USE MORE OF YOU "SIC" KIDS IN TOWN!
HMM! YOU KNOW, WE OUGHT TO THINK ABOUT CHANGING THOSE INITIALS!
END.

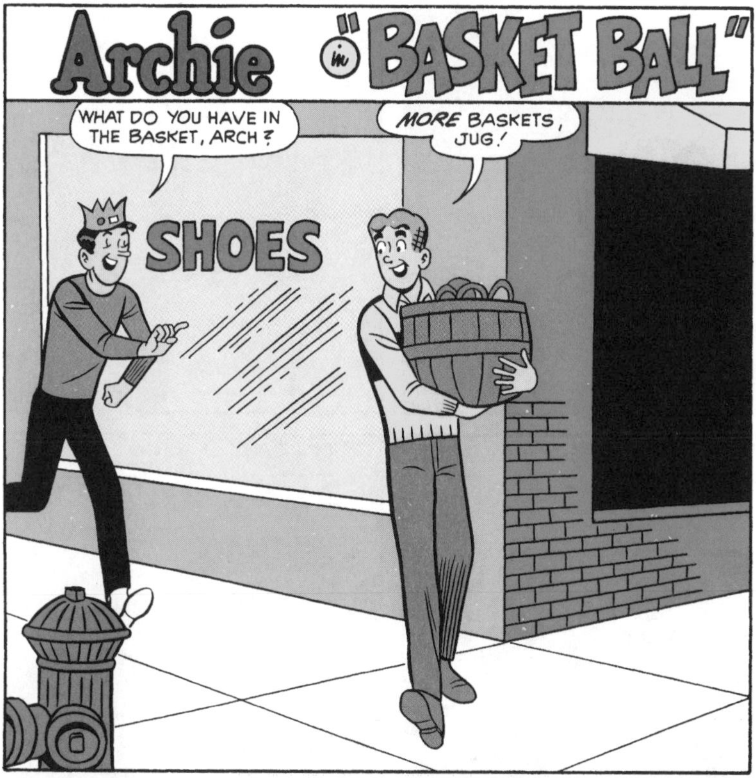
Archie in "BASKET BALL"
WHAT DO YOU HAVE IN THE BASKET, ARCH?
MORE BASKETS, JUG!
SHOES

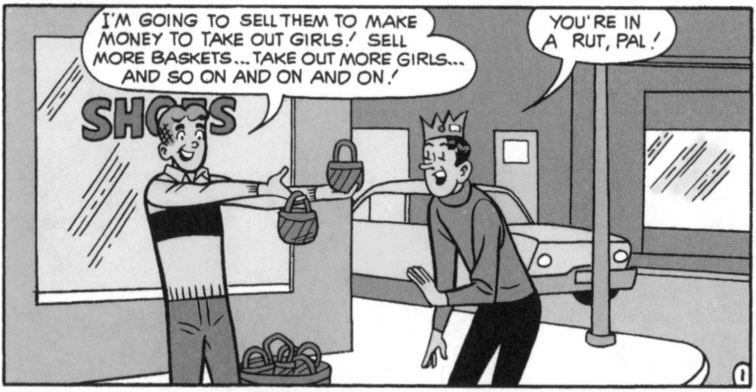
I'M GOING TO SELL THEM TO MAKE MONEY TO TAKE OUT GIRLS! SELL MORE BASKETS... TAKE OUT MORE GIRLS... AND SO ON AND ON AND ON!
YOU'RE IN A RUT, PAL!

Story: Frank Doyle Art: Bob White
Letters: Bill Yoshida Colors: Barry Grossman

Originally printed in EVERYTHING'S ARCHIE #14, JUNE 1971

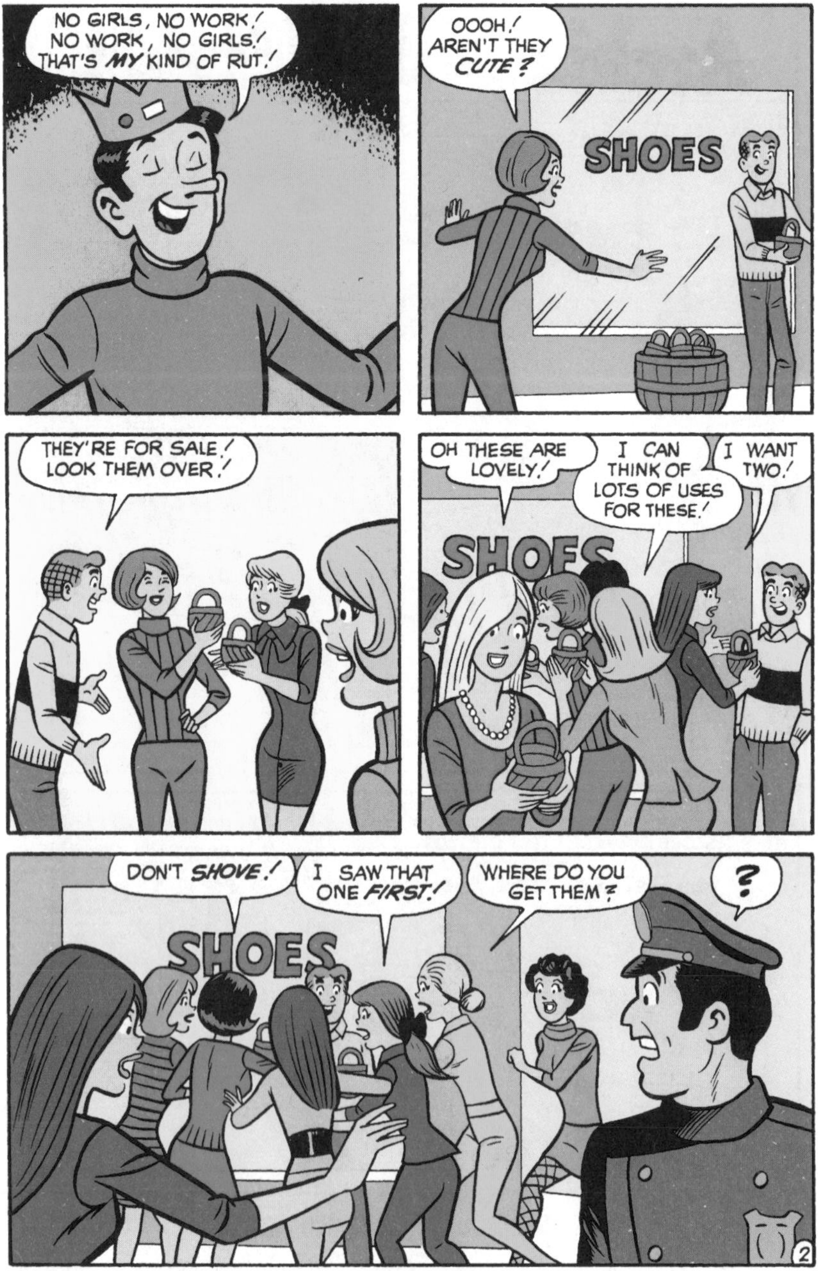
NO GIRLS, NO WORK! NO WORK, NO GIRLS! THAT'S MY KIND OF RUT!
OOOH! AREN'T THEY CUTE?
SHOES
THEY'RE FOR SALE! LOOK THEM OVER!
OH THESE ARE LOVELY!
I CAN THINK OF LOTS OF USES FOR THESE!
I WANT TWO!
DON'T SHOVE!
I SAW THAT ONE FIRST!
WHERE DO YOU GET THEM?
?
SHOES
2

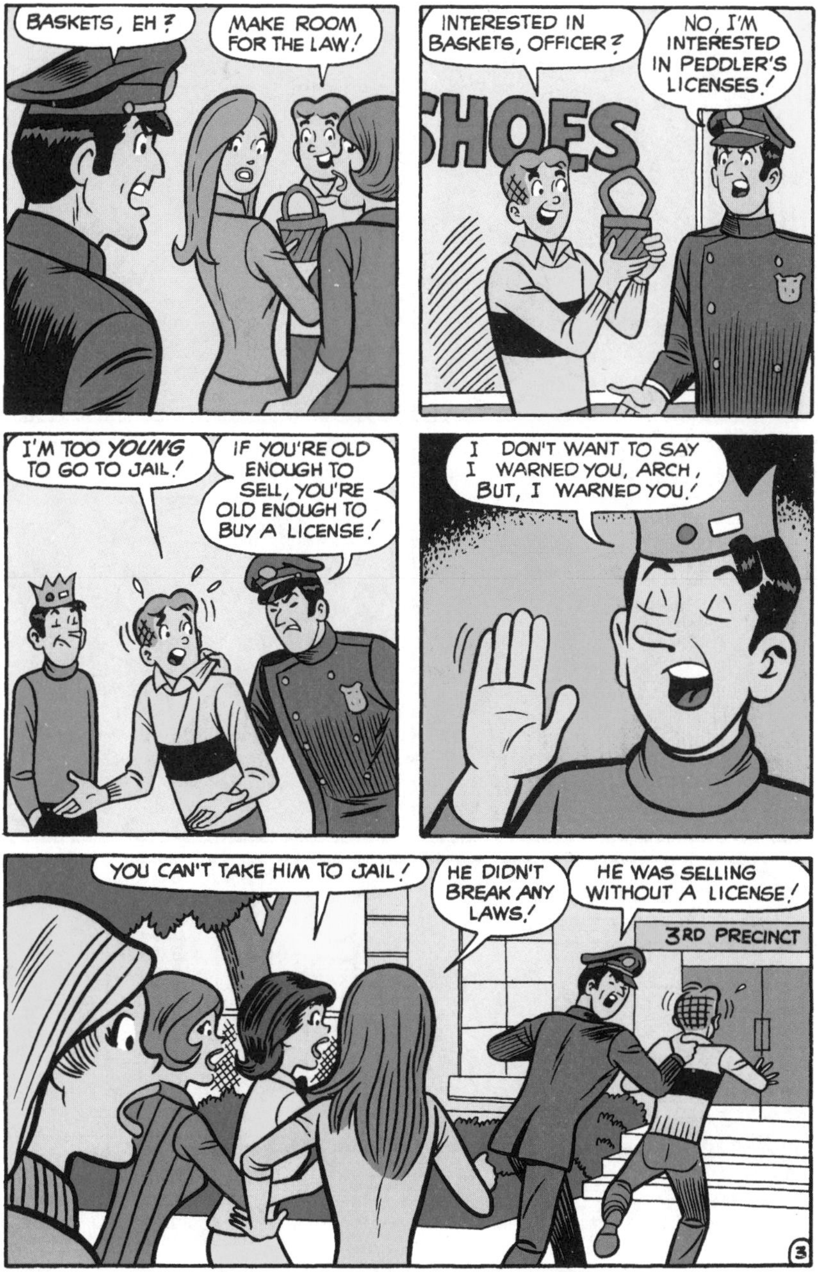
BASKETS, EH?
MAKE ROOM FOR THE LAW!
INTERESTED IN BASKETS, OFFICER?
NO, I'M INTERESTED IN PEDDLER'S LICENSES!
SHOES
I'M TOO YOUNG TO GO TO JAIL!
IF YOU'RE OLD ENOUGH TO SELL, YOU'RE OLD ENOUGH TO BUY A LICENSE!
I DON'T WANT TO SAY I WARNED YOU, ARCH, BUT, I WARNED YOU!
YOU CAN'T TAKE HIM TO JAIL!
HE DIDN'T BREAK ANY LAWS!
HE WAS SELLING WITHOUT A LICENSE!
3RD PRECINCT
3

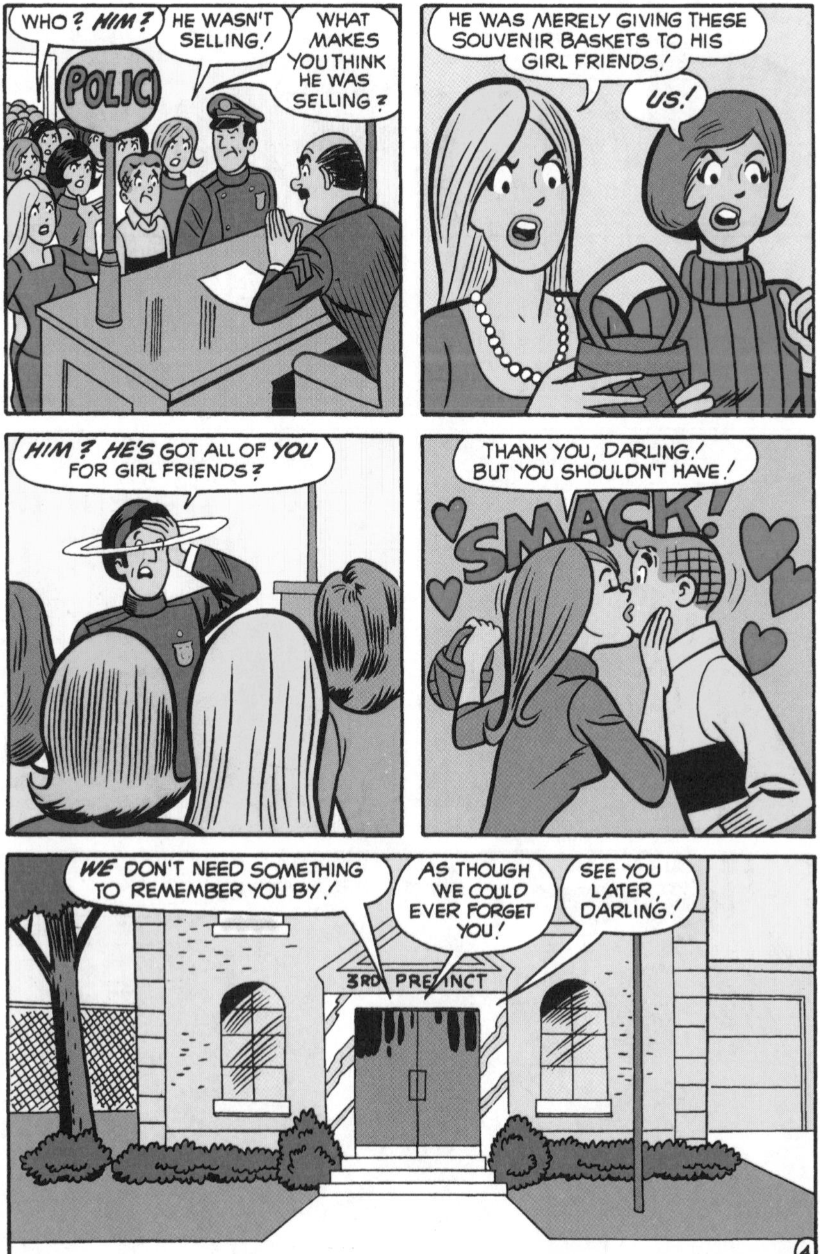
WHO? HIM?
HE WASN'T SELLING!
WHAT MAKES YOU THINK HE WAS SELLING?
POLIC
HE WAS MERELY GIVING THESE SOUVENIR BASKETS TO HIS GIRL FRIENDS!
US!
HIM? HE'S GOT ALL OF YOU FOR GIRL FRIENDS?
THANK YOU, DARLING! BUT YOU SHOULDN'T HAVE!
SMACK!
WE DON'T NEED SOMETHING TO REMEMBER YOU BY!
AS THOUGH WE COULD EVER FORGET YOU!
SEE YOU LATER, DARLING!
3RD PRECINCT
4

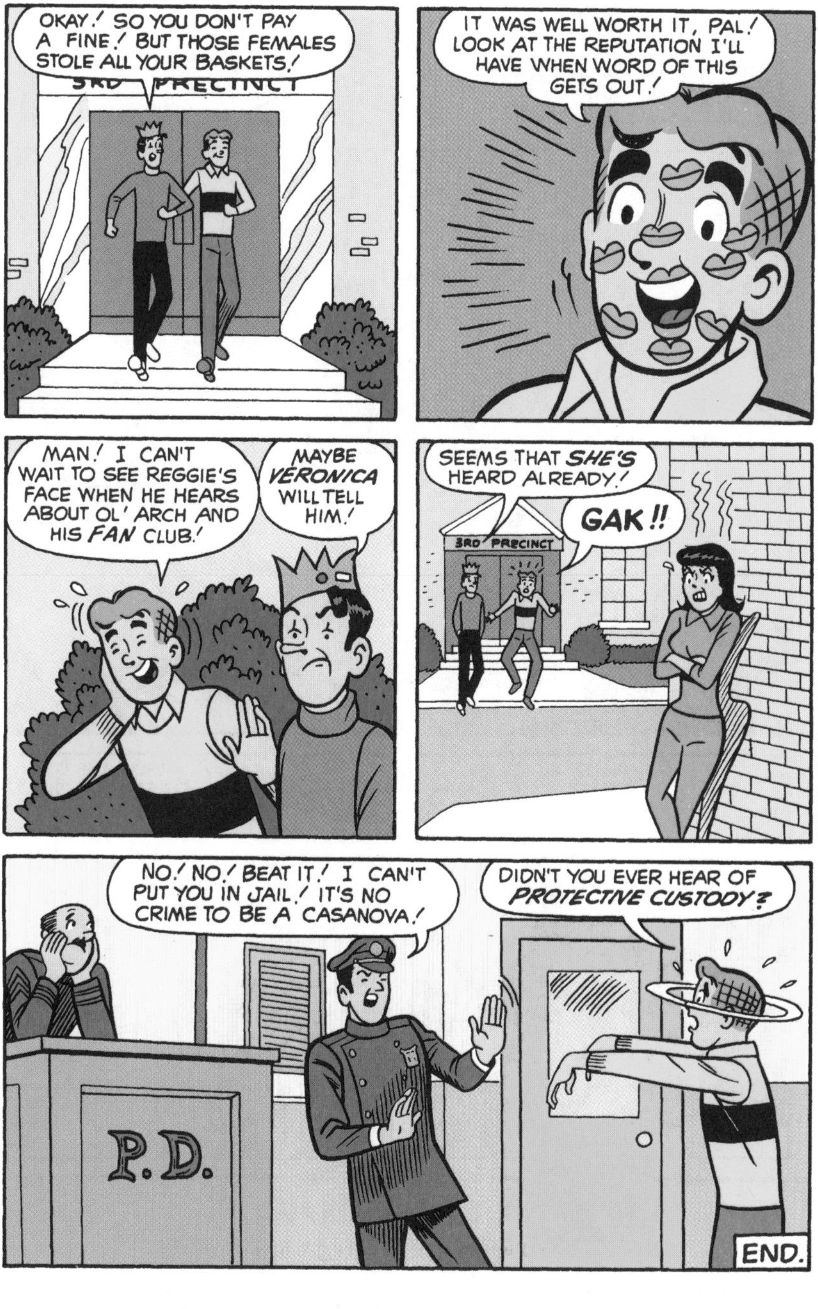
OKAY! SO YOU DON'T PAY A FINE! BUT THOSE FEMALES STOLE ALL YOUR BASKETS!
3RD PRECINCT
IT WAS WELL WORTH IT, PAL! LOOK AT THE REPUTATION I'LL HAVE WHEN WORD OF THIS GETS OUT!
MAN! I CAN'T WAIT TO SEE REGGIE'S FACE WHEN HE HEARS ABOUT OL' ARCH AND HIS FAN CLUB!
MAYBE VERONICA WILL TELL HIM!
SEEMS THAT SHE'S HEARD ALREADY!
GAK!!
3RD PRECINCT
NO! NO! BEAT IT! I CAN'T PUT YOU IN JAIL! IT'S NO CRIME TO BE A CASANOVA!
DIDN'T YOU EVER HEAR OF PROTECTIVE CUSTODY?
P.D.
END.

MISS GRUNDY -in- TEST RUN!

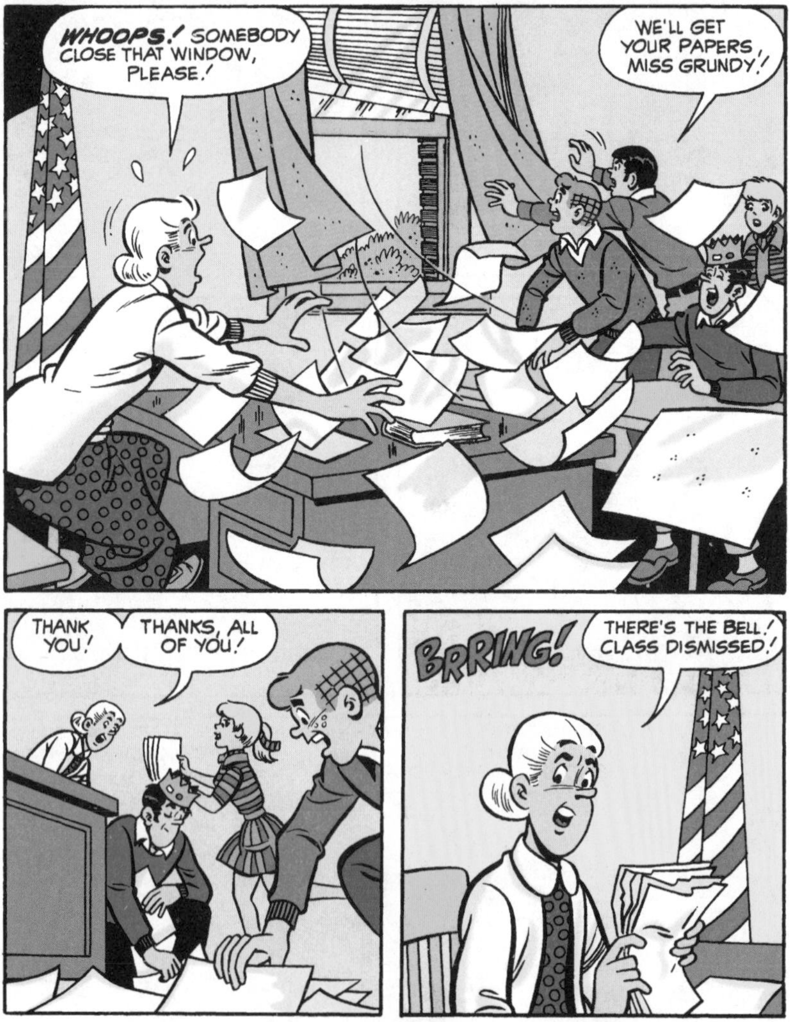
WHOOPS! SOMEBODY CLOSE THAT WINDOW, PLEASE!
WE'LL GET YOUR PAPERS, MISS GRUNDY!!
THANK YOU!
THANKS, ALL OF YOU!
BRRING!
THERE'S THE BELL! CLASS DISMISSED!

Story & Pencils: Al Hartley

Inks: Jon D'Agostino Letters: Bill Yoshida

Originally printed in EVERYTHING'S ARCHIE #15, AUGUST 1971

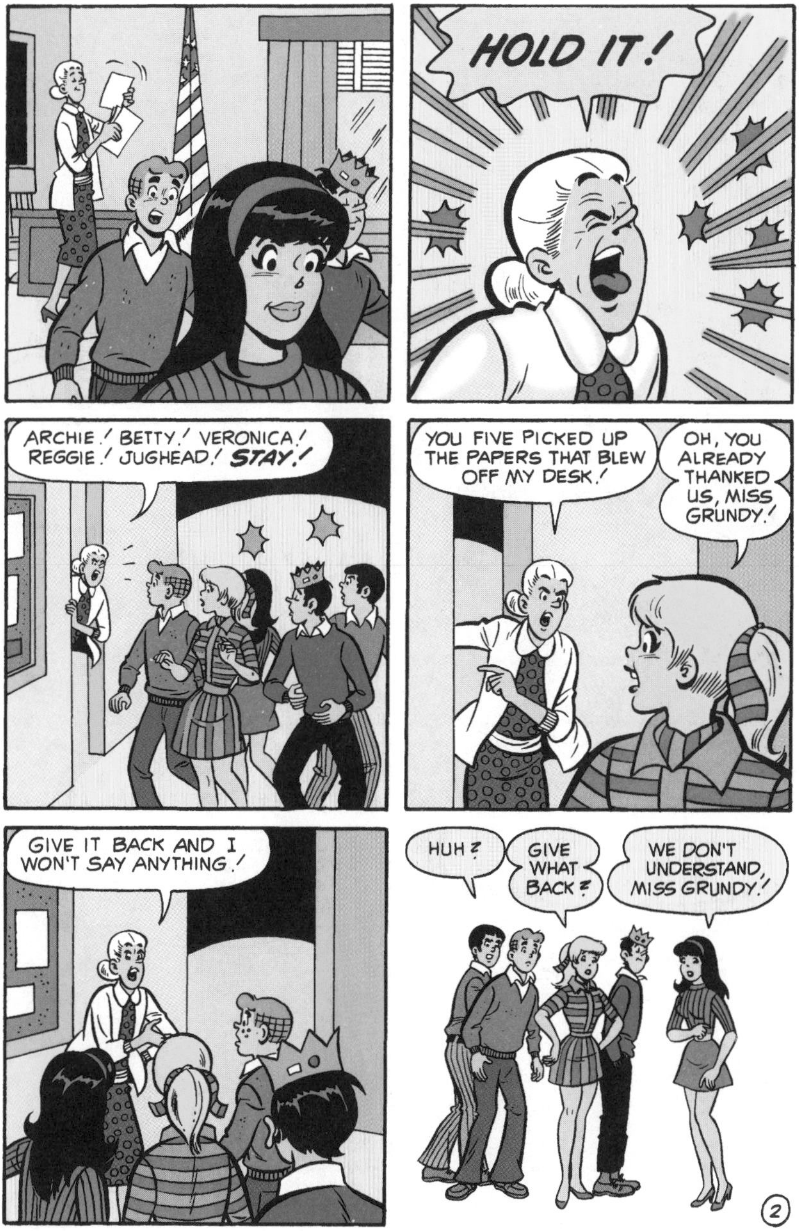
HOLD IT!
ARCHIE! BETTY! VERONICA! REGGIE! JUGHEAD! STAY!
YOU FIVE PICKED UP THE PAPERS THAT BLEW OFF MY DESK!
OH, YOU ALREADY THANKED US, MISS GRUNDY!
GIVE IT BACK AND I WON'T SAY ANYTHING!
HUH?
GIVE WHAT BACK?
WE DON'T UNDERSTAND, MISS GRUNDY!
2

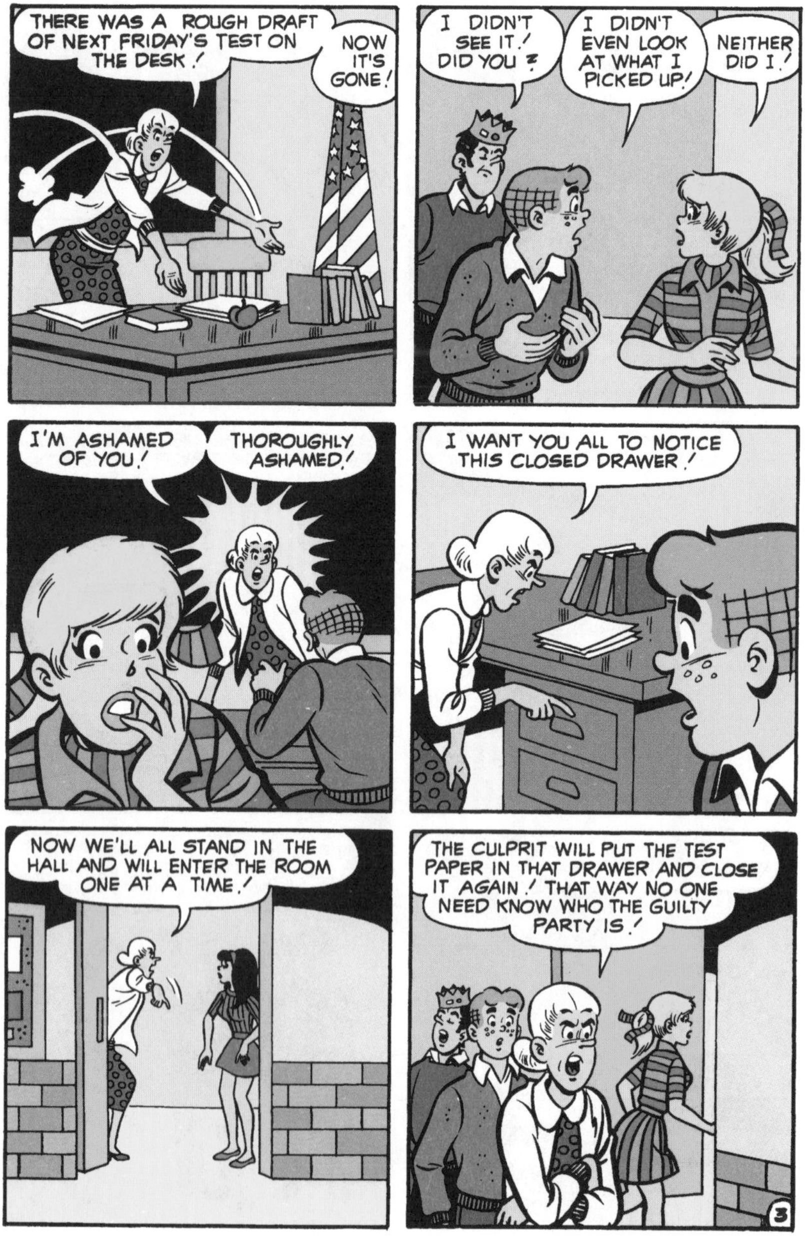
THERE WAS A ROUGH DRAFT OF NEXT FRIDAY'S TEST ON THE DESK!
NOW IT'S GONE!
I DIDN'T SEE IT! DID YOU?
I DIDN'T EVEN LOOK AT WHAT I PICKED UP!
NEITHER DID I!
I'M ASHAMED OF YOU!
THOROUGHLY ASHAMED!
I WANT YOU ALL TO NOTICE THIS CLOSED DRAWER!
NOW WE'LL ALL STAND IN THE HALL AND WILL ENTER THE ROOM ONE AT A TIME!
THE CULPRIT WILL PUT THE TEST PAPER IN THAT DRAWER AND CLOSE IT AGAIN! THAT WAY NO ONE NEED KNOW WHO THE GUILTY PARTY IS!
3

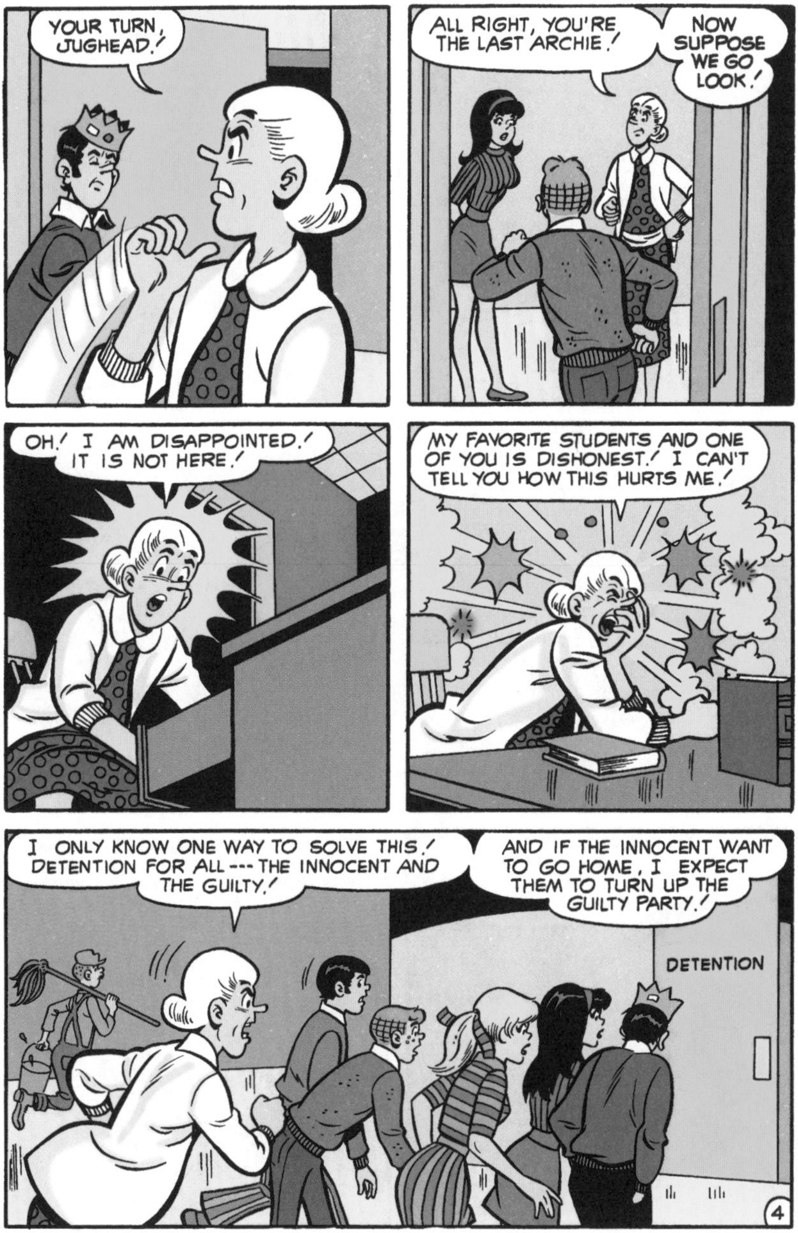
YOUR TURN, JUGHEAD!
ALL RIGHT, YOU'RE THE LAST ARCHIE!
NOW SUPPOSE WE GO LOOK!
OH! I AM DISAPPOINTED! IT IS NOT HERE!
MY FAVORITE STUDENTS AND ONE OF YOU IS DISHONEST! I CAN'T TELL YOU HOW THIS HURTS ME!
I ONLY KNOW ONE WAY TO SOLVE THIS! DETENTION FOR ALL --- THE INNOCENT AND THE GUILTY!
AND IF THE INNOCENT WANT TO GO HOME, I EXPECT THEM TO TURN UP THE GUILTY PARTY!
DETENTION
4

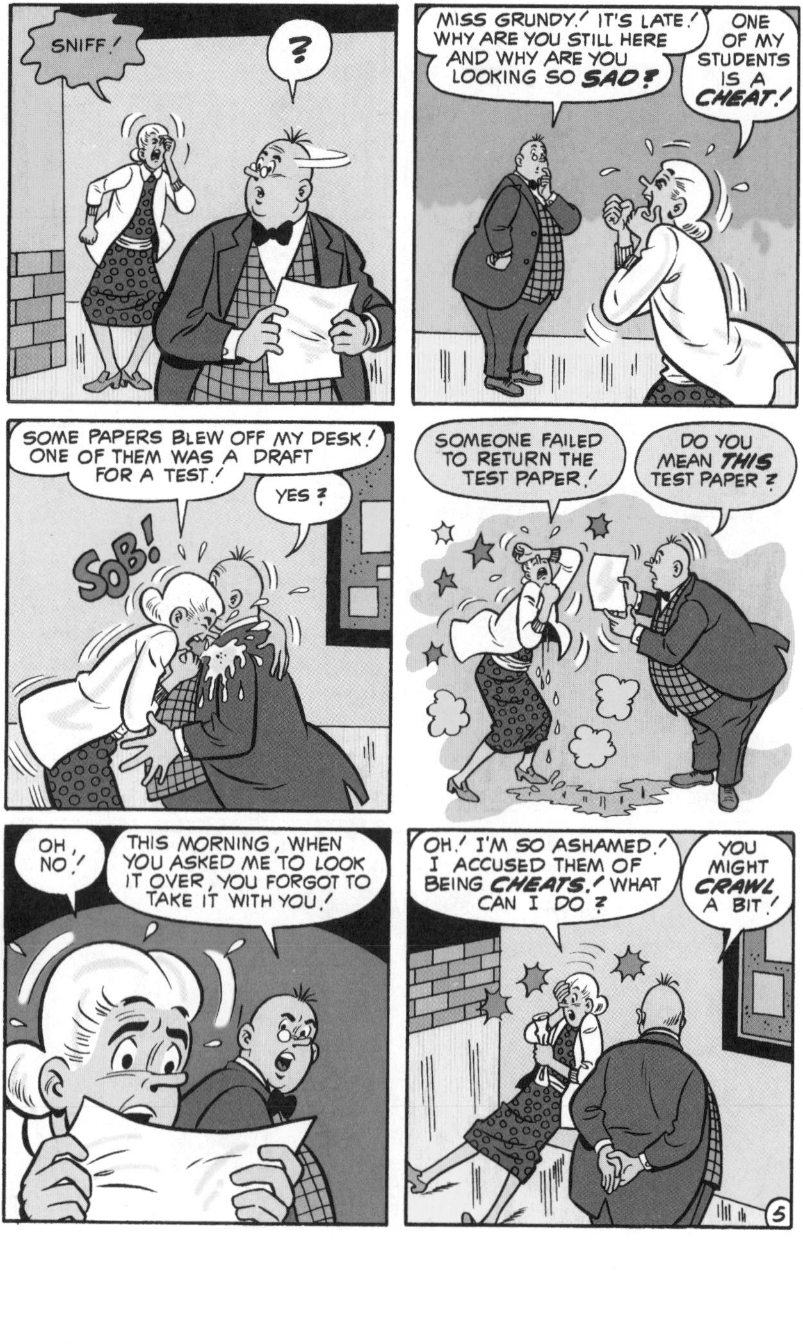
SNIFF!
?
MISS GRUNDY! IT'S LATE! WHY ARE YOU STILL HERE AND WHY ARE YOU LOOKING SO SAD?
ONE OF MY STUDENTS IS A CHEAT!
SOME PAPERS BLEW OFF MY DESK! ONE OF THEM WAS A DRAFT FOR A TEST!
YES?
SOB!
SOMEONE FAILED TO RETURN THE TEST PAPER!
DO YOU MEAN THIS TEST PAPER?
OH NO!!
THIS MORNING, WHEN YOU ASKED ME TO LOOK IT OVER, YOU FORGOT TO TAKE IT WITH YOU!
OH! I'M SO ASHAMED! I ACCUSED THEM OF BEING CHEATS! WHAT CAN I DO?
YOU MIGHT CRAWL A BIT!
5

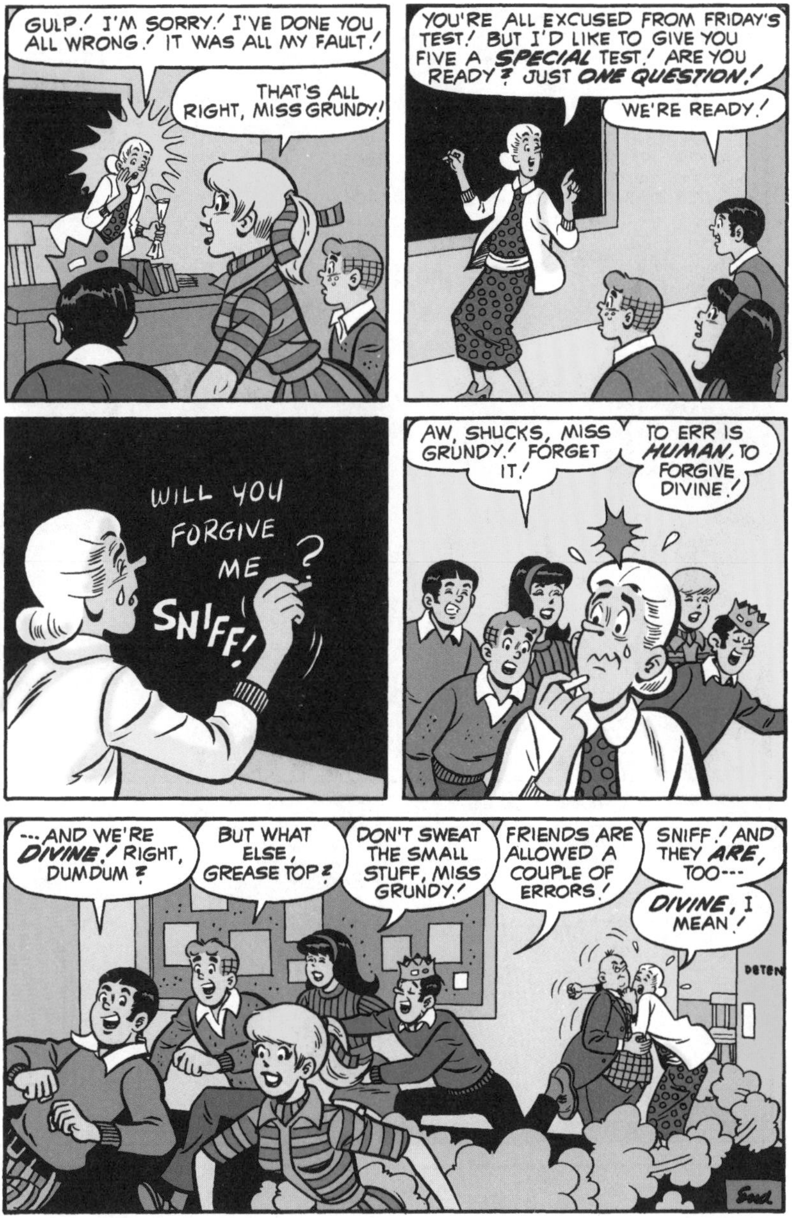
GULP! I'M SORRY! I'VE DONE YOU ALL WRONG! IT WAS ALL MY FAULT!
THAT'S ALL RIGHT, MISS GRUNDY!
YOU'RE ALL EXCUSED FROM FRIDAY'S TEST! BUT I'D LIKE TO GIVE YOU FIVE A SPECIAL TEST! ARE YOU READY? JUST ONE QUESTION!
WE'RE READY!
WILL YOU FORGIVE ME ?
SNIFF!
AW, SHUCKS, MISS GRUNDY! FORGET IT!
TO ERR IS HUMAN, TO FORGIVE DIVINE!
---AND WE'RE DIVINE! RIGHT, DUMDUM?
BUT WHAT ELSE, GREASE TOP?
DON'T SWEAT THE SMALL STUFF, MISS GRUNDY!
FRIENDS ARE ALLOWED A COUPLE OF ERRORS!
SNIFF! AND THEY ARE, TOO---
DIVINE, I MEAN!
End

DILTON TEACH-IN in Wet and Wild

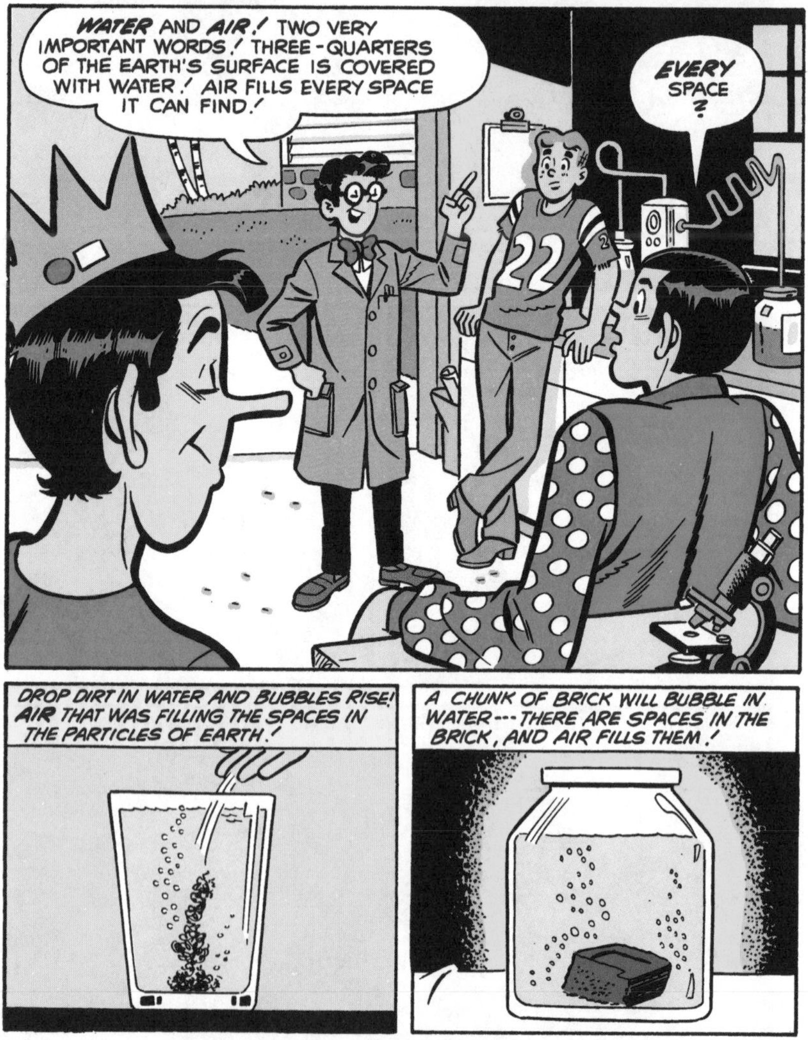
WATER AND AIR! TWO VERY IMPORTANT WORDS! THREE-QUARTERS OF THE EARTH'S SURFACE IS COVERED WITH WATER! AIR FILLS EVERY SPACE IT CAN FIND!
EVERY SPACE?
22
DROP DIRT IN WATER AND BUBBLES RISE! AIR THAT WAS FILLING THE SPACES IN THE PARTICLES OF EARTH!
A CHUNK OF BRICK WILL BUBBLE IN WATER---THERE ARE SPACES IN THE BRICK, AND AIR FILLS THEM!

Story: George Gladir Pencils: Dan DeCarlo
Inks: Rudy Lapick Letters: Bill Yoshida

Originally printed in EVERYTHING'S ARCHIE #15, AUGUST 1971

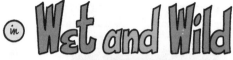

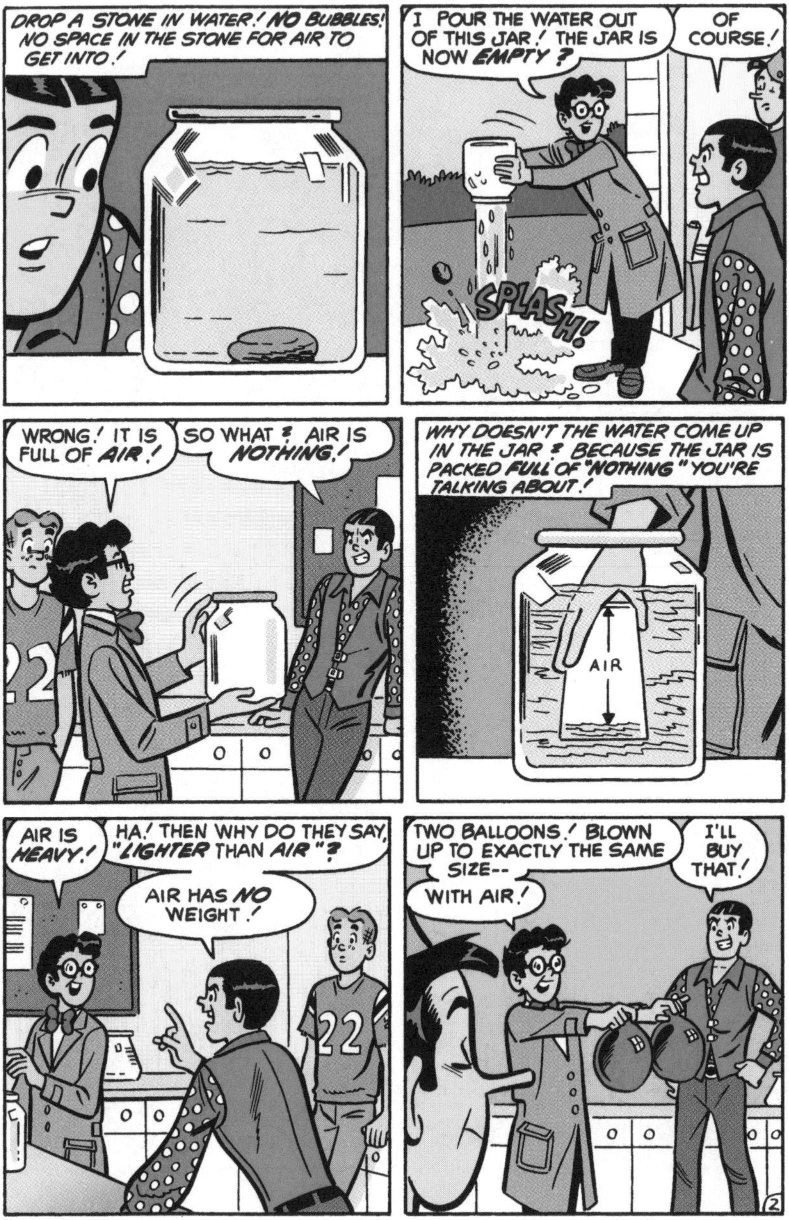
DROP A STONE IN WATER! NO BUBBLES! NO SPACE IN THE STONE FOR AIR TO GET INTO!
I POUR THE WATER OUT OF THIS JAR! THE JAR IS NOW EMPTY?
OF COURSE!
SPLASH!
WRONG! IT IS FULL OF AIR!
SO WHAT? AIR IS NOTHING!
WHY DOESN'T THE WATER COME UP IN THE JAR? BECAUSE THE JAR IS PACKED FULL OF "NOTHING" YOU'RE TALKING ABOUT!
AIR
AIR IS HEAVY!
HA! THEN WHY DO THEY SAY, "LIGHTER THAN AIR"?
AIR HAS NO WEIGHT!
TWO BALLOONS! BLOWN UP TO EXACTLY THE SAME SIZE--
WITH AIR!
I'LL BUY THAT!
2

PERFECTLY BALANCED! RIGHT!

SO?

HERE'S A PIN! BREAK ONE OF THOSE BALLOONS THAT ARE FILLED WITH THAT *"WEIGHTLESS"* AIR!

RIGHT ON, DILTON BABY!

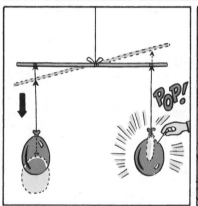

POP!

THE ONLY THING WE LOST WAS THAT "WEIGHTLESS" AIR-- YET THE OTHER ONE SUNK DOWN! HMM?

SONOFAGUN! THAT AIR IS HEAVY STUFF!

NOW! WATER CAN BE SOLID - LIQUID --OR GAS! LET ME SHOW YOU HOW!

DO THAT!

HOW ABOUT ICE CUBES? AREN'T THEY *SOLID WATER*?

THE KID'S RIGHT!

3

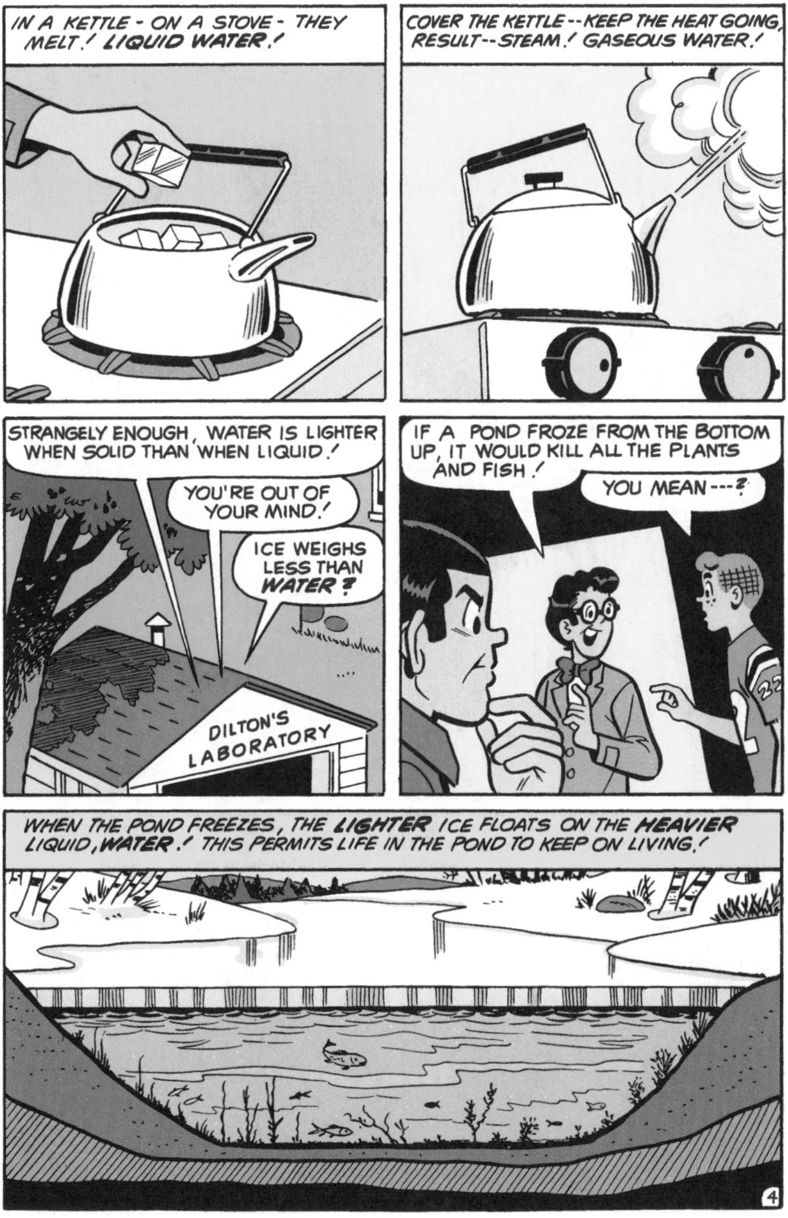
IN A KETTLE - ON A STOVE - THEY MELT! LIQUID WATER!
COVER THE KETTLE--KEEP THE HEAT GOING, RESULT--STEAM! GASEOUS WATER!
STRANGELY ENOUGH, WATER IS LIGHTER WHEN SOLID THAN WHEN LIQUID!
YOU'RE OUT OF YOUR MIND!
ICE WEIGHS LESS THAN WATER?
DILTON'S LABORATORY
IF A POND FROZE FROM THE BOTTOM UP, IT WOULD KILL ALL THE PLANTS AND FISH!
YOU MEAN---?
WHEN THE POND FREEZES, THE LIGHTER ICE FLOATS ON THE HEAVIER LIQUID, WATER! THIS PERMITS LIFE IN THE POND TO KEEP ON LIVING!
4

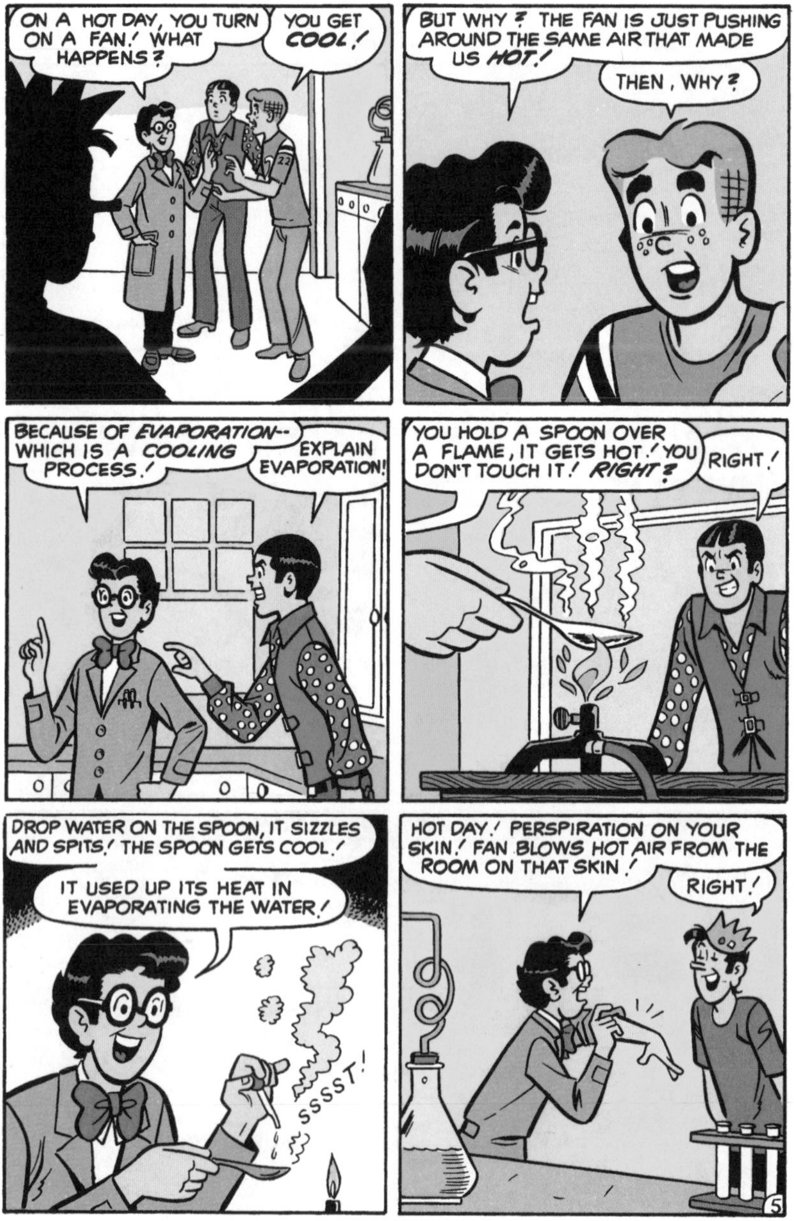
ON A HOT DAY, YOU TURN ON A FAN! WHAT HAPPENS?
YOU GET COOL!
BUT WHY? THE FAN IS JUST PUSHING AROUND THE SAME AIR THAT MADE US HOT!
THEN, WHY?
BECAUSE OF EVAPORATION-- WHICH IS A COOLING PROCESS!
EXPLAIN EVAPORATION!
YOU HOLD A SPOON OVER A FLAME, IT GETS HOT! YOU DON'T TOUCH IT! RIGHT?
RIGHT!
DROP WATER ON THE SPOON, IT SIZZLES AND SPITS! THE SPOON GETS COOL!
IT USED UP ITS HEAT IN EVAPORATING THE WATER!
SSSST!
HOT DAY! PERSPIRATION ON YOUR SKIN! FAN BLOWS HOT AIR FROM THE ROOM ON THAT SKIN!
RIGHT!
5

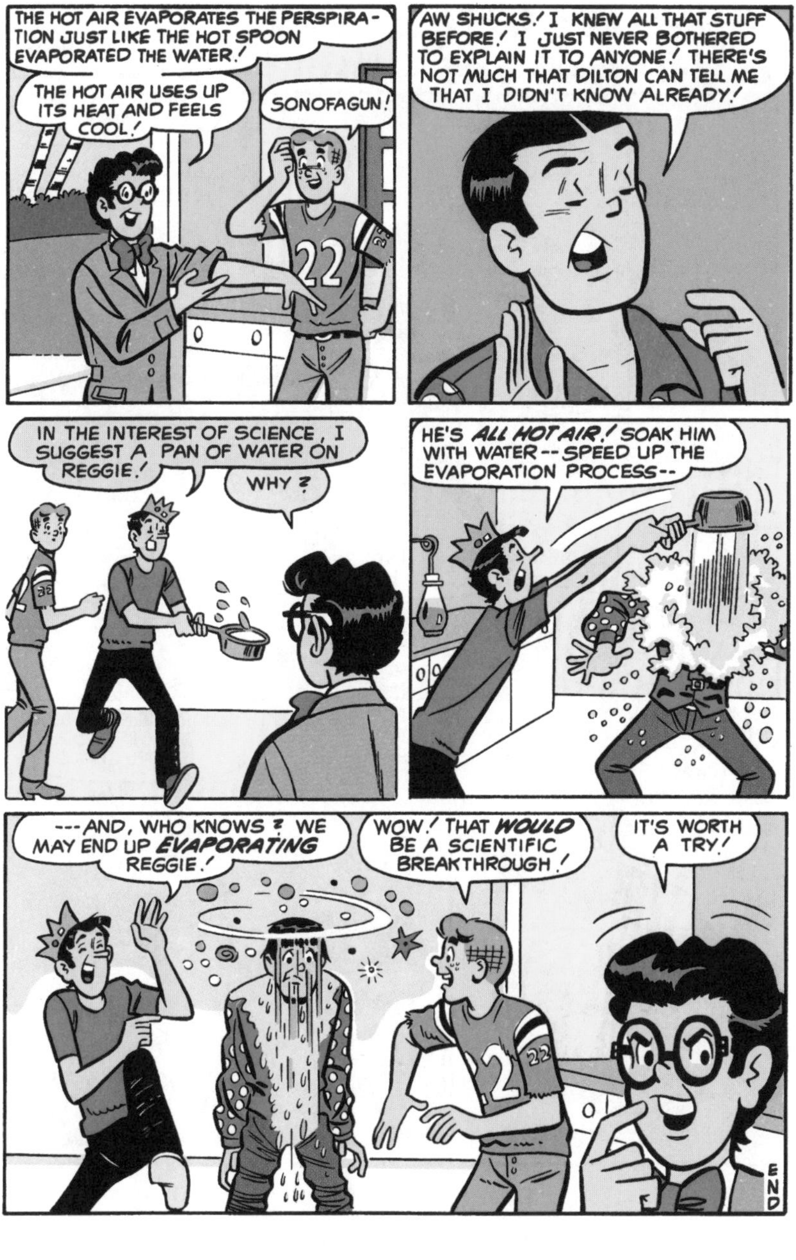
THE HOT AIR EVAPORATES THE PERSPIRATION JUST LIKE THE HOT SPOON EVAPORATED THE WATER!
THE HOT AIR USES UP ITS HEAT AND FEELS COOL!
SONOFAGUN!
AW SHUCKS! I KNEW ALL THAT STUFF BEFORE! I JUST NEVER BOTHERED TO EXPLAIN IT TO ANYONE! THERE'S NOT MUCH THAT DILTON CAN TELL ME THAT I DIDN'T KNOW ALREADY!
IN THE INTEREST OF SCIENCE, I SUGGEST A PAN OF WATER ON REGGIE!
WHY?
HE'S ALL HOT AIR! SOAK HIM WITH WATER -- SPEED UP THE EVAPORATION PROCESS --
--- AND, WHO KNOWS? WE MAY END UP EVAPORATING REGGIE!
WOW! THAT WOULD BE A SCIENTIFIC BREAKTHROUGH!
IT'S WORTH A TRY!
END

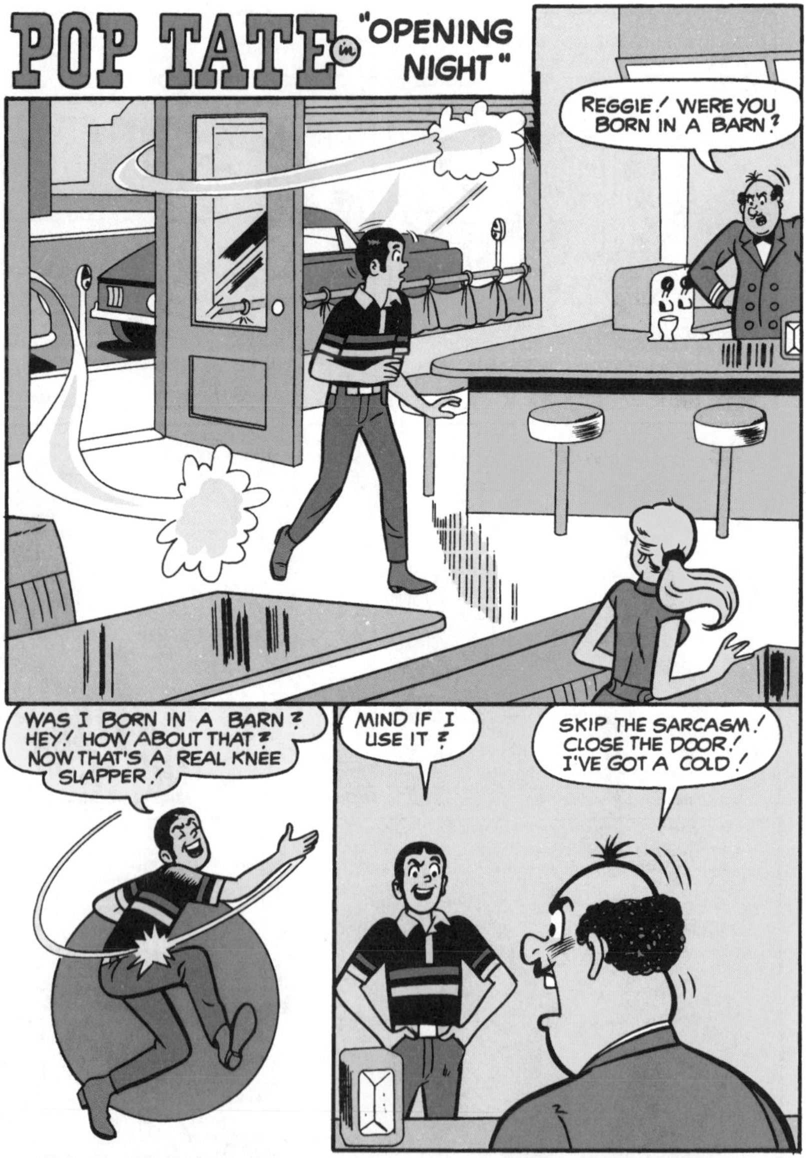
POP TATE in "OPENING NIGHT"
REGGIE! WERE YOU BORN IN A BARN?
WAS I BORN IN A BARN? HEY! HOW ABOUT THAT? NOW THAT'S A REAL KNEE SLAPPER!
MIND IF I USE IT?
SKIP THE SARCASM! CLOSE THE DOOR! I'VE GOT A COLD!

Story: George Gladir Pencils: Bob Bolling
Inks: Rudy Lapick Letters: Bill Yoshida

Originally printed in EVERYTHING'S ARCHIE #15, AUGUST 1971

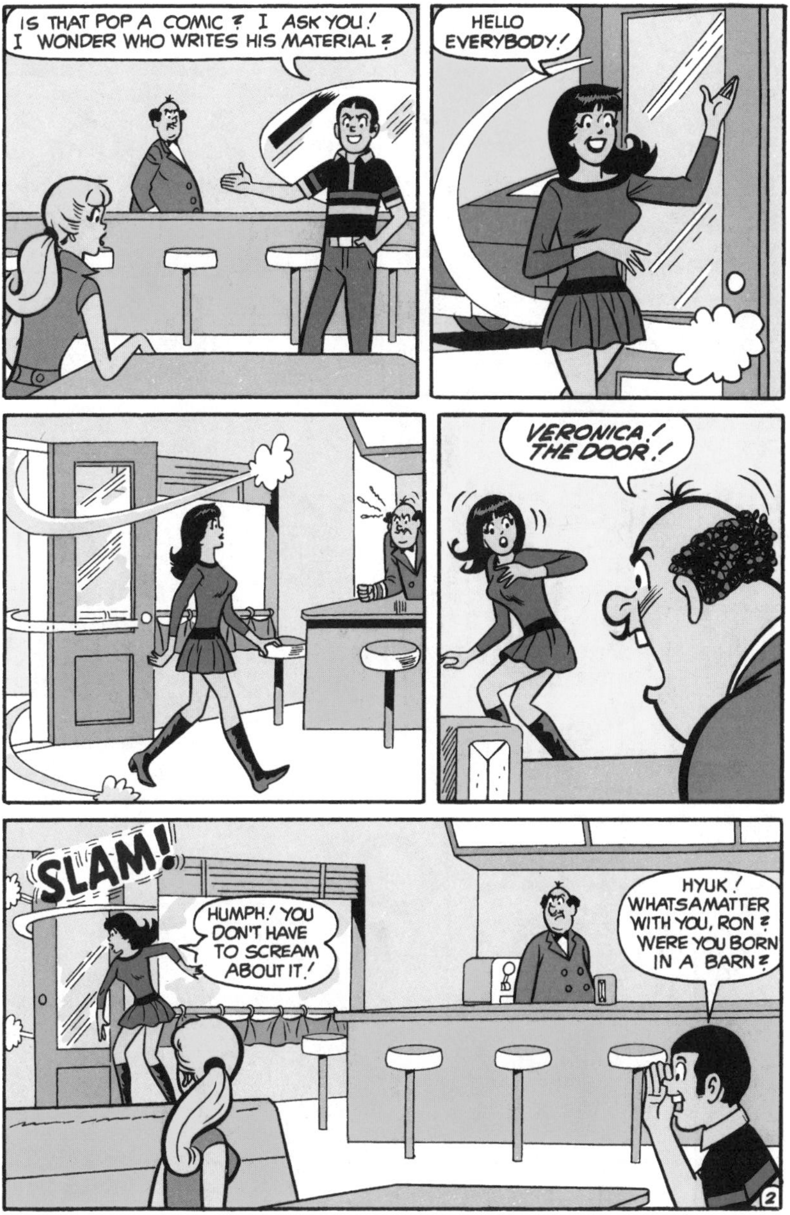
IS THAT POP A COMIC ? I ASK YOU! I WONDER WHO WRITES HIS MATERIAL ?
HELLO EVERYBODY!
VERONICA! THE DOOR!
SLAM!
HUMPH! YOU DON'T HAVE TO SCREAM ABOUT IT!
HYUK! WHATSAMATTER WITH YOU, RON ? WERE YOU BORN IN A BARN ?
2

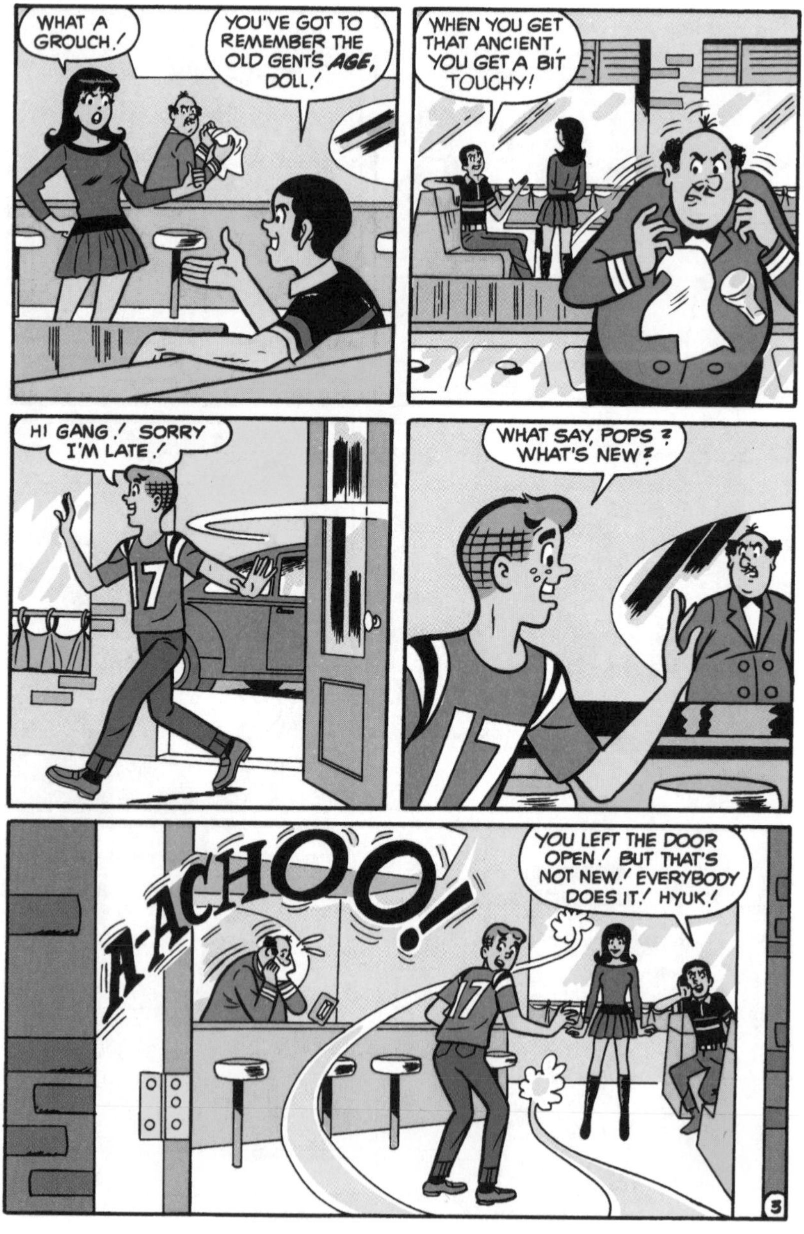
WHAT A GROUCH!
YOU'VE GOT TO REMEMBER THE OLD GENT'S AGE, DOLL!
WHEN YOU GET THAT ANCIENT, YOU GET A BIT TOUCHY!
HI GANG! SORRY I'M LATE!
WHAT SAY, POPS? WHAT'S NEW?
A-ACHOOO!
YOU LEFT THE DOOR OPEN! BUT THAT'S NOT NEW! EVERYBODY DOES IT! HYUK!
3

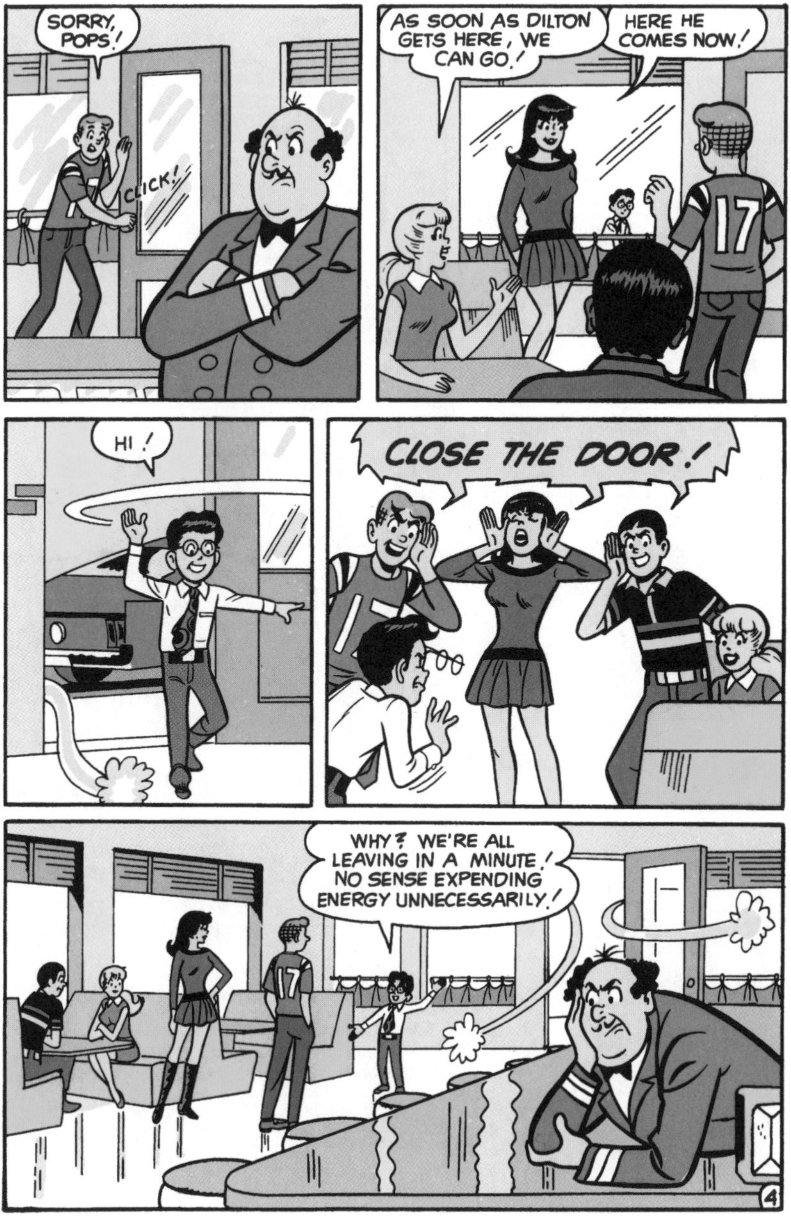
SORRY, POPS!
CLICK!
AS SOON AS DILTON GETS HERE, WE CAN GO!
HERE HE COMES NOW!
HI!
CLOSE THE DOOR!
WHY? WE'RE ALL LEAVING IN A MINUTE! NO SENSE EXPENDING ENERGY UNNECESSARILY!
4

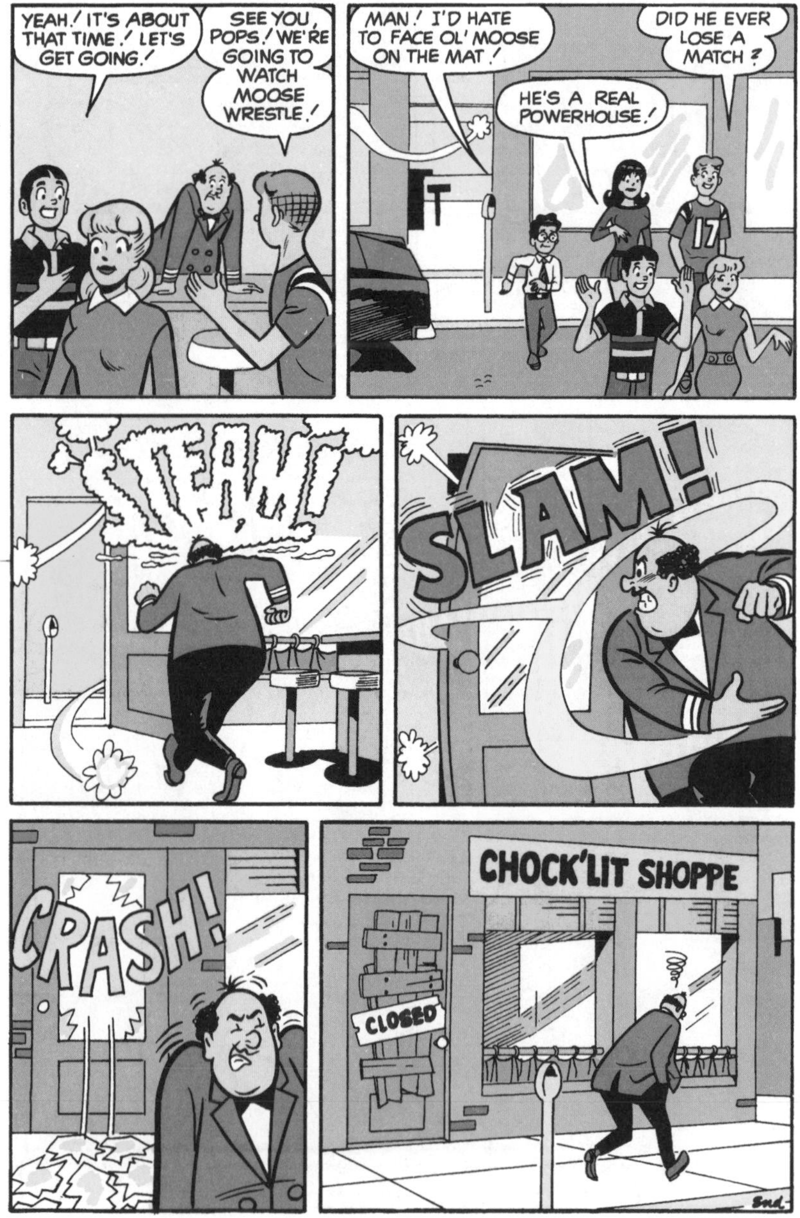
YEAH! IT'S ABOUT THAT TIME! LET'S GET GOING!
SEE YOU, POPS! WE'RE GOING TO WATCH MOOSE WRESTLE!
MAN! I'D HATE TO FACE OL' MOOSE ON THE MAT!
HE'S A REAL POWERHOUSE!
DID HE EVER LOSE A MATCH?
STEAM!
SLAM!
CRASH!
CHOCK'LIT SHOPPE
CLOSED
End

THE Archies "SUMMER PRAYER FOR PEACE"

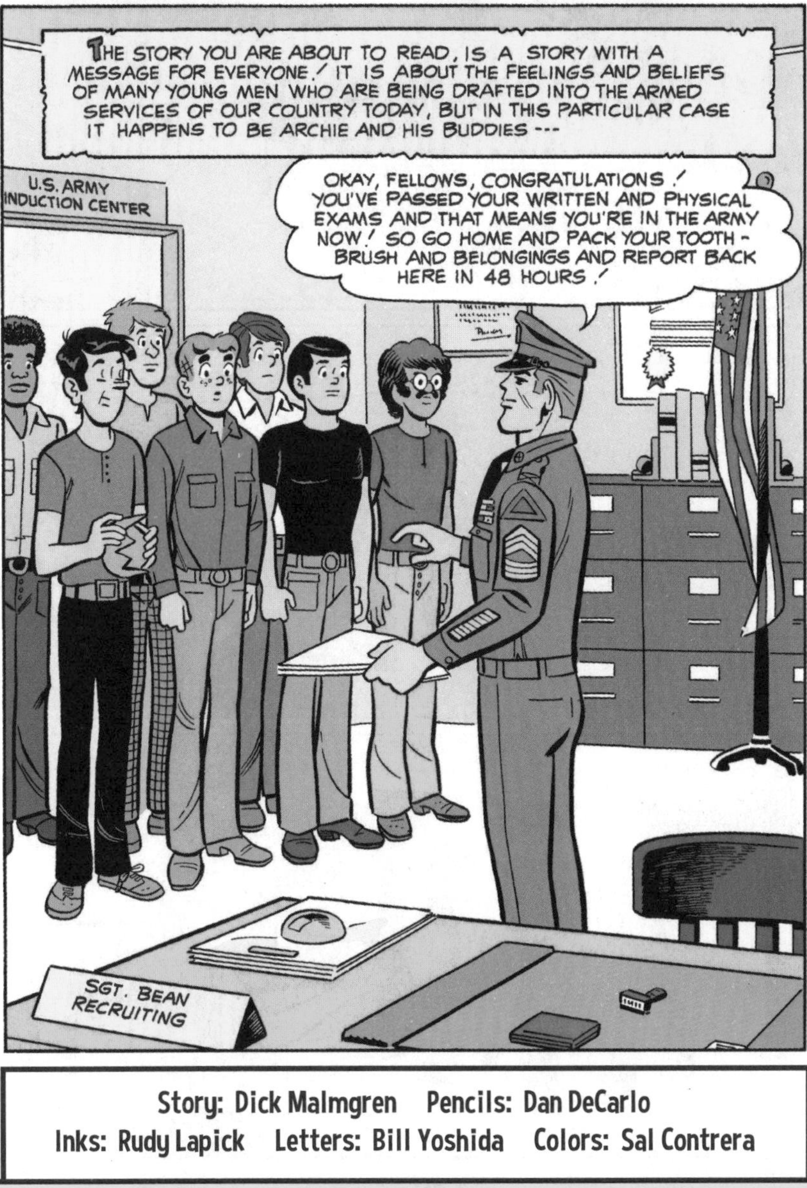
THE STORY YOU ARE ABOUT TO READ, IS A STORY WITH A MESSAGE FOR EVERYONE! IT IS ABOUT THE FEELINGS AND BELIEFS OF MANY YOUNG MEN WHO ARE BEING DRAFTED INTO THE ARMED SERVICES OF OUR COUNTRY TODAY, BUT IN THIS PARTICULAR CASE IT HAPPENS TO BE ARCHIE AND HIS BUDDIES ---
U.S. ARMY INDUCTION CENTER
OKAY, FELLOWS, CONGRATULATIONS! YOU'VE PASSED YOUR WRITTEN AND PHYSICAL EXAMS AND THAT MEANS YOU'RE IN THE ARMY NOW! SO GO HOME AND PACK YOUR TOOTH-BRUSH AND BELONGINGS AND REPORT BACK HERE IN 48 HOURS!
SGT. BEAN RECRUITING

Story: Dick Malmgren Pencils: Dan DeCarlo
Inks: Rudy Lapick Letters: Bill Yoshida Colors: Sal Contrera

Originally printed in EVERYTHING'S ARCHIE #16, OCTOBER 1971

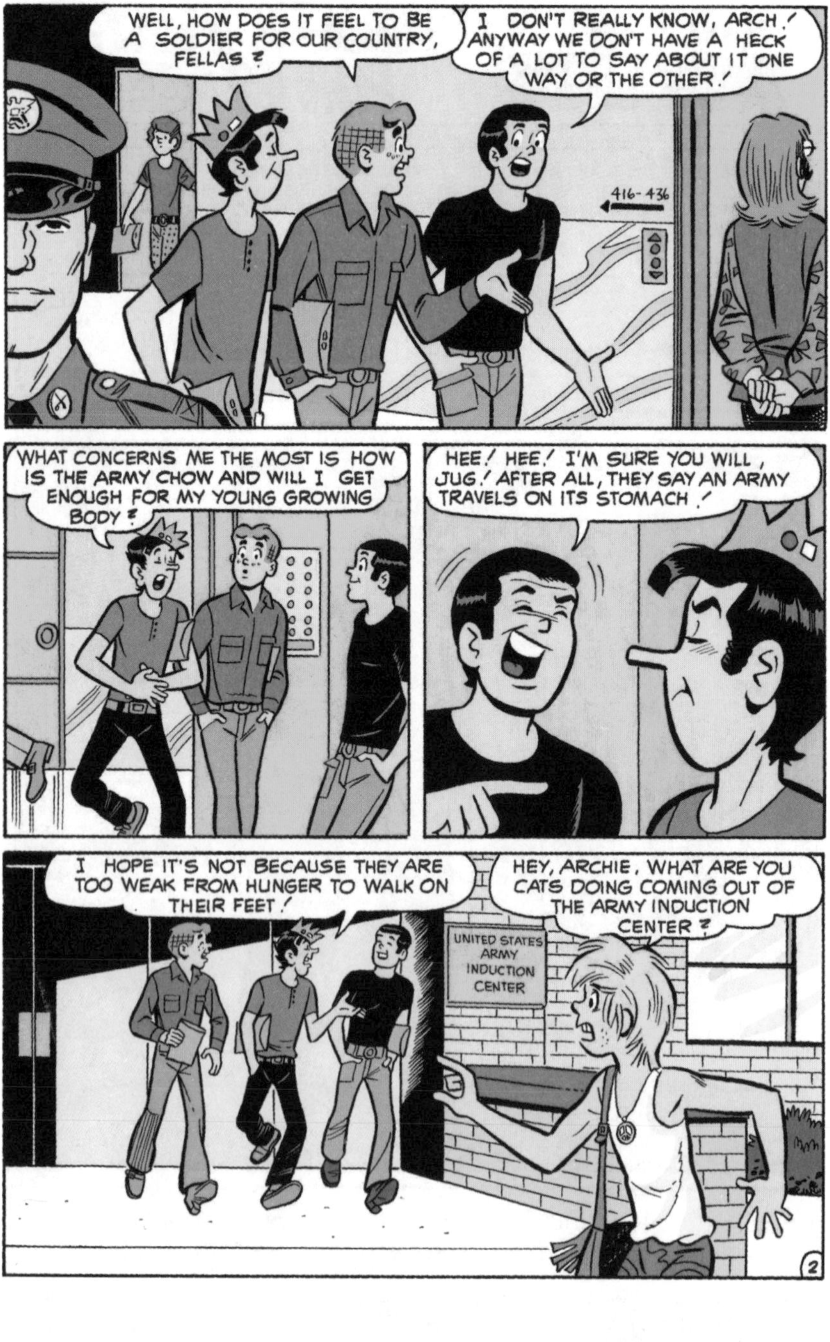
WELL, HOW DOES IT FEEL TO BE A SOLDIER FOR OUR COUNTRY, FELLAS ?
I DON'T REALLY KNOW, ARCH! ANYWAY WE DON'T HAVE A HECK OF A LOT TO SAY ABOUT IT ONE WAY OR THE OTHER!
416-436
WHAT CONCERNS ME THE MOST IS HOW IS THE ARMY CHOW AND WILL I GET ENOUGH FOR MY YOUNG GROWING BODY ?
HEE! HEE! I'M SURE YOU WILL, JUG! AFTER ALL, THEY SAY AN ARMY TRAVELS ON ITS STOMACH!
I HOPE IT'S NOT BECAUSE THEY ARE TOO WEAK FROM HUNGER TO WALK ON THEIR FEET!
HEY, ARCHIE, WHAT ARE YOU CATS DOING COMING OUT OF THE ARMY INDUCTION CENTER ?
UNITED STATES ARMY INDUCTION CENTER
2

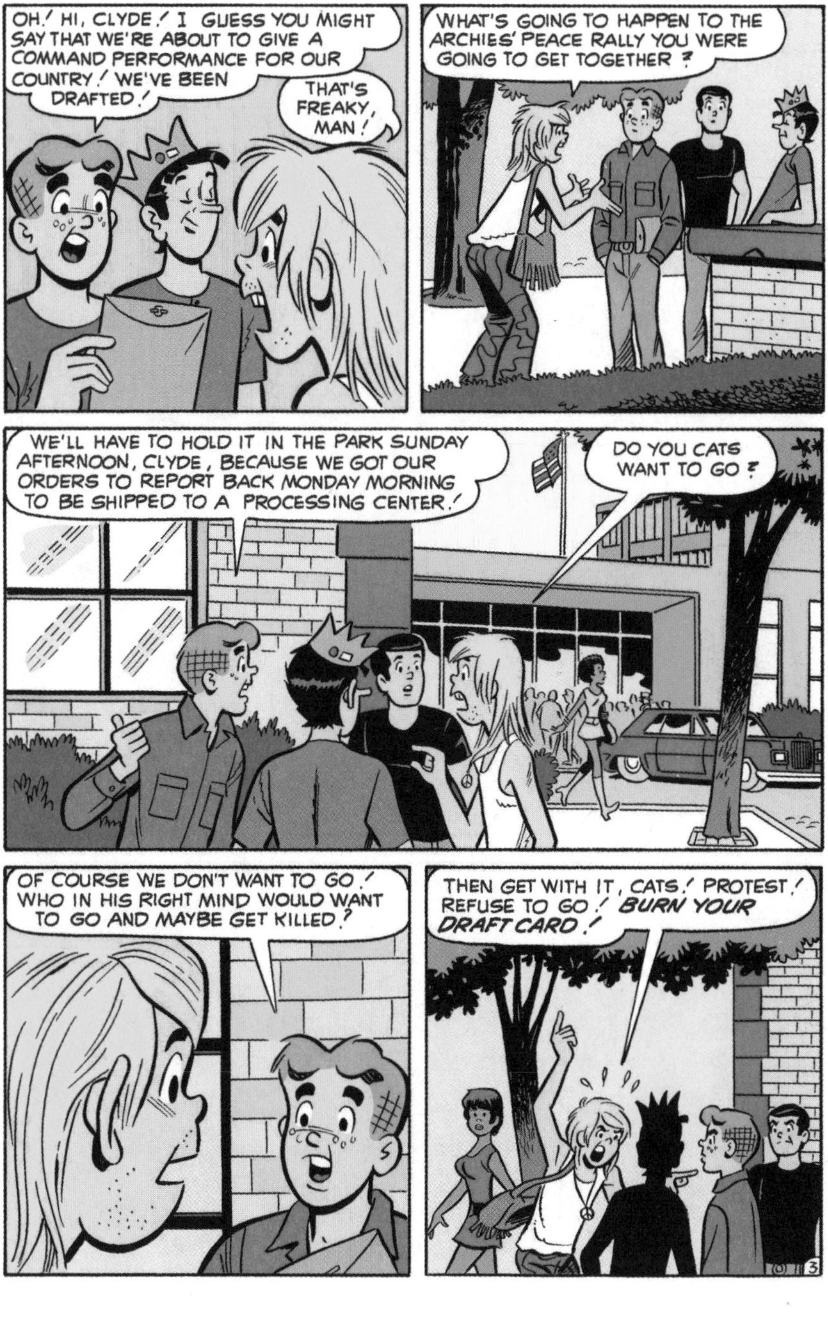
OH! HI, CLYDE! I GUESS YOU MIGHT SAY THAT WE'RE ABOUT TO GIVE A COMMAND PERFORMANCE FOR OUR COUNTRY! WE'VE BEEN DRAFTED!
THAT'S FREAKY, MAN!
WHAT'S GOING TO HAPPEN TO THE ARCHIES' PEACE RALLY YOU WERE GOING TO GET TOGETHER?
WE'LL HAVE TO HOLD IT IN THE PARK SUNDAY AFTERNOON, CLYDE, BECAUSE WE GOT OUR ORDERS TO REPORT BACK MONDAY MORNING TO BE SHIPPED TO A PROCESSING CENTER!
DO YOU CATS WANT TO GO?
OF COURSE WE DON'T WANT TO GO! WHO IN HIS RIGHT MIND WOULD WANT TO GO AND MAYBE GET KILLED?
THEN GET WITH IT, CATS! PROTEST! REFUSE TO GO! BURN YOUR DRAFT CARD!

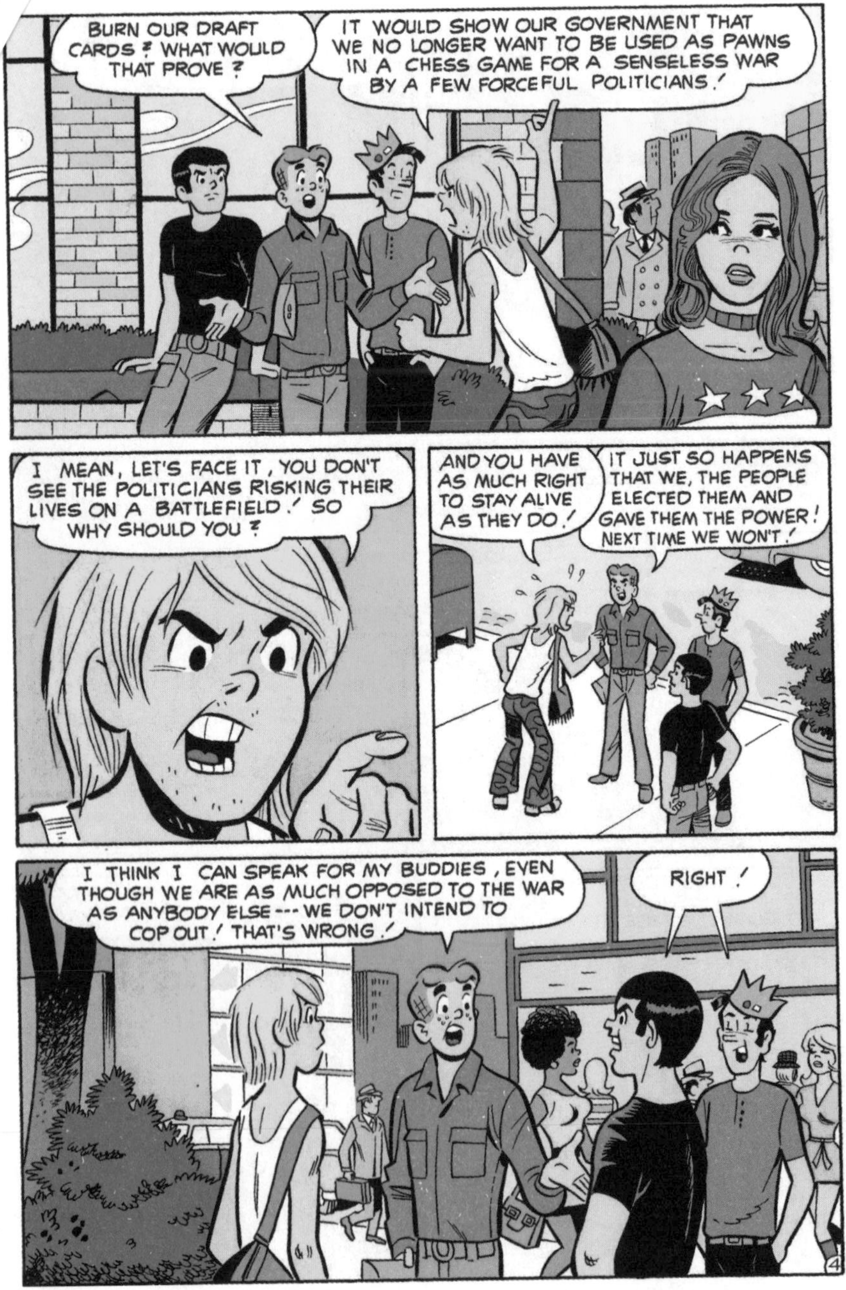
BURN OUR DRAFT CARDS? WHAT WOULD THAT PROVE?
IT WOULD SHOW OUR GOVERNMENT THAT WE NO LONGER WANT TO BE USED AS PAWNS IN A CHESS GAME FOR A SENSELESS WAR BY A FEW FORCEFUL POLITICIANS!
I MEAN, LET'S FACE IT, YOU DON'T SEE THE POLITICIANS RISKING THEIR LIVES ON A BATTLEFIELD! SO WHY SHOULD YOU?
AND YOU HAVE AS MUCH RIGHT TO STAY ALIVE AS THEY DO!
IT JUST SO HAPPENS THAT WE, THE PEOPLE ELECTED THEM AND GAVE THEM THE POWER! NEXT TIME WE WON'T!
I THINK I CAN SPEAK FOR MY BUDDIES, EVEN THOUGH WE ARE AS MUCH OPPOSED TO THE WAR AS ANYBODY ELSE --- WE DON'T INTEND TO COP OUT! THAT'S WRONG!
RIGHT!
4

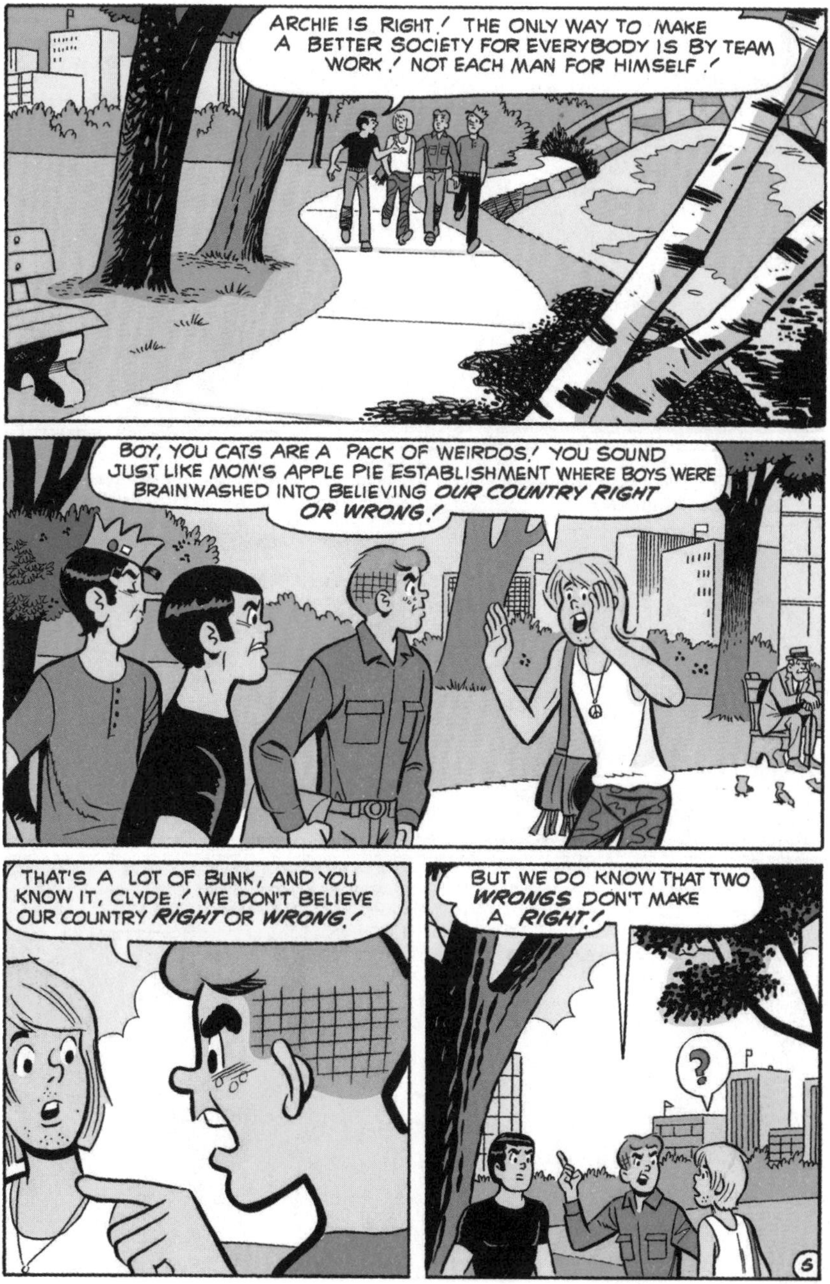
ARCHIE IS RIGHT! THE ONLY WAY TO MAKE A BETTER SOCIETY FOR EVERYBODY IS BY TEAM WORK! NOT EACH MAN FOR HIMSELF!
BOY, YOU CATS ARE A PACK OF WEIRDOS! YOU SOUND JUST LIKE MOM'S APPLE PIE ESTABLISHMENT WHERE BOYS WERE BRAINWASHED INTO BELIEVING OUR COUNTRY RIGHT OR WRONG!
THAT'S A LOT OF BUNK, AND YOU KNOW IT, CLYDE! WE DON'T BELIEVE OUR COUNTRY RIGHT OR WRONG!
BUT WE DO KNOW THAT TWO WRONGS DON'T MAKE A RIGHT!
?
6

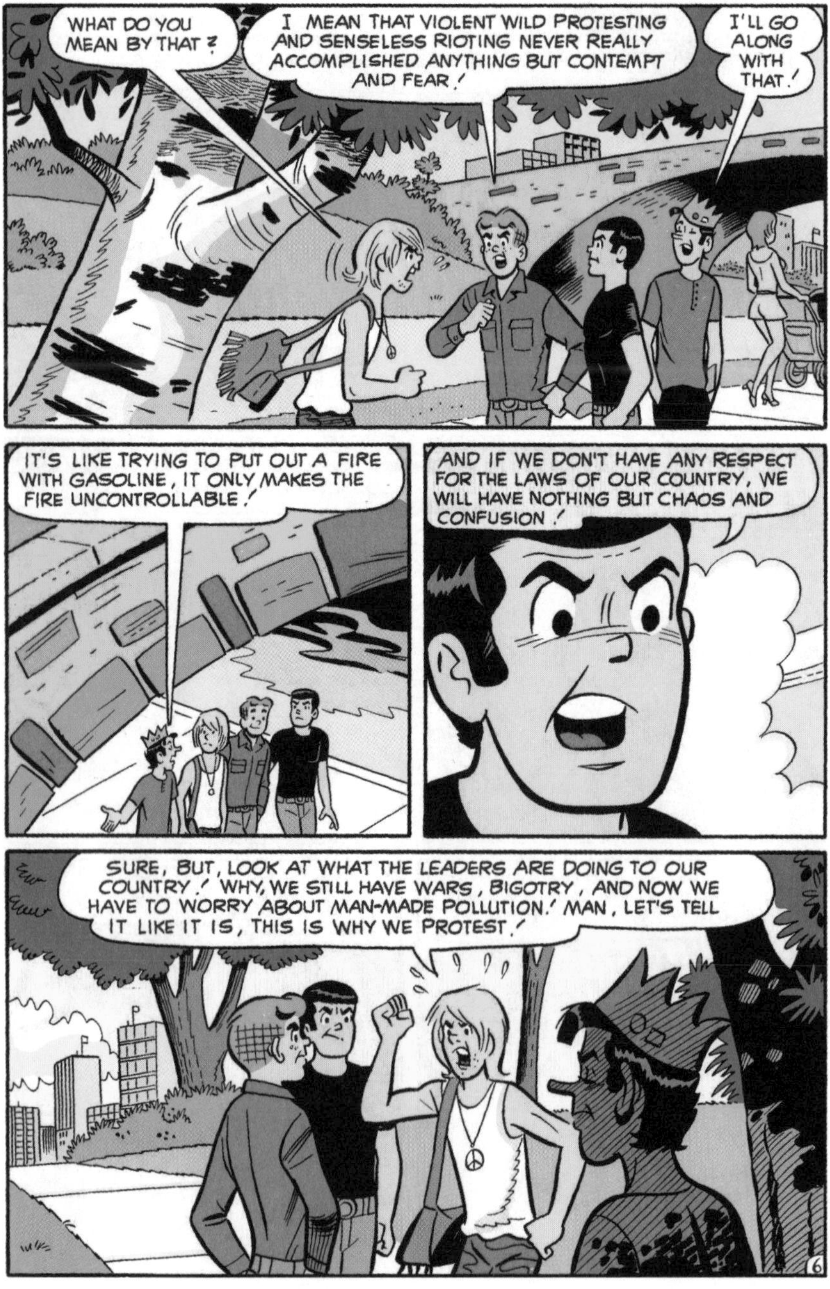
WHAT DO YOU MEAN BY THAT ?
I MEAN THAT VIOLENT WILD PROTESTING AND SENSELESS RIOTING NEVER REALLY ACCOMPLISHED ANYTHING BUT CONTEMPT AND FEAR!
I'LL GO ALONG WITH THAT!
IT'S LIKE TRYING TO PUT OUT A FIRE WITH GASOLINE, IT ONLY MAKES THE FIRE UNCONTROLLABLE!
AND IF WE DON'T HAVE ANY RESPECT FOR THE LAWS OF OUR COUNTRY, WE WILL HAVE NOTHING BUT CHAOS AND CONFUSION!
SURE, BUT, LOOK AT WHAT THE LEADERS ARE DOING TO OUR COUNTRY! WHY, WE STILL HAVE WARS, BIGOTRY, AND NOW WE HAVE TO WORRY ABOUT MAN-MADE POLLUTION! MAN, LET'S TELL IT LIKE IT IS, THIS IS WHY WE PROTEST!
6

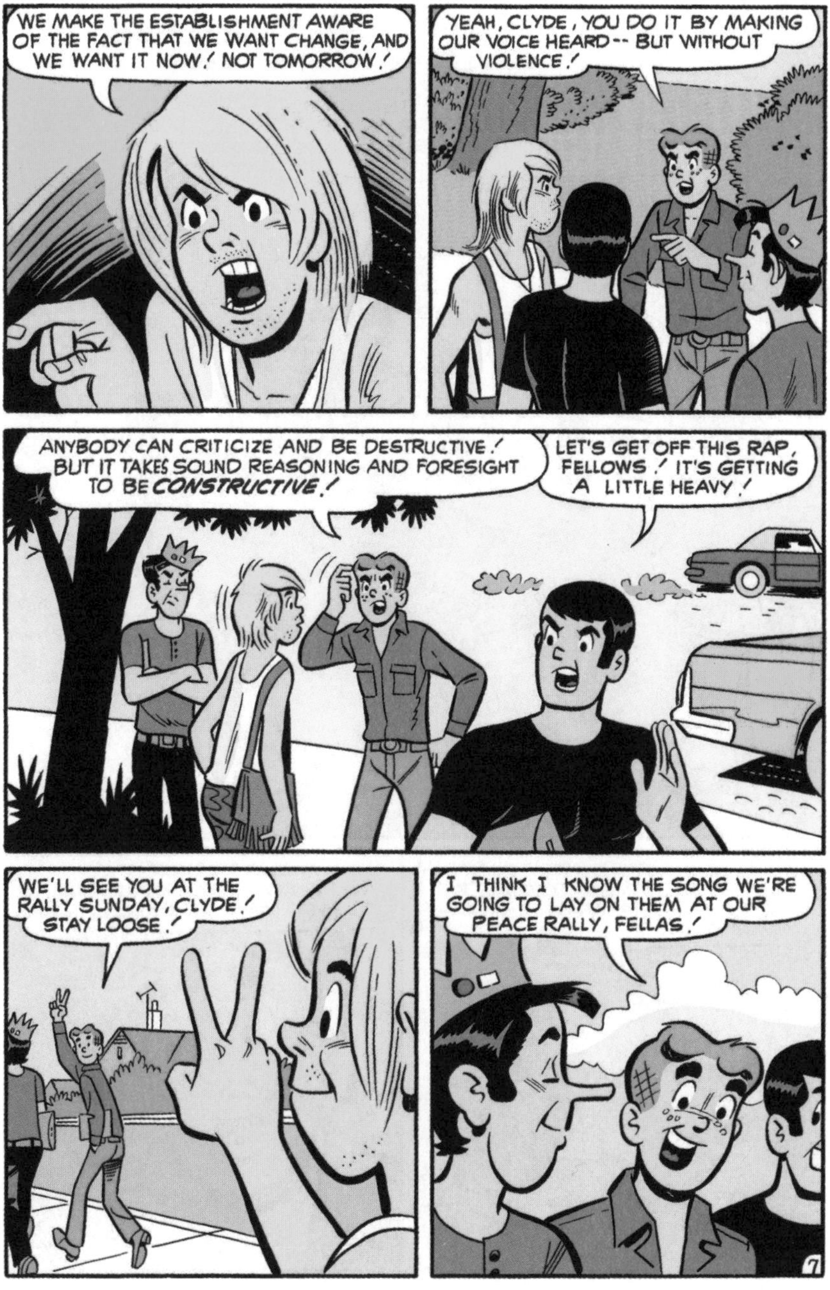
WE MAKE THE ESTABLISHMENT AWARE OF THE FACT THAT WE WANT CHANGE, AND WE WANT IT NOW! NOT TOMORROW!
YEAH, CLYDE, YOU DO IT BY MAKING OUR VOICE HEARD-- BUT WITHOUT VIOLENCE!
ANYBODY CAN CRITICIZE AND BE DESTRUCTIVE! BUT IT TAKES SOUND REASONING AND FORESIGHT TO BE CONSTRUCTIVE!
LET'S GET OFF THIS RAP, FELLOWS! IT'S GETTING A LITTLE HEAVY!
WE'LL SEE YOU AT THE RALLY SUNDAY, CLYDE! STAY LOOSE!
I THINK I KNOW THE SONG WE'RE GOING TO LAY ON THEM AT OUR PEACE RALLY, FELLAS!
7

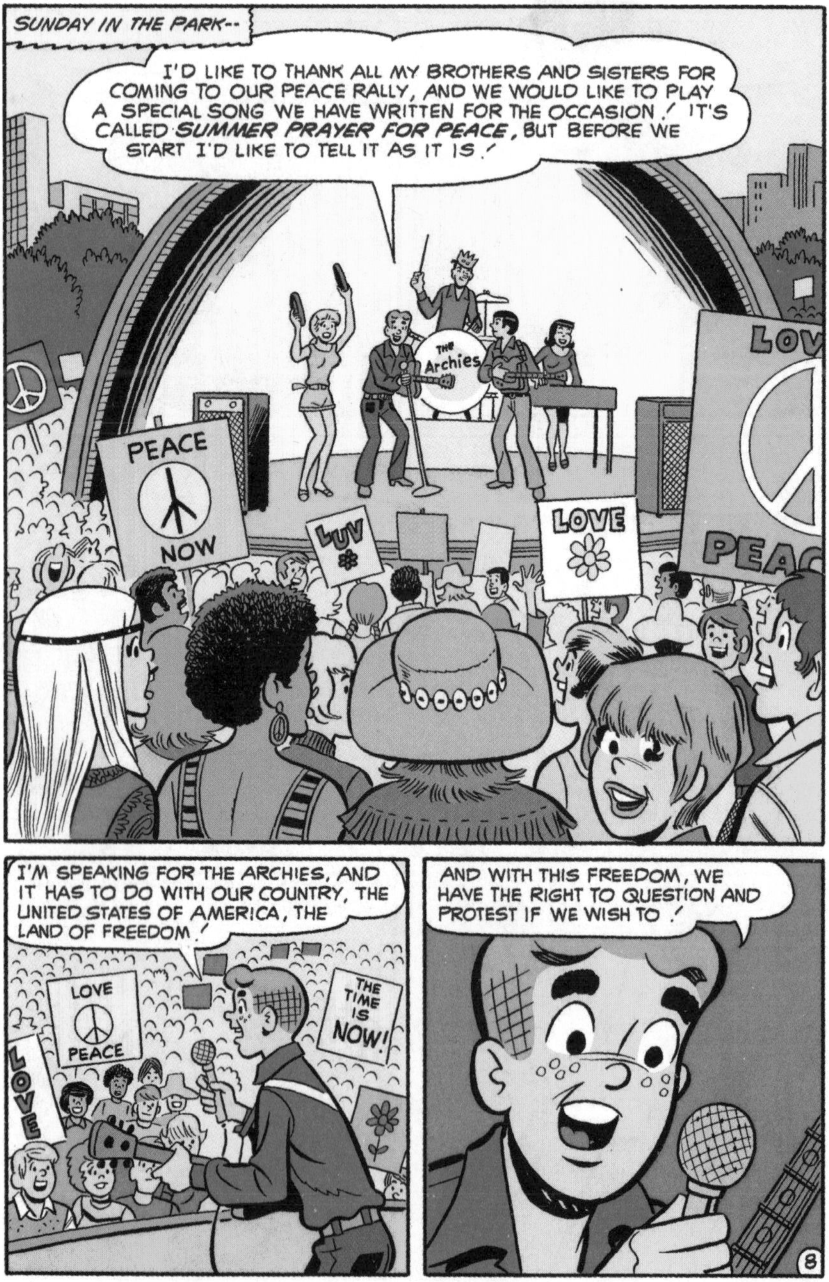
SUNDAY IN THE PARK--
I'D LIKE TO THANK ALL MY BROTHERS AND SISTERS FOR COMING TO OUR PEACE RALLY, AND WE WOULD LIKE TO PLAY A SPECIAL SONG WE HAVE WRITTEN FOR THE OCCASION! IT'S CALLED SUMMER PRAYER FOR PEACE, BUT BEFORE WE START I'D LIKE TO TELL IT AS IT IS!
THE Archies
PEACE NOW
LUV
LOVE
LOV
PEA
I'M SPEAKING FOR THE ARCHIES, AND IT HAS TO DO WITH OUR COUNTRY, THE UNITED STATES OF AMERICA, THE LAND OF FREEDOM!
LOVE PEACE
THE TIME IS NOW!
LOVE
AND WITH THIS FREEDOM, WE HAVE THE RIGHT TO QUESTION AND PROTEST IF WE WISH TO!
8